NOBLEMEN WITH BAD INTENTIONS

Looking into her reflection, she managed to settle two fabric butterflies back into her hair and wrap the dangling threads of a third around some seed pearls in the flowers at her shoulder. She must have groaned aloud, because her fashion critic laughed. When she looked up, he stood nearby with a gold stickpin in hand.

"Try this." His grin raised both hackles and gooseflesh.

She watched in disbelief as he pulled out the fabric of her bodice, jabbed the pin through a flower, and threaded it through from behind.

She should be kicking him like a Missouri mule, should be giving him a painful lesson in how American girls dealt with "bounders." But, truth be told—tall, dark men with bad intentions had always been her weakness, and he was taller and darker than most, and from what she could tell, his intentions were spectacularly bad.

"There," he said with a wry smile, lowering his hand. "If you can overlook the fact that those two appear to be mating, you'll be fine."

"Mating?" Her eyes flew wide as she realized what he'd done. "You, you—" She caught herself before she uttered a curse and drew a fiercely controlled breath instead. "What is her name? This mama you slunk in here like a polecat to avoid."

His grin dimmed and he paused a moment, studying her. She had caught him off-guard.

"A gentleman does not discuss the ladies in his life."

"Is that so?" she said, lifting her chin as she headed for the door. "Well, I'm sure I'll recognize her when I see her. She'll be the one with the shotgun"—she raked him with a look—"and the horse-faced daughter."

BOOK YOUR PLACE ON OUR WEBSITE AND MAKE THE READING CONNECTION!

We've created a customized website just for our very special readers, where you can get the inside scoop on everything that's going on with Zebra, Pinnacle and Kensington books.

When you come online, you'll have the exciting opportunity to:
- View covers of upcoming books
- Read sample chapters
- Learn about our future publishing schedule (listed by publication month and author)
- Find out when your favorite authors will be visiting a city near you
- Search for and order backlist books from our online catalog
- Check out author bios and background information
- Send e-mail to your favorite authors
- Meet the Kensington staff online
- Join us in weekly chats with authors, readers and other guests
- Get writing guidelines
- AND MUCH MORE!

**Visit our website at
http://www.kensingtonbooks.com**

A Good Day To Marry A Duke

BETINA KRAHN

ZEBRA BOOKS
KENSINGTON PUBLISHING CORP.
http://www.kensingtonbooks.com

ZEBRA BOOKS are published by

Kensington Publishing Corp.
119 West 40th Street
New York, NY 10018

First Printing: December 2017
ISBN-13: 978-1-4201-4347-8
ISBN-10: 1-4201-4347-6

eISBN-13: 978-1-4201-4348-5
eISBN-10: 1-4201-4348-4

10 9 8 7 6 5 4 3 2 1

Printed in the United States of America

For Michael, Sarah, and Lauren.

*May you find a love that will help you become
the person you are meant to be.*

Prologue

This was the moment she had been waiting for, her time to shine.

She had the perfect horse—seventeen intimidating hands and black as midnight—and the perfect riding habit—scarlet coat with a black overskirt that hid her trousers, and a saucy top hat cocked at an eye-catching angle—

The Bellington Hunt had gathered in the estate's stone-paved court and the barrel-chested hunt master was making the rounds, glad-handing the men and flattering the few ladies who would soon be riding over hill and dale in pursuit of a fox and a pack of baying hounds. The morning was brisk and sunny, with wisps of mist lingering among the stately oaks that dotted the grounds. The horses snorted and stepped sharply, anxious to be off, while the riders laid wagers on who would be first at the kill and quietly appraised the saucy young thing holding the reins of a strapping black stallion.

They were staring at her, so she lifted her chin and stared right back. And when the hunt master introduced her to nearby gentlemen, she thrust out her hand and gave them a shake they'd remember. She glanced at the other lady riders and thought: *Sidesaddle Sadie's, every one of them. Have to be hoisted up and tucked into stirrups like babies in buggies. Well, no mounting block for me, no sir! The minute that horn sounds, they'll see Daisy Bumgarten's a horsewoman who don't need coddling. I'll throw this soft bunch of city boys some gen-u-ine competition.*

"Daisy!" Her mother's fierce whisper penetrated her concentration, and Daisy looked down instantly to make sure her skirt didn't reveal what she wore beneath. Her mother gave her reddened cheek a kiss and straightened her hat to a more demure angle, giving the impression of a doting mother come to see her daughter off. Daisy knew better. She had come to remind her daughter how much was riding on this opportunity.

"Don't stare." Elizabeth Bumgarten gave her arm a covert squeeze. "Remember your manners. Rein in that beast of yours and hang back. Stay in the middle of the pack—try to keep company with the other ladies. And avoid fences. No proper lady could keep her seat going over a fence."

"Mount up!" the hunt master bellowed. "We're soon away!"

Every horse and rider in the yard was suddenly in motion, including Daisy.

"Be sure . . . use the . . ."

Mounting block. Daisy didn't need to hear it to know what her mother intended as she led her horse through the press and around that confounded contraption. With a quick look over her shoulder to be certain she was out of sight, she grabbed the saddle and jumped up to slip her boot into the stirrup. Swinging her leg over the saddle, she smiled. *Let's see any of these other gals mount half so slick.* She pulled her skirt up to tuck out of the way. The horn blew, the hounds tore off at a wicked pace, and a shout went up as the riders bolted out of the yard and across the nearby field.

Daisy's last coherent thought before excitement seized her every sense was that her mother hadn't even noticed she was using her western saddle.

The horses were lathered and smelly, the riders were windblown and red faced, and the hounds barked triumphantly as they jumped around the dismounting riders in the same courtyard two hours later. The male hunters vied with bourbon-bold bluster for recognition of their prowess on horseback. Hip flasks—silver and monogrammed—were passed around, and one found its way into Daisy's hands. She grinned at its owner, tilted it up, and took a long, fiery swig of Kentucky's finest.

Raucous male laughter burst around her as she swiped her mouth with the back of her sleeve and thrust the flask back into her benefactor's hand. She'd done it—she had led the pack and jumped half a dozen fences and proved her mettle in grand style. And they toasted her performance in true camaraderie with their best liquor. She was too busy basking in the heat of their admiring gazes to notice the rush of footsteps behind her. It was only when her mother snagged her arm and spun her about that she realized she was in trouble.

"Daisy, dear, you must be exhausted from such exertion. You simply must come along to rest and change for tea," Elizabeth Bumgarten said through lips pressed as tight as barrel staves. Her eyes were intense and her grip was fierce. Daisy allowed herself to be dragged away from the rest of the hunting party, praying that her mother hadn't witnessed that impulsive gulp of bourbon. The heat of the draught lingered nicely in her throat and belly, fortification that would no doubt be necessary.

She was escorted firmly through the mansion's main hall,

up the grand, carved, mahogany staircase, and around a gallery to one of the rooms set aside for the visiting ladies.

The China Blue bedchamber was filled with wrapped dresses hung from wardrobe doors and was piled with valises, hatboxes, and small trunks. Discarded tissue, recently shed shoes, tins of perfumed powder, ribbons, and hairbrushes littered the floor and dressing tables. Mercifully, it was empty of ladies and ladies' maids just now, so no one else would hear the blistering Daisy was about to receive.

"How dare you present yourself to these people in that— that—" Her mother glared at Daisy's overskirt, which was still turned up in front and tucked at her waist, and then at her woolen trousers. Daisy half expected the fabric to burst into flames. "What in Heaven's Holy Name did you think you were doing dragging those things along?"

"I can't ride sideways, Ma. I damn near killed myself the last time I tried. *You* try takin' a fence on one of those death traps." Recognizing the mistake of mentioning fences, she lifted her chin. "Unless you'd rather I just wore a damned skirt and let my naked legs show?"

"How dare you use such language with me?" Her mother backed her against the wall beside an open wardrobe and leaned in, an inch from Daisy's nose, where she inhaled sharply. "You've been *drinking*!"

"Just a nip. To get the blood flowin'." Daisy winced. She sounded too much like her beloved Uncle Red just now, and she was fairly sure her mother wouldn't miss the similarity.

Elizabeth blanched and her mouth worked without sound. A moment later both her voice and her color returned with a vengeance.

"You know we're here on sufferance. If Mrs. Barclay hadn't intervened to get us an invitation—this is our one chance to show we're more than just a bunch of raucous, ill-mannered western—"

A gaggle of feminine voices burst into the stuffy chamber,

and a second later the mahogany door swung open to the sound of Mrs. Townsend-Burden's grating, high-pitched laughter.

"Did you see the woman's face?" she crowed. "Purely mortified."

"Rightly so," said a voice as yet unfamiliar, but betraying the tortured vowels of Boston proper. "And those bloomers. Good God—even Amelia Bloomer has given those up by now."

"They're not bloom—" Daisy's whispered protest was cut off by her mother's hand across her mouth. The gowns hanging from the wardrobe doors hid them, but they wouldn't go unnoticed for long. Spotting the open doorway to the adjacent bathing room, Elizabeth impulsively yanked Daisy into the white-tiled chamber and pressed a finger to her own tightly clamped mouth, ordering silence.

"And riding *astride* with the *men*," the Townsend-Burden woman continued. "Brazen creature."

"Uncouth is what she is," came a third voice. "Where is that girl of mine? These shoes are killing me." That plummy, distinctive voice lowered. "No doubt she's given the men more than an eyeful this day."

The laughter was sharp as cats' claws.

"Did you see her this morning before they started out? Not waiting to be introduced . . . smiling, laughing, and shaking hands like . . . like a *man*. Mark my words: that one knows too much."

"A hussy, that's what she is. Far too bold to be anything else."

Daisy's chest tightened as she watched the fire in her mother's eyes flicker and damp. She wanted to look away, but the pain she read in Elizabeth's face kept her riveted. This was what her mother had brought the family to New York to do. For the last three years Elizabeth Bumgarten's every action, every hope, every expenditure had been focused on getting them into society, on getting her girls well fixed in the world.

Daisy had mostly ignored or pretended amusement at her mother's aspirations and the lessons, fittings, and exposures to "culture" that resulted. In truth, she had resented them and the implication that because she and her sisters were new to moneyed life, they were somehow inferior and had to work to become worthy of notice. Deeper still, she had chafed at her mother's constant watchfulness that said she was not to be trusted around men. Thus motivated, she had found ways to escape most of her mother's attempts to transform her.

Until now. Until she heard her mother's fears and dire assessments coming from the mouths of others, ridiculing her mother's attempts at her daughters' betterment and naming Daisy a hussy—a judgment that was a bit too close to the bone.

"Just goes to show what money cannot buy," the third woman said, her cultured tones dripping disdain. "Breeding, manners, and good taste. The chit and her pathetic mother will never set foot in my ballroom, I can tell you that. On that Mr. McAllister and I quite agree."

With the drop of that name and the mention of a ball-room, the identity of the third guest was made clear. Mr. McAllister. *Ward McAllister*. Even Daisy knew that name. That meant their third detractor could be none other than Mrs. John Jacob Astor herself. The queen of New York society. The creator and self-appointed keeper of the Four Hundred. She had apparently deigned to attend the "boring country house party," after all.

Daisy watched her mother's shoulders round and her face redden with humiliation. The verbal scalding went on until the ladies' maids descended to help their mistresses freshen for tea.

By the time the women exited the chamber, Daisy and her mother were pressed back into a corner behind the porcelain water heater, having missed detection by the slimmest of margins. Daisy stepped out cautiously and peered into the bedchamber, which now resembled the workroom at the rear of a dressmaker's shop. When she turned back, her mother was staring at her with a desolate look.

"It seems you've gotten your wish," Elizabeth said bitterly. "You won't be troubled with manners and prissy clothes and 'expectations' ever again."

"It's not too late," Daisy said anxiously. "I'll behave. I won't look at a single man and I'll use my best Sunday manners. You'll see—"

"I have already seen. And so have *they*," Elizabeth said, her voice low and choked with anger. "As of this day, we are social pariahs. But know this, girl—you have not only ruined my hopes, you have ruined your sisters' as well. Their reputations, their expectations are forever tarnished by your headstrong, selfish behavior." She strode toward the bedchamber, but paused in front of Daisy for one last salvo.

"I hope you're proud of yourself."

Chapter One

London, two years later

"You don't have to do this, girl," Uncle Red said as they paused on the front steps of the Earl of Mountjoy's palatial London home.

"Yes, I do." Daisy struggled for breath against her wickedly tight corset. She had worked fervently for the last two years to come to this moment. A little suffocation and a few spots before her eyes were a small price to pay for climbing onto the social register. A girl had obligations, after all—sisters to marry off and a mother with badly bruised pride.

This was going to make everything she had done wrong, right. She was going to marry a nobleman—a top nobleman—and take him home and watch Mrs. Astor choke on "that Bumgarten tart's" good fortune. Assuming, of course, that she survived the night in this damned corset.

"You want a nip to brace you up?" Uncle Red patted the conspicuous bulge in the breast pocket of his coat. His concern was downright sweet, considering his own duress . . . being stone-cold sober and stuffed into a cutaway with a starched collar that was choking him senseless. But if anyone could sympathize with a body it would be Redmond Strait. Her blustery, ruddy-faced uncle had a sentimental streak about as wide as the massive silver vein he'd discovered in Nevada.

"I'm fine, Uncle Red. Truly." She lied through her teeth; she could really use a nip just now. "Couldn't be better. My feet are positively itching for a dance."

Red sighed at her determined expression and took her at her word. The minute they handed over their invitation to the liveried footman, he smacked his mouth thirstily and struck off in search of the nearest punch bowl.

Daisy paused at the bottom of the great expanse of marble steps leading up to the ballroom, dreading the climb in an elaborate gown that had to weigh fifty pounds and made her look like she'd been caught in a florist shop explosion. Silk flowers were stitched to embroidered vines running riot over her narrow satin bodice and half bare shoulders—not to mention those absurd butterflies the countess had insisted on plastering all over her. She looked down at her waist, grabbed an eye-catching blue insect, and tugged until the threads that held it gave with a pop.

With a fierce sense of satisfaction, she gathered her skirts to proceed, but then someone clutched her elbow.

"Come with me, Miss Bumgarten." Lady Evelyn Hargrave, Countess of Kew—Daisy's sponsor and guide on her matrimonial quest—had eyes narrowed to slits and lips frozen into an icy smile. The force she used in spiriting her protégée out of public view told Daisy she was in trouble.

The countess ushered her down a long hallway and into a dimly lighted room filled with stuffed bookcases, heavy leather furnishings, and the smell of old cigars. As the door closed, the countess turned on her.

"Where in Heaven's name are your gloves?"

Daisy sighed and produced lengths of limp kidskin from the folds of her dress. She was in for it. The English were

obsessed with gloves, wore them morning, noon, and night—
sometimes ate in the damned things.

"I believe I have made myself perfectly clear on this
matter." The countess yanked them from her and smoothed
the wrinkles caused by her moist hands. "Ladies never
appear in public without gloves."

"They make my arms feel like sausages," Daisy said as
the countess held one out for her to insert her hand.

"They wouldn't if you—" The countess bit off the rest,
but Daisy finished the comment in her head: *didn't have
such unladylike arms*. She couldn't help it that her body had
what old Chuck Worth in Paris had called "a remarkably
physical aspect." She'd spent much of her life wrangling
horses, carrying saddles, and hefting bales of hay back at her
home in Nevada, and three years of city living in New York
before she headed to Paris and London hadn't been enough
to soften all of her contours.

The countess struggled with the row of tiny leather-
covered buttons, paused suddenly, and looked up with
splotches blooming in her cheeks.

"Where are your butterflies?"

"I felt silly in them, so I—I—"

Daisy opened her other hand to reveal the squished blue
silk. The countess's mouth opened and worked, but produced only a gurgle. Daisy wondered if she were strangling
on her own juices.

There's a thought.

"We paid a small fortune to have those hand painted to
resemble rare and exotic specimens." The countess snatched
the faux insect and tried to restore it, then stopped dead.
"There are supposed to be two in your coiffure and two more
at your shoulder. What the devil did you do with them?"

Daisy wished the woman would just come out with a
good, old-fashioned "hell's fire" or "damnation" and get it
off her chest. Her blanches of disappointment were far too

much like Daisy's long-suffering mother's. With a huff, she opened her reticule to reveal the four crumpled butterflies she had removed on the way to the ball.

The countess closed her eyes briefly and looked as if someone were lighting a pyre around her feet.

"You have engaged me to assist you in your quest, Miss Bumgarten. I cannot do so if you refuse to follow my advice." She drew back irritably. "I shall be waiting by the stairs to accompany you, should you decide to cooperate."

Daisy watched the door close and then glowered at the gloves and butterflies.

"I'm a grown woman." She tossed her reticule onto a nearby chair and started to button the wretched accessory. "I shouldn't have to walk around frumped up like a goddamned flowerpot!"

"I agree." Deep male tones startled her.

She clasped a hand over her racing heart and looked around to find the top of a head sticking up behind the back of a sofa.

"What are you doing there?" she demanded.

"Escaping a certain young lady's irate mother. At least, I was before you and your governess barged in."

"The countess is *not* my governess." Daisy drew herself up with true indignation. "Eavesdropping is—you might have had the decency to say something, announce your presence."

"And miss such a fascinating conversation?" A face wearing a wince appeared. "Oh. I see what you mean about the flowerpot."

He began to rise. And rise. Daisy found herself watching a tall, broad-shouldered man unfold from the sofa . . . longish hair, arresting face, elegant evening clothes that sat casually on a leanly muscled frame. What she could see in the dim light gave her a very bad feeling. Well, not so much bad as wicked, the kind that started just behind her navel and curled upward and downward into alarmingly excitable territory.

With a flush, she jerked her gaze back to her glove buttons and tried to concentrate on stuffing the buttons through the loops. But he moved around the sofa toward her and she soon found herself looking up . . . and up . . . and up. He came to a stop barely an arm's length away, and she took a half step back.

He was tall and dark and—her heart tripped over the obvious—handsome. His face was framed on strong, patrician bones; he had a long, straight English nose; and his curved mouth bore a decidedly sensual cast.

"I agree with you, by the by. The butterflies look theatrical." *Tall, dark, and clever.*

In other words, trouble. She groaned privately. Men who eavesdropped and commented boldly on a lady's appearance had no scruples. Much less what the Brits called "proper sensibilities." Men like him believed that rules were made for other people.

When he reached for her hand and began to fasten her glove, she felt a tingle in places she wasn't supposed to know that ladies possessed. She tried to withdraw her hand, but he held it fast.

"It's almost impossible to do these one handed." He slid buttons through loops with long, expert fingers. She glanced up and away, but not before she caught the way his dark hair lay in smooth, feathered layers. No sticky pomade there. Nothing but soft, silky—

She shook herself mentally, refusing to listen to the siren call of her own wayward impulses. She had come to England to marry a duke, and marry one she would. If it killed her.

Why, then, was she allowing this cad—the British equivalent of a "varmint"—to behave so presumptuously? Another of the Brits' favorite words: "presumptuous." The Brits were a wordy bunch.

"I believe I can manage the rest on my own," she said, yanking her hand back and refusing to look at him again.

He took a step back, spread his coat to prop his hands on his waist, and watched as she smoothed the glove and fumbled with the buttons.

"You're American," he said, and she could tell from his voice he was smiling, probably the same superior expression she'd seen on so many English aristocrats. "But not from Boston."

"Thank God," she said from between clenched teeth. The damned buttons were putting up a fight. "Nevada. That's out west."

"I know where it is," he said. "Next to California."

"Give the man a prize," she said irritably, regretting it the minute the retort left her lips. But he just laughed in low, mesmerizing tones that made her bones and determination both soften.

"At that rate, you'll be here until the closing dance." He brushed aside her resistance to finish her buttons. This time she looked up, which turned out to be a bad idea. He had long, dark lashes that she could almost *feel* against her skin. "If I'm not mistaken, that is a Charles Worth gown."

"It is."

"Not his usual work." One eyebrow rose.

"It was made specially for this ball."

"I imagine so. The duke is known to be a nature lover."

She reddened. He knew exactly the point of her having bought and worn such an extravagant dress and was far too amused by it to suit her.

"So am I," she said defiantly. "I love flowers. And butterflies."

"Ah, yes. The butterflies. In your hair, were they?"

As the last button was fastened, she jerked her arm back and looked around for a mirror. The best she could do was a dark picture under glass that allowed her to see her reflection. She carried her reticule to the console below the picture, where she managed to settle two butterflies back into her hair and wrap the dangling threads of a third around some seed pearls in the flowers at her shoulder. She must have groaned aloud, because her fashion critic laughed. When she looked up, he stood nearby with a gold stickpin in hand.

"Try this." His grin raised both hackles and gooseflesh.

"I couldn't possibly." She dropped her gaze and found the butterfly she'd applied hanging to one side, as if it had expired from the indignity of having to appear on that dog's dinner of a dress.

"Well, I could," he said, taking the butterflies from her and stabbing both through with the stickpin. She watched in disbelief as he pulled out the shoulder of her bodice, jabbed the pin through a flower, and threaded it through from behind.

When the butterflies were secured, his hand remained in audacious contact with her liberally exposed skin. He ran the backs of his knuckles slowly around the neckline of her bodice. She froze; unable to protest, unable to even swallow as he reached the exposed top of her left breast and paused, stroking, sensitizing that all too susceptible flesh.

She raised her chin to tell him just how vile his behavior was, but he was leaning close enough for her gaze to get caught in the hot bronze disks of his eyes . . . worldly eyes that advertised understanding of a woman's deepest desires and the promise of pleasures well practiced and perfected. Unfortunately, there was more as well: humor, intelligence, and a piqued bit of sensual curiosity. A deep tremor of interest rocked her, awakening nerves and raising an alarm.

She should be kicking him like a Missouri mule, should be giving him a painful lesson in how American girls dealt with "bounders." But, truth be told—tall, dark men with bad intentions had always been her weakness, and he was taller

and darker than most, and from what she could tell, his
intentions were spectacularly bad. Right now every muscle
in her body was taut with expectation and her lips ached for
contact of a sort she'd sworn to forgo until she had spoken
respectable vows.

"There," he said with a wry smile, lowering his hand. "If
you can overlook the fact that those two appear to be
mating, you'll be fine."

"Mating?" Her eyes flew wide as she realized what he'd
done. "You, you—" She caught herself before she uttered a
curse and drew a fiercely controlled breath instead. "What
is her name? This mama you slunk in here like a polecat to
avoid."

His grin dimmed and he paused a moment, studying her.
She had caught him off-guard.

"A gentleman does not discuss the ladies in his life."

"Is that so?" she said, lifting her chin as she headed for
the door. "Well, I'm sure I'll recognize her when I see her.
She'll be the one with the shotgun"—she raked him with a
look—"and the horse-faced daughter."

Chapter Two

Ashton Graham, second son of the fifth Duke of Meridian, watched the tart-tongued American exit the earl's study and grinned. Worth gowns and the Countess of Kew as a sponsor; whoever she was, she'd spent a bundle to attract his brother's eye. *Poor thing, thinking that Arthur could be swayed by satiny curves and a calculated show of bosoms. Even magnificent bosoms.* His knuckles tingled where they had stroked her breast. To his knowledge his brother, the sixth Duke of Meridian, had never shown the slightest interest in the females of his own species.

However, the American with the big, bold eyes and exquisite skin could be the first. Wit, beauty, experience; she was no greensick tyro. And, clever chit, she was probably on to something with those butterflies. His brother was obsessed with the things—all manner of six-legged beasties, in fact. Artie was quite the devoted naturalist and collector.

Ashton checked his appearance in the same picture the Nevada girl had used as a mirror. As he straightened his tie, his gaze landed on a swatch of blue caught between the wall and the rear of the console table. It was an ornate silk butterfly that looked the worse for wear.

The thing was the exact color of those patch-of-sky eyes

that had registered anticipation at his touch and suggested a deliciously inappropriate knowledge of the pleasures it promised. With a quiver of anticipation he tucked it into his lapel and promised himself he would see that luscious little American again.

Halfway up the stairs to the busy ballroom, Ashton spotted his uncle, Lord Bertram Graham, headed straight for him. He glanced frantically around, but in the middle of the staircase there was no hope of escape. The old man seized his arm with a "my-dear-dear-boy" and hauled him up the steps and through the upstairs hallway to a private sitting room.

Ashton groaned quietly as he stepped inside and found himself facing a contingent of half a dozen family elders, headed by his father's formidable elder sister, Lady Sylvia Graham Upshaw. There was trouble. He could see it in their razor-sharp stares.

He approached Aunt Sylvia first. She wore full mourning black with demi-veil and mantilla, despite the fact that her husband had been dead the better part of thirty years. Her hand, properly gloved though it was, felt as cold as a corpse's bum cheek. The old girl sucked the warmth and vitality out of everything unfortunate enough to fall in her vicinity.

"My dear aunt." He prayed the tension that made his jaw clench would pass for upper-crust diction. "You look the very picture of health."

"Whereas you look the very picture of profligacy," the old girl said, causing the hoary heads at her back to exchange nods of agreement.

Ashton braced, scrambling to think which of his peccadilloes had landed him in the court of family opinion this time.

"I take it I am in trouble," he said, aiming his most beguiling smile at the old aunts. Two responded with furtive delight, while Aunt Sylvia hiked one side of her nose as if she'd detected something sulfurous.

"What you are *in*, is luck," she declared. "You have a chance to be useful to the family for a change. We have finally found a task that will employ your natural proclivities to the family's advantage."

That gave him a moment's pause. His natural proclivities? According to them, all he was good at was high living and moral scandal.

"I don't believe I understand," he said, truly puzzled. The family must really be in trouble if they were calling on him for help. Pedigree and finance were hardly his long suits, and the desiccated old gourds that shepherded the family fortunes cared little for anything else.

"A situation has arisen that cannot be tolerated. Your brother, as usual, is oblivious. He sees nothing but what is under his cursed specimen glass. It is up to us to protect him and our family heritage from the predations of that gauche American."

"A *dollar princess*," Uncle Bertram clarified with an aggrieved look.

"Dollar princess?" Ashton echoed, knowing full well what they meant.

Over the last ten years, rich American heiresses had arrived in England in droves and had been met with open arms by impoverished but eligible noblemen. These opportunistic alliances of old English blood and new American money were encouraged by no less than His Royal Highness Albert, Prince of Wales. "Bertie" found the American girls pretty, and spirited, and unconventional enough to keep pace in his cosmopolitan social set. It figured that the family creaks and groans would disapprove; they'd never thought much of the queen's eldest son and heir.

"It's that rich American chit the Countess of Kew is steering through ballrooms and parlors all over town," Uncle Bertram said, dipping into his snuffbox for a pinch. "Seems she has set her cap for your brother."

The American he had just encountered in the library. He glanced down at his lapel, stirring at the memory of her honey-blond petulance.

"Arthur is considering marriage?" he said, trying to imagine it.

"Who knows what that boy has in his head," Sylvia said with an ill-restrained snarl. "Besides moths."

"Butterflies," Bertram corrected.

"*Whichever*. He's taken notice of this girl and permitted the countess to introduce them. We cannot allow him to do anything foolish." Sylvia seemed to resettle herself for a pronouncement. "We have plans."

"For Arthur?" Ashton wondered if his brother had a clue.

"He is going to marry the Countess of Dorchester."

Ashton couldn't hide his astonishment. "Won't that trouble her good husband just a bit?"

Sylvia's scowl deepened. "He's on his deathbed."

"Could go at any moment," Cousin Albertine put in, clearly pleased.

"Or not." Old Uncle Seward felt obliged to counter Albertine's optimism. "He's lingerin'. Been draggin' it out for weeks. Makin' a disgraceful fuss over departin' for the hereafter."

Aunt Sylvia glowered at Seward, then turned back to Ashton. "Out of concern, we've sent our personal physician . . . who, in addition to easing the earl's distress, will discreetly convey our desire for a closer connection to the countess herself."

"Can't allow that hound Norwich to get his foot in the door there," Uncle Bertram broke in, hanging his hands on his vest. "He's lusted after that estate for years. Prime pheasant country, you know. Big, fat birds—"

"Meanwhile"—Sylvia wrenched them back to the point at hand—"we must deal with this upstart American."

"Can't have Arthur getting notions about women and marriage until after old Dorchester snuffs it," Bertram declared.

"Which is where you come in, Nephew." Sylvia looked him up and down. "You have the skills and experience to see that this creature is distracted from all thoughts of matrimony with the duke."

He thought of the determination in the American's brazen eyes and voluptuous lips. A frisson of anticipation slithered through him.

"And if she should prove impervious to distraction?" he asked.

"She is as fresh and forward as they come," Aunt Sylvia declared. "I am sure you can find a way to make yourself more interesting than Arthur."

This was almost beyond belief. He'd lost count of the times the old trots had chastised him for his prodigal living and indiscreet romances. Now they wanted to sic him and his intemperate ways on an upstart American who had the audacity to set her sights on the family coronet.

He glanced from one hooded gaze to another and read in those determined stares a shocking bill of license. They wanted him to do more than just distract her; they wanted him to seduce her.

The thought spun in his mind like a coin on its edge, then fell with a sweet, remunerative-sounding *clink*. The American was quite the little package. Lovely. Rebellious. Apparently quite rich. He smiled. It was a combination tailor-made for his kind of trouble. Then it occurred to him that there were yet other possibilities in the situation. He had attended the ball tonight hoping for a chance to plead for an increase in his dwindling stipend.

"Distraction," he said smoothly, "can be a very expensive business."

Every visible part of Aunt Sylvia puckered at the mention of "expense."

"I suppose"—she glanced to the others, who seemed more appalled by his demands on the family's beleaguered treasury than they had been by a suggestion that he seduce on command—"accommodations can be made."

Chapter Three

In the glittering, mirrored ballroom, Daisy squirmed as she watched the duke wend his way toward her through the revelers. Men kept blathering on about the latest election and women kept thrusting their homely daughters forward, slowing his progress. The countess's hand on her wrist, hidden between their skirts, reminded her she had to wait for the duke to acknowledge her.

It was a unique torment for an American, waiting on one's betters, and a particular irritation for Daisy, who was not used to having to wait for men of any station to acknowledge her. It wasn't like she and the duke hadn't been properly introduced. They had "taken tea" together for three days running, and she had already suffered through two of his lectures on *Lugubrious butterfli-mi-cus,* or some such.

The duke's legs came into view first, then his waist and discreetly padded shoulders. Nothing about him was long and lean and well muscled, which was probably a very good thing. He was taller than average and his grooming was impeccable, from his perfectly pomaded hair right down to his handsomely polished shoes. What did it matter that his hands weren't strong and sure fingered? A tingle in her breasts made her recall the feel of—*no!*

She struggled to raise both her gaze and the tone of her thoughts. The duke's hair was a medium brown, his eyes were a medium gray, and his modest lips seemed perfectly sized for sedate ducal smiles. Unlike the library stranger's perfect teeth and broad, sensual lips that promised magnificently abandoned pleasures. Phantom sensations of that rakish mouth nibbling its way across her—

The countess squeezed her hand again.

Chastened, Daisy averted her gaze and tried to think about something, anything else. Ribbons. Horses. Pomegranates. *Horses wearing ribbons and eating pomegranates.* Up came rebellious visions of *her* wearing just ribbons—thick, satiny ribbons—and being fed pomegranates by—

"Miss Bumgarten."

She looked up to find the duke had arrived with a coterie of hangers-on and was reaching for her hand. His gaze fastened with delight on her gown, and her heart sank. He was captivated, all right, by the damned butterflies.

"Your Grace." She made a half curtsy, summoned her brightest smile, and reminded herself of the impact he would have on Mrs. Astor when they visited New York. The gorgon of society would suddenly find that her famed ballroom held New York's Four Hundred plus two.

"Unless I am very much mistaken," the duke said eagerly, "you have a *Melanargia galathea* and a *Parnassius apollo* in your hair."

"Is that what you call them?" she said. Glowing with delight took an appalling amount of effort for some reason. "The little things landed as I stepped out of the coach, and I didn't have the heart to make them leave."

He smiled as his gaze fixed on the butterflies impaled together on the stickpin at her shoulder. "And how clever of you to pair a Purple Emperor with a Cleopatra on your gown." His eyes widened. "A rather aberrant pair, however.

I don't believe in the wild those two would ever frequent the same bush, much less attempt to procreate."

"Your Grace," the countess intervened anxiously, "the music is delightful and Miss Bumgarten has not yet had her first dance."

"Truly?" The duke seemed genuinely dismayed. "What an intolerable state of—oh." He blushed. "Forgive me. The sight of your butterflies was such—I'm not much for tromping around a ballroom floor, but if you have your heart set on a dance, Miss Bumgarten—"

She placed her hand in his and two interminable dances later she retired to the side with tortured toes and a face frozen in a grimace of a smile. The duke, it seemed, was not given to self-deprecation for humor's sake. When he said "tromping about a ballroom," he did indeed mean tromping . . . and pitching and galumphing . . . like a steer with a belly full of locoweed. But her abused feet and his frequent apologies were outweighed by his comments on her "grace" and "pleasant demeanor."

"Ladies," the duke had confided as they danced, "put me on edge. So many rules to observe in their company. Things not to say, where not to look, what not to bump. But you, Miss Bumgarten, you are effortless to be around." He warmed to his subject. "You listen so easily, dance so easily, and laugh so easily. *Easy*, Miss Bumgarten, that's what you are!"

Easy. She reddened. The duke was not the first to offer that opinion, but he was certainly the first to intend it as a compliment. Having finally roused the duke's masculine interest, she was just starting to feel some confidence in her enterprise when disaster struck in the form of a tall, dark figure with sinfully handsome eyes.

"Sin" was the word to keep in mind, Daisy told herself as her library stranger boldly planted himself before her and the duke. And she'd already had more than her share of in-

Iquity, thank you very much. Her breath caught as her gaze fell to the splash of blue on his lapel.

"Arthur, you sly dog. Monopolizing the most enchanting creature on the dance floor," he said. "The least you can do is introduce us."

"Really, sir—" she sputtered, eyes narrowing on the sight of her blue butterfly in his lapel.

"Thoughtless of me." The duke smiled guiltily. "Ash, meet Miss Daisy Bumgarten, of Nevada. That's 'out west,' as the Americans say." He turned to Daisy. "May I present my brother, Lord Ashton Graham."

His brother? Her heart gave a convulsive thump in her chest. How could she have known? She glared at him over a fierce little smile. There was some family resemblance. And she did recall the countess mentioning that the duke had a brother somewhere . . . a scapegrace out of family favor.

Her breast tingled alarmingly. Trouble. Within two minutes of laying eyes on him, he had been feeling her breast like a peach for the plucking. If she had half a brain, she would keep at least a couple of county lines between herself and the nimble-fingered wretch.

"Great Heavens, Ashton"—the duke broke into her thoughts—"you've got a Common Blue on your lapel. No, an *Adonis* Blue!" His excitement was quickly overtaken by confusion. "Whatever are you doing wearing a *Polymmatus bellargus*?" His gaze suddenly flew to Daisy's butterflies and back, as if he were struggling to make sense of such a coincidence. She could see from the onlookers' faces that they were making a connection, one that if allowed to develop might sink her matrimonial hopes altogether.

"They're all the thing," she said as airily as possible.

Lord Ashton's fascinating mouth quirked up on one end and he stroked his lapel. "Indeed. Everyone's wearing butterflies this season."

"They are?" Duke Arthur looked quickly at nearby guests

for additional signs of the infestation. "Don't tell me I'm on the verge of becoming fashionable."

"I wouldn't go that far." Lord Ashton broke into a sardonic smile that made Daisy want to kick him. Just then, the music began again, and he held out a hand. "Perhaps Miss Bumgarten will honor me with a dance."

She almost groaned aloud.

Social success, the countess had drilled into her, was as much about knowing what and whom to refuse as it was about knowing what and whom to accept. She made a show of consulting the dance card she had left mostly empty in order to be free to spend time with the duke. Before she could craft a convincing lie, the library-lurking lord seized her hand, trapped it on his arm, and steered her onto the dance floor.

As they merged into the flow of couples already dancing, she refused to look at him and was actually grateful for those blasted gloves that prevented skin-to-skin contact.

"You have some nerve, wearing *my* butterfly," she muttered, desperately bolstering her defenses against the heat radiating from him.

"Seemed a shame to waste it," he said, leading her expertly in the waltz, "seeing how expensive it was. You may thank me by removing that scowl from your face. People are staring."

"Thank you for what?" She glanced around them and did indeed note curious eyes aimed their way. She forced herself to relax.

"For rescuing you from social infamy. Everyone in the ballroom has been watching you and Arthur, counting the steps you've taken and the minutes you've spent together. One more dance and you would have been labeled a gauche American title hunter. The sound of doors closing to you all over London would have been deafening."

"You're saying you saved my reputation?"

"I'm generous that way," he said with an infuriatingly handsome smile, no doubt the undoing of many a susceptible young girl. Fortunately, she was neither that young nor that susceptible.

"One thing you are not, sir, is gallant."

"'One thing you are not, *my lord*, is gallant,'" he said.

"What?" The correction infuriated her. It was all she could do to keep from leaving him flat-footed in the middle of the dance. She glanced around at the people watching and settled for mentally calling him names that would have dropped the countess like a plank.

"You really must brush up on forms of noble address if you're aiming for a title yourself," he said. "When in doubt, use 'my lord.' It's safe for every rank but dukes, who are addressed 'Your Grace.' My brother is oblivious to such things. Unfortunately for you, the family elders are not. They have rather exacting standards."

"Then they can't be overly happy with you," she said testily. "Unless I miss my guess, you're more accustomed to violating standards than upholding them." She was rewarded with additional space between them.

"Careful, Miss Bumgarten." His voice deepened. "Such remarks might lead one to wonder how you came to be such an expert on men."

It was a perfect opening.

"A body doesn't have to have been bitten to recognize a snake."

He threw back his head and laughed, a full, resonant sound that set something deep in her chest quivering. Sweet Jesus. Vibrations spread through her like ripples on a pond, and she bobbled a step.

"You are so American." He covered her misstep with annoying grace.

"What the devil does that mean?"

"It means"—he leveled an amused look on her—"that

you speak your mind regularly and emphatically, damn the consequences. The prince must adore you."

"What prince?"

"Wales, of course. What other prince is there? You have been presented to Bertie, have you not?"

"Not," she said defensively. "Apparently he's busy yachting."

"Well, I'm certain you'll get on famously. He has a penchant for pretty American girls with sharp wits and bags of money."

He wasn't the first to call her pretty, but he was the first to make it sound like a hanging offense. Arrogant piece of humanity, issuing judgments on her person and lecturing her on manners and decorum when he was clearly used to doing whatever he pleased to whomever he pleased. He was the walking, talking embodiment of the arrogance of the British male. From government minister to stable hand, they all blustered and swaggered as if they were personally responsible for creating the empire.

The instant the music ended, she left him in the middle of the dance floor.

Ashton watched Daisy Bumgarten sail away a second time, sensing that she was trying to escape her interest in him as much as his admittedly caddish behavior. The way she reacted in the library, the way she met his eyes and melted beneath his touch; she was attracted to him.

Virgins as a rule sensed the danger his sensuality posed and avoided him like the plague, but there was no such wariness in Miss Bumgarten's gaze. Was that just the American in her or a sign of something more interesting . . . like . . . a desire for a little sensual adventuring?

The sound of his brother's voice made him look around.

Arthur was holding forth on some point of naturalist's lore that was making his listeners' eyes glaze over.

Imagining Daisy Bumgarten with his elder brother, Ashton winced. Vibrant and dull as ditchwater. Calculating and clueless. She was spirited and plain-spoken and unpredictable . . . a disastrous combination in a wife, much less a duchess. Yoking them together for life would be like harnessing a plow horse to a panther.

A flood of boyhood images came back to him: Arthur tromping through mud and muck about the estate park with a book in one hand and collecting net in the other, squinting with concentration, oblivious to guests and obligations and even his own importance. A surge of nobility seized him. Artie. Once again in his ancillary, "spare to the heir" life, he had to protect his poor brother—this time, from the matrimonial schemes of Daisy Bumgarten.

After she left Lord Ashton on the dance floor Daisy spotted the countess in the ballroom doorway trying discreetly to attract her attention. The moment she came within reach, she seized Daisy's arm and steered her out into the upstairs hall.

"The duke's family has summoned your uncle for a word."

The news stunned Daisy. "What kind of word?"

"I'm not certain." The countess was clearly unsettled. "It is too early for negotiations. But, the duke *has* shown extraordinary interest."

Hope roused at the sound of those blessed words: extraordinary interest. By the countess's best estimates, marriage negotiations were still at least a couple of balls, a few house parties, and several gallons of afternoon tea away. Why would they want to speak with Red?

"Your uncle was well into his second punch bowl." The

countess took a whiff from the vial of smelling salts she had taken to carrying. "God knows what he's saying to them."

"You mean, now?" Daisy's heart stopped as the full impact of it struck. "He's with them this very minute? Where?"

The countess pointed to the opposite upstairs hallway and a heartbeat later Daisy was striding down it, hot on her uncle's trail.

"What do you think you are doing?" The countess panted a bit as she worked to both keep up and maintain some sense of decorum.

"Drunk or sober, Uncle Red can talk a dog down off a meat wagon," Daisy said to herself as much as to the winded countess. "But he needs somebody to keep him on track."

"Not you." She pulled Daisy to a halt. "That is unthinkable."

"It's either me or you."

After a moment, the countess wilted around the edges.

"The man is utterly unmanageable," she said defensively.

"Then it has to be me."

"B-but your presence would be *unmaidenly*."

Daisy groaned silently. That again. Why was the whole damned world obsessed with maidenhood?

"Well, they won't be getting a 'maiden,' they'll be getting a duchess, and I think they should know that right up front."

Chapter Four

Latching on to the sound of voices, Daisy and the countess located the source in a cozy upstairs parlor tucked away at the back of the house. There, a well-marinated Redmond Strait stood before a half dozen wizened countenances that bore an uncanny resemblance to human remains they'd seen in the British Museum's Egyptian Exhibit. Three old ladies sat around a tea table while an equal number of old gents loomed behind them. At their head was a veritable prune of a woman swathed from head to toe in what Daisy had learned was British deep-mourning attire.

Red hitched around at the sound of their entrance and grinned sloppily at the sight of his niece. The countess stammered apologies and, in a choked voice, introduced herself and her protégée. The duke's family elders spoke not a word of greeting to either.

"As I said," the one called Lady Sylvia addressed Uncle Red, "we are duty bound to see to the young duke's interests and honor." The others at her back nodded, all but one old gent who was listing badly to one side, looking as if he might be slipping into rigor mortis. "After all, there are standards to be maintained."

Daisy gave Uncle Red an elbow in the ribs and, sensing the gravity of the moment, he rose to the challenge.

"Well, our Daisy—she ain't exactly standard." His chuckle made Daisy wince; under the influence, Uncle Red always imagined himself a wit. "But she does take a bit o' maintainin'."

The old lady cut a look at Daisy's wearable flower garden, and Daisy decided then and there that she would *never* be invited to Christmas dinner.

"Coming back to the matter at hand," Lady Sylvia continued, "it has been rumored that your niece has blood ties to an old English family. Were that not a possibility, we would not be having this interview. Proper bloodlines are critical to the honor of an old and venerated title like Meridian. Before permitting further contact between the duke and your niece, we must ask for proof of these claims to noble blood. To which noble house are the Bumgartens related?"

This was what she got, Daisy told herself, for recounting family lore as if it were fact. Uncle Red shook his head, seeming confused by the talk of ventilation and old ties and bloody houses.

"Bumgartens?" he blurted out. "Why, they're common as fleas on yer ol' hound dog."

Daisy's heart stopped, the countess's jaw dropped, and the old fossils registered astonishment.

"It's yer Straits that got a kiss o' blue in their blood," he continued, meeting Lady Sylvia's gaze squarely. "That's Daisy's mother's name. Lizzy Strait—'Lisbeth. Just like our Daize here is really Marguerite."

"Well, then." Lady Sylvia gave Daisy a look that could have parboiled a lobster. "To what noble house can the Straits be traced?"

He looked down at Daisy and blinked.

"Tell them . . . those names you talked about . . . remember?" she whispered, tightening her hold on his arm.

"Oh." He shook free of Daisy's grip to rub his chin, broaden his stance, and tilt his head back.

Daisy held her breath. She had seen him talk his way out of saloon fights and claim-jumping suits and late-night muggings, all while deeply under the influence. She had hopes that he could manage to say something coherent, until he opened his mouth and began to *sing*.

Dear Lord. It wasn't even a melody. More a chant with a rising and falling cadence that was littered with odd names and comments about lands acquired and children born under some blanket or other. It was a bizarre performance she had seen part of once before, a few years back, when Red was three-sheets-to-the-wind and feeling even more sentimental than usual. But until this moment, she had never connected it with the vague and oft-embroidered story she'd been told about the Strait family's beginnings.

Red's drone began far back in the mists of time with a fellow named Beaufort—a name that sounded appallingly made-up to Daisy. This "Beaufort" fellow took sides against some king or other, and there were battles and knights and ladies who defied their fathers to wed. Along the way there were Wear-ricks and Woodpiles—at least that was what they sounded like when Red droned them. A bunch of Nibbles and dead sons and somebody who fled to "the colonies" just ahead of a hangman's noose.

Daisy was desperate to shut him up, but he shook off her attempt to halt him and settled deeper into his trance. Her visual appeal to the countess for help went unnoticed; the poor woman was fanning herself, clearly waiting for a socially acceptable time to faint. Worst of all, the Meridian family fossils were staring at her uncle as if he were a freak of nature, like a two-headed calf or a talking pig.

Her matrimonial hopes were going down with all flags flying, and no nudges or tugs on coattails could break Red's dogged concentration.

Then came a subtle shift in the names and she recognized the Howards, Palmers, Meades, Hazeletts, and finally the Straits. Her heart sank as she realized what was done was done. Come the morning, she'd have to start looking for another duke, or lower her sights to an earl or—if it came to that—even a baron.

Red's chant ended as abruptly as it began, leaving him a little spent. He lurched forward, dropped both fists on the table with a thump, and gave the old trots a toothy grin.

"That enough for you Me-rid-ians? 'Cause that's all I got."

Not an eye blinked and not a breath was taken.

Daisy braced for the blistering rebuke that was surely coming their way. She was wholly unprepared for the old lady to turn to her relatives with an angry nod that elicited a response in kind.

"We shall have to have documentation." Old Lady Sylvia poked her head out of her shell of black bombazine like a peevish old turtle. "Testaments of authenticity."

Documentation? For a drunken rant?

The countess roused from her shock enough to assure Lady Sylvia that they could and would most certainly provide proof.

"In a fortnight," Lady Sylvia added a stipulation.

"But we may have to range afar to delve into estate records and parish archives," the countess protested. "It may take more than—"

"Two weeks," the old lady insisted, her countenance tight with intolerance. "We shall have guests at Betancourt in two weeks' time. Present your proof then and we shall see what we shall see."

Suddenly past her limit, Daisy stepped between Uncle Red and the old lady with a fierce expression.

"We'll be there. With all the proof you need." She caught the old woman's eye and held it, refusing to defer. "Count on it."

"What I am counting on," Lady Sylvia responded acidly, "is the duke's brother. Lord Ashton will represent our family in the matter, to inspect your 'proofs' and determine if they are authentic."

It took a moment to sink in. Daisy couldn't have been more shocked if they'd tossed a bucket of cold water in her face. The duke's brother with the roving hands and dangerous eyes? Sweet Jesus. He was going to pass judgment on her heritage?

"How do we know the duke's brother would recognize such 'proof' if it jumped up and bit him in the—"

"Lord Ashton is something of a scholar," the old lady declared with enough volume to suggest it was her final word on the subject. "He is exceedingly knowledgeable on the documentation of England's glorious history. We shall trust his assessment. He is, after all, a prime Meridian."

Lady Sylvia sank back into her veiling with a wave that signaled the interview was over.

Her face on fire, Daisy threaded her arm through Uncle Red's and helped the countess turn him toward the door. His performance seemed to have taken the starch out of him; he was wobbly on his—

Standing between them and the door was the duke's tall, dark, and arrogant brother. His long, muscular legs were spread, his arms were crossed, and his expression fairly glowed with intensity. Daisy cringed. How long had he been there? Had he seen Uncle Red's performance?

Against her better judgment she allowed her gaze to be drawn to his and saw a slow-forming smile curl the edges of his mouth.

Of course he had.

Ignoring the shiver that ran through her, she forced her chin up and dragged Uncle Red around him and out the door.

"What the devil was all that?" she demanded of Uncle

Red as they maneuvered him toward the main staircase. He seemed confused by her irritation.

"Your ancestors," the countess supplied, leaning past Red to scowl at Daisy. "The scions of noble houses are all taught to recite their genealogy. We should have had someone looking into it, documenting it. Why didn't you tell me about any of this?"

"I didn't know. I'd heard a few stories, but"—she turned on Red—"where did you get all that malarkey you dished out back there?"

"My pa taught me it." Red teetered precariously and Daisy motioned for help to the countess, who looked around to see who was nearby before taking a supportive grip on Red's arm. "Said it was for me to learn and say. Like his pa taught him. An' his pa before him."

Daisy groaned at the challenge they faced—proving a lineage based entirely on rum-soaked memory. By the time they got Red down the stairs and sent a footman for their carriage, all she could think about was the promise of trouble on Lord Ashton's handsome face.

"I need a drink," Uncle Red muttered, smacking his lips. She could have throttled him. But then he grinned that sweet, lopsided, utterly stewed grin of his and she sighed instead.

"Me too."

Ashton watched his quarry collect her dignity and exit the interview with a crimson face. The part where she tried to get the old boy to shut up was priceless. And Aunt Sylvia's horror at the prospect of being related, even remotely, to jug-bit Redmond Strait was enough to make his night.

He made a sardonic bow to the family and sauntered out, trying to scrub the vision of Daisy Bumgarten's hypnotic blue eyes from his head.

How did she know about the chant? How did she know to

pick those particular families? And how did she get the old boy to muff the names so convincingly? He rolled his shoulders and sternly refocused his thoughts. The only thing that really mattered was that he'd just learned how resourceful she truly was. He mustn't underestimate her.

By the time he reached the grand staircase, she and the countess were already on the lower level, ushering her uncle to the front doors.

So she wanted to be a duchess, did she? His smile took on a wicked cast. It was time Miss Bumgarten learned a few of the facts of noble life.

Ashton rose earlier than usual the next morning, dressed to the nines, and presented himself at his quarry's London address at half past ten.

As he was admitted to the sizeable house, he noted the marble-clad foyer, sweeping curved staircase, and portraits and gilt-framed landscapes that lined the entry hall. Daisy had surrounded herself with the trappings of old English aristocracy, perfect for receiving guests and insinuating herself into London society. The countess's influence, no doubt.

"Miss Bumgarten is not yet receiving callers," he was informed by the imperious old butler. Ashton thrust his hat and gloves into the servant's hands with patrician imperative.

"I am not a 'caller,' per se. I am here on important family business. Inform Miss Bumgarten that Lord Ashton Graham is waiting in the drawing room. And"—he held up a finger as the man started to sputter—"I'll need some coffee. I had something of a late night."

"Really, sir—this is most—you cannot possibly—"

The butler trailed anxiously after Ashton but knew better than to interfere. Proper servants knew to honor all requests—even outrageous ones—from noblemen. And

Miss Bumgarten had managed to acquire proper servants to staff her proper house.

Ashton grabbed the ornate handles and pulled open the massive drawing room doors to reveal a shocking tableau of enterprise and exhaustion. Coffee cups, a drained brandy decanter, several half-finished cigars, and carelessly shed shoes littered tables and carpet respectively.

A guttural snuffling sound drew his eye to the figure of Redmond Strait sprawled over a club chair, snoring away. The westerner's collar and evening coat had been tossed aside and his vest and viciously starched shirtfront were flung open. His stocking-clad feet rested on an ottoman and his arms hung limply over the sides of the chair.

On the windowed side of the grand chamber Daisy Bumgarten was face down, on a card table littered with well-used writing paper, pens, and ink. The laces of both her gown and corset had been loosened. Her bodice was spread enough to reveal tantalizing expanses of bare back, and her breasts were in very real danger of spilling out of her slackened bodice onto the tabletop. A choking sound from the butler told Ash that the servant was just as shocked as he was by the sight.

"R-really, m-milord." The butler's stammer said that such a tawdry scene exceeded even his most jaded expectations.

"As I said," Ashton managed, his gaze fixed on Daisy's luscious dishabille, "critical family business. Coffee, man. Trust me when I say that your mistress will need it."

As the butler hurried out, Ashton strolled forward and forced his gaze from his quarry's delectable figure to the papers on the tabletop beneath it. He picked up one page and perused the bold script, thinking that it suited her before registering that he held a list of names, locations, and offspring.

He glanced around, reading in those pages and the room's disarray what had taken place. She'd come straight home and spent the balance of the night documenting the old boy's ramblings and picking his brain for details of her lineage. His narrowed gaze came back to her. Or making up said details. Many a title-hungry mama had resorted to embroidering or even fabricating a family tree in order to snag a husband for—

He halted and frowned at Redmond Strait.

Where was that ambitious mama, anyway? What was Daisy Bumgarten doing rambling about the continent in the care of a rummy old uncle and a sponsor whose respectability and social connections clearly had been bought?

Deferring that question, he pulled another page from under her elbow and looked it over. Damn, if she hadn't copied the old boy's words exactly, mistake by priceless mistake. He gave in to the urge to stare at her. Just now, sprawled over her writing like a schoolgirl over her sums, she didn't look like a wily and ruthless title hunter.

He bent to speak directly into her ear but found himself inhaling the perfume of her warmth, tracing her unguarded features with his eyes, sweeping her half-naked back with a tactile glance. She seemed so fresh, so sensual, so—*Get on with it, man, before you start salivating.*

"Miss Bumgarten." He smacked a hand on the tabletop, startling her awake. She jerked up, blinking in confusion and batting down a piece of writing paper stuck to her cheek. He grinned at the sight she made with her eyes widened by shock and a blot of ink on one cheek, deliciously unaware that the tops of her nipples were peeping over the rim of her bodice. "I suggest you pull yourself together. You're in danger of satisfying my rather prurient curiosity."

Chapter Five

Daisy froze for an instant, her heart pounding as a specimen of Prime, Grade A English beef came into focus. She could have sworn she was still asleep, still dreaming about that very face with its kiss-me-witless-lips and strip-me-naked eyes. It wasn't until Lord Ashton stepped behind her and began to pull her laces that she knew for certain it was no dream.

"Aghhh—what are you—"

She tried to shoot to her feet, but her ball gown lagged behind, held down by its own ponderous weight. With a strangled cry, she sank back to collect her gown about her before lurching up again.

"What the devil are you doing here?" Crimson-faced, she turned on him and followed his gaze to her breasts, which were doing their best to escape her corset. She pulled her gown higher and wrapped her arms around it to hold it in place.

"Saving your modesty, it seems." He strode around her, turned her by the shoulders, and seized her corset laces. "Against every impulse in my flawed mortal frame."

He yanked hard enough to make her gasp.

"Will you stop that?"

He pulled her back toward him by her laces and leaned to her ear.

"Most ladies say that when someone is trying to get them *out* of their clothes." Those words—uttered with finger-tingling intimacy—brought her resistance to a halt.

"I guess you would know," she snapped.

"Yes," he responded with a wicked chuckle. "I would."

The moment he finished tying off her corset she turned to give him a royal dressing down. But Uncle Red chose that moment to stir.

"You want him to know I caught you half naked in the drawing room?" Lord Ashton whispered, reaching for her shoulders to turn her again. "Horrors. Think of the scandal."

If he thought that, she told herself, he seriously under-estimated Uncle Red's tolerance for breaches of etiquette, not to mention her own *in*tolerance for being told what to do. She wrenched free and backed away just as Uncle Red reached his feet.

"Who the devil are you?" Red demanded, rubbing his bleary eyes.

"This is Lord Ashton, Uncle Red. He's here to . . . to . . ."

"Authenticate your niece's lineage," Lord Ashton said with aristocratic aplomb.

Red scowled and scratched his chin, chest, and belly thoroughly.

"He's the duke's brother." Daisy tried to clarify things. "He's supposed to make sure those names you recited last night are real."

"Actually, I believe I'm here just to certify your proof of that. A small but important distinction." Lord Ashton stepped over to the card table, giving the still open back of her gown a pointed glance as he passed. "And I must say, I am surprised to find you have already made a start toward documenting her forbearers." He lifted a page to peruse. "But then, you Americans are known to be an industrious lot."

"Awww," Uncle Red growled. "It's too damned early to be puttin' up with the likes of him." He headed for the door, continuing his morning scratch. "I need me some coffee."

"I took the liberty of ordering some," Lord Ashton said even as Uncle Red lumbered out. Shrugging off Red's rejection, he unbuttoned his coat and seated himself with a flourish in her former seat at the card table.

Liberties. Daisy watched him settle into her chair as if he belonged there. He had perfected the art of the disarming intrusion. She had never met a man so ready to seize control at the slightest opportunity. You'd think *he* was the duke instead of his brother.

"What have we here?" He perused her notes. "'Beaufort' . . . a rather grand point of origin for your family tree, I must say." He scanned another page, then another. "Your 'Woodpiles' are most likely 'Woodvilles,' you know . . . a controversial family who supplied England with a queen and a lot of upstart nobles. These 'Nibbles' I suspect to actually be 'Nevilles.' You do have cheek, you Bumgartens, claiming connection to some of England's most famous noble houses."

She snatched the papers from him but stopped short, distracted from uttering a few air-sizzling epithets. The names actually made sense?

"What famous houses?"

"Come now. Why not just confess that you plucked a history book off the shelf and wrote down every name you came across?"

Her eyes narrowed. On their ranch in Nevada she had been taught that there were animals in the wild that a body should never run from. Apparently that bit of wisdom applied to civilized society as well, for it was clear to her now that Ashton Graham was just such a beast.

Flashes of sensual heat notwithstanding, she had to make him understand she did not intend to abandon her quest.

"I'm not much for history books. But if I were, you can

bet they'd be American ones, not English." She crossed her
arms and narrowed her eyes. "If Uncle Red says his pa made
him memorize those names, then he did. I can't imagine how
else he'd come by them otherwise—him being just a hard-
drinking old prospector from the Nevada hills."

He looked her up and down; the corner of his mouth
pursed as he studied her testy declaration, then went back to
sorting through the pages.

"What have we here? A Palmer, a Howard, and a Fitzroy."
There he stopped with his finger on the last name. His face
darkened. "You claim to have a *Fitzroy* in your lineage?"

"Apparently." She tried to read the change in his de
meanor, but found too few clues in his sudden intensity.
"What does that mean?"

He mulled it over. "A Palmer and a Fitzroy."

"Sounds faintly Irish. I know you English have a grudge
against them, but—"

"It is not Irish. 'Fitzroy' is purely English. 'Fitz' means
'born from,' 'roy' refers to the royal—'the king.'"

"Born from"—she was more focused on his attitude than
his words—"a king?" Her heart sank when she realized he
was serious. Her knees weakened. Damn and blast Uncle
Red for claiming royal connections! What had he gotten
them into?

She snatched the page from his hands and found the
name that had caused such a change in him. "Charlotte
Fitzroy?" She looked up. "Who was she? Anybody . . .
special?" She had almost said "anybody *real*?"

He stared at her for a long moment, suspicion slowly
melting into a frank examination of her face. His gaze kept
coming back to her right cheek. She could feel there was
something on it, but refused to touch it and give him the
satisfaction of knowing his scrutiny made her self-conscious.
He rose and she found herself facing a wall of a chest and the
abundant heat of a big, male body.

Damn.

Tall and dark. With wicked possibilities in his eyes. Her breast tingled where he had touched it. Double damn. Her *skin* remembered him.

"Why do you want to be a duchess?" he asked, his voice husky.

"Why wouldn't I?" She took a step backward. "Duchesses wear rich clothes and fine jewels . . . attend fine parties and balls . . . go to grand soirees and ceremonies. They have armies of servants to see to their every need and admirers to flatter every mood. They live in palaces and ride in great carriages—"

"All of which you have right now, if even a small part of your reputed wealth is real," he charged. "What do you need a duke for?"

There was no reason not to tell him, she reasoned. Doing so might legitimize her quest a bit and reaffirm her own sense of purpose.

"The standing, of course. As you pointed out, I already have the best of everything else. Why not the best husband possible?"

A laugh burst from him, surprising her.

Damned enthralling sound.

"Sorry. I'm just having trouble picturing my brother as 'best husband' material. Good God, woman, you've listened to Arthur and even danced with him. Surely you have higher aspirations than that."

His bluntness shocked her, until she realized he was trying to draw her into agreeing with him. Her face flamed with indignation, and she tossed the papers back onto the table and drew herself up straight.

"All right, if you insist on knowing . . . I have three younger sisters. *Three*. They're lovely, accomplished, sweet-natured girls who are totally shut out of the snooty ranks of society in New York because their fortune is too new. An 'old' title will balance out our 'new' money and gain society's acceptance for them."

"So, you're sacrificing yourself on the altar of familial obligation."

"Hardly a sacrifice, I think, marrying a top nobleman."

"Hardly an informed opinion, I think, that would lead you to marry into a family and a society you know nothing about." He huffed amusement and looked her over. "What do you know of a duchess's life?"

She strode to the window, threw back the heavy velvet draperies to admit more light, and turned to face him.

"On an ordinary day, a duchess sleeps until ten o'clock, emerges at noon, receives callers until four, takes tea until six, then dresses for dinner at nine . . . after which she indulges in 'entertainments.' She's abed by two and up again at ten for a lengthy toilette and another round." Daisy crossed her arms, grateful for the beams of bright sun warming her mostly bare shoulders. "She attends the opera and the races with equal verve, hosts fox hunts and shooting parties, sponsors charities and is a patroness of the arts. She is a guiding light for the duke's household and the world at large. She holds duty dear and her family's welfare even dearer."

All of which had been memorized from the countess's numerous lectures, for just such an occasion. The way Ashton seemed to be re-evaluating the situation as he edged toward her made the effort seem worthwhile.

"You have conducted a thorough study indeed." He gave a courtly nod. "But I fear you have left off the foremost duty of a duchess."

"Which is?" she said archly, emboldened by her success.

"To give the duke an heir." He leaned forward, letting his gaze drift downward to her well-displayed bosom. "To furnish the duke's bed and bring forth a healthy son from what transpires there."

He would bring *that* into the discussion. She rolled her eyes, hoping the gesture would distract from her overheated cheeks.

"That takes no special talent or attention to duty."

"A view probably not shared by numerous queens of the realm who were divorced, beheaded, or replaced for failing at that very thing."

"Millions of women give birth to male children each year. The proof is plowing fields, swabbing ship's decks, and mucking out horse stalls all across the country." A reckless impulse made her add: "Who knows—I may find that particular duty quite pleasant with your brother."

That took some of the smugness out of his expression.

"You overestimate Arthur," he said, straightening. "He is hardly the amorous sort."

"Every man is 'the amorous sort,' given the proper occasion."

"Once again, Miss Bumgarten, you invite the question of how you became such an expert on men." He strolled still closer, spreading his coat to prop fists on his waist.

She was prepared for the question this time.

"I grew up on a ranch in Nevada, where men outnumber women five to one. I lived among and worked alongside all kinds of men. I'd have to be a 'dim Dora' indeed not to have learned something about them."

He assessed that comment and her steady, unapologetic regard.

"I think you'll find 'cowboys' and dukes of the realm are cut from very different cloth."

"Oh? Dukes are too grand to be moved by the sight of a well-turned ankle? Too high-minded to appreciate the scent of a lady's hair or the warmth in a pair of flirting eyes? Can you honestly say they are never affected by the brush of a fan against their sleeve or the feel of a woman's waist as she is

assisted into a carriage?" She laughed quietly at the way his
eyes darkened and his chin jerked back.

"Arthur is a devout naturalist. A virtual hermit," he said,
with growing irritation. "Comfortable only with his bugs
and his peering glass."

When she didn't respond immediately, he looked down at
her. She smiled, feeling solid ground under her feet for the
first time that morning.

"I believe I can say with some authority that your brother
is as susceptible to such things as the next man."

He stiffened visibly, his face a slate she found hard to
read. He didn't like the notion of his older brother being
human enough to desire and take pleasure? Or was it the
idea of Duke Arthur taking pleasure with *her* that he found
objectionable? She smiled at that thought.

"Your Lordship!" came the countess's strained voice from
the doorway, causing them to break apart and back away
from each other. Daisy's sponsor bustled into the room with
a harried air, her face flushed, smoothing her dark skirts
nervously. "A most pleasant surprise."

"The duke's brother was just attempting to tutor me on
the duties of a duchess." Daisy's voice carried a bit too much
determination. "I told him that I would have no difficulty
with what is required."

The countess halted halfway across the chamber, reading
in their proximity and posture that something personal had
transpired between them. Blotches of color appeared in her
pale cheeks.

"Well, of course not," she said emphatically, taking in
Daisy's half-laced bodice. "A young lady of superior breeding and fine old lineage—Miss Bumgarten will be a jewel
in the Meridian crown."

"Yes, well. What she is and what she will be remains to
be seen." Lord Ashton tugged down his waistcoat and
stepped to the table to lift a page from the pile of papers.

"The *Beauforts*? Half of England makes claims to their seed and with good reason; they were a potent and tempestuous lot and—conveniently—most of their family records have been destroyed. There is no way to prove or deny claims to them."

"None at all?" Daisy's heart sank and she glanced at the countess, who was scowling pointedly at her half-laced gown and making a furtive swiping gesture toward her cheek. The potential collapse of Daisy's hopes eclipsed the countess's inscrutable hints. Then it struck her that she was taking his word for it. The library-lurking, eavesdropping, freehanded varmint—why in the world would she ever believe *him*?

"Well, if there is no way to prove we come from Beauforts"—she dug deep into her pride and squared her shoulders—"we'll have to find someone else, someone further down the list . . . like . . . like that Fitzroy girl, that Charlotte." She ignored the way the countess moved closer and motioned more openly. "If she was a king's daughter, she has to be listed in records somewhere."

"King's daughter?" The countess halted mid-hint, her jaw dropping.

"I believe the countess is trying to tell you that you have ink on your cheek," Lord Ashton said, tossing the page back to the table and producing a handkerchief. He positioned himself in front of her, holding the linen ready, and ordered, "Stick out your tongue."

"I beg your pardon." Daisy was confused by both his proximity and his demand. What the devil was he—

"Have it your way," he said, then moistened his tongue, gave the cloth a long, slow stroke with it, and turned the dampened linen on her.

"Hey!" He held her by the arm and wiped her cheek as if she were a newborn calf that needed licking. "How dare you?" she growled, finally succeeding in shoving one arm aside. "Get your paws off me!" A moment later he released her and backed away, leaving her wrestling with the impulse to kick him someplace that would leave his future kids dizzy.

"Charlotte Fitzroy?" he said, his voice sounding a bit huskier than it had a moment ago. He tucked his handkerchief back into his breast pocket. "The living expert on the Fitzroys is at Oxford. Queen's College. Professor Broadman Huxley. And if you can get information out of that old prune, you're a better man than most."

Her spit-cleaned cheek burned like it had been washed in lye.

"I *am* better than most men," she snapped, flinging a finger toward the hallway, demanding he exit. "I am a *woman*."

The wretch threw back his head and laughed—*laughed*—as he struck off for the front door. He arrived at the archway to the hall at the very moment the butler arrived with a rattling cart laden with coffee and morning buns.

"Ah. Just in time." He paused to pour himself a cup and cream and sugar it properly. Then he stood for a moment with the cup in one hand and the other propped insolently on his waist. Only when he had drained the cup did he hand it off to the bewildered manservant with a "Damned fine coffee" and stride out.

Daisy's teeth were clamped so hard that her jaws hurt.

"That," the countess said, glaring after him, "is no gentleman."

"Gentleman, *hell*—he's a low-down, sneaky, egg-suckin' hound." Ignoring the countess's cringe at her language, she collected the skirts of her weighty ball gown into her arms—revealing the stockings and garters she had rolled down to her ankles for comfort—and headed for the stairs. Just inside the archway to the hall, she paused at the coffee cart, poured herself a cup, and threw back a big gulp.

"But maybe a useful hound." Her eyes crinkled at the corners and a slow, crafty smile appeared. "Jonas," she

addressed the butler, "bring down our trunks out of storage."
She turned a full, knowing grin on the countess. "We're
going to Oxford. Wherever the hell that is."

Just down the street, minutes later, Ashton sat in a two-
seater cab watching the doors of Daisy Bumgarten's house
and trying desperately to purge the memory of the texture of
her skin from his senses. He kept seeing that ink on her
cheek—not just a smudge, but an entire word absorbed
from the inked velum her face had rested on. One word.
Damned if he hadn't felt a jolt of prescience the moment she
raised her head.

Wife.

Before long, a young boy came running out of the alley
beside the house to perch, breathless, on the step of his cab.

"Th' under houseman . . . 'e's jawin' about havin' to drag
out them big trunks agin, an' the cook, she's complainin'
about all th' food she's laid in goin' bad if there's nobody
there to eat it."

"Good work," Ashton declared, flipping the boy a gold
coin that made the urchin's eyes pop as he detached from the
cab door and scurried off.

Rapping on the roof with his knuckles, he called out to
the cabbie, "Severin House in Grosvenor Square. And make
it quick."

She had taken the bait.

Chapter Six

Ashton blew through the front doors of the stately but somewhat past its prime Severin House, shouting orders for his valet to assemble his kit and sending a serving boy to the local livery to have his horse ready for the train in half an hour. As he headed for the main stairs, a voice from the drawing room halted him in his tracks.

"Ashton, old chum."

Oh, God. Not now. He turned his head.

Reynard Boulton, heir of the Viscount Tannehill, thorough reprobate and spectacular gossip, was leaning against the door frame with his arms tucked across his chest and his legs crossed at the ankles. A sly look of assessment lighted his face as he took in Ashton's exquisitely groomed appearance and evident unease.

"In need of money again?" Ashton raised his chin and continued to the staircase and up. "Out of luck, I'm afraid. I'm skinned myself."

"You wound me," Reynard said with exaggerated petulance, pushing off with his shoulder and sauntering to the center of the hall. "Suggesting that I only seek you out to put the touch on you." He sniffed, making a show of forgiving the slight. "As it happens, I come bearing news."

Ashton stopped dead in the middle of the stairs. His very skin contracted. To ignore such an entrée would be to court disaster. "The Fox," as Reynard was known in fashionable circles, had a nose for scandal unequaled in the Western Hemisphere. If there was disgrace or depravity to be uncovered, the Fox found it first. If recklessness and ruination titillated society's imagination, it was the Fox who supplied the details. If trouble and discord beset noble houses, the Fox was the first one to lay it about. And sometimes—chilling thought—even to stir it into existence.

The fact that he had brought news to Severin House could only mean that one of its hapless residents had fallen under Reynard's jaundiced gaze and was about to become the subject of a campaign of curiosity. Since Ashton's own waywardness had long since been diced and digested by society's appetite for scandal, it could only be his poor brother who was about to fall under the Fox's quizzing glass. And there could only be one aspect of his brother's dull life that would be of interest to London's premier gossip.

"News of what?" Ashton turned fully on the step, staring down at the future viscount. "Or should I say 'whom'?"

"Surely you won't make me divulge this juicy bit here in the hallway," Reynard said, with a wicked glint in his eye. "I've had a long night of it, Ash. Haven't been to bed yet, and I'm positively famished."

"Damn it, Reynard—I've a train to catch."

"Oh? And where are we going that requires such urgency? Hmm?"

Trapped. *We.* He wouldn't put it past Reynard to follow him all the way to Oxford, if he didn't hand over something. Swearing softly, Ashton stomped back down the steps, instructed the butler hovering nearby to lay on breakfast in the dining room, and led the treacherous Fox down the hall and into that little used chamber.

Coffee, scones with cream, and peach preserves were

served immediately, thanks to the cook's penchant for rising early and being prepared to provide whoever had furnished the upstairs beds the previous night with a suitably romantic breakfast. She always kept morning-appropriate delicacies at the ready, along with effective remedies for grievous overindulgence and intimate infestations. She was worth her weight in gold, their cook.

"Ummm." Reynard savored the aroma of the coffee and scones. "Your cook is a marvel, Ash. Where did you say you found her, again?"

"I didn't." Ash sipped, feeling his empty stomach tighten in complaint around the coffee. "In fact, I make it a point never to say."

"Selfish of you," Reynard said, dishing himself heaps of peach preserves. "But then, I do appreciate the desire to protect a valuable asset." He carefully bisected a scone and slathered it with clotted cream.

"About this juicy bit you have . . ." Ashton probed with less finesse than he would have liked. He needed to get past this and on to the station.

"You're not eating?" Reynard studied him and chewed thoughtfully.

Ashton glared, hating the way Reynard was dragging this out. He grabbed a scone, ripped it open, and spread it with cream and preserves. When he'd taken a huge bite, Reynard smiled.

"Now, isn't that better? Never take news on an empty stomach."

"What news?" Ashton demanded, aching to be rid of Reynard.

"Word is that your brother is the object of a matrimonial campaign."

Ashton managed what sounded like a hearty laugh—only part of which was forced. "Artie? Matrimonially targeted? Don't be absurd."

"Is it absurd that the only female he squired around the floor at Mountjoy's ball was a rich American with a countess for a sponsor?"

How the devil—it took Ashton a supreme bit of effort to make his face and body appear casually alert.

"You were there?" He tipped a bit more coffee into his cup. "You saw this for yourself?"

"I arrived shortly after, but whispers were to be heard. And several of your family members were spotted arriving . . . Lady Sylvia, I believe, and the estimable Baron Beesock—your Uncle Bertram—and your Uncle Seward, among others. A veritable gathering of the family elders." Reynard pursed his mouth and narrowed his eyes. "Wouldn't have figured the Meridians for offering up the family coronet to the highest bidder."

"I fear you have it wrong, Fox. Artie is as clueless as ever. The family creaks and groans insisted he attend, hoping to see some signs of life in him. Did your sources not tell you that there was another who danced with that entrepreneurial princess?"

"Another?" Reynard paused, digesting that, and reached for more coffee. "Who might that have been?"

Ashton let his answer begin with raised eyebrows, and then slowly added a broadening smile until he was the very picture of smug insinuation.

"You?" Reynard sat back, surprised but quickly dismissive. "An untitled, penniless second son?"

"Yes, well." Ash's grin tightened at that reminder of how little he had to offer. "It makes as much sense as *Artie* marrying a beautiful, filthy-rich heiress."

At that moment, the butler arrived with eggs, kippers, potatoes, and bacon. The pause gave Ash a moment to collect himself and realize that Fox probably already had the wealthy American in his sights, watching as she made forays into London society. He relaxed in earnest this time. Before him sat a potential source of knowledge about Miss Bumgarten.

"So what do you know about this well heeled American?" he asked, not bothering to hide his curiosity. "I take it you've seen her and probably even been introduced."

"Not yet, but I have done some investigation." Fox piled his plate with food before continuing. "Family fortune made in silver, and quite a sum. She is a beauty, though not of the delicate Pear soap variety. Walks at a fast clip, pours her tea into houseplants when no one is looking, rides a huge, black devil of a horse—*everywhere*—and laughs loudly enough to give her sponsor the vapors."

"You're certain she's here to snag a title? Perhaps she's just on a grand tour, acquiring a much needed bit of continental polish."

"A wardrobe of Worth gowns, a house near Hyde Park, and a pile of invitations engineered by the Countess of Kew?" Fox stuffed a kipper in his mouth and talked around it: "If she were just touring, she'd have taken a hotel suite and made friends with whatever displaced French nobles she found in the lobby." He chewed, swallowed, and grinned. "No, no, my boy, she's on the hunt. And it will be entertaining to see where she aims her considerable arsenal of feminine wiles." He eyed Ashton while helping himself to more potatoes. "And as for Artie's missing attractions . . . I assure you, a dukedom can make up for any number of manly deficits."

Ashton appeared to take that into consideration while, in fact, reeling from the possibility that Fox might be right—at least where Daisy Bumgarten was concerned. She was a determined wench; he'd give her that. And Artie had partnered her through a whole dance or two, which had to be something of a social milestone for him. He recalled the fond way Artie had gazed at her silk butterflies, and he froze.

Good God. Had his elder brother actually been gazing at the chit's bosoms? If so, things were worse than he thought. He had to get to Oxford and Huxley right away.

"Lovely breakfasting with you, Reynard, but I must be on

my way." He rose, plopped his napkin by his mostly bare plate, and finished his coffee in a couple of gulps. "Family business. Uncle Seward's birthday, you know." And he turned on his heel and strode out, leaving the Fox with a mouthful of food and a look of surprise.

"Wait—the old cod was actually *born*?" he called after Ash.

Reynard chuckled at the irritable way Ash waved off the comment as he made his escape. His news seemed to have lit a fire under the usually unflappable Meridian spare. Now why was that?

He intended to find out. If there was anything Reynard Boulton couldn't countenance, it was the existence of a secret he didn't possess. He sighed, poured himself another coffee, and tucked into the eggs again. No sense in letting a proper breakfast go to waste. It would be simple enough to find out where Ashton Graham was headed.

The train to Oxford seemed to take forever. Daisy paced the aisle of the richly appointed first-class cabin between the countess's and Uncle Red's knees, checked on their horses in the baggage car three times, and fidgeted through the countess's lecture on the history and structure of the university they were about to visit. When she got to the part about the importance of the "dons" and the protocol with which they must be addressed, Daisy groaned aloud.

"You must listen, Miss Bumgarten." The countess shook her finger. "Whatever you do, show proper deference for the professor. As a rule, Oxford dons are not fond of women. It hasn't been that many years since the faculty wasn't even permitted to marry. Most colleges were founded by donations made as a duty to the church, you see. Historically the university produced clerics for the Church of England. Celibate and abstemious ones, at that.

"Women have always been considered lesser intellectual lights, unequal to the rigors of scholarship, so having a young woman poking around in his field of study may offend Professor Huxley. He must be approached carefully and with great attention to his scholarly sensibilities."

There was that word again. "Sensibilities." Daisy sighed and straightened the peplum of her jacket. She was sick of hearing about Englishmen's easily offended sensibilities. You'd think they were all delicate flowers, to hear the countess talk. But to her it was just another way of saying "thin skinned" and "poor loser." The English male took major offense at being challenged or discomforted in any way. He couldn't bear being outdone at cards, on horseback, or even in conversation.

"Don't worry, Countess," she said with a wicked smile. "I'll behave. Before I'm through, he'll be dishing up facts on Charlotte Fitzroy like they're bangers an' mash."

The countess closed her eyes and groaned quietly, no doubt regretting ever allowing Daisy and her uncle Red to hear about the unique culture and cuisine of the neighborhood pub. Now they couldn't let a day pass without a reference to "bangers an' mash" or "bubble an' squeak" . . . usually accompanied by riotous laughter.

As the train pulled into the Oxford station, Daisy let down the window to stick her head out, and in came coal smoke, laden with the tang of machine oil, the smell of greasy food from the box-vendors, and the sweat-and-wet-wool odors of the mass of humanity crowded onto the platform. She coughed and quickly raised the window glass.

Red found them a cab and made arrangements for a second one to carry their luggage and Daisy's newly hired lady's maid, Collette, and groom, Banks. Daisy's horse, Midnight Dancer, and Uncle Red's favorite mount, Renegade, were inspected and tied on behind the second cab, with Banks seated on the luggage to watch over them.

Soon they were rolling through the city with Daisy's nose practically pressed against the window. Everywhere she looked something was pointing heavenward; spires and steeples topped every major building.

"I see what you mean about this place." She glanced at the long-suffering countess out of the corner of her eye. "More da—danged churches than anyplace else on earth. No wonder they're all abstainers."

"Abstainers?" Red, who had dozed through the countess's earlier lecture, looked horrified and headed to the other side windows for evidence.

"The architecture," the countess said pointedly, peering at Daisy from under her hat brim, "is meant to elevate the inhabitants' thoughts to a higher plane. A clear lesson on how one is expected to *behave* in these precincts."

The brick-paved streets soon gave way to cobbled lanes lined with ancient houses, shops, and the fronts of grander establishments that the countess informed her were the "colleges" of the famed center of learning. Everywhere the streets were thick with young men garbed in black robes, some carrying books and folders and striding purposefully, others carrying a snout-full of drink and struggling to stay upright. Red looked vastly relieved as they passed a noisy ale hall, and he scratched his bristled chin.

"May be my kinda place, after all."

The Holloway House was a dignified stone structure, provided with all the modern conveniences, including indoor plumbing "en suite." Lush, parklike gardens stretched off toward one of the college greens. A small livery lay behind the main grounds and a well-regarded dining establishment took up a significant part of the main floor. At least they would be comfortable during their search for proof of her connection to Charlotte Fitzroy.

The countess announced she needed time to rest and refresh from the journey, but Daisy was eager to get started. After the countess retired, she wasted no time in setting off with Red to find Queen's College. Following directions from the concierge of the hotel, they soon located the place.

An imposing iron gate opened onto the street, with a gatehouse beyond guarding the entrance to a quadrangle formed by buildings made of light-colored stone. A hound-faced fellow in a dark suit, wearing a bowler hat, confronted them the minute they stepped through the ornate arch. When they asked after Professor Broadman Huxley, he scowled and said the professor wasn't there. It took a winsome smile from Daisy and the offer of a fragrant cigar from Red to get him to divulge that the professor didn't lecture or give tutorials these days; he was "emeritus" . . . whatever that was. A young fellow in a black robe strolling through the gate heard him and paused to translate "emeritus" into "pensioned" for them. Apparently, the illustrious professor now spent most of his time on the college's estates.

"But it's important that we speak with him about his work on the Fitzroys." Daisy produced a look of distress calculated to elicit gentlemanly assistance. "Could you point us in the direction of his estate?"

At the younger fellow's insistence, the porter drew them something of a map. While he worked, Red slipped out to locate the nearest ale hall and secure a nip of the Irish and bottle of Scottish whiskey to say thanks.

They arrived back at Holloway House to find the countess standing in the lobby with her arms crossed and her foot tapping in annoyance.

"You walked into the town without a word to me?" she said.

"I was eager to get started," Daisy said, producing the map. "We went to the college and found out the professor is 'rusticating.'"

"He's what?" The countess looked taken aback.

"Rusticating? That's what the young fellow in the black robe said." Daisy looked to Red, who nodded affirmation.

"'Rusticating' is a term used when a student is sent down from college for some breach of rules or standards," the countess declared. "Surely a renowned professor like Huxley was not expelled for misconduct."

"Well, I don' know what he did, but he got a pension fer it," Red put in, roundly confused.

That mollified the countess, who raised an eyebrow. "A sad attempt at humor, then. Come. It is much too late to begin scouring the countryside for this 'estate.' We should have dinner and begin our search the first thing in the morning."

Chapter Seven

"Wha' do ye want?" A round dumpling of a woman with graying hair and the scent of flour and cinnamon about her answered Daisy's knock on the cottage door the next morning. The porter's map had proven exceptionally true, but it would have helped a great deal to know that "estate" was their hoity-toity way of saying "farm." Englishmen. Daisy, Red, and the countess passed the place three times before realizing the picturesque cottage, outbuildings, and pens populated by all manner of farm animals were indeed their destination.

Daisy adjusted her jacket, glanced around the neat gardens, and smiled. "We have come to see Professor Huxley. This is his home?"

The old girl gave them a thorough once-over, openly assessing the carriage, the fine clothes, and the fancy horseflesh.

"Wull, 'e don't tutor these days. And anyways, he ain't here."

"He can't 'ave strayed far—not with such a handsome lass in th' house," Red said, with a wink that brought color and a surprised grin to the housekeeper's worn face. Daisy watched him charming the woman and wondered where he had picked up the word "lass."

"He be out in the far shed." The woman pointed over her shoulder with her thumb. "Bessie's calvin' an' he's . . . tendin' 'er."

"Would you mind if we wait, dear lady?" Red asked with a flourish.

She studied his grand appearance and gallant talk, but must have decided that purposeful flattery was better than no flattery at all, for she smiled coquettishly and gave a small dip at the knee.

"Becky's th' name, sarr. Housekeeper fer th' perfesser." She regarded Daisy and the countess with less approval, but stepped back and waved them forward. "In with 'e, then, and I'll put a kettle on. Could be a spell b'fore he's finished."

Red and the countess followed the housekeeper inside, but Daisy paused on the doorstep, then turned without a word and strode off through the gardens in search of her quarry.

The place was an idealized miniature of a working farm . . . everything half scale and what the gentry would call "quaint." The cottage sat amidst a well-tended garden of hollyhocks, daylilies, nasturtiums, and asters, and was climbed by prolific red roses. Hedge roses climbed sheds and fence posts along a path of well-laid bricks that swept through flocks of ducks, geese, and chickens, then later broadened to include a vine-covered arbor complete with a stone bench. Each paddock, fence, and shed was neatly whitewashed and the barn itself was a brick, hip-roofed structure with carved stone cornices and no small number of furbelows. It was nothing less than idyllic. Exactly the kind of place a high-minded professor might choose to live out his twilight years.

As she approached the farthest shed, she heard a man's harried voice floating from it and hurried to the edge of the half wall that made up the sides of the structure. Inside, an older man in plus fours, rubber boots, and tweed coat and vest paced beside a doe-eyed cow lying on a bed of straw. The beast's sides bulged; she was indeed in the throes of giving birth.

"Come now, Bessie, let's get on with it," the professor implored. "This is a fully natural process. Part of intricate weave of the fabric of life. A touch of the grand and eternal mystery." Exasperation began to show as he pointed to a book lying atop the far wall. "You've heard what Erasmus and John Locke had to say: Nothing worthwhile comes without effort. Put your heart into it and give it a proper push."

"Professor?" Daisy called, standing on her tiptoes to lean over the side of the shed. "Professor Broadman Huxley?"

The man turned partway, scowled at her, and declared "Not now" with a dismissive wave. "I'm engaged in a tricky bit of animal husbandry, here."

Daisy frowned. "I have traveled a long way to see you, Professor. All the way from New York."

"If you've waited that long, you can wait a bit longer," he said irritably. "This poor creature is giving birth and in need of instruction."

He knelt by the cow, produced a small book from his jacket pocket, and began to read to her in a language that sounded suspiciously like Latin.

"What the devil are you doing?" she called.

He turned halfway, clearly annoyed. "Dipping into philosophy from the wisdom of the Greats. The classical masters are full of it."

"They're *full of it* all right," she muttered. The old boy was thick as cow pies. Stepping around the shed for a better look, she spotted a pair of hooves protruding from the cow's rear quarters. While she watched, the cow's muscles contracted and the forelegs were thrust out further, and then retreated as soon as the contraction passed. The same ineffectual process was repeated twice more before it struck her what was happening.

"Is it her first calf?" she called to the professor. He bristled and read louder. "I said: Is she a first-calf heifer? How long has this been going on?"

"I don't know who you are, young woman"—he turned, still squatting, red faced, and irritable—"but your presence here is both inappropriate and unwanted. Be so good as to remove yourself and allow me to minister to this poor creature."

"Minister?" Daisy was struck forcefully by the old boy's high-handed dismissal, but fought past her annoyance to concentrate on the emerging crisis. "Reading to her is not going to do a bit of good. She's got a big calf." She pointed. "Look at the size of those legs and hooves."

Before he could respond, she had removed her gloves and was around the open end of the shed, unbuttoning her jacket.

"Now, see here—" He stood and spread his arms to bar her from the sight. When she darted around him to look closer at the business end, he gasped. "Come away from there, this instant! This is most unseemly!"

"It's not just unseemly, it's downright dangerous." She draped her jacket over the nearest shed wall and rolled up her sleeves. "Most cows give birth out in the pasture with no trouble, but sometimes—especially with first-calf heifers— a calf may be too big for a cow to birth by herself. That's what's happening here, and if we don't help her, she'll go into shock and she and the calf will die—you'll lose them both."

"You cannot possibly—this is no business for a lady," he said, then glanced anxiously at Bessie, who had begun to make odd panting noises. His eyes flew wide.

"Rope, we need heavy rope," Daisy ordered, turning him by the shoulders and shoving him toward the stall opening. "Or chains."

He halted, staring at Bessie with distress, and Daisy barked: "Now."

A second later, he scrambled out of the shed and headed for the barn. While he was gone, Daisy knelt beside Bessie's head and stroked her stoic face. "It's all right, girl. We're going to get your baby out, safe and sound. It may be your first, but I've been through this dozens of times."

A sudden, powerful wave of feeling swept her, taking her back in time and across an ocean, taking her to spring calving, first-calf heifers, and a stirring of new life that made everything seem possible. For the first time in months, she was intensely homesick. How many times had she sat at a cow's head with a lantern while the ranch hands hauled a calf into the world? How many times had they relented and let her help because they needed an extra pair of hands? Old Jake and Lefty and Fred . . . they had treated her like a princess one day and an annoying kid sister the next. If only she could see them, hear them laugh, and have a snort of whiskey with them again.

The professor came running back with two ropes, one of which seemed sturdy enough. She switched to the business end of the birthing and prayed she remembered the wrap and knots correctly.

"Are you certain you know what you are doing, young woman?"

When she looked up, the professor was teetering between imperious skepticism and naked hope. The way he wrung his hands—he was still uncertain he should be allowing a young female to meddle in such messy business. When she tugged on the ropes to test the knots, his eyes bulged. The impact of what they were about to do finally struck.

"Been pullin' calves since I was knee-high to a prairie dog."

"You're going to pull the calf out?" He staggered a step.

"*We're* going to do it—you and me, Professor."

He produced a handkerchief and mopped sweat from his

brow and she took a moment to tuck her skirts back out of the way.

"We wait for the next contraction—till the legs start coming out again—and then we pull like their lives depend on it, because they do."

They positioned themselves and waited until the legs started to move. They started to pull. "Harder—put your back into it!" she shouted. Despite their best efforts, the legs halted and slid back inside.

"Don't die on me, Bessie!" the professor pleaded, rushing to stroke the cow's head. "If you'll just help me get this calf out, right and proper, I'll never pester you with Aristotle again!"

"We need help, another strong back," Daisy said, thinking of Uncle Red, back at the cottage, and maybe the coachman. But, both were on the downhill side of fifty and no longer used to physical exertion. Then she looked up and found a tall, broad-shouldered answer to their dilemma bearing down them.

At that moment, in the brilliant morning sun, she could have sworn Ashton Graham had a halo of light around his imposing frame. The sure, confident way he walked, the sway of those shoulders . . . By the time he reached the shed, she had to struggle to shake off that unsettling effect.

"Just in time," she greeted him. "Take off your coat and get in here."

Ashton battled through momentary confusion, taking in the half-delivered cow, his old professor's anxiety, and Daisy Bumgarten's rolled sleeves and partly raised skirts.

"Good God, Miss Bumgarten." He stood gripping the sides of his half-shed suit coat, already complying with her demand. "What have you—"

"Now, Mr. Graham."

She turned her attention back to the cow and he found himself entering the shed hatless and in shirtsleeves. She explained that the heifer's calf was too big and they were waiting for the next contraction to begin pulling again. He stared at her in disbelief.

"You expect me to . . ."

"I most certainly do," she said emphatically, and for a moment those blue eyes contained a flash of lightning.

Her sleeves were rolled to the elbows, her half-tucked skirt was littered with straw, and her skin was flushed with warmth. Her honey-blond hair was being teased out of its proper coif by contact with her standing collar. He couldn't recall ever seeing a woman in such circumstances, but he couldn't imagine any of his numerous female acquaintances looking more appealing than Daisy Bumgarten while pulling a calf out of a cow.

He positioned himself on the rope behind Daisy and before the professor, and began to pull when she gave the order. "Harder." So he wrapped his hand with the rope and really put his back into it.

The legs didn't retreat fully this time and Daisy shot a grin over her shoulder.

"It's working. We may get it with this next round."

In fact, two more contractions were required to convince Bessie's body to finally heave the calf out onto the straw. The sudden release sent Ashton and the professor thudding back against the shed wall and Daisy falling back atop Ashton. As she struggled up, she flashed a smile at him and headed for the calf and Bessie. He lay against the wall, stunned, feeling the lingering imprint of her body against him and her hand on his thigh as she pushed away.

The little beast was dark and wet, but it already moved and gasped for its first taste of air.

"Get up, girl, you've got to see him—he's beautiful!" she

coaxed the mother as the little calf struggled to his feet.
"And he needs a good licking."

Ashton got to his feet and helped the professor up. Together they watched in silence as Bessie inspected and
cleaned her calf. It wasn't long before the calf was attempting to stand on legs that were hugely out of proportion to the
rest of him.

"Purely miraculous," Huxley whispered, his voice choked.
"Good job, my girl—good job!" He rushed toward them
and Daisy braced with expectation. But he lurched past her
and threw his arms around the little cow's neck.

A soft smile lit her face as she watched the professor
blink away tears and mumble thanks for Bessie's safe deliv-
ery. Her cheeks were rosy, her lips curved into a perfect bow,
and her eyes—those blue eyes were suddenly as clear and
fathomless as a summer sky. Ashton stared, spellbound.

She looked like a Madonna . . . soft and appealing, giving
and wise in a way he'd never seen in a flesh and blood
woman. Moments later she stepped in to dry the little calf
with some straw and then the hem of her skirt. She laughed
as the calf nuzzled her, and the full, throaty sound sent ripples of reaction beneath his skin.

"Not me, little fella. Your ma's the one with the chuck
wagon." Ashton had no idea what that meant—some god-
awful Americanism, no doubt—but she looked up at him
with such genuine delight, he couldn't help but smile.

"Isn't he beautiful?" she asked in a voice that was pure
music. "So new, so *perfect*." A second later she was on her
knees beside the little beast, running bare hands over his
sturdy little frame and knobby legs.

The professor joined her in adoring the newborn and together they giggled like children. For a moment, Ashton was
drawn into it with them, aroused in soft places he had forgotten existed inside him. His chest grew tight and his knees

were a little spongy. He stood absorbing the wonder of the moment until Huxley turned to Daisy and snatched her hands into his.

"Thank you, thank you, dear lady. Don't know what I would have done if you hadn't happened along. I owe you a debt." He looked chagrined. "And I don't even know your name."

"Daisy Bumgarten, Professor. From Nevada. In the States."

The bottom dropped out of Ashton's stomach.

The Grand Old Man of English History, the feared "Hatchet of Scholarly Hopes," the once dreaded Don of Doom . . . blubbering over a cow and slathering gratitude on a dollar princess who fancied herself an expert in bovine midwifery. What the hell happened to his razor-tongued old mentor?

Never mind Huxley—what the hell had happened to *him*?

Chapter Eight

Rattled and not a little appalled by his momentary wallow in sentimentality—*over a cow*—Ashton tugged down his vest, snatched up his coat and hat, and strode out of the shed. He was halfway up the path to the cottage when he realized he was leaving Huxley in Daisy Bumgarten's clutches. Making an abrupt about-face, he retraced his steps and arrived just in time to hear Daisy extracting an agreement from Huxley to meet her at the Bodleian Library to review documents from his former collection. That took a moment to sink in. His crusty old tutor had donated his remarkable collection of primary source documents to a library?

"All of it? Even your collection of letters?" he said, staggering mentally.

"All of it," Huxley said proudly. "I had my go at it, and I'm on to far more worthy and profound things."

"Like cows," Ash said shortly, working to keep the curl from his lips.

"Like cows," Huxley echoed, with unabashed pleasure before turning to Daisy. "You must stay to luncheon, my dear." He swept Ashton along with Daisy toward the cottage. "And you, too, Ashton. We must have something of a celebration.

My first calf, delivered safely. Thanks to our clever Miss Bumgarten."

Well, this wasn't going the way he'd planned.

Ashton sat back from the modest dinner table in Huxley's cottage and schooled his features. He had intended to reach the old boy first, appeal to his scholarly prejudices in explaining Daisy Bumgarten's search, and recruit his professorial pride in opposition to her. But he hadn't counted on Huxley having retired to the blessed back of beyond, and she got here first. Now his old tutor was bubbling on about the glories of nature and the duty of mankind to "dress, till, and keep" the earth. A biblical imperative, he called it. His mentor had taken a dive into *religious* philosophy in his waning days and hadn't yet surfaced.

"Arcadia is what it's called. Creation unspoiled," Huxley explained. "Humankind living in a sylvan paradise, in harmony with the Almighty, and nature, and with one another. A veritable Garden of Eden. The Greats have all written about it, and artists of every age have attempted to capture it." He got a far-off look in his eyes that made Ashton want to shake him. "Of course, I can only glimpse it here . . . times like today . . . rare, luminous hints of the glory that can be."

"Yeah, well, glory some days," Redmond Strait put in before taking another gulp of wine. "Hellish heat, struggle, and pain other days. Ever seen what's left of a cow after a mountain lion gets through with it?"

The professor looked taken aback and Daisy quickly intervened.

"I believe what Uncle Red means is: some places are more like this 'Arcadia' than others. Out west, things get pretty rough at times. It's eat-or-be-eaten most days. Mountain lions, wolves, bears, coyotes, buzzards—all kinds of varmints have an eye on a rancher's stock."

"Why, I recall times, back in my prospectin' days—" Red launched into a tale of his adventures in Nevada's mountains and flats that had the professor wide-eyed with both horror and fascination.

Ashton watched with ill-concealed annoyance as the pair charmed his old tutor with outlandish stories of western grit and bravado . . . fabricated, no doubt. He would have called a halt or strode out, but Daisy Bumgarten's glances at him during the telling reminded him that he was here for her . . . to enchant and distract her. Right now there was nothing he wanted more than to abandon this whole ridiculous mission.

"So, hardly a place for civilized folk, this 'West' of yours," Ashton said when Red paused for another swig of wine.

"A place where men have to be strong to survive," Daisy countered with a fierce little smile. "And women have to be even stronger."

"Speaking of women"—Ashton turned to Huxley— "Miss Bumgarten is in search of a forbearer, one Charlotte Fitzroy. I take it you have agreed to help her look for documentation of that connection."

"I believe there may be documents in my collection pertaining to such issue." Huxley dragged his attention from Red long enough to reply.

"Well, that will be interesting," Ashton said with a small smile. "Considering there are two Charlotte Fitzroys."

"What?" Daisy sat forward, all attention now. "*Two* Charlottes?"

"Indeed. And it's always been something of a muddle to figure out which is being referred to in a given document, right, Professor?"

"Ah. I recall now; one a Countess of Yarmouth and the other a Countess of Lichfield . . . both sired by Charles the Second."

"Both named Charlotte?" Daisy looked with dismay to the countess.

"A feminine derivative of 'Charles,'" Ashton said, trying to hide his pleasure. "Royal mistresses were keen to attach their offspring to their fathers via names, and Charles had numerous mistresses. The trick, Miss Bumgarten, will be to discover which, if any, contributed to your line."

"Low down, egg-suckin' weasel," Daisy muttered as she rode up to the whitewashed stable that served Holloway House. She had ridden furiously on the way back, abandoning Red and the countess in the coach to let Dancer stretch his legs and work off some of her own tension in the process. She was windblown and overheated and determined to make sure Ashton Graham—she refused to call him "Lord Ashton"—didn't interfere with her quest for documentation of her ancestry. She should have guessed something was up when he so helpfully volunteered the professor's name and whereabouts.

She slid from Dancer's back and waved away the stable boy. She'd handle her own tack and brush down her horse. Despite the countess's horror, she insisted on doing it regularly. She found it calming. Grounding. And if she were going to get through this next couple of weeks, she needed to have both feet planted squarely in her greater purpose. Besides, English saddles were easy to heft compared to the western ones she'd grown up on.

With each stroke of the brush, some of her anxiety melted away. She paused to stroke Dancer's head and ears and pressed her forehead against his. Her heartbeat slowed as she murmured softly into his neck. The smell and the sturdy feel of him brought back memories of home. Her real home, in Nevada. The dry, rugged landscape, the painted sky—every color in creation strewn across the sunset—the smell of horses and leather, of ever-present dust and mesquite; it was a feast for the senses. It was a beautiful and proud, difficult and unapologetic land . . . not for the soft or self-obsessed. How she wished that she could go back to the ranch for a few short hours—immerse herself in the smells of coffee boiling and bacon sizzling in the—

"*Tsk, tsk,*" a voice broke the quiet. "What would the countess say?"

She turned with a start and found Ashton Graham leaning against the stall opening, his arms folded and his eyes roaming her with speculation.

"What are you doing here?" she demanded, flushing with heat.

"Stabling my horse."

"Here?"

"I am staying at Holloway House, and this *is* their livery." He turned that assessing gaze on Dancer and the curry brush in her hand. "They have staff to see to that, you know."

"I prefer to do it myself," she said, drawing herself up straighter. "Dancer means a great deal to me, and where I come from, a person sees to his or her own horse. It's a personal obligation that begets a personal bond. You take care of your horse and your horse takes care of you."

"And does he?" He had that look in his eyes, that bone-melting, meet-me-in-the-hayloft kind of look. "Take care of you?"

"He will if the time comes," she said, wishing the varmint wasn't so close or so tall or so damned male. Parts of her she was determined to ignore began to tingle. Unrepentantly. Curse his broad, nubile lips. . . . It was something of a task to watch him talk without licking her own in anticipation. As she struggled with her responses, he moved closer and ran a hand over Dancer's hip and down his flank.

"Beautiful animal," he murmured, closer still. Then his

gaze transferred to her and his deepening tones invaded her skin. "Every line pure perfection."

"You don't have to be much of a judge of horseflesh to see that." She took a step back, scowling. "He's the best damned stallion in the state of Nevada . . . maybe in the whole western U.S."

"Quite a claim." He slid closer, watching her like a hawk does a rabbit.

She retreated around Dancer, giving his head a stroke as she ducked beneath the stall rope. "My daddy—God rest his soul—was a keen judge of horseflesh and bought a couple of Arabians to breed into our quarter horses. Midnight Dancer, here, is a result." She busied her hands with the brush, giving Dancer long, firm strokes that hid the way her hand trembled. "Strength and nimble footwork paired with increased endurance. Silver River horses are known all the way to Sacramento and San Francisco."

"Silver River?"

"The name of our ranch: Silver River. That's what water looks like coming down over rocks in the mountains. Pure silver. And that's where our money came from: silver." She looked up from brushing and he was ducking under the stall rope himself, running hands over Dancer like he was in a buying mood. She'd nip that in the bud. "He's not for sale."

"Everything has a price, Silver Girl." He stopped by her shoulder and she could feel his gaze on her. Every inch of her skin came alive with expectation; she had gooseflesh in places she didn't want to think about. Curse his hide. Against her own better judgment, she lowered her hand to her side, staring straight ahead, waiting to see what would happen.

She wasn't sure what to expect, but it wasn't the way he ran a knuckle down the side of her face as if he were memorizing it. Nor was it the way he withdrew enough to touch only the wisps of hair the wind had teased out of place during her ride. Along her face, then by her ear, and along the nape of her neck . . . it tickled. Deliciously. It made her want to lean into his hand. She swallowed hard, resisting, until he gave a low, nerve-tingling laugh . . . a wicked sound that said he knew exactly what was happening in her.

Varmint. He was using her own impulses against her, hinting that he knew things about her, maybe things she didn't know about herself. Well, she did know, all too well, how responsive she was to tall, dark men with bad intentions. But knowing didn't stop her from turning to face him and looking up into those handsome autumn-forest eyes. What she read there surprised her; sensual gamesmanship, certainly, but also flat-out curiosity.

And there was something else in his eyes, something that had nothing to do with his purpose here. It was desire. He truly wanted to kiss her, exactly the way she wanted to kiss him. Then she knew: this desire, this longing for a taste of the forbidden, was going to dangle between them until the deed was done and the impulse laid to rest.

Damn it.

Taking a deep breath, she tilted her head, raised her face, softening her mouth in an unmistakable offer. Down came his face, his lips parting as they met hers, and she plunged headfirst into a potent stream of sensation.

Warm and soft and yet firm and responsive, his mouth made heat bloom in her core and streak down the backs of her legs. Sweet Nevada, it was perfect the way he fitted his mouth to hers and coaxed her lips apart. She swayed and shifted on her feet, widening her stance. Only their lips were touching, but her whole body responded with an urge to mold against him and absorb every sensation his tall, muscular frame could offer.

His tongue traced the opening between her lips with light, tantalizing strokes that drew her deeper into the kiss. And suddenly her hands were sliding up his chest and gripping his lapels, hauling his mouth harder against hers. Tilting her head, she searched for more delicious variations and found them, soft, delicate pairings and firm, passionate matings with those lush contours. He tasted faintly of coffee with a hint of sweetness. It was lovely, unlike anything—any*one*— she had tasted before.

When his mouth slid from hers and across her hot cheek she was too intoxicated to think of ending it. His mouth glided down her ear, his breath hot, and he pressed his lips against the sensitive side of her neck. She had unbuttoned her collar and the top button of her blouse in the warmth of the stable and now he nudged it aside to explore the tender skin at the base of her throat. She had the vague sense of him releasing yet another button, and sagged against whatever was holding her up. He nudged aside her blouse and nibbled her skin, sending shivers through her that lodged in her breasts and started a fire in their tips. Closer—she wanted him closer—

Sounds from outside the box stall penetrated her pleasure-stuffed senses as he straightened and looked toward the stall's open door. Voices and the clop of hooves down the center alley jarred her back to reality. She was caught hard in Ashton's arms and was pressing against him like she was trying to climb inside his skin.

"Good God," came a voice that with only two words managed to announce the officious nature of its owner. "Ashton Graham, is that you?"

Ashton released the delectable Daisy like she was a hot poker and for a moment almost panicked. Her collar was askew and blouse buttons had been loosed, her lips were kiss-reddened, and her eyes were wide and dark-centered. His own face was hot and his lips felt thick and conspicuous. Damn and double damn. Anyone who saw them now . . . He shoved her frantically behind the horse and turned just in time to face Reynard Boulton.

The wretch had followed him to Oxford.

"Whatever are you doing here?" Reynard's voice carried a hint of accusation as he poked his head through the stall opening. "I thought you were headed to Sussex to attend Uncle Seward's birthday *fete*."

Ashton forced a taut smile, knowing that Reynard's gaze missed nothing when he was on the hunt.

"Had to stop by my old mentor's house for a chat, first," Ashton said with a calmness that surprised him. "Huxley's gone rustic, and I'd hoped to convince him to abandon such nonsense and resume his chair at Queen's."

"And did you convince him?" Reynard stepped inside the stall and craned his neck to look around Ash, searching for whoever had been entertaining him moments before. Ashton folded his arms and leaned in the direction Reynard was looking, to interfere with his view.

"Hardly. The old boy's balmy. Donated his entire collection of source documents to the Bodleian. Now spends his days nursemaiding cows and spouting rubbish about 'keeping' the earth and the nobility of animals. A tragic waste. Annoying as hell to have to listen to."

"Well, I was worried there for a minute that you'd joined him." Reynard slid around him to focus on the impressive beast behind him. "Damned fine horse, old boy. A new acquisition?"

"It is not." Daisy Bumgarten stepped around the horse with a brush in her hand and engaged Reynard with a tart look. "This is my horse, Mister—"

"Boulton. Reynard Boulton, at your service." The Fox nodded gallantly and looked to Ashton to complete the introduction.

"May I present Miss Daisy Bumgarten of Nevada. That's in—"

"The States, yes, I know." The Fox smiled a bit too broadly as he approached Daisy and accepted the hand she offered. "I've heard of you, Miss Bumgarten . . . that you're something of a horsewoman."

"I would be pleased to answer to that description, Mr. Boulton," she said, her smile warming over the wretch's elegant features and striking eyes. She had managed to restore her buttons and smooth her hair, but nothing could have blanched the color from her lips. She looked like she'd been eating cherries all day and the juice could still be savored on her lips. Reynard's gaze slid to Ash's clamped mouth.

"What brings you to Oxford, Reynard?" Ashton demanded, hoping to divert him.

"I've a nephew—my eldest sister's boy—being hooded." He transferred his gaze back to Daisy. "She's asked me to look in. I say, Miss Bumgarten, it's a pleasure to meet you. Are you staying here at Holloway?"

"I am. The countess insisted it was the best place to stay in Oxford."

"The countess?" Reynard stepped back to take her in, inspecting her behind a gentlemanly smile. "And which countess would that be?"

"Lady Evelyn Hargrave, of course," Daisy said, matching his scrutiny with a boldness that surprised Ashton. "Countess of Kew. An old friend of the family and my guide through the deep waters of London society. And how do you know Lord Ashton, Mr. Boulton? Are you a friend of his brother's?"

Ashton smiled at the brief flash of irritation in Reynard's eyes. The Fox, heir to an old title, would not stoop to correcting her address, but he was vain enough to take umbrage at being termed a mere "mister."

"We were at school together, Ash and I, then at university," Boulton said, retreating into superiority. "Though he lingered long after I left."

"Old friends." She gave Ash an inscrutable smile. "Then you'll have a dinner companion tonight." She turned her back on the pair to finish brushing down her horse.

Ashton schooled his face to a cultivated indifference and strode out of the stable. Inside, he was simmering. Damned high-handed of her to dismiss him like a stable boy after he'd just saved her from ignominy at the hands of society's most ruthless gossip hawk. She should be kissing his—

"So you see?" Boulton caught up with him on the hotel path. "She has set her sights higher than a 'spare,' after all."

"Damn you, Boulton, for barging in where you're not wanted. You have the most abysmal timing."

And the bastard laughed.

"It's a gift."

Chapter Nine

The countess was waiting in her rooms when Daisy returned to Holloway House. She looked Daisy over, took a sniff, and wrinkled her nose.

"You smell like *horse*. I feared as much, so I took the liberty of having Collette draw you a bath." She nodded to the little maid, who hurried into the tiled bathing chamber to add more hot water to the porcelain tub. "But before you bathe, I must have a word with you."

Daisy unbuttoned her jacket, wondering what she'd done now.

"You do know that Lord Ashton is no friend of your efforts to find documentation of your lineage?"

"Of course, I know that," Daisy answered crossly, though she couldn't say who annoyed her more at the moment, the countess or herself. She tossed her jacket aside and started on her blouse buttons.

"He's a wastrel, a womanizer, and a high-liver," the countess continued, "whatever his academic credentials."

"I know tha—What 'credentials'?" She paused in the middle of disrobing, frowned, and fixed her gaze on her long-suffering mentor, who seemed pleased to have her undivided attention.

"I did some checking while you were dillydallying with that beast of yours. Apparently he *has* been awarded degrees by the university; they've actually made him a doctor of philosophy. He studied further at the Sorbonne in Paris and at Heidelberg University. Each place, he cut a wide swath through the local society. I fear he may try to use his glib tongue and fancy education to worm his way into your confidence. Or *worse*." She wrung her hands, looking quite unsettled. "There are those who say he is utterly without morals or conscience."

Daisy stood stock still, staring at the countess but seeing Ashton Graham's slow smile and I-know-what-you-want look. She scowled.

"You needn't worry about me, Countess. Once bitten, twice shy." She stalked into the bathing chamber and closed the door forcefully, but not before she heard the countess's anxious voice.

"You've been bitten? Where?"

The bathtub was steaming nicely by the time Collette left her to soak in deliciously rose-scented water.

"Idiot," she muttered. She'd come within a hair's breadth of scandal earlier. What if his old school friend had walked in on them kissing? Her eyes widened. Or was that the plan? Let someone catch them kissing, and ruin her reputation. In the eyes of upper crust society, a girl who would kiss a man she wasn't engaged to would do any number of immoral things. How could she have forgotten? How could she have been so . . . so . . . susceptible?

She looked down at her bare body and answered that one.

She just was. It was the way she was made, whether her mama and fancy-pants society liked it or not. It was her burden to bear, the flaw in her body and soul: vulnerable to temptations of the flesh. Was it marked on her somehow? She often wondered that. She ran hands over her face, shoulders, and arms. How did he know? And he *knew*. She was certain of it.

The last thing she needed was that velvet-tongued devil hanging around, occupying her thoughts and haunting her senses. And he was—after that kiss—haunting the edges of her thoughts and expectations. And desires.

Continuing her self-examination, she admitted that her moment of decision in the barn had been a fraud. Down deep, she had known it wouldn't settle anything between them, that it would only tempt her and encourage him to more of the same. She had enjoyed it, damn it, just like she knew she would. She had reveled in it, right down to the way her toes curled in her boots.

And it danged-well couldn't happen again. *Ever*.

The Bodleian Library was a warren of stone-clad buildings that nestled near the Radcliffe Camera, an ornate circular building that had come to represent the collections that made the library one of the scholarly prizes of the Western world . . . so they were informed by the countess on the ride over. They led a reluctant Uncle Red into the arch and column-lined reading room that now occupied the main floor of the Radcliffe. Professor Huxley was waiting and led them out and down the street to the main entrance of the venerable Bodleian.

"More walkin'," Red grumbled, trudging along the ankle-turning cobblestones. "All just to sit in a room with a bunch o' books."

"This is necessary, Uncle Red," Daisy said, slipping her arm through his. "We have to prove whose blood runs in my veins."

"It's yer blood, girl." Red glowered. "How could it be anybody else's?"

The Radcliffe they had just left, the professor explained,

had become little more than a reading room. The major collections were now housed in the halls and storerooms of the buildings Bodley himself had endowed . . . which turned out to be a fancy way of saying he'd paid for them.

It was something wealthy people did on both sides of the Atlantic: pay to put their names on buildings.

They rambled through hall after ornate hall while the professor narrated the history of each. Even the countess's hat feathers were drooping when they finally came to a plain rectangular hall crammed with ranks of bookshelves jutting from the walls. Oak reading tables and glass cases holding open books and documents were clustered in the center of the hall. Shaded windows and the few overhead lamps provided inadequate light. It was a dim, quiet place with a musty, old-book taint to the air.

"These are the historical collections," Huxley said quietly, requiring them to lean in to hear him as he beckoned them along toward one of the glass cases. "Where my source material resides."

He peered into the case, squinted, and craned his neck to scan the documents under glass. Then he snapped upright, looking distressed.

"Where is it? The charter? The king's restoration document—it was right here. The roster of nobles signing to pledge allegiance to the crown—" He bustled off in search of "that cursed librarian," leaving them to cool their heels.

The countess sat down primly at one of the tables, and Red groaned and sprawled beside her in a chair, propping his feet on the table. The countess narrowed her eyes and nudged his shoe to insist he remove his feet from the table. It took a second, more forceful push to make him comply.

Minutes passed before the professor reappeared with a nervous-looking minion of the library who kept trying to explain that the Huxley Collection had been removed to secure storage. The professor was having none of it.

"I gifted this institution with the work of a lifetime," Huxley said, drawing himself up in outrage. "The crème de la crème of British historical scholarship. The empire's intellectual lifeblood. You cannot simply lock such documents away in a vault!"

"A vault?" Red sat up with a jerk. "Fer what?"

"Papers dealing with the monarchy and empire," the countess informed him in clipped tones. "Apparently some documents are considered too precious or too delicate to be stored on mere shelves." She gave a dismissive wave at the overburdened bookcases around them.

"Papers. *Humph*." Red slouched back into his chair in disappointment.

"Surely, Professor, you could ask that some of your papers be brought out for us to have a look?" Daisy entered the fray, turning her best smile on the library assistant, who was wringing his hands. "If the professor asked for certain documents, you could get them for him, right?"

The little assistant swallowed hard and glanced over his shoulder, caught between the professor and another dire but unnamed force.

"Of course he could," came a deep voice from the entrance.

Daisy's heart sank toward her stomach. *Him* again.

Ashton strode straight into the middle of the threesome and turned the assistant by the elbow. "I'll be pleased to help." He propelled the little fellow quickly down the aisle between the ranks of bookcases. "I know my way around the historical collections. I can pick out exactly the things the professor will need."

"Really, Mister Graham—" Daisy snapped, taking several steps toward them before he and the librarian disappeared around a corner. The sound of a substantial door slamming stopped her from following.

Professor Huxley seemed relieved to have his former student pursuing a solution to the problem, muttered, and seated himself to wait. Daisy paced between the bookshelves, glancing at the leather-bound books, ribbon-wrapped folios, and collections of journals all around her. Somebody had put numbers and letters on everything, and out of sheer boredom she pulled a book from the shelf to inspect.

The typeface was ornate and difficult to read. She was still trying to make sense of it when the sound of a door opening and heavy footsteps drew her back to the center of the hall.

"This is a disgrace." Ashton strode down the aisle carrying armfuls of leather folios tied with ribbon. Behind him came the gray-faced assistant laden with books and more folios. When he reached the table where the countess, Red, and the professor sat, Ashton laid the documents out carefully, then turned to Huxley. "You won't believe where they've put your collection. A charwoman's closet. In with the mops, buckets, and brooms."

"Shelf space is at a premium—" The assistant was overwhelmed.

"A charwoman's closet? Priceless documents—the writings of kings and details of the monarchy itself are treated like discarded penny papers?" Huxley bounded to his feet and glared at the trembling assistant, who hastily emptied his arms of items and wisely gave no excuse. "I must see the head librarian," he roared at the assistant. "Now!"

As the professor stormed out with the assistant in tow, Ashton turned his attention to the folios he'd rescued and ran a hand over the heavy covers. He stared in horror at the residue left on his fingertips. "Mildew. Dear God." He opened one packet and gingerly slid the documents out onto the table. His eyes widened. "Look at this. There should be cotton weave between each page, and you can smell the must. Damn fortunate we came today—another two months and the damage would have been irreversible."

Daisy leaned in to pick up one of the documents and he quickly blocked her hand with his. "Not without proper gloves."

"I'm wearing gloves," she said, glaring at him, recalling their first, shocking encounter. "I *always* wear proper gloves."

"They're kidskin," he said, meeting her glare with one of his own.

"The best danged kidskin money can buy." She raised her chin.

"Leather contains oils. You need plain cotton to protect the documents." He produced two pairs from his inner breast pocket and thrust one at her.

"Gloves for *reading*?" Horrified, she looked to the countess, who merely blinked what was probably Morse code for "shoot me now."

"These documents are rare and must be handled carefully," he said, donning his own gloves. "Some are hundreds of years old. The pigments in the inks are susceptible to light and moisture and are already in a perilous state. Much more of this neglect and the work would be lost forever."

Daisy grudgingly removed her leather gloves and donned the ones he provided, staring between him and the pile of books and documents that might hold the key to her family's past and her future.

"How do you know about ink and documents?" she asked.

"I studied under Huxley at Queens. When researching history, you have to learn about handling old sources of information, old documents."

Daisy watched him lay out the pages, inspecting each for what he hoped not to find. He seemed truly worried about the papers . . . not the kind of thing she imagined would bother a high-living rake like him. He seemed perfectly at ease checking the documents for damage and checking curled edges for pliability. And those supple, long-fingered hands . . . she could almost imagine them curling and un-curling around . . .

She crossed her arms and took a step back from the table.

The books had fared better than the loose documents. One hefty volume on the offspring of Charles II bore the name of Broadman Huxley on the spine. As Ashton selected it and leafed through the thick pages, Daisy couldn't help edging close to peer over his arm. Remembering the feel of it tight around her, she barely managed to keep her hands tucked firmly beneath her arms.

"Does it say anything about Charlotte Fitzroy?" she asked, her voice higher than usual. She swallowed hard and edged back several inches.

"I believe there may be some mention of—" He paged through the front, paused, and then flipped quickly to the middle of the book. "Ah. Lady Charlotte Fitzroy Lee, Count-ess of Lichfield."

"What does it say about her?" Daisy was suddenly consumed with curiosity and forgot the need for distance. "When was she born? Where did she live? Did she have children?"

"According to Huxley she was contracted in marriage in the year 1644, at the age of nine years," he read aloud.

"What?" Daisy grabbed his arm to pull the book closer and see for herself. Her eyes widened on the line he indi-cated. "That's—disgusting. Marrying off a child? Who would do such a thing?"

"Her parents or guardians, one must assume," he said dryly. "However, she wasn't actually wed until two years later."

"Two? But that would make her . . . eleven, at most twelve

years old." Daisy frowned. "But surely they didn't—they wouldn't have made her—"

"Presumably they did." He gave her a sidelong glance. "Because she gave birth to her first child at thirteen."

The countess's gasp echoed in the hall. "That poor, poor child."

"How old was the beast they married her to—thirty-five?" Daisy grabbed the book from Ashton, scanned it, and looked up in disbelief.

Lord Ashton-with-the-smoldering-eyes gave a slow smile. "Her beast of a husband was all of thirteen years old when they were married. He fathered a child on her when he was not yet fourteen. It seems both the men and women of your lineage start young."

"Assuming she is an ancestor of mine. There was a second Charlotte Fitzroy, after all. What does the book say about her?"

He took the book back, went to the front, then turned to a page near the one they had been reading.

"'Lady Charlotte, Countess of Yarmouth,'" he read. "'Born to Elizabeth Killigrew Boyle in 1650 and acknowledged by HRH Charles the Second. She married the Honorable James Howard, by whom she had one daughter. In 1672 she married William Paston, who inherited his father's title and became the Second Earl of Yarmouth. By him she had four more children.'"

"She sounds respectable." Daisy bit her lip, appalled by her thinking.

"Really? Yarmouth fought two duels over her 'virtue.'"

She winced. "Well, at least she had her children within a marriage."

"Not exactly a high standard." He flipped back a few pages. "Charlotte, the Countess Lichfield, and her first and *only* husband, Edward Lee, Earl of Lichfield, lived together for forty-two years. Together they had eighteen children. As opposed to the Countess of Yarmouth's paltry five." He gave her a taunting smile. "Your odds of finding an ancestor probably lie with the more fertile Charlotte."

Daisy took a step back, her jaw drooping. "Eighteen children? The woman was brought to childbed eighteen *times*?"

Chapter Ten

A scuffling sound interrupted and as Daisy turned she caught a whiff of the tobacco smoke settling in a wreath around Uncle Red's head. She glowered, but before she could speak, the countess smacked Red's arm, nearly causing him to drop the cigar he was enjoying.

"Hey—"

"How dare you!" The countess sprang to her feet and took Red by the ear, forcing him—protesting—to his feet.

"Damn it, woman—that hurts!" He jerked and twisted, trying to escape.

"Outside with you, this minute!" the countess snapped. "Of all the irresponsible—thoughtless—smoking that filthy thing around priceless historical documents!" She didn't relent for an instant as she dragged him, howling, out of the hall.

Daisy's shock became a chuckle that grew to a hearty laugh at the sight of the usually demure and decorous countess taking wild and woolly Uncle Red in hand. Seconds later she found herself looking up into Ashton Graham's glowing face. He had been laughing, too, and traces of pleasure lingered in his gaze as it roamed her. He took a step that brought him against her skirts. A bolt of expectation shot through her, leaving scorch marks on every hungry and traitorous nerve in her body.

"Where were we?" His voice was thick as wild honey. "Ah, yes. Eighteen children, Daisy Bumgarten. In forty-two years of marriage, Lady Charlotte spent almost half of them pregnant."

"I believe the proper term is 'in a family way.'" She licked her lip.

"Eighteen years *pregnant*. No riding horses or hosting hunting parties or attending operas or balls—watched constantly—every bit of food inspected and measured, every exertion and diverting pastime prohibited, all contact with frivolous society disallowed. You see, a duchess's pregnancy isn't about a baby, it's about an *heir*. And believe me, families take no chances that the heir to a title might be endangered by the whims of a mere *mother*." She could feel him leaning, closing on her, watching her reaction. "That's the lot of a woman lucky enough to snag a duke for a husband. I wonder what Lady Charlotte would counsel if she could talk to you across the years." He moved still closer and she retreated another step, feeling his heat and determination crowding her. "Would she warn you against seeking attachment to a title—an elevated one at that?"

"Doesn't much matter what she'd say. That was two hundred years ago. People don't marry off their daughters at twelve anymore." She took another step back, but the distance between them didn't seem to widen. "And I've never been a meek little thing like Charlotte, not even when I was twelve. Just ask my mama."

"Oh, I'll take your word for that." He advanced again and she backed into a bookcase that stopped her retreat. That look in his eye—that hungry coyote look—she couldn't run from that and live with herself.

"Look, I've traveled and learned and read plenty of books. I know a few things about the world. I've talked to sea captains and lawyers and horse breeders and professors and a passel of noblemen from here to Rome, Italy."

"I bet you have." His mouth quirked up into a wicked smile that hit her pulse like a hammer. "And I bet every damned one of them wanted to do this—"

His lips came down on hers and her whole body caught fire. The heat welled from deep in her body to explode and spread quickly under her skin. She had no more chance of stopping it than she had of heading off a stampede of long-horns by waving a hankie. When she slid her arms up and around his neck and pressed her body against him, the rumble from his chest could have been a taunt of victory, but in her steam-filled head it sounded more like hungry approval.

His supple lips drew hers into luscious, ever-changing combinations that spread pleasure through every denied and long-suffering part of her. Her determination melted. Her skin came alive, tingling, yearning, needing exactly what she had sworn to abstain from until she was safely married.

The bookcase behind her began to creak and she could hear the slide and plop of books falling over as she was pressed back against the shelves. She ended the kiss to take a breath and glimpsed his arms braced wide on either side of her and his hands fiercely clasping the wooden shelves. It took a minute for her to realize he gripped the shelves to avoid touching her.

Surprised, she looked up into his face.

His eyes shone, but in them she saw no taunt or ridicule, no gloating at having aroused her. She saw only wanting. She'd heard it called a dozen things, most in nervous leering or self-righteous condemnation: the itch, desire, craving, lust, hunger, wanting, lechery, heat, the burning. All of that was in his eyes, but there was more, something deeper and more important than just physical pleasure. There was *need*.

His lips covered hers again, inundating that thought with

waves of sensation that made her sigh against his mouth and mold eagerly against his body. This time his hands came, too. His touch was gentle as he traced her curves at first, but grew firmer, more possessive as he pulled her tighter against him. The quiet hum of his chest against hers relayed the pleasure he found in exploring her shape. She wanted more, needed him against her bare—

Approaching voices froze them lips to lips, bodies pressed hard together. She pushed him back, breathless with panic. Before she could manage a word, he grabbed her by the arm and pulled her around the bookcase and out of sight of Huxley, the countess, and whoever else had just entered the hall.

"Well,"—she heard the countess—"where did they go?"

"Ashton?" Huxley called out. "Where the devil are you?"

She clapped a hand over her kiss-swollen lips and stared at Ashton with wide eyes. He grabbed the biggest book he could find from the shelves around them and shoved it into her hands.

"Here, Huxley." He stuck his head around the end of the row of bookcases. "Trying to find the latest Burke's. Much of the stuff on the shelves is refuse . . . useless and inaccurate . . . schoolboy scribbling. Yet, they store *your* precious primary sources in a charwoman's closet."

"Well, I've brought the head librarian here to see and account for such shabby treatment," the professor said with indignation.

"About time." Ashton strolled out of the stacks with an open volume in his hand. "Inspect, if you will, the professor's life's work, sir. And explain, if you can, the carelessness with which such precious sources have been curated."

The head librarian was a portly, well-starched fellow used to holding his own with the nobs and swells of his world. Daisy peered through a crack above the books as he stretched his portly neck past his starched collar and collected his dignity.

"I am certain the misplacement of Professor Huxley's materials can be explained by our shortage of storage and display space. A regrettable situation, surely, but one that can be remedied."

What followed was a loud and furious discussion of the importance of various documents and books and the manner in which they should be held.

Daisy pressed icy hands to her flushed cheeks and calmed her breathing, grateful for the chance to regain her composure. She spotted an opening at the far end of the rank of bookcases, slipped through it, and walked down the rank of farther bookcases toward the center aisle. She exited looking down, as if she were engrossed in the massive volume in her hands. The countess noticed her, but turned back to the confrontation, and she noticed Uncle Red standing not far away with his fists clinched in anticipation, itching to see fists fly.

Relieved to be spared their scrutiny, she closed the book and joined watching the conflict. The librarian finally had enough and stalked out with the professor close behind. The assistant librarian looked to Lord Ashton as if awaiting instructions, so Ashton gave him some.

"We need unbleached cotton vellum, and plenty of it."

The man hurried out the rear of the hall, and Lord Ashton turned to look through the folios, selecting two that had suffered only minor damage.

"What are you doing?" she asked, putting a table between them as she watched.

"These folios hold a small portion of the letters the professor has collected and studied over the years." He pointed to elegant numerals painted on the bottom of one packet. "These are all marked with the years your Lady Charlottes lived. Some bear the royal seal and others the mark of noble houses. Some are official correspondence and others are personal. We shall have to go through them one by one if you want to uncover any possible links to your ancestry."

"We?" She propped hands on her waist. "You intend to search, too?"

He paused to study her irritable question, then produced one of those slow smiles that never failed to weaken her knees.

"I do." He raised one eyebrow. "And believe me, that is the first time I have ever spoken those two words to a lady."

A second later, Uncle Red guffawed and the countess hid a quiet laugh behind a hand.

Daisy sat down furiously at the table and reached for one of the folios of letters. He put a hand out to stop her from opening it until she'd heard his rules for the proper handling of such old and important documents. By the time he finished she was ready to chew saddle leather and spit tacks.

Whatever his game was, she would bet stacks of silver dollars it wasn't to help her prove her royal ancestry. That meant she had to watch his every step, his every move. And that meant she was going to be tempted by those devilish eyes and that delicious mouth, again and again.

Curse his hide.

The morning faded into afternoon and the documents piled up. Letters—who knew people wrote so much about so little? Exchanges of property, news of births and deaths and the occasional marriage, visits, and permissions asked and granted. Everything was made to sound important with fancy wording. Worse still, the writing itself was nearly impossible to decipher without help. *His* help. Ashton had obviously read and interpreted many such documents before—which began to undermine her distrust of his abilities. They took turns reading Huxley's book regarding the Charlottes and verifying what he said with the letters and documents in the folios.

Late in the day, when lamps had been lit and Uncle Red and the countess both had begun to snore, Daisy looked up from the letter she was trying to decipher and caught him pouring over something with an official-looking seal. It had come from the same folio as the letter she was holding.

"What is that?" she asked, rising with her letter.

"Record of a Royal Navy promotion. Commodore Fitzroy Henry Lee." He pointed to the name and frowned. "Promoted to vice admiral."

"Who was he, again? I think he's in the professor's book."

"Charlotte of Lichfield's son. Her seventh, I believe." He consulted Huxley's book. "Yes. Appointed Commodore Governor of Newfoundland, Canada, in 1736." Then he scowled. "Was removed from that post later," he read, "accused of drunkenness and debauchery." He looked back at the warrant of promotion with confusion. "Don't know how that could be. He was promoted to vice admiral after his dismissal and return to England."

"Look at this letter . . . from Lady Charlotte to an *F*-somebody. I can make out some of it. She's writing about temperament or something. And 'integrity and duty' over something."

Reluctantly, he dragged his attention from the warrant to the letter. She retreated to her chair, arching her back to relieve the strain, and watched him devour the script. He was truly interested in this search, she realized, or at least in the history it resurrected. He'd apparently spent a great deal of time at the university deciphering and studying old papers. It seemed out of character for a man with such a fast and loose reputation.

He was something of a puzzle, Ashton Graham. Only then did she recall Old Lady Sylvia's confidence in his ability to discern the truth of her heritage. What was it she called him? For the life of her, she couldn't recall.

"Good God." His exclamation brought her back to the

present. "It's a letter from Lady Charlotte to her son 'Fitz.' And from the sound of things she wasn't happy with him. She's talking about his removal from the governorship in Newfoundland."

He read slowly: "'Intemperance has ever been your downfall. But if you will return to the true faith and change your ways, you may still recover your reputation. You still enjoy our uncle's favor—if you would but seek to do the honorable thing, and in the matter of the child, do as integrity and duty require, you may yet be restored to the bosom of your family and country.'"

Daisy winced. "Child? Does she mean his child?"

"Huxley's book lists him without any offspring." He looked thoughtful. "But apparently he was something of a high-liver and a heavy drinker. Who knows what he got up to in the colonies?"

"So hard-drinkin' Fitz got booted out of Canada in disgrace and went home, where his uncle got him promoted? Who was his uncle?"

"She said 'our' uncle," Ashton replied, glancing at the warrant. "He was apparently Charlotte's uncle as well. That can only be one person: James the Second, the king himself. Huxley says Charlotte was known to be his favorite niece among all of Charles's children. He was very fond of her and her children, so perhaps he intervened to clear Fitz's record and give him this promotion."

"But there was something about a child. Was that in Canada? Did he have a child while he was in America?"

"Good question." He began to look through the other letters and documents in the folio. She came around the table to look over his shoulder as he read aloud. Most of the letters were to Charlotte from her daughters and sons, but occasionally a letter from Charlotte to one of her children surfaced. At the very bottom of the folio was a small piece of paper written in masculine hand . . . the name of a church . . . with

numbers and a date . . . attached to a name. Gemma Rose
Howard.

"What could that be?" she asked, seeing nothing of value
in it. But it had been included with family letters and pre-
served.

Ashton studied it, and then looked at her with an intensity
that set her back a few inches.

"I believe it's a parish registry citation." He pointed a
gloved finger at the line. "Temple Church . . . thirty-six is
likely a volume number, ninety-one would indicate a page,
and the date of entry is October third, 1747. There are two
'Temple' churches that I know of, one in London, and another, older one in Bristol. It would make more sense for it
to reference Bristol, if it is tied to Fitz. The city is a major
port for the Royal Navy, a place that Fitz would have spent
time. And that 'Temple' is one of the oldest churches in
England."

"A registry for what?" she asked, sensing that this might
prove more important than she realized.

"Marriages and deaths." He paused, and then as he said
the final word, she understood. "And births."

"So someone named Gemma Rose Howard is registered
there. Maybe that rascal Fitz married her there."

He cracked a half smile. "If it were a marriage, I believe
both parties would be listed in the citation. There is only one
name, so I would be willing to bet it is a birth or a death."

"Do you suppose they still have those records?"

"It's a very old church, and such records are not always
kept under the best of conditions. But it is possible they're
still available."

"And how would I find out if they are?"

"You could write the dean of the parish or vicar to ask for
answers. But even if they grant your request, which could
take weeks or months, you can't count on a thorough or
verifiable search." He studied her upturned face. "The only

way to be certain you get the proper information is to go to Bristol and search the records yourself. And should you need reminding, you have a mere eleven days left to produce some proof of a noble connection."

"Do you think . . . is it possible that we might find proof of a connection in this Gemma Rose Howard?"

"All of the other children of both Charlottes are accounted for in Burke's or in the professor's work. The errant admiral may be your best chance at a connection. But, who knows who Gemma Howard was or why she was included in this batch of documents?"

This close to him, her skin had begun to itch in alarming places and her gaze fixed on his mouth like a honeybee on a flower. She swallowed hard, trying to force her mind past this momentary distraction. He was sensual and wicked— an invitation to sin that she could not accept.

"Daisy, Daisy . . . you have no idea what you're getting yourself into," he said softly, running a knuckle down the side of her face.

"Why do you keep trying to talk me out of marrying your brother?" she said, trying for more irritation than she was able to muster.

"The title 'duke' is not just part of a man's name or a pronouncement of his authority; it is a designation that defines his entire world. It's land and estates and the people who work for and tend them. It's a never-ending stream of obligations and duties to people both above and below your station. It's a deluge of debts and taxes and legal requirements, contracts, and entailments. It's a whole extended family—those long-since born and those yet to come— attached to and dependent on one man's fortunes and decisions. Everything he has, everything he does, everything he *is* must serve his obligations, his heritage. And everyone in his life serves that blessed title as well."

"Even his younger brother?" she asked, searching his face and finding there a raw bit of truth she hadn't expected.

"Especially his younger brother," Ashton answered, feeling those words resonating deep within him. "A younger son studies and trains and prepares for power . . . then spends his days marking time . . . waiting . . . hoping the time never comes that he must step into his brother's shoes. That is the lot of the 'spare' to the title. Wanting it, but afraid of wanting it." His eyes clouded. "I have spent my whole life serving my brother's title as his second . . . a stand-in that has never been required, and one I pray is never needed.

"Arthur may be myopic, boring, and oblivious to most of humanity's doings, but he has a good heart and a sound intellect, should he ever decide to use it for something besides bug classifications. He was trained to do his duty as the Duke of Meridian and will someday rise to that mantle. But it will take everything he has to fulfill a role he neither wants nor feels confident in."

"What are you saying?" She stirred, on the edge of insight, searching. "You think you'd make a better duke than he would?"

The heaviness in Ashton's chest slid deeper inside him. His lecture had brought up all-too-familiar feelings of being resigned to his fate and yet restless and miserable within it. He gave a rueful smile.

"I would never say that. I have no desire for my brother's coronet."

Was she standing closer? Were the blue eyes prying into his soul reaching for more than just—

"Then what do you desire, Ashton Graham?"

Chapter Eleven

Her voice was low and full of invitation.

For some reason he was reluctant to accept with his usual enthusiasm. Vulnerable and sexually curious, she was asking for his attentions in the most elemental way. She was also out of her country, out of her culture, and totally out of her depth. There were so many ways this could go wrong for her, and he was bound by his family's orders to seek out every bloody one of them.

For the first time since he'd accepted his elders' ignoble charge, he acknowledged true distaste for this mission. A moment of panic ensued, but he wrestled it back into the depths of his stained soul and squared his shoulders.

"I *desire* a good cigar, a stout Scotch whiskey, and a good book."

She drew back as if she'd been smacked, reddened, then marched over to her uncle to riffle through his breast pocket for one of his treasured cigars. Thrusting it into Ash's hand with enough force that it broke in half, she glared and then reached for Huxley's book.

"Well, you have two out of three right here," she said, using the hefty tome to smack him hard enough in the mid-section to cause him an involuntary grunt. He scrambled to catch the book before it tumbled out of hand and watched with a mixture of relief and regret as she shook the countess and her uncle awake and bundled them out of the hall.

He stood for a long moment holding the book against him, staring at the doorway, and listening to her angry departure. Taking a deep breath, he felt himself settling back into his insulating worldliness and began to tidy up the documents, placing velum carefully between the pages of the letters as he returned them to the folios.

It was a good quarter of an hour later that he stood looking at the tidy pile of historical mystery he had just uncovered. Struck by a thought, he searched for that square of paper with the Temple Church citation and found it missing. He looked again. Then, a third time.

She had taken it. The minx.

He grinned.

He knew exactly where she was headed.

The next afternoon, in the midst of preparations for Bristol, Daisy and Red managed to take Dancer and Renegade for a good ride. She spent some time in the stable afterward, brushing Dancer and making certain he was well fed and treated to a carrot. At every sound of hooves on the brick alley or rattle of harness chain, she turned, half dreading and half anticipating Ashton's appearance. She refused to admit disappointment at his absence but, in her heart, she knew it was there.

She had spent a long, fruitless night going over the lineage she had copied from Uncle Red's ramblings. It seemed there were indeed a couple of Howards several generations back, but her attention was repeatedly diverted by the way every name she read called up an annoying association with *him*. The way Ashton Graham corrected the names of her forbearers, the disdain in his aristocratic face, the physical hunger he either didn't bother to hide or hid too well . . . every encounter between them had left a trace of longing in its wake. When she finally turned down the lamp and slid between the cool covers, she felt hot and restless and beset by memories she had spent five years trying to purge.

The sweet smell of new hay, the dark velvet of the Nevada night sky sprinkled with stars, the feel of a man's hands on her bare skin, a tongue circling her nipples, a young, hard body between her naked—

"No," she said aloud, and turned over to bury her face in the down pillow. "Absolutely not. Never again. Not until I'm a damned duchess."

That night became one more sacrifice on the altar of family ambitions. As she lay there, tortured by what might have been and what would never be, she turned Ashton's words over and over in her head. He had laid out in no uncertain terms the sacrifices she would be making in becoming the Duchess of Meridian. Her life would become an asset to the title. Every bit of her wardrobe, every friendship she made, and every social occasion she attended would be accounted as adding to or subtracting from some invisible tally of ducal prestige. If Ashton were to be believed, even her future children would be little more than property of the damned coat of arms. The closer she came to her goal, the more alarming those prospects seemed.

But as the night wore on, her spirits sounded the depths and started to rise. Yes, she would have to make sacrifices as the duchess of the house of Meridian, but she was no stranger to the grind and constraint of duty. Daily, she made sacrifices that were required by her family's fortunes and future—for her beloved sisters and generations yet to come, who were depending on her. Did his fancy-pants lordship think being a younger son was harder than being an eldest daughter?

She rose from her bed, lighted a lamp, and wrote a letter to her mother asking for any information she might be able to find on the Howards that Red claimed as forbearers. On impulse, she added that if all went as planned, a certain duke would soon be making a happy announcement in the *Times*.

By the time Collette knocked discreetly on her door the next morning, her letter was ready for posting, and she had banished both her doubts and her troublesome desires. She was determined once again to complete her quest. She was going to prove her lineage, delight the Duke of Meridian, and wrangle him to the altar. See if she didn't.

Packing and making travel arrangements consumed much of the next morning—that and posting both her letter and the endless stream of notes Lady Evelyn was penning to acquaintances in Bristol's environs, announcing their visit. She explained to Daisy and Red that they needed to make advantageous friendships in places other than London, and since much of the Royal Navy was berthed at Bristol—not to mention commercial trading companies that used the port—it seemed prudent to call on the countess's dear friends in that city. Until they had a firm invitation, they would have to postpone progress toward that destination. It dealt a blow to Daisy's hopes of hot-footing it to Bristol on horseback and discovering the truth about the mysterious Gemma Howard.

"What is all of this?" Daisy stopped in the middle of her chamber at Holloway House to stare at the slew of garments laid out on the great four-poster bed. Collette stood nearby with her hands clasped, looking eager, while the countess rose from a chair at the tea table and smoothed her skirts.

"It is high time you got back. That beast of yours is better groomed than most men I know."

"Shouldn't all this be packed?" Daisy scowled and indicated her favorite pale sea-foam-blue dinner gown.

"We still haven't heard from Lady Regina and so we're

attending a dinner party tonight," the countess said, drawing herself up to face what she was certain would be opposition to her announcement. "At the home of my dear friends the Viscount Shively and his wife, Lady Esseme."

"This evening?" Daisy thought of a rebuttal based on the countess's emphatic rule: "Never accept an invitation on short notice."

"Lady Esseme and I were girls together in Sussex. She only just learned we are in town—my own fault for not contacting her earlier. I had to plead urgent family business and beg forgiveness. But the invitation is in hand and while we wait for word from Bristol, this will be a perfect opportunity for you to cultivate acquaintances in this area. You never know when they may become important." She must have sensed Daisy's looming objection, for she stated flatly: "I have accepted for the three of us."

Daisy's mouth worked silently. The countess had already sealed the deal; there was no backing out now.

"Fine," she said irritably, looking to Collette. "Draw me a bath, then." She looked closer at the sea-foam-colored satin gown lying on the bed and shot a narrow glance at her satisfied sponsor. "And I see you've already decided what I'm to wear."

Daisy straightened and peered at herself over her half-bare shoulder, inspecting the rear view of her best dinner gown in the pier glass. The blue-green satin shone in the lamplight, seeming almost iridescent when she moved. Thank Heaven the delicate drape and lace-crusted rear required no frame. The countess and old Chuck Worth were united in their disdain for the current craze that made women look bizarrely misshapen in the hindquarters. Only her most expensive dinner and ball gowns had rear drapery of any consequence. Most of her dresses lacked bustles altogether.

She had overheard enough of the countess's and the couturier's whispered consultations to realize they hoped the simplicity of the styles he created for her might make her seem more demure and girlish. That had amused her at first, but it seemed less entertaining now. It was probably a portent of the judgment and constant scrutiny yet to come.

Clothes. *Mere clothes*, she told herself. Not something she felt strongly about—as long as they didn't require her to be laced too tightly. But when she turned to face herself in the mirror, she realized there was method in their madness. She did look younger and "fresher" and better still, *eligible*.

Uncle Red was less than thrilled to be stuffed into his white-tie dinner clothes and trundled out to meet a bunch of stiff-necked, long-nosed nobs. A word he'd picked up in the local alehouse: "nobs." Short for "nobles." When he voiced that sentiment, the countess pounced on him like a duck on a junebug. He was not to utter that word tonight or ever again. These were people of a rank and class that could aid his niece's progress toward a most advantageous marriage.

Then, as they rocked along toward the viscount's comfortable home, the countess's conscience got the better of her and she turned to the sulking Red with a bit of salve for his pride.

"Just think," she said, proving how closely she had read his nature, "this will be a new audience for your Nevada stories."

He froze for a moment, studying her before breaking into a sly smile.

"I knew it." He sat up straight with a wicked laugh. "You listen to my stories."

The countess gave him a haughty look. "I could hardly escape hearing them. You tell the same ones everywhere you go."

"And you like 'em, don't you, Evie girl?"

The countess clamped her teeth, looking like someone

was trying to pull them out by the roots. "They do, I suppose, have a gritty, simpleminded sort of charm."

Red laughed, smacked his knee with his hand, and sat back, wholly untouched by the barbs in her compliment.

"You like me, Evie. You know you do." And for the rest of the ride, Red hummed a bawdy saloon ditty Daisy prayed he'd forgotten the words to, and he watched the countess's irritation with undisguised pleasure.

Chapter Twelve

The viscount's home was a stately stone manse set in a park of venerable oaks and elms. Liveried footmen met Daisy, the countess, and Red at the door and showed them into a large salon decorated in gold silk damask, thick Persian carpets, and down-stuffed Louis Quatorze furnishings. Daisy's heart quickened as a dozen faces turned to greet her. After the last two days, she could only think that each of them was assessing her and cataloging her value by some inscrutable noble standard.

Lady Esseme turned out to be a short, round woman with a pretty face and a contagious laugh. Her husband, the viscount, was moderately tall, dignified, and not without a streak of dry humor in his conversation. When he learned Red had spent most of his life in America's untamed west, he informed his wife that Red must be seated beside him at dinner so he could ask a thousand and one questions as they dined. Present also were a baron, another viscount, their lady wives, and a pair of dowagers who didn't seem to like each other much. One had brought her nephew with her.

Daisy was busy trying to memorize a dozen names with a trick the countess had taught her, when she found herself being drawn forcefully by their hostess to meet a younger

man "of some renown." She looked up and found herself
caught in the pale gray gaze of Reynard Boulton, who was
being introduced as a something-or-other to the Viscount
Tannehill. Tannehill was the other viscount present—the
exceptionally thin man whose name she had just committed
to memory by comparing him to a stork.

"Miss Bumgarten." He broke into a brilliant smile and
reached for her hand almost before she offered it. "How
lovely to see you again."

"And you, sir," she answered, her mouth suddenly dry
as dirt.

"You have met?" Lady Esseme asked, glancing at the
countess, who seemed taken aback.

"I had no idea." The countess's smile was thin as she
glanced at Daisy. "Who introduced you?"

"Ashton Graham," Boulton answered for her. "Lovely to
see you again, Lady Evelyn." He released Daisy to take the
countess's barely offered hand. "We met at Holloway House.
In the stables, actually." He turned that diamond-sharp gaze
on Daisy. "Miss Bumgarten was caring for a magnificent
beast of a horse and I wangled an introduction out of Ash.
You mustn't blame Miss Bumgarten, Countess, I have a way
of getting what I want, and I most certainly wanted to meet
the lovely Miss Bumgarten."

"He is such a rascal," Lady Esseme said, rapping him on
the sleeve with her fan. She tilted her head toward Daisy and
lowered her voice. "Don't doubt for a minute that he speaks
the truth. He *does* get what he wants. But he's so charming
and so devilishly handsome that we have to forgive his devious ways."

Far from taking offense, Boulton laughed and placed a
hand over his heart. "My errors and indiscretions go before
me, announcing to the world that I am sinful and flawed, but
also"—he waggled his brows—"*fun*."

Lady Esseme's laughter drew the others into it and even

Daisy chuckled at his audacious manner. It was only when they went in to dinner and she found herself seated beside him that she realized she would have to be on guard. Her dear, departed father had always said: "When a man tells you what he is, you'd best believe him." Reynard Boulton had just pronounced himself an unrepentant sinner and a self-centered scapegrace . . . with an interest in her. His words to her as serving began confirmed it.

"Fair warning, Miss Bumgarten. Tell me nothing you wouldn't want to see printed on the front page of the *Times*." He managed to look abashed, but the expression disappeared so quickly, she realized it was an act. "I cannot keep a secret to save my soul. In fact, I can't keep a secret to save anyone's soul." Then he chuckled and turned that charming smile on her again. "Now, tell me everything you know about everyone you know."

She stared at him for a moment, wondering how a man could be so openly wicked and yet be accepted in such elegant company.

"I am afraid I have to disappoint you, Mr. Boulton. I'm new in England and haven't met many people."

"But you have met Ashton Graham, so you must have had *some* sort of adventure."

"In a library?" She winced for effect.

"And the stables." The words were strung together with oily insinuation. "Mustn't forget where I saw you together."

"You were in the stables, too, Mr. Boulton. Did *we* have 'an adventure' as well? Lands, what imaginations you Brits have." She shook her head and concentrated on the soup being ladled into her bowl.

"You didn't tell that scapegrace anything, I hope." The countess whispered in her ear as the ladies retired to the sitting room while the gentlemen brought out their cigars.

"He jests about not being able to keep a secret, but in fact, he has made tales of indiscretion and scandal his vocation. Guard your every word. And for Heaven's sake, do not mention the duke's name. Mr. Boulton will use whatever you give him to sink you like a rock."

Forewarned is forearmed, Daisy thought later as she saw him bearing down on her across Lady Esseme's golden salon. A "gossip-hawk" who apparently saw a tasty morsel in her. She sighed tightly. Could he somehow sense the mother lode of indiscretions she harbored inside her fancy clothes?

She smoothed her skirts around her on the sofa near the card table, where gentlemen and ladies were partnering for a game of vingt-et-un. Through dinner she had responded to Boulton's questions with bits of western wisdom and cowboy lore that gave him a laugh but nothing more. She could tell that by the end of the meal he was frustrated by her simple but effective defense, and the look in his eye as he settled beside her on the settee said that in this next round he would be sharper.

"So, what do you think of our friend Ashton?" He came right out with it, no beating around the bush.

"Oh." She adopted a smile. "I hardly know him well enough to call him a friend or to have formed an opinion. Except that he seems to know a lot about historical matters. I've recently become something of a family historian myself. Interesting stuff, history. It's so . . . old."

He laughed in spite of himself and eyed her in a way that said he was revising his idea of her. "Historian, eh? A rather bookish interest for such a vibrant, horse-loving young woman, wouldn't you say?"

"An interest sparked by my travels. All those dusty old ruins with columns and castles with turrets. You know in Rome, Italy, they have one temple from the time of Julius

Caesar that is still standing?" She let her wistful admiration shine. "We don't have anything like that in the States." She sighed for effect. "I guess we're busier making history than studying it."

"Be sure to tell Ashton that," he said with no trace of sarcasm. "I'd love to hear his response."

"Why? Would he find it 'cheeky'? I think that's the word."

"He would find it a sacrilege. He's drunk deep from the well of academia, and believes those of us who bear no initials after our names are lesser lights in the firmament." He swept a hand across an imaginary sky.

"So, he's a snob?"

"Absolutely. And a hypocrite. All mind over matter, until the 'matter' has lovely curves and pouty lips. Then his true nature comes out."

"True nature?" She blinked. More than once. And it worked.

He gave her a patronizing smile and she silently blessed the countess and old Chuck Worth for giving her such an effective disguise.

"He's something of a rake, Ashton Graham. In with the fast crowd at St. James. Carouses with the prince when he's got the gilt."

"Guilt?"

"Gilt. As in gold, my dear. He's often strapped for funds, but the ladies don't seem to mind. Prominent names have been linked with his."

"How disturbing. Professor Huxley led us to believe he was something of a scholar."

"The old cod would. Ash was his favorite student. He tried everything to get Ash a seat on the faculty, but the dons wouldn't hear of it. He was a libertine, they said—unfit for the sober and godly pursuit of knowledge."

"Tell me more." She leaned in and saw his eyes narrow ever so slightly. She smiled. "Forewarned is forearmed."

He smiled and patted her hand, eager to recount an old story for a new audience. "The duke's and Ashton's father died early on, and Arthur became heir to their bachelor uncle's title. Artie was a quiet, bookish child, but Ashton was the opposite. If it hadn't been for their old nurse, he wouldn't have survived the thrashings up to age seven. That was when they were sent away to school. Eton. There, Ash stood up for his brother—scrapped and fought back when they called Artie a toady little bookworm—which, in fact, he was. Always had his nose buried in some tome or other and hated the playing fields and 'manly' pursuits of pranks and fighting. When he became the duke at twelve, they reeled him home and set tutors on him. Ash stayed on at school, where he became the opposite of Artie: brash, stubborn, quick with his fists, and fond of the suds."

"Suds?" She frowned.

"Ale. He went on to university, where he did well in spite of his loose-living ways. A social whirlwind, he was—invited everywhere for his presentable looks and entertaining wit—until the mamas started to complain and the papas started to threaten. There were rumors of duels, and he withdrew to more jaded company. Raked Hell itself, it is said. Make no mistake, my dear, he is most amusing company. Until he isn't. I won't trouble you with a list of families who have barred him from their doors."

"Then, I must be wary of his presence from now on," she said, watching the way he studied her face. What was he trying to do? Warn her of the dangers of Ashton's company, certainly. But why would he do that?

"What are you doing in England?" he asked in lowered tones.

She felt a sudden chill. He was a student of scandal; did he sense there was more to her than a painstakingly acquired facade of manners? Had he heard things? London was full of well-heeled travelers. . . .

"Have you ever been to New York, Mr. Boulton?"

"I have not had that pleasure," he said, with a barely concealed condescension that hinted he had no idea of her reputation on the other side of the Atlantic.

"If you had, you would know why I decided to travel. It is big, dirty, and bustling, and the darnedest collection of human beings you can imagine. Park Avenue swells who light cigars with twenty-dollar bills, down to laborers who work dawn to dusk and still can't buy enough food to keep body and soul together. Filth, smoke, and factories of all kinds taint the air, but the city still seems to collect people and money from all over the world." She looked past him into a sudden, unwelcome vision: Mrs. Vanderbilt and her covey of acid-tongued gossips. "And those with hour-old fortunes work to distance themselves from those whose fortunes are only half an hour old."

After a moment, he spoke, giving her a start.

"So, yours is a half-hour fortune, is it?" he asked. His intense gray eyes said he already knew the answer.

"Silver has no age, Mr. Boulton." Her entire body tensed. "It has existed since the beginning of time and will continue until the end. We Bumgartens are just fortunate that it landed in our lap for—"

"How selfish of you to take up all of Miss Bumgarten's time, Mr. Boulton." Lady Esseme descended on them with a glint in her eye. Daisy looked around to find the countess watching anxiously from across the room, and she rose with a rueful expression.

"Mr. Boulton was tutoring me on the finer points of family history." She gave him a determined smile that she hoped would quell any questions raised by her responses. "For which I am most grateful, sir." With that, she joined her hostess and the countess at the newly vacated card table, and breathed a sigh of relief.

It was another full day before the countess received a reply from her friend in Bristol and still more time before they were able to acquire tickets on a train. First class, it seemed, was very much in demand . . . though when she saw the first-class cabins bound for Bristol, Daisy wondered why. The compartments were not half as plush as the ones from London to Oxford; they were paneled in mismatched oak, their brass fittings were worn, and the finish on the leather upholstery was beginning to crack. But in all honesty, no amount of comfort or luxury could have soothed Daisy as the repetitive clack of the wheels on rails rasped against her nerves.

By noon, she was pacing again and insisting on trekking back to the baggage area to check on the horses. Red and the countess had tried to convince her that Banks would see to their beloved mounts, but she insisted on visiting them herself.

She stopped in the dining car, where she obtained a couple of carrots, and then made her way through general seating to the baggage car. She opened the door, expecting to see Banks draped across a shipping crate or propped against a grain bag beside the horses, but stopped dead at the sight of Ashton Graham stroking Dancer's head and feeding him an apple.

The sound of the door alerted him to another's presence. He glanced over his shoulder, then went back to petting her horse. She drew herself up and quelled the urge to press a hand to her racing heart.

"What are you doing on this train?" she demanded, hoping that she sounded more composed than she felt.

"How else was I to get to Bristol? I suppose I could have ridden horseback for days or hired a coach. But I'm not as fond of saddle sores as you apparently are, and coaches are slow and expensive. All in all, a train seemed the best choice."

"And you just happened to choose the same train we're on?" She reached for Dancer's halter and scowled. "You followed us."

"I did," he admitted, relinquishing the horse to her. "I have to know where and how you obtain documentation of your ancestry. How else am I to authenticate your findings?"

It was plausible, curse his hide. Why did everything he said have to seem so reasonable, when every sensible conclusion about his involvement warned that he was not to be trusted? She stroked Dancer's head and neck. As the countess never failed to remind her, he was here at his hostile and condescending family's insistence. And yet, to this date, he had been more help than hindrance.

Why was that? And why would he bother to try to talk her out of her pursuit of his brother when he could just discredit her findings? Lord knew, the evidence for a noble ancestor was slim enough.

"You're homesick," he said, his voice low, lulling, and too damned close for comfort.

"What?" She turned halfway to frown at him in the dim light filtering through the screened upper windows.

He stood close by with his long legs spread, his arms crossed, and his gaze intent.

"Why would you say that?"

"That's why you visit your horses so frequently and insist on taking care of them personally. You miss your home out west."

It was a declaration of just how keenly he'd studied her. It should have alarmed her and sent her storming back to the safety of her first class accommodations. Instead, she felt a worrisome warmth rise inside her.

He had guessed a truth that she could not, would not reveal to anyone. If her beloved Uncle Red knew how she really felt, he would pack her up and head for New York in a heartbeat. And the countess had invested so much time and effort, and recruited so many of her own personal connections to her protégée's progress that it would be seen as her personal failure if Daisy withdrew now. It was a campaign in which she could no longer retreat. She must win or . . . *win*.

"Suppose I am. What of it?"

"Why don't you go home, Daisy Bumgarten? Back to your horses and big sky and magnificent mountains."

"You know why," she said, refusing to meet his gaze. From the warmth in his voice, she already knew what she would see there. She offered Dancer a carrot and the big horse gave it a halfhearted nibble.

"English noble life is not for you." He stepped closer and she pulled back. "You deserve better than a marriage that is nothing but a contract to duty and obligation."

"You're trying too hard. Hanging crepe all around, trying to convince me to pack it up and go home. Why is that? If noble life is as bad as you say, why do families like yours fight fang-and-claw to hang on to every last shred of it?"

He was silent for a moment, and then stepped to the other side of Dancer's head.

"Because they're arrogant, greedy, and too lazy to strike out and make a life for themselves." His low, resonant voice vibrated her very fingertips.

The big horse turned to him, nuzzled the hand he offered, and then butted his head into Ashton's chest, insisting on a cuddle.

Daisy's jaw dropped as Ashton smiled and stroked the horse's head. Dancer only did that to one other person in the world—*her*. Curse that four-legger's faithless hide. She had always thought animals were superior judges of character. Dancer was apparently as lacking in moral fiber as she was—because right now all she wanted to do was curl up in Ashton's lap and have him stroke and caress her the same way! Watching his hands— those strong, beautiful hands— moving gently over Dancer's lustrous coat, she felt her resolve melting like butter on a hot biscuit.

"Does that describe you, too?" she said, trying to put at least a few brash words between him and her warming skin and weakening knees. "Arrogant, greedy, and too lazy to make a life for yourself?"

"I confess to a history of free-spending and high-handed ways. But I would like to think at least some of my pursuits have had a higher purpose." He didn't look at her.

"Like your study of history," she said. "You might have been a professor, except for those free-spending, high-living ways."

"Who told you that?" He looked over Dancer's neck with a frown.

"It's true, then. You wanted to be a professor and were refused."

"Just as you wanted to be a New York debutant and were refused," he countered. "New money, new manners, and too much spirit. So you decided to prove your worth and advance your sisters with a duke for a husband." He stepped around Dancer to confront her. "And you picked Artie. Naive, good-hearted, easily dazzled Arthur, Duke of Meridian." He loomed over her, his hands clenched at his sides. "Can't you see that marrying him would be disastrous for you both?"

"You think I would embarrass him," she charged, desperate to put words between them. His male scent was pouring like steam into her blood.

"Your manners, when you decide to use them, are impeccable," he countered.

"You think I couldn't make him happy."

His laugh came from deep in his chest and had a knowing edge.

"Sweetness, you could make a fence post happy."

Chapter Thirteen

It took a moment for the various ways that statement could be taken to coalesce in Daisy's turbulent thoughts.

"You are rotten to the core, Ashton Graham."

His gaze connected with hers like flint striking steel. Sparks of response showered through her, and she felt it coming, inevitable as sunrise. He was going to kiss her and she was going to respond. She would probably regret it afterward, but for now, the desire for his lips against hers and the urge to press her body against his big, potent frame were overpowering.

"There we disagree, sweet Daisy. My core is perfectly sound. If you'll permit me to demonstrate—"

He grabbed her hand and reeled her against him, never taking his gaze from hers. She met his kiss with desire of her own. He filled her arms, her head, and her lungs—she drank him in on every breath and craved more. His mouth was demanding one minute, soft and giving the next, producing sensations so intense she was momentarily overwhelmed. Her nerves, her very bones began to resonate with a kind of need she had never felt before.

He ran his hands over her body, tracing the lines of her

stylish traveling clothes and groaning against her mouth in appreciation. She ran her hands inside his coat and beneath the edges of his vest, tracing his sides and back, finding his shape exactly as she imagined it—strong, lean, and male. Compelled to greater exploration, she grasped handfuls of flesh and fabric, wanting to be closer, to claim and possess his body . . . needing to feel his strength and hardness around her . . . inside her.

"*Mmmmmore,*" she hummed against his mouth, setting up a delicious vibration in their lips and a tingle that spread through her face and down her throat.

"*Mmmmmmy* thoughts exactly." He returned her murmur, then pulled back enough to work her jacket buttons.

Without breaking that bone-melting kiss, she dispatched his vest buttons and started on his shirt. Somewhere in the midst of the kissing and peeling and touching, they maneuvered further back in the car to where several hay bales lay stacked together, topped with a rough blanket. Through the haze in her senses she recognized Banks's hat and grooming satchel and a couple of the penny dreadfuls he was known to read in his spare time. She sank onto the blanket and Ashton sank with her, then over her. She sighed silently as his body replaced her anticipation with steamy pleasure.

Her jacket and blouse were soon open and her breasts were bare above the demi-corset the countess insisted she wear. He nudged the top of that constraint aside and ran his face over the tip of her breast. That wrung a groan from her that made him chuckle and free her other breast to the same attention. She tugged down her corselet, baring more of herself and reveling in the erotic stimulation she had tried to convince herself no longer existed.

He cupped and massaged her breasts, then nuzzled and began to tease her nipples with his tongue. When he suckled sharply on one, she gasped but pulled his head harder against her, demanding more. He obliged until her whole body quivered with expectation and she writhed sensually beneath him, seeking a more satisfying blending of their bodies.

This, *this* was what she'd both wanted and feared from the moment they'd met. He somehow knew her desires, sensed her body's paths to pleasure and her sensual predilections. His touch seemed tailored to the exact movement and pressure that drove her excitement to the brink.

She pushed him up for a moment, overwhelmed, seeking his gaze while struggling to catch her breath.

She lay beneath him, open and undone, bared to his pleasure. Ashton watched her sultry, instinctive movements, studying her naked breasts and the heat that bloomed in her cheeks and turned her eyes to molten silver. She was breathtaking. An enticement to sin and a passage to paradise rolled together into one irresistible feminine form. He had never known a woman like her, and it struck him that he would probably never know one like her again. She was one of a kind. Forthright, unpretentious, and unintentionally seductive. She didn't have to pose, pout, or preen. Sensuality radiated from her like a rare, entrancing fragrance.

"You are so beautiful," he murmured, wishing he had not said those words so many times before that now they sounded trite. He had never truly appreciated their full power before now, and that thought lodged in the back of his mind. As he ran his fingertips over her face, around her throat, and down the center of her chest, she curled around his touch and then rose to pull his mouth to hers again.

"You are, too, Ashton Graham," she murmured against his lips. "You're a tall, gorgeous, swagger of a man with a silky tongue and eyes that could melt Winter itself. I don't know how the women of London can bear to let you leave the city."

Her lips trapped his half-formed laugh in his throat and it came out a growl of need as his arms wrapped around her and she pushed him back so that her chest lay atop his. She threaded her fingers through his thick, soft hair as she licked his lips and kissed him within an inch of his sanity. His whole body was responding . . . skin, heart, loins. He was slowly losing his grip on all reality outside the luscious and irresistible Daisy Bumgarten.

The one small part of his consciousness that had not yet succumbed to glorious sensation detected the rumble of the wheels when the door opened. Years of secret liaisons and illicitly snatched pleasures had tuned his perceptions to sounds that might indicate discovery, and once again those defenses served him well.

"Oi, me dancin' boy. Lookie what I brought ye." It was Banks.

"Sap-headed pony-jack—yer spoilin' 'em with them apples." That was Daisy's uncle.

Daisy had frozen beneath Ashton with eyes wide with dawning horror. He pressed a finger to her love-swollen lips and motioned her to stay before pulling away and frantically buttoning his shirt and vest. To her credit, she seemed to understand and helped, even as she stuffed herself back into her own clothes. As soon as he was presentable he rose from the pallet and made a show of yawning and stretching. Running his fingers through his hair to disarrange it further, he turned and stepped around the horses.

He had managed to grab one of Banks's penny dreadfuls and stuck his thumb in it as if keeping a place. "There you are. Hope you don't mind." He strolled forward holding the book up for Banks to see. "I saw your book—thought I'd have a peek. Must have drifted off. No reflection on your taste in reading matter, Banks old man, I just had a late night."

"What the hell are you doin' here?" Red demanded, scowling.

"No tickets available, so I paid a small fee to sit back here with the baggage," he said, looking as sincere as a man in the middle of a bold-faced lie could look. He'd had plenty of practice at that kind of deception, so his face—though still slightly flushed—was fairly convincing.

"Where's Daisy? She came back for a look at the horses." Red looked around and started around the horses.

"She was here?" He stifled a purposeful yawn and stepped into Red's path. "I had no idea. Must have been while I was dozing back there." Red frowned, looked around the baggage, barrels, and bales, and relented.

"Didn't see her on the way back." Red chewed on that a moment before giving him an out. "Must've gone to the priv—necessary, then."

"Say, I'm famished." Ashton rubbed his stomach. "Care for a bite of food and a drink? I've been meaning to ask you about Nevada. I hear you're quite the expert on both silver and horses. And they have some wonderful Irish whiskey in Dining."

It was as if he'd waved a magic wand. Red broke into a grin and he could almost see the old fellow salivating as he rubbed his bristled chin.

"Hell, yeah."

Daisy sat as taut as a bowstring on the cushioned seat of the carriage the countess's friend, Lady Regina, Countess of Albemarle, sent to the station for them. She had hoped to stay in a hotel and avoid the manners and endless courtesies required of a guest in a grand house, but once the invitation was extended, she had little say in the matter. According to the countess, to decline after announcing their presence in a way that practically begged an invitation would be unthinkable.

Of course, there was that business of "making friends" among the nobility, which was turning out to be time-consuming and exhausting. What she wouldn't give for a good hard ride and some time alone in the country.

The thought of horses brought a blush of warmth to her cheeks. She had managed to put herself together after that incident in the baggage car, but the pleasure Ashton had roused in her and the sensual hunger that lingered afterward now refused to be shut away in the inner strongbox she'd always trusted to contain it. Blast his hide. He was on her mind. He was on her skin. The taste of him was sure as hell on her lips. She found herself licking them and stopped, praying the countess hadn't seen her do it.

Ashton Graham had freed her passion.

God help her, it felt wonderful. She was alive and hungry and eager for sensual encounter. Five long years ago she had forsworn men and pleasures of the flesh, and in the time since, she had come to believe that she had put that part of her life and its mistakes behind her. It was a shock to find her headstrong desires free and focused on the one man in all of England she had no business desiring.

He was Duke Arthur's brother, for Heaven's sake. Everything served the title, he said, even him. Especially him.

Which meant he was up to something. Most likely, preventing her from marrying his brother. He said she was beautiful and had excellent manners when she decided to use them. And he found her desirable, which meant his objections to her marrying Arthur had to do with that pile of "family obligation" horse manure he'd warned her about. It boiled down to one miserable conclusion; he believed what his wretched family believed. She wasn't good enough for his precious brother.

With all of her money, hard-won manners, and willingness to sacrifice for her family and the dukedom, she wasn't any more respected on this side of the Atlantic than she had been on the other. She wasn't one of *them*.

Maybe it truly did come down to blood and history, and if it did, she had to somehow prove to him and to the duke's arrogant family that she *was* one of them . . . that whatever was in her blood, it was potent enough to meet their damned challenge and win.

By the time they arrived at Marlton, the Earl of Albemarle's seat, she was sitting straighter and her eyes were narrowed over so slightly. Determination had relaxed the knot in her stomach and replaced her anxiety. She felt fortified by her own logic and a fresh conviction that the next man to set hands to her naked body would be her *husband*.

They were greeted in the marble-clad center hall of Marlton by Lady Regina herself, surrounded by a dozen uniformed staff and portraits of hundreds of years of ancestors. The two countesses hugged warmly and their obvious affection for each other put Daisy at ease. She was heartened to think that maybe there could be true friendships among nobles, after all.

"Delighted to meet you, my dear," tall, slender Lady Regina said as she gave Daisy a kiss on each cheek. "We've heard intriguing snippets about our dear Evelyn's protégée. All good, I assure you. I can't wait to hear all about New York and Philadelphia and the great American West." She turned to Red. "And you must be . . ."

"Redmond Strait." The countess stepped in to finish the introductions. "Our dear Daisy's uncle."

Lady Regina's eyes widened. "The cowboy!"

"Well, not exactly that, ma'am." He caught the countess's look of dismay at his address and corrected it. "I mean, milady. I owned half interest in the ranch, but mostly I did the prospectin' and openin' mines."

"No matter." Lady Regina waved away his modesty. "You're from the untamed West and that will be good enough for the earl." She leaned closer to him with a twinkle in her eye. "He is mad about cowboys and reads everything he can about them."

"I look forward to meetin' yer husband, milady. Sounds like a straight-shootin' kind of a fella."

The Lady of Albemarle fairly giggled with delight.

"I'm sure you're exhausted from the trip down from Oxford, so I've planned a simple family dinner tonight. Just the earl, myself, and the dowager—his mother." She scooped up Daisy's and the countess's arms in hers to lead them up the sweeping staircase that dominated the hall, leaving Red to fall in behind. "But we have another guest arriving tomorrow and I thought we should have a few of our friends in for a little party." She lowered her head toward Daisy as they climbed the stairs. "I've never made his acquaintance myself, but he corresponds with the earl regularly. He's something of a naturalist, they say, the young Duke of Meridian."

Daisy and the countess stopped dead on the stairs, dragging Lady Regina to a halt between them. The countess was too stunned to speak.

"But, Lady Regina, we've already met." Daisy's heart skipped beats and she was suddenly flushed with pleasure. "The duke and I are on the way to becoming . . . *good friends.*"

That same night, while Daisy was dining quietly with the Earl and Countess of Albemarle, Ashton sat in the bar of the Grand Hotel, located in the heart of the city of Bristol, drinking whiskey and brooding on the confusing nature of his interactions with the delectable Daisy Bumgarten. He was making headway with her, no doubt of that. His sincerity and forthrightness were slowly winning her over, and she was so susceptible to his usual seductions that it was almost crimin—

"What the devil are *you* doing here?" When he looked up, his uncle Bertram stood nearby with his fists propped at his waist, wearing a scowl. "You're supposed to be"—he stepped closer and lowered his voice—"dealing with that Bamgarter wench."

"Bumgarten," he corrected, more sharply than he intended. "And I am dealing with her. She is here to look for records of one of her ancestors."

"Here? In the hotel?" Bertram started and looked around the bar in horror.

"No. She is staying with one of the countess's friends. I am here to 'oversee' her findings, remember? Using the meager funds I was provided for this project," Ashton said irritably. "What are *you* doing here, Uncle?"

"I've come to meet your brother. He's off on a beetle-headed search for some crawly bit or other, and he needs a minder. Insisted on coming down to see some gardens he'd heard about. We had no idea that Bamgarter chit would be here or we'd never have allowed it."

"Bumgarten," Ashton gritted out again. Bertram didn't seem to notice. His reference to Artie needing a "minder" struck Ashton as mean and petty. But then, mean-and-petty was standard fare from the family grisards.

"You must keep your Aunt Sylvia apprised of your whereabouts." Bertram looked around for a chair he deemed fit to support his precious arse and finally settled on one, glowering. "We understood you were in Oxford. What is the chit doing here?"

"I believe I just said. Tracking a potential ancestor, as

required. The countess finagled them an invitation to stay with the Albemarles."

"Albemarles?" Uncle Bertram's jowls quivered under the impact of that name. "Good God, man. That's where he's headed."

"Arthur?" Ashton's jaw slacked in disbelief.

"Who else? He's been invited to visit the gardens at Marlton . . . Albemarle's pile." Bertram's ruddy face paled. "Good God. They'll be there *together*."

Chapter Fourteen

The weather was unseasonably warm and sunny the next morning, so a stroll through Marlton's expansive gardens was a must, according to Lady Regina. Daisy was itching to get on with her ancestor search at the Temple Church, but those infernal "courtesies" required a trek through the gardens with her host and hostess first. She prayed they could get it over quickly.

She should have known better.

As the talkative earl and his lady wife prepared to squire Daisy, Uncle Red, and the countess around the gardens, they had their guests change into sensible walking shoes and a wrap that could be shed if they became too warm. The group was a full quarter of an hour into the walk before they reached the first set of plantings.

The gardens were the pride of Marlton, Lady Regina explained, and a great part of its fame. The flowers and shrubs were visited by rare butterflies and by birds on migrations—whatever the heck those were. The gathering of such rare specimens attracted naturalists from all over England, now including the young Duke of Meridian. Daisy chaffed privately at the realization that her upcoming meeting with the object of her hopes was made possible by a few posies and some six-legged critters. She wondered fleetingly what they'd done with the butterflies she'd worn at the Mountjoy's ball.

The term "garden" was inadequate to describe the wealth of plantings and multitude of colors that rolled across Marlton's massive acreage. It had begun as an arboretum, the earl said, planted by a tree-loving ancestor. But it hadn't taken long for flowering shrubs, hedges, and patterned plantings of flowers to make their way into the preserve. For the last hundred years, each earl had managed to add something new and unusual. The present earl, Lord Robert, had installed what he called "topiaries". . . bushes cut into fanciful shapes and figures that were nothing short of remarkable. One was shaped like a bear, another like a rabbit, and a third was laid out like a rank of chess pieces on a grassy board.

A small army of gardeners was tending the breathtaking beds and medallions of color made up of asters, bells of Ireland, verbena, valerian, phlox, sweet Williams, nasturtiums, freesia, dahlias, delphiniums, and primroses. How the earl and Lady Regina could remember what each was called was beyond Daisy. She struggled to memorize a few. Whenever they approached, the workers respectfully faded back to allow them full access and smiled proudly as the earl complimented their skill and dedication.

Awestruck, she forgot for a time the pressing nature of her mission. She had seen a number of estate parks in England and on the continent, and was no stranger to the public gardens and conservatories in Paris and London. But nothing could compare to the size and splendor of the gardens that generations of Albemarles had created here.

They strolled the gravel paths and paused to smell flowers, listen to fountains, and enjoy the various vistas created by the garden's architects. Most fascinating were a set of tall, tightly woven hedges that looked like walls. Lady Regina insisted on leading them to a blossom-sheltered bower at the center of the maze and mischievously related that when a young man and young woman reached the center of the maze together, they were required to kiss to assure good luck.

Red stepped close to the countess with a wicked gleam in his eye.

"Not on your life," she said with a blush, and fled with laughter at her back.

It was well into the afternoon before they returned to the house and Lady Regina insisted on providing a light "luncheon" before sending them off to their rooms for a rest. Daisy paced and fretted in her elegant ivy themed room, while Collette watched anxiously and tried to get her to lie down. In the end, she sent Collette to the housekeeper for writing supplies and penned a letter to the dean of the Temple Church asking for access to records corresponding to the date on the paper she had found in Huxley's collection.

Only after Collette carried the letter to Banks with instructions to exercise Dancer by riding into the city to deliver it, did Daisy surrender to the need for a rejuvenating nap. After all, as the countess had pointedly advised, that night she could be seeing the Duke of Meridian and had to be at her best.

The earl's carriage collected the duke from the train station late that afternoon; Daisy was afforded a view of his arrival from her window on the second floor. His hair was a tad too long, his suit not at all stylish, and his broad gestures conveyed boyish excitement as the earl greeted him and ushered him inside. She turned from the window, squared her shoulders, and set about dressing to become a duke's fondest desire.

Later, as she joined the countess to descend the stairs to dinner, she was pleased to see her sponsor's smile of approval. She had chosen a sky-blue dinner dress that was intended to bring out her eyes, and Collette had put her hair up into a lovely cascade of curls that included a pair of silk butterflies already proven to draw the duke's delight.

The salon was filled with people, every one of whom wanted to meet Daisy and her uncle. Introduction after introduction proceeded along familiar lines: the earl, viscount, countess, lady, honorable sir, missus, dowager, or simple reverend mister . . . and she was Miss Bumgarten from Nevada, America. Hands were shaken or kissed, pleasantries exchanged, travel, weather, and gardens were all referenced. Suddenly there was a rustle of interest among the guests and they looked to the salon entrance.

Daisy turned to see what caused it.

"Miss Bumgarten!" The duke rushed forward a few steps before remembering himself and slowing to a more dignified pace. "How wonderful to see you."

"Your Grace." She managed a small curtsy and a warm, winning smile as he reached for her hand. "This is such a pleasant surprise."

"Isn't it, though?" He ignored the other guests, who watched their meeting with keen interest. Not even the earl's throat clearing could divert his attention. "I had no idea you were visiting Marlton's gardens, too. What a marvelous coincidence. Who would have thought? But then, who can fathom the clever doings of Fortune herself?"

Before she could respond, a stout, white-bearded, old fellow in immaculate dinner attire appeared at the duke's side to clasp his arm with not-so-subtle force. The duke seemed unfazed. "Dear Miss Bumgarten, I would have you meet my uncle . . . Bertram Graham, Baron Beesock."

"Baron." She gave him her hand, but the icy look on the old man's face made her wonder if it would be frostbit when she got it back.

"Miss Bamgarters." He bit off the words and gave a

Prussian-stiff dip over her hand. It was only then that she remembered where she had seen him before; he was one of the family elders in the Earl of Mountjoy's upper room.

A second later, he was whisking the duke away to greet other guests, and the countess appeared at Daisy's side with a raised eyebrow that said she had seen the baron's mispronunciation of her name and the crass way he spirited the duke away from her. Daisy nodded to her, took a steadying breath, and then turned brightly to engage their host and fellow guests.

When dinner was announced, Lady Regina led them into the dining room on Uncle Red's arm. Albemarle escorted his mother, the dowager, and Daisy was surprised to have the duke appear at her side and offer her his arm. She cast a subtle glance around and discovered the countess had performed the ultimate sacrifice—throwing herself in the baron's path and dousing him with enough charm that he couldn't refuse to escort her.

Whether it was the countess's influence or simple curiosity about the pairing on her hostess's part, Daisy was seated beside the duke at dinner. She warmed as he took the chair beside hers and turned to her with a smile that could almost have been called shy.

"I am so glad to see you here, Miss Bumgarten. I know you said you enjoy gardens and butterflies, but people say such things to me—knowing I study them. I had a feeling that your interest was more genuine, and I am gratified to be proven correct. Have you seen the gardens?"

"I have only been here a short time, Your Grace, but the earl and Lady Regina personally squired us around the gardens. The plantings took my breath. Such colors and shapes. A surprise around every turn. And the butterflies . . . just thick around the flowers."

"It seems you've already captured some in your hair." He reached out to touch one of her butterflies and inadvertently brushed a curl on the nape of her neck. Surprised, she gave a small "oh." He withdrew with a look of chagrin, but a moment later she met his glance with a smile and he relaxed. His face seemed a bit leaner than she remembered, somehow more mature.

"I've heard of Albemarle's gardens for years." He paused as the serving began, then continued when the footmen had moved on. "Don't know why I've never come before. Just too absorbed in my studies, I suppose. And there is always so much to do." He shrugged. "I've determined to see more of nature for myself. And I've you to thank, Miss Bumgarten. You are my inspiration."

"I am?" She felt an unexpected wave of warmth at his earnest compliment. "How wonderful of you to say so, Your Grace."

"When I saw how eager you are to travel and learn and see other places and other people—well, I realize how isolated I have been, and I am determined to remedy that. Starting with good Albemarle's gardens."

"Just wait until you see the topiaries they have installed," Daisy said. "They're such fun. Though I believe you'll like the butterfly garden best."

"They have a butterfly garden?" He pressed a hand to his heart. "I won't sleep a wink tonight."

At that moment a voice was raised down the table: his uncle Bertram was recounting a tale of the duke's younger days. . . . "He fell into a muddy stream bank area while searching for a specimen and returned to the house covered head to toe with mud and oblivious to rugs and upholstery . . . thinking of nothing but his precious salamander." There were polite chuckles as the other guests looked to the duke for a reaction. His ill-concealed discomfort silenced that end of the table.

"Well, salamanders can be quite a prize for twelve-year-old boys," the countess said, trying to relieve the awkwardness.

"Twelve? That was just last year!" Uncle Bertram roared with laughter, oblivious to the fact that he was the only one laughing.

The duke stiffened and Daisy could have sworn he shrank inside his coat. Unable to help herself, she reached for his hand beneath the table, and when he looked over in surprise, she squeezed it and gave him a smile.

The rest of dinner was more enjoyable. Uncle Red recounted a few prospecting stories and the earl related a tale or two he'd read about cowboys on a cattle drive. Red and Daisy were called on to confirm that thousands of cattle were moved to railheads across vast open spaces, and that the drives sometimes took weeks. But they did have to say that this was less common since the railroads had spread over so much more of the country. Long, brutal cattle drives were no longer as necessary.

By the end of dinner the duke seemed to have recovered his spirits and spoke about the recent theories of naturalists about the habits of birds and even butterflies. Once again his uncle made pointed comments about his eccentric interests, but this time his remarks were ignored, even by the countess, who chose to converse with the guests seated opposite her instead of listening to him.

Later, when the gentlemen joined the ladies in the salon, the baron did his best to prevent Arthur from seeking out Daisy and was partly successful. She watched as Arthur was forced to sit hands of cards he had no interest in and suffered through displays of piano skill that ranged from pleasant to cringe worthy. Eventually the aging baron's stamina and vigilance waned and the duke sought out Daisy for a chat.

"I must apologize for my uncle," he said with a tepid smile. "He grows older and less discreet by the year. Whatever goes through his head comes out his mouth, without a care for how it may be received. And yet, I cannot be too hard on him. He and my aunts have always worried and fussed over me, and tried to direct and protect me."

"No doubt," she said. *And what they were trying to protect him from, right now, was her*. Daisy slipped her hand between them and risked another touch of his hand. "My mother has been much the same. She didn't want me to tour the continent and come to England. But in the end, I recruited Uncle Red and wrote letters and contacted the countess— and—here I am."

"Such pluck. You are without a doubt the pluckiest female I have ever known, Miss—May I call you Daisy? I feel like we have been friends forever." When she nodded, it was as if the sun dawned in his face. "And do please call me Arthur—at least out of company. So few people do."

By the time she trooped up the stairs at the end of the evening, Daisy was glowing with the success of her time with "Arthur." When the countess arrived in her room later, she, too, was flushed with excitement.

"Now is not the time to rest on our laurels," the countess forced herself to caution. "We still have to find evidence to satisfy the family elders." Then she smiled. "But having the duke's *interest* might sway things in our direction no matter what the outcome of your ancestry search."

Chapter Fifteen

Daisy rose early the next morning, dressed in an India-cotton dress printed with bluebells and carried a broad-brimmed sun hat in preparation for an outing. She appeared in the breakfast room to find that the other guests who were staying had the same idea: to be out and about in the splendid weather. One of the earl's friends arranged pairings for a game of lawn tennis, another mounted a ride to the ruins of a nearby abbey, and several ladies insisted on a personally guided tour of the gardens. When the duke appeared, it was with his uncle, who steered him away from her. The old coot. She smiled sweetly and sipped her coffee.

As expected, the duke chose to enjoy the gardens, with the earl and Lady Regina as guides. The ladies who had insisted on the tour chatted eagerly about the wonders to come. There were *"ah's"* aplenty and questions about the designs and names for the various plants and parts of the gardens. "The Moroccan," a great rectangular planting designed to look like a Persian rug, was Lady Regina's declared favorite. As they walked, each person picked out a part that spoke to them. For the duke, it clearly was the butterfly garden.

With the earl's encouragement, he followed the stepping stones into the midst of the flowers and brushed the plants gently to stir a flutter of wings. Butterflies rose in a cloud around him and he raised his hands and laughed at the sensation of wings brushing his skin. Daisy watched his joyful response with pleasure that was dimmed seconds later by the sight of his uncle Bertram's narrowed eyes. He must have felt her watching him, for he quickly turned that glare directly on her.

Nothing could have put steel in her spine quicker than that arrogant look, a warning if she'd ever seen one. From that moment, she looked for a chance to part the duke from his uncle. It wasn't long before she found one.

The maze loomed in the distance and the group neared it. She worked her way toward Arthur, caught his eye, and nodded in a way that suggested he step aside and wait for her. He slowed his pace and soon they were at the rear of the group fast disappearing into the maze.

"Come with me," she whispered, taking his hand and heading along the edge of the maze.

"Where?"

"Everywhere," she whispered loudly. "There is so much to see here." She pulled him into a run, laughing, and he followed self-consciously, looking over his shoulder. He kept pace as she hiked her skirts and led him through the arboretum, past plantings of holly and berry bushes and through groves of dogwoods, cherry trees, and exotic flowering almonds. They emerged from a planting of pines to more floral plantings centered on fountains and then to a long, rose-covered arbor that arched like a perfumed tunnel above the path. It was strangely pleasant, walking with him, saying little, sharing the beauty of the place.

After a time, they arrived back at the butterfly garden and she stopped just inside the opening in the brick wall that surrounded it, motioning him in ahead of her.

"After you, Your Grace."

"This . . . this is remarkable," he said, once again using

the carefully positioned stepping stones among the flowers, hands out at his sides to gently stroke the blossoms and send the butterflies hovering. "Adonis Blues, Pearl-bordered Fritillaries, Painted Ladies, Swallowtails, Red Admirals—it's a compendium of the best species seen in England."

"I thought this part would be your favorite," she said, clasping her hands behind her and skirting the edge of the flowers as she circled the garden. "I believe those lovely tall, blue flowers are delphiniums"—she pointed them out— "and I heard the earl name these allium and those daylilies. Those he called snapdragons, and those"—she waved toward a stand of stalks bearing bracts of stunning flowers— "lupines."

"It's a banquet for butterflies," he declared, grinning at her. "I tried to plant some of these same varieties and create a butterfly garden, but my flowers don't thrive like this, and only a local species or two of butterflies visit them. This is magnificent."

"We'll have to ask the earl his secret, then," she said, enjoying the wonder in his expression. Standing there in the middle of the garden, drenched in sunshine and buoyed by excitement, he seemed taller than she recalled. His smile was broader and his eyes shone in a way she had never seen before. It struck her that he was a man as well as a duke, and if she were to make good on her determination to marry him, she would have to see him that way. What was it Ashton had said about his brother? He had a good heart and a sound intellect. She could see now that was true. He just had not been required to use that brain and those talents in productive ways.

"If you had the chance to do anything you want," she asked, lifting her skirts to step on the stones that led to him in the center of the garden, "what would you do?"

He paused for a moment, looking around him as if searching the flowers for an answer. He turned to her as she neared.

"I would want to be a good duke, of course. It's my duty. I owe it to my family and my tenants and the uncles and aunts who raised me."

She studied him. "And if you didn't have to worry about your 'duty,' what then? What would you do simply because you love to do it?"

"I believe, Daisy Bumgarten, that I would do exactly what you have done: travel." He offered her his arm and she took it. He led her to the brick wall at the edge of the garden and picked her up bodily to set her on the wall.

"Ohhh!" She was almost as surprised by where he had put her as she was by the fact that he had easily manhandled her. Then he pulled himself up on the wall, twisted neatly, and settled to a seat beside her. "Well, that was a surprise," she said, laughing.

"I like sitting on walls," he said with a mischievous grin. "It gives one a change of perspective—a different view of things. We have quite a few walls at Betancourt."

"Betancourt?"

"Our family home. I was always climbing the roofs and walking the walls as a boy. Gave Uncle Bertram and Uncle Seward palpitations. I still do it when no one is watching. It's a way to be alone and collect my thoughts."

She studied him for a moment, struck by his need to escape to the tops of walls to have some peace in his own home. His uncle's vile, controlling behavior seemed even more despicable.

"So, if you were to travel, where would you go?" she asked. "Paris? Rome? Florence?"

"Egypt," he said with a firm nod. "I would love to see pyramids and camels and rug and spice markets. Then, there's the rest of Africa, too. There is an intriguing theory, you know, about what happens to many of our birds and butterflies in winter. It has been proposed that they go from England all the way to Africa and back, with the seasons.

Migration, it's called. I'd love to go with them someday and be the one to confirm it." He clasped his knees, seeming not to know what to do with his hands.

"As it is, I've studied and catalogued a hundred local species, but there is so much more to do. If I could only . . ." He sighed and was silent for a moment. "You need to discover something important to be invited into the Royal Society." He halted for a moment. "And I would love to go to America and see the buffalos and the mountains and the cowboys. And China. The temples, palaces, and Great Wall there are more than a thousand years old."

"You've read about these places?"

"I have. Wonderful places with such thrilling sights."

"Then why don't you go? At least to one or two of them. Egypt or America."

"I have . . . obligations." He frowned, seeming uncertain whether or not to reveal: "Travel takes money. *Everything* takes money. Repairing walls and replacing roofs, repointing brickwork and restacking chimneys. Not to mention keeping the staff—whom you actually have to *pay* these days—and buying comestibles and coal for the fires and hay and oats for the blessed horses. Don't ask me why we have to keep so many horses. Don't see why they can't just walk most places. I do." He sighed and his shoulders rounded. "Money. They talk of nothing else, these days. Apparently it is not exactly in great supply."

His odd opinions and quixotic jumps of topic would have been amusing if she hadn't realized they came from his ignorance of society and even of his own situation. He showed not even a glimmer of recognition that she thought of him as a matrimonial prospect, which meant he had no idea that she and his family elders were locked in a battle of sorts for the right to his hand in matrimony.

"Arthur, surely there is a way to remedy such a situation for—"

"There you are!" Uncle Bertram's voice crashed through the hedges outside the wall and Bertram himself quickly followed. The duke was startled, swayed, and looked over his shoulder at his panting, ruddy-faced chaperone. "What the devil are you doing up there?"

"Oh, Uncle, I—I was . . . I just wanted to . . ." Arthur was suddenly fifteen years old again, clammy-handed and stammering.

"His Grace wanted to see the butterfly garden again, and I knew the way and offered to show him," she asserted, struggling to keep her tone respectful. "Butterflies are his passion, after all."

The minute she uttered the word "passion" she knew it was a mistake.

"His Grace does not have *passions*, young woman. He has mere *enthusiasms*." He speared poor Arthur with a glare. "Come down this minute, Your Grace. That is most undignified."

Daisy watched the duke's jaw clench, but he complied with his uncle's order and slid from the wall. He delayed departing to reach up for her, and she let her hands linger on his shoulders a moment after he set her on the ground. As she thanked him, she could see Uncle Bertram struggling to contain his indignation.

She watched them stalk back to the house and could imagine the dressing-down his uncle was giving him. But then she saw them jerk to a halt, saw Arthur square his shoulders and speak, and then watched him stride away, leaving his uncle standing on the path.

"Good for you, Arthur," she muttered as she took another turn around the butterfly garden before setting off for a long walk to vent the steam in her blood.

Visions of Arthur's life at Betancourt, under Uncle Bertram's and Aunt Sylvia's hostile regard, weighted her steps. She was beginning to understand Ashton's view that elevated rank has more obligations and constraints than privileges. Poor Arthur had been isolated and deprived of a broader vision of the world—a prisoner of his own importance. She stopped on the path, thinking of the way—after so short an acquaintance—he'd named her his inspiration and confided his heartfelt hopes and dreams in her.

Sweet Heaven Above.

The duke didn't just need a wife, he needed a savior!

Chapter Sixteen

The great house, Marlton, was cool and quiet, and he'd had a hard night. While he waited for the earl to return to the house and receive him, Ashton sank into a large, pillow-stuffed chair, stretched his legs out before him, and nodded off for a bit. He was just sinking into a delicious dream of warm flesh and hot blue eyes when voices intruded and he was rattled awake.

"Can you not see? She's an ambitious title seeker. Pure and simple."

Good God. It was Bertram winding up for one of his harangues.

"Just because you see money in everything you look at, doesn't mean others do. She's a fine young woman with a sound mind and caring nature."

Damn it all. That was Arthur. And the "she" under discussion had to be Daisy Bumgarten.

Ashton wrestled with the urge to announce his presence before it went further, but he didn't want Arthur to question his appearance and purpose there. Even his usually oblivious brother knew he wasn't welcomed with open arms in polite society.

"She's a crude, grasping bit of baggage who doesn't

know her place," Bertram railed with compressed fury. "She'll waggle her bustle at you and soon have a ring around her finger and another through your nose. She'll lead you around like a moon-struck calf."

"Uncle, I will not listen to slander against a young woman who has shown nothing but courtesy and kindness to me. I have better things to do."

Arthur strode out, the sound of his heels smacking the marble entry floor the only sign of his outrage. Ashton heard his uncle muttering and moving about, so he popped his head over the edge of the chair.

"You're wrong, you know," he said, giving Bertram a start. His uncle wheeled and glowered at him. "She doesn't wear bustles."

"Damn your eyes—what the hell are you doing here?"

"Waiting for a certain 'grasping bit of baggage' to return. We have business at the old Temple Church—which, if you are luckier than you deserve, will keep her out of your hair for the rest of the day."

"Does Albemarle know you're here?" Bertram asked, glancing at the door behind him.

"Not yet. I'm waiting for him to return from his gardens. The butler put me in here." He sniffed. "Without even an offer of refreshment."

"No doubt he's heard your reputation and won't risk the help," Bertram snarled, stalking closer to the chair where Ashton was sprawled. He lowered his head and his voice. "For God's sake, man, get on with it. Compromise the chit before she gets her hooks into your brother. We've barely a week before she's due at Betancourt to present her 'proof.' I take it you'll see to it that said proof is insufficient, or better yet, fraudulent." The venom in his voice took on an oily quality. "That would add dashes of shame to her abject unsuitability."

Ashton rose slowly to tower over his uncle.

"I'll do what must be done," he bit out, forcing his hands to unclench. "Now, if you don't mind, I've a 'grasping bit of baggage' to see."

Daisy walked slowly, deep in thought and staring at the path as she approached Marlton House. She didn't notice the figure standing on the terrace until she was close enough to recognize him and stop dead.

Sons of Thunder. What was *he* doing here?

A breeze had come up, and now tugged at her sun hat, threatening to tip it off, so she removed it and clutched the brim of it tightly before her.

Ashton was dressed in a handsome charcoal suit and stood with his feet spread and one hand clasping the other wrist, waiting. He seemed perfectly at ease and utterly focused. On her.

His gaze felt like a physical touch and her heart responded as if it would jump out of her chest to run to him. She was suddenly aware of every aspect of her body; the touch of the breeze against her bare throat, the feel of her clothes rustling against her body, the motion of her legs, the sway of her hips. Each sensation was somehow linked to the man watching her, waiting for her. She swallowed hard as she mounted the steps onto the stone terrace.

"What are you doing here?" she asked.

"Everyone keeps asking that." He pursed one side of his mouth. "I should think it would be obvious to *you*. I am here to verify your ancestral documentation. I spent the morning at Temple Church, waiting for the dean. He said he would wait for us until six o'clock, which is the time he leaves for home and supper . . . which he is unwilling to delay one single minute. So if you'll get a shawl or wrap of some kind, we'll be on our way. I have a cab waiting."

"I can't just up and go with you, unchaperoned," she said,

raising her hat like a shield against her breast. "It wouldn't be proper."

"It's a church, Daisy," he said, leaning close. "I'm hardly apt to ravish you in the nave."

"You didn't seem to have any scruples about doing it in a library."

"Nor"—he smiled wickedly—"did you."

"Varmint." She stepped furiously around him, entered the salon, and headed for the nearest servant. Her uncle, she was informed, was in the library having a cigar. She had the footman carry a message that she needed him straightaway, and soon he appeared in the entry hall with his cigar still in hand. A heady cloud of whiskey vapor collected around them as he listened to her predicament. Catching a footman by the sleeve, he sent his regrets to the earl, whom he had intended to hustle in a game of billiards, and asked for his hat.

While he waited, she raced upstairs to retrieve a shawl and a reticule from her room, and the threesome were soon in a coach being driven into the heart of Bristol.

"Did you ask him about the citation?" she asked. Ashton looked at her blankly and she clarified: "The dean. When you spoke, did you ask about the records?"

"Not really. He was anxious to leave for luncheon, which he does every day, promptly at one o'clock—which he called 'two bells.' Pretentiously nautical." He raised one eyebrow. "Besides, I don't have the citation. When you left the library the other day it mysteriously disappeared. I was counting on your *bear-trap* of a mind to recall it."

"Bear-trap," Red echoed, chuckling. "Good one."

She reached over, grabbed his cigar, and tossed it out the window.

"Hey!" Red was a little too whiskey-mellowed to take serious offense, but he looked to Ashton with indignation.

"I know," Ashton commiserated. "She's hard on cigars."

It was all Daisy could do to keep her lip from curling. She

moved closer to the side of the coach and stared doggedly out at the scenery.

The nearby sea port and its military vessels had clearly shaped Bristol's development as a city. Everything from shop signs to street names bent to a nautical theme, and the striped middies and black caps of sailors were thick in the streets near the river.

Temple Church sat in the middle of the city, accompanied by a bell tower that leaned off center and made Daisy cock her head three different ways to make certain she was seeing it properly. Ashton noticed.

"Yes, it is leaning to one side. Like the Tower of Pisa in Italy. Same problem, I believe." He offered her his arm, but she took Red's instead.

The dean of the parish met them at the rear of the church and directed them to a side door in the sanctuary. He lighted a lantern from a table in the hallway, and led them down a set of worn stone steps to an arch-braced cellar that seemed to stretch for miles.

It was chilled and gloomy. All manner of crates, shelves, cast-off benches, and tables were stacked around, as well as banners, brass candle stands, iron grillwork, and unused lamps from pre-gaslight days. The dean lighted an oil lamp and then continued down one row of the cellar arches to a set of shelves that had once been covered by doors . . . the rusting hinges were still attached.

"These"—the dean waved to great, leather-bound books that slumped against each other and lay in disorder on the shelves—"contain the history of the parish of Temple Fee and Redcliffe Fee—which merged some time ago to make our parish. Help yourselves." He turned to go.

"Wait," Daisy said, reaching out but not touching him. "Can you tell us anything about the records? Are they all here, or are there other documents to be found?"

He studied her with a put-upon expression. "They're

numbered." With that he stalked off, taking his lantern with him and leaving them to the mercy of the one questionable-looking oil lamp in a sea of darkness and liturgical leavings.

She lifted one of the volumes, blew off the dust, and looked it over.

"Here." She held the spine to the light and tried to read the numbers on it. Ashton and Red leaned in to see. "Does that look like forty-eight?"

They agreed and she opened the volume. Her heart sank at the faded condition of the ink and the embellishments of the script that made it all but unreadable. It was nearly as bad as the papers in the professor's collection.

"We need more light," Ashton said, and headed back to the place the dean had found the lamp. There was some metallic rattling and a muffled curse as something fell, but he returned shortly with another lamp that seemed to still have some fuel in it.

Red helped Ashton pull a nearby table over and wipe its top with a handkerchief. Then he rambled off with the second lamp to locate some chairs. Soon they were seated at a blocky old table on bare wooden benches that would have made church pews feel comfortable by comparison.

With both lamps providing light, Ashton was able to decipher the script and then show Daisy how to interpret the writing. The going was slow for her at first, but with both of them searching, he said, they would find the records faster. The volume she had picked up turned out to be a register from the early 1790s and covered a period of approximately ten years. The records of all of the births (by baptisms), deaths, and marriages in the parish slowly materialized before them.

"What was the number of the volume in the citation?" Ashton asked Daisy as he looked over the shelves. "Thirty-something?"

She delved into her reticule and produced the yellowed

paper she had secreted from the professor's collection. She opened it, avoiding Ashton's accusing look. "Thirty-six. If you're right about this being a citation."

"Then let's look for that number." He grabbed one of the lamps and went back to the shelves.

She joined him and picked up one dusty old register after another, sneezing at the cloud of dust they created. Then came the second disappointment of the afternoon: some of the numbers were worn off or so badly damaged that they were unreadable. Worse yet, some of the volumes were water stained and the leather bindings were mildewed.

"This is appalling," Ashton said, gingerly examining the registers. "These are records that go back hundreds of years, and look how they are treated." Daisy paused to watch him testing corners and smoothing damaged pages. She stared at his hands, remembering the feel of them on . . .

She shook herself out of that slide toward indiscretion and looked around for Red. He was prone on a nearby bench with his hands clasped and eyes closed. Any moment now he'd begin to snore; Red could fall asleep in the middle of a damned stampede!

"This one has no number, and the ink is barely readable," she said with disappointment.

Ashton came to have a look and together they deciphered the date of the initial entry: forty years after the date they sought. They set it aside. The next volume had a forty-four painted on the spine, and the one after that, a twenty-four. They began to rearrange the registers on the shelves according to number, and to place the numberless ones in a stack on the table.

A quarter of an hour later, they had arranged all of the numbered volumes on the shelves in order, but hadn't found volume thirty-six. They turned to the unnumbered registers on the table and began to look for opening dates. In the next to the last volume, they found entries beginning in 1738.

Given that each register contained roughly ten years' worth of records, they might have found the volume they sought.

Daisy's heart beat faster as they settled side by side on the bench and Ashton pulled one of the lamps closer. She could tell from the tension in his expression that he was just as excited as she was. Each page carried history forward in time until they reached the sought-after page ninety-one.

There was the citation—the ink less faded than many of the entries.

"It's a birth," she said reverently, running a finger along the line beneath the words. "There's her name: Gemma Rose Howard. 'Baptized on October third, 1747,'" she read aloud. "'Mother: Hannah Violet Howard of Redcliffe. Father: Fitzroy Henry Lee, Commodore, Royal Navy. Witnesses: Sadie McLeod, godmother, and Eli Cornwallis, Royal Navy, godfather.'"

"The disreputable commodore had no wife, but he clearly had a daughter," Ashton said, putting pieces of the story together. "And the family knew it—because this citation"—he held up the paper Daisy had taken from the folio—"was with their letters and other documents. This has to be the child Lady Charlotte was urging him to make his 'duty.'"

"This proves Gemma Howard was the great-granddaughter of King Charles the Second," she said, sitting back, feeling a little dizzy. Was it possible the lineage Red had memorized was true?

"So she was," he said, the working of his mind visible in his eyes. "Though, what it proves about you is still to be established."

"Well, there are Howards several generations back in my lineage—I remember my mother mentioning them. I'm fairly sure they were in the States. . . . Maine or Massachusetts. I've written my mother for any information she might be able to find on them."

She stared at the entry, trying to imagine the baby girl

and what her life might have been like. "Why wouldn't he marry Hannah? She bore him a child and he was there at the baptism."

He expelled a heavy breath. "Maybe it turned out for the best for Gemma Rose and her mother. Perhaps they went to America and Hannah found a husband and raised a family. Maybe she lived to a ripe old age and was revered by all."

"Or maybe she mourned the loss of the love of her life for the rest of her days," she countered, though with less conviction than she would have liked. "Maybe she died young and penniless and desperate." In her mind's eye, Daisy conjured possible futures for the child who may have been the anchor of her family's past. "Poor little girl. That's a rotten thing to do . . . beget a child on the wrong side of the blanket and expose her to shame and ridicule for the rest of her life."

"Not necessarily. It happened to Charlotte, and she ended up with a good marriage, a comfortable life, royal favor . . . lots of children and grandchildren."

"Her father was a king, not a navy officer accused of drunkenness and debauchery who refused to acknowledge his daughter," she said, scowling.

"Not so. He signed the register as the father. That's proof he cared about what happened to her."

"If it truly was him," she said.

"I would lay odds it was. They didn't let just anyone sign a church register. The participants had to be known in the parish or vouched for by an upstanding parish member." He frowned, still studying the bold signature on the page for clues. "Maybe he had a reason for not marrying her."

"What? That she was lowborn? Part of the *common* folk. Charlotte's letter said he should do right in the matter of the child, not the mother." She frowned thoughtfully. "Maybe his family thought she wasn't good enough for him." She turned to look him straight in the eye. "Families do that—sit in judgment on prospective brides."

He considered her personal connection to that statement for a moment.

"Don't take it personally. Meridian elders sit in judgment on everyone, including their heirs and spares."

That was probably true, she realized, considering Uncle Bertram's disgraceful behavior. He was as condescending to Arthur as he was to her.

"If I prove my lineage to your family, do you think they'll accept me?"

"They're not known to be *accepting* of anyone." He looked away.

"Your uncle was vile to Arthur this morning. . . . Treated him like a child, ordering him around, pulling him this way and that. Last night he openly ridiculed Arthur at dinner."

"That's Uncle Bertram. Unpleasant to everyone."

"But especially to Arthur. I felt horrible for him." She looked up and found him watching her with an intensity that spurred her heart to extra beats. "Your brother is odd at times, I'll admit. But he's mostly just bookish and hasn't been out in the world much. He's sharp about some things, and gentle, and courteous. He's really very sweet."

"You've gone soft on him," Ashton accused, one corner of his mouth quirked up in that wicked half smile of his that started her bones melting.

"And why wouldn't I?" she said, battling her fascination with his lips. She knew just how they would taste and feel—how they could tease her sensitive—"He needs someone to stand up for him and care for him and help him take his rightful place in the world."

"Yes, well, it can't be you."

"Oh? And why not?" She could hardly breathe. He was so close . . . he filled her senses and invaded her very breath. Parts of her that had no business making themselves known were tingling with anticipation.

Alarmed, she rose and stood with her hands clasped, but

she was unable to make herself move away or to take her eyes from his handsome mouth. She wanted so badly to touch that face, to run her fingers over every slope and curve—to memorize every—

"I'll tell you why not." His words came low and slow and vibrated her very fingertips. "Better yet, I'll show you."

He seized her arms and pulled her off balance and onto his lap. The next instant he was kissing her within an inch of her life. His mouth was hard and demanding at first, but softened as she responded and wrapped her arms around his neck. She shifted against him, savoring the feel of his body beneath her and smiling against his lips as his hands moved over her waist, claiming it. She held her breath as he slid his hands down her skirts to trace the contours of her leg.

Moments later he dragged her petticoats higher and slid his hand past her garters to her bare thigh. She held her breath as he reached her knickers and the sensitive curve of her hip. She wanted more . . . his touch on her bare skin, his hands caressing her body, his strength around her, his hardness inside her.

She was barely conscious of shifting, moving to straddle him, to press her burning need against him. They were now face to face, exploring each other and the lush, instinctive synchrony of their bodies molding, moving, rubbing. When she stiffened and shuddered, momentarily lost in a flash and rumble of pleasure, she sensed it was exactly what she wanted—*needed*—this release of tension, this freedom from constant restraint. She melted against him, feeling deliciously flushed and open to him.

With just a few kisses and knowledgeable touches he'd led her into a warm shower of pleasure. She kissed him deeply, feeling his hardness against her sensitive and hungry flesh. She wanted to be naked and horizontal and to have him deep within her, driving them both toward even greater—

She froze as the realization of what just happened made

it through the steamy haze muddling her mind. She opened her eyes and looked around.

They were in a church—Merciful Heaven!—and Red lay snoring just a few feet away. She was straddling the rogue's lap with her skirts raised halfway to Heaven, and her body was burning for more. When she tried to move away, his hands on her waist held her against him.

"That's why it can't be you," he said, his voice thick with unspent passion.

Because she had just disgraced herself. Because she had abandoned her morals yet again and been betrayed by her body's lustful cravings. Shame flooded her face. She squirmed out of his grasp, stood on shaky legs, and turned her back to him to right her skirts. Her hands trembled.

Seconds later, he was on his feet behind her.

"Arthur could never give you that," he said, putting his hands on her shoulders and turning her around. She turned her head, frantic to avoid what she was certain would be a gloating expression. He lifted her chin to make her meet his gaze.

"You're not a weak, wilting lily of a deb. You're a strong, determined, passionate woman. You need someone to match your strength." He stroked her cheek to coax her to meet his gaze. "Noble or common—what matters in a marriage is that a man and a woman are equally matched. The church fathers called it 'equally yoked,' though I believe what they meant by that was that believers should marry believers, not heathens. All the same, it works to say that people should marry their equal." He gave her a wry and tender smile.

"Like it or not, Daisy love, the Duke of Meridian will never be your equal." He tapped her temple. "Not here." He tapped her chest above her heart. "Nor here." He leaned closer and breathed against her lips: "And certainly not here." His mouth caressed hers so gently, so lovingly, that tears welled within her closed eyes.

He wasn't condemning her for her knowledge of carnal pleasures; rather, he was saying his brother was woefully ignorant of such things. Was he right? Did her knowledge of passion make her an unsuitable wife for a man who had little or no experience of it?

She pushed away, scrambling for emotional footing, trying to make sense of his motives. As she gathered her shawl around her, she shivered and blinked to clear her vision. Did he care anything about her, or was he just using her own passions to get her to abandon pursuit of his brother?

In his presence she couldn't think straight; he had her wits roped and tied. Why was he luring her into forbidden pleasures, and then rescuing her from her own headstrong urges? Was he just another treacherous Meridian, using his gift for temptation to destroy her hopes? While the other family members sneered and bullied to get their way, he flattered and seduced. But did that make him any less dangerous?

At that moment she remembered what Lady Sylvia had called him in that upper room at the Earl of Mountjoy's. "*A prime Meridian.*"

He was that, all right.

She had fled his pull on her desires and now found herself at the limits of the lamplight. She turned to find him watching her, staring at her with what could only be called lust in his eyes. At least that much was true. He wanted her almost as much as he wanted her to give up Arthur.

Almost.

That put things into perspective. Taking a steadying breath, she strode back to the table, shook Uncle Red awake, and grabbed the volume containing Gemma Howard's baptismal record.

"What is it?" Red sat up, smacking his lips dryly, looking around.

"We found it, Uncle Red. We found Gemma Howard in the book and we have to get that 'dean' fellow to make out a paper saying who her parents were and when she was baptized. Come on."

She looped an arm through her uncle's and led him briskly to the stairs, leaving Ashton standing in the lamplight.

She wouldn't listen, Ashton realized, his hopes sinking. She wasn't going to give up her pursuit of Arthur, no matter how ardently he tried to persuade her they were mismatched. Time was running out. By the end of the week, she would be at Betancourt with the family and a number of other notables . . . where the family elders expected he would discredit her lineage even if he had to falsify it.

But what if it were true? What if her ancestry could be traced back to Charles II, the Restoration king? Two weeks was an absurdly short amount of time to prove any sort of history, much less a family lineage that spanned two continents, but they had made a promising start. The scholar in him rebelled at the idea of patently lying about history, no matter how small it was in scope. The past was foundation to the present, Huxley had drilled into him years ago, and to deny or falsify it was to undermine the future.

Her future.

There was only one path left. Her personal history included more than she pretended. She was no shrinking virgin, that was clear. Much as he despised the idea, he would have to use her own unknown past and whatever gave her such a delicious eagerness for pleasure against her.

Chapter Seventeen

That very night, Ashton Graham appeared as a dinner guest at the Earl of Albemarle's table, along with at least a dozen other engaging guests. The duke was delighted to have his younger brother at his side and embraced him heartily, while their tight-lipped uncle was less welcoming.

Daisy was seated opposite the duke at dinner that night and struggled to be an attentive listener as he related his afternoon in the gardens collecting specimens. He described in exhaustive detail his scientific observations, techniques of capture, and preservation . . . then went on to discuss where in his collection he intended to place these new acquisitions.

Twice Daisy tried to change the subject, but "collecting" was all the duke could think about. The elaborate seven-course meal the Albemarles provided sat largely untouched before him. She found herself wishing he would drink a few glasses of wine; he was wound as tight as a clock spring.

Down the long table, Ashton was entertaining both ladies and gentlemen with tales of Ascot races and yachting and the prince's royal faux pas. She glanced his way and felt a spur of envy that they got to enjoy his scandalous company. During the serving, he looked toward her, as if drawn by her gaze, and their eyes met. She ached to reach across the candelabra, crystal, and linen . . . past the silks, starched collars, and fancy manners . . . to touch him. She wanted to be the woman sitting beside him, enjoying his jaded opinions and droll stories of London society.

And more . . . She wanted to know how he spent his evenings, what books he read, which foods he couldn't resist, whether he could drive a four-in-hand, and where he would go if he could live anywhere in the world. In truth, she wanted to know him in more than just the biblical sense.

Oh, God.

She paled so abruptly that the duke halted mid-discourse and asked if she were feeling quite well. She produced a fair imitation of a smile and bade him continue his fascinating comparison of the butterflies of western and southern England . . . while she gripped the table edge in a quiet panic.

She had more than just a fascination for Ashton Graham. She had feelings of a kind—she forced her gaze back to the duke—she might never have for Arthur. Her heart sank, leaving a hollow in her middle as she searched her future husband for something, anything to pin a hope on.

Her gaze snagged on his chin and slid to his mouth. Not broad and sensuous, but pleasant and perhaps even promising. She watched his mouth as he spoke, and gradually began to take hope.

It was time she redirected her passionate leanings toward the duke. Given time and proximity, she would surely begin to have the same feelings for him that she was having for Ashton. It was her regrettable nature to be susceptible to the temptations of the flesh. And Arthur, as far as she could tell, was indeed made of flesh.

By the end of dinner her spirits had rebounded and she had made up her mind. She had to kiss Arthur. And soon.

* * *

"Goodness, Daisy, I've all but talked your ears off," the duke said as they strolled on the half-lit terrace outside the salon where their hosts and the other guests were gathered. It had taken a bit of doing to maneuver him outside and alone; in his presence, everyone seemed to show an unprecedented interest in butterfly collecting.

"Nonsense, Your Grace," she began.

"Arthur," he corrected.

"Arthur," she repeated with true pleasure. "I love to see you share your favorite occupation. I've learned a lot about insects and butterflies from you. And I think you are very wise to think of cultivating beehives along with your orchard."

"Don't know why we haven't done it before now." He paused at the stone baluster that edged the terrace and looked down at her in the moonlight. "It seems like I've been waking up to a lot of things in recent days. There is so much to do . . . a great house to maintain, estates to run, people to sort out. Some of our servants should have been pensioned off years ago and replaced with younger backs and knees. And I had no idea how much land belonged to us until a week ago. I went to my father's study—which is usually occupied by Uncle Bertram, who doesn't like his things disturbed—and I discovered maps showing far-flung parcels of land belonging to Betancourt."

"You don't say. That sounds like a big responsibility. You know, you need help, Arthur. Someone with a sound mind and a strong constitution to help you take stock of your obligations and get them in hand."

"Well, my aunts and uncles—"

"Are getting on in years themselves," she opined, feeling only a little guilty for pretending concern. "It's hardly fair to burden them."

"I suppose that's true." He looked at her and slowly cocked his head, as if seeing her from a different perspective. She met his gaze and felt a mild surge of relief that he was finally

paying attention to her. When he stepped closer, she broke
into a flirtatious smile and put a hand on his arm.

"Of course, it's true," came a strong voice from the terrace
doors. She withdrew a step. Curse his hide! "Anyone can see
the old cods are going dotty. I was starting to fear they would
drag you with them."

"Ashton." The duke's face lit with good humor. "I must
say, I'm glad to see you're back in society. I hope this means
you'll be coming to Betancourt more." He looked to Daisy
with widened eyes. "Oh, I nearly forgot. We're having people
in next week. You must come, too. The family will be thrilled
to see you. Miss Bumgarten, here, is coming."

"Really?" Ashton gave her a duplicitous smile. "How
lovely. I'd be delighted to come home for a visit."

She gave him a fierce glare that Arthur missed.

Ashton offered her his arm, which she ignored as she
headed for the door.

The next morning Daisy persuaded the duke to accompany her for a ride. He was not well acquainted with horses
and not much of a rider, he confessed, but he agreed to try
since she had her heart set on it. When he was younger, his
uncles had discouraged him from spending time in the stables
or riding over the estates, so he had become accustomed to
walking.

Once again, Arthur turned out to be more honest than
diplomatic. He sat stiff as a board and bounced in the saddle
as if every step the horse took required an equal and opposite reaction. Daisy reined in Dancer to stay close to him and
offer a few suggestions intended to make him more comfortable in the saddle and with the reins. She shared with him
distracting tales of her early rides and some western lore regarding horses.

In the end, she suggested they gallop a bit to let the

horses work off some energy and promised it would smooth out his ride. She was relieved to see that he used his heels to make his mount go and he managed to hang on as they set off across open fields and veered along hedgerows. Frequently she took the lead and chose the path, and when she looked back he was smiling—at least she hoped it was a smile.

To his credit, he persevered, improved, and was often on her heels as they crossed bridges, avoided stone walls, and rounded haystacks in fields. Was it her imagination that he sat more at ease in the saddle and used the reins more effectively now?

The duke was red faced and panting, and she was breathing hard herself as they slowed to a walk and turned back toward the stables. Arthur insisted he was in fine fettle, and to her eye, he did seem invigorated by the exercise. When they came upon the horse trail Lady Regina had described to her, she knew she had found the perfect spot to maneuver him into a kiss.

Marlton's bridle path was an old cart road lined with mature trees that had grown tall enough to meet overhead and shade the area. It had become a picturesque venue for riders wishing to cool down their mounts before a final jog back to the stables.

Sunlight slanted through the leaves and danced across the duke's ruddy face, giving him a robust appearance. She smiled and asked if he wished to dismount and walk a bit in the shade. He smiled back, his eyes alight with pleasure as he expounded on the beauty of the place and how much he appreciated her tutelage in horsemanship. He spoke of tending to his stables when he returned to Betancourt, and promised her a tour of the main estate on horseback when she visited.

She was supposed to wait for him to help her dismount.

She leaned this way and that, trying to see around his mount, and finally spotted his boots on the far side.

"Your Grace? Arthur?"

A groan from his location galvanized her and a moment later she swung down from Dancer's back and hurried around to see what was wrong.

Arthur stood bent at the waist, his legs spread awkwardly and his arms dangling from his shoulders. "I—I can't move," he croaked.

"Truly?" Alarmed, she rushed to help him straighten, inserting herself under his left arm. "You can stand, can't you? Lean on me and I'll help."

A massive groan accompanied his effort to straighten and he grabbed his lower back and squeezed his eyes shut. Seconds later, he laid his head back and took several labored breaths. "God in Heaven," he muttered, clearly in pain. "What's happened to me?"

"I've heard of this," she said, running her hands over his midsection before realizing how inappropriate that was and simply wrapping her arms around his waist to help him keep his balance. "You're just unused to riding and your muscles have seized up. You'll be fine in a few minutes. Here, we'll walk it off . . . get your blood circulating again."

"Arghhhh!" He nearly fell flat on his face as she urged him forward. "I can't walk—I can't even move my legs!"

This was bad, she realized. Very bad. The worst case of city-slicker stumble she'd ever seen. She looked around frantically, hoping for a stump or a felled tree where he might sit and recover. There was nothing of the kind in the vicinity; she had to come up with some way to get him back to the house.

"Your Grace, I'll have to rub your limbs to get the blood moving again. We're too far from the house to go for help.

Here"—she turned him toward his horse—"hold on to the saddle and don't move."

"What are you—ohhhh—aghhhhh—"

That was the way Ashton found them: Daisy on her knees behind Arthur rubbing and massaging his legs with appalling familiarity, and Arthur gripping the saddle of his horse and moaning as if in great pain or great pleasure—it was impossible to say which. Ashton dismounted and rushed forward calling his brother's name.

"Oh!" Daisy fell over onto her rear in the grass. Her eyes were as big as Wedgwood saucers. "What are you—"

"Never mind *me*. What in bloody hell do you think *you're* doing?"

"I'm all seized up," Arthur said, the same moment she explained.

"He's got cramps."

"I got off the danged animal and my legs won't work."

"I was just helping him get the blood circulating again."

Ashton stared at the pair for a minute, taking in the excuses. Daisy was sprawled on the ground wringing her clever little hands, and Arthur was red faced and wincing in discomfort and deep humiliation.

"I'll bet you were getting his blood going," he muttered, glaring at her before transferring his displeasure to his brother. "And you. Whatever possessed you to ride off to God-knows-where on a horse?" He jammed his gloved fists on his waist. "You never ride. You hate horses."

"I do not," Arthur declared, drawing himself up as straight as he could. "I simply have not had much experience with them, and it's about time I learned to handle them. I have duties. And some may require that I ride out to oversee Betancourt's business." He sagged, but raised his chin, striking a determined pose. "I've just . . . overdone it a bit on my first day out."

"Dear God." Ashton glanced at Daisy. "I suppose you're responsible for this newfound interest—irrepressible horse-woman that you are."

She scrambled to her feet and brushed grass and debris from her split skirt. Copying Arthur, she lifted her chin and then resettled her hat.

"He wanted to learn and I was happy to accompany him. Now if you're through chastising us, please lend a hand and help me get your brother back to the house."

With a growl of frustration and more muttering, he helped Daisy tie the horses in series and then stationed himself under one of Arthur's arms while she tucked herself under the other. They walked slowly, arms around the suffering duke, who soon announced that he thought his circulation was improving; he was beginning to feel things again. Unable to stop himself, Ashton glanced at the bulge in the front of Arthur's trousers.

"Yes, I can see that," he said, hating the fact that he sounded jealous in his own ears.

There was quite a commotion when they returned to Marlton with the duke barely mobile and clearly in pain. He was carried upstairs and put straight to bed to await the earl's doctor.

A nasty sprain, the doctor announced gravely to a re-lieved Earl and Countess of Albemarle, an outraged Uncle Bertram, and a host of curious guests. Liniment, the doctor prescribed, and a strong willow bark tea. Within a week the young duke should be good as new.

Privately, he told Ashton that it was the worst case of saddle-soreness he'd ever seen. "Get him up and walking as soon as you can," he advised. "Don't let him cripple up because he's afraid it will hurt when he moves."

At the countess's urging, Daisy offered to read to the duke, to help him pass the time. Uncle Bertram inserted himself before the sickroom door to reject her offer, saying that she'd done quite enough already. The old man insisted on sitting by his nephew's bedside himself. Ashton chuckled at the news of his uncle's unprecedented urge to tend a sickbed and snuck Arthur a bottle of strong brandy, relabeled "tonic," to help him through his recovery.

Whether it was the quality of his uncle's nursing, the brandy, or the boredom, Arthur emerged from his room the very next day, walking stiffly on a cane and insisting he was well on the way to recovery.

"Splendid, then you're fit to travel. We're needed at home," Uncle Bertram declared, and immediately requested use of the earl's carriage to take them to the railroad station.

Arthur didn't argue with his uncle. He collected his new specimens for transport, then bathed and dressed carefully, while the earl's man packed for him. There was no hurry, he insisted, when Uncle Bertram paced and warned that they might miss the train.

"If so, there will be another later, Uncle," Arthur said, firmly but politely. Bertram glowered at Ashton as if it were his fault, and dragged him into the salon for a quick, private word.

"What a disaster! Get it done, boy. Finish the chit," he snapped, leaning in. His face contorted in a way that made him resemble an irritable badger. "See that she loses interest in your brother . . . or else." Threat delivered, he stalked outside to wait for his nephew.

Arthur thanked the earl and Lady Regina for extending him such gracious hospitality, then sought out Ashton, who had retreated to the billiards room.

"I want you to know, Ash, that I've missed you. And I'm

heartened to think that you'll be coming home at last—even for just a visit."

They shook hands and gave each other a manly half hug.

"I look forward to seeing you again, Artie." Ashton looked down, then quickly picked up a billiards cue and began to chalk the point. "Take care of yourself. Especially if you intend to further your acquaintance with horses."

Arthur grinned and lifted the cane the earl had loaned him. "I am counting that any future lessons will be less painful."

"It wasn't a total loss. The stick makes you look almost debonair." He waggled his brows and Arthur exited laughing.

Daisy stationed herself near the great stairs in the center hall, waiting for Arthur, hoping to say good-bye and perhaps give him a peck on the cheek to think about on his way home. Thus, she was surprised when he pulled her into a nook beside the stairs.

"I am so sorry about your injury, Your Grace," she began.

"Arthur," he chided.

"Arthur," she echoed gratefully, knowing that his insistence that she use his given name meant she was forgiven. "Are you sure you're all right?"

He surprised her by laying his cane aside and taking her hands in his.

"My dear Daisy, I am better by the moment. I want you to know that I will be so very pleased to see you next week at Betancourt. You're a breath of fresh air for me . . . a window onto a world I have ignored for too long."

Before she knew what was happening, he drew her close and lowered his head to press her lips with his. It all happened so fast. Her impressions were of warmth, simple pressure, and a faint scent of sandalwood. Then it was over and he was withdrawing with a tenuous smile.

"I—I look forward to seeing you again, dear Arthur," she said.

Smiling broadly, he picked up his cane, turned on his heel, and she could have sworn that he no longer limped as he strode out the center hall to the waiting carriage.

She touched her lips and fought the sinking feeling in her middle. It wasn't a proper kiss, really. It was too sudden. She was unprepared.

She bit her lip.

And sagged.

There wasn't the slightest tingle in it.

Chapter Eighteen

"What is *he* still doing here?" The countess stood by the window in Daisy's room that overlooked the entry court. "Whatever possessed the earl to ask him to stay? After the way he absconded with you the other day—thank Heaven, Redmond had the good sense to insist on going along."

Daisy stood openmouthed, listening to the first complimentary words the countess had ever aimed her uncle's way.

The countess drew her to the window to watch Ashton climbing aboard a big roan and setting off for God-knew-where.

"Scandal follows that man like night follows day, and for the same reason. It's his very nature," the countess declared. "He's a scoundrel, born and bred, and he always will be. Not an honest or sincere bone in his body."

Daisy pursed her lips at that.

"I'm not so certain, Countess." To forestall her sponsor's concern, she explained: "He has been nothing but helpful in searching out my possible ancestors, and has behaved in a gentlemanly fashion." *Mostly.*

The countess clasped her forehead and gave a small groan.

"He's used his charm on you, dear. It's his most potent

and treacherous weapon. He'll have you thinking he's helpful . . . then secretly noble . . . then selflessly heroic. And it will all be to his purpose, trust me. There are plenty of noblemen of that ilk. Charming wretches whose sole purpose in life is the satisfaction of their base and selfish desires."

Daisy had thought those very things of him . . . until . . .

"I know he doesn't want me to marry his brother, Countess. He's said as much. But, I can't think selfishness figures into it. Nor my 'common' roots, or being from America, or having new money. He simply says the duke and I are mismatched."

"What?" The countess whirled to face her. "That's absurd."

"He believes that sooner or later I would be miserable being a duchess—having to deal with all that propriety and restraint, and the burden and responsibilities of the title. He says Arthur and I have such different natures that we would end up making each other miserable."

"It's his misery he's truly concerned with . . . his lot as his brother's second." The countess took her hands and pulled her to a seat on the chaise. "Don't you see his game? If his brother doesn't marry and produce an heir, he might still inherit the title himself someday." She squeezed Daisy's hands. "Scheming wretch. That's his motive, mark my word.

"Daisy, dear, you and the duke will get on fine together. He needs your verve and spirit and you need his . . . thoughtful and methodical manner. You'll provide balance for each other and produce a dignified and harmonious household. You'll see, dear. Don't you worry." She patted Daisy's hands and rose with a determined nod. "I'll see that Regina keeps the scoundrel away from you at dinner tonight."

Daisy sat for a few minutes, ruminating on that, bringing memories of her time with Ashton to mind and scouring them for evidence that what the countess believed might be true. Was he purely self-serving and ambitious? Was he determined to see his brother die a bachelor without an heir?

She thought of his descriptions of noble life and the burden of bearing a title . . . some of which she now saw had a basis in reality.

But then, she saw how the Earl and Countess of Albemarle got along. They seemed to enjoy each other's company and to work together to make their estate beautiful and their life together fulfilling. Was that not a possibility for her and Arthur?

Feeling embattled and a little suffocated in her elegant room, she traded her embroidered slippers for walking shoes and grabbed a hat and shawl to go for a walk in the gardens.

Outside it was sunny and the afternoon air was sweet with the scent of banks of flowers in bloom. She removed her hat and turned her face to the sun, ignoring the countess's adamant advice to avoid the sun on her skin at all costs. She had spent years with the sun on her face and needed it now as a tonic for her spirits.

She faced so many obstacles and unknowns and there was no one to talk to about it, no one who would understand her true situation. The walking helped, as it often did. The crunch of gravel underfoot and the swish of her skirts combined in a rhythm that calmed her thoughts and led her heart to relax beneath its burdens. She thought of the cliffs overlooking the river bordering their ranch, where she would go when her mother's expectations became too much. She smiled softly. She understood Arthur's escape to the walls of his home all too well.

Ashton saw her walking up one of the garden paths and reined up in the shelter of the trees at the end of the bridle path. She wore a simple, pale blue, cotton dress and carried the sun hat from the other day—the one that made her look like a girl in a painting. Her hair was down and being teased by a breeze. He sat for a few minutes, watching her wend her way through colorful flower beds, beneath rose-covered arbors, and around topiaries. The sight of her, so lovely and at ease, produced a hollow feeling inside him.

She was something he'd never imagined existed; a wild combination of innocence and experience, determination and self-doubt, with independence of thought and a great hunger to belong. She was earthy and elegant, simple and complicated, tantalizing and terrifying. She was at his fingertips and, yet, so far beyond his reach.

He was supposed to seduce and compromise her—destroy her dreams and her sisters' hopes—this remarkable young woman whose provocative spirit and nubile body invaded his dreams at night.

She approached the tall hedges and feathery ornamental plantings that marked the start of Lord Robert's maze. Ashton sat back in the saddle and watched until she disappeared between the green walls, then he kicked his horse into motion and soon dismounted at the maze entrance. He tied his mount where it could graze, brushed his sleeves, and strode into the maze.

He had no idea what he was going to say to her, but he wanted to talk with her, touch her, be with her. By week's end she would be at Betancourt and plunged into a sea of scrutiny and intrigue she would not fully recognize or understand. She would slip beyond his reach forever.

The grass muffled his steps as he came up behind her. Her skirts swayed as she walked to a rhythm known only to her, her honey-blond hair trailing down her back, and her royal blue shawl and straw hat dangling from her hands. He paused, watching, deeply pleased by the sight of her.

"Daisy." His call startled her so that she jumped.

"Arghh!" She whirled, clasping a hand to her chest as if to contain a racing heart. "What are you doing here?" She frowned. "If you're seeking solitude, you'll have to find another spot. This one is taken."

"I'm not seeking solitude." He set his hands to his waist and shifted his weight back onto one leg. "I'm seeking you."

"Me?" She raised her broad-brimmed hat like a shield before her. "What do you want with me?"

"Besides your welcoming presence?" He laughed softly, then strolled toward her and looked at the hedge walls. "I'm not sure. I just feel there is something more I need to settle in my mind about you."

"What more needs to be explained? You know the extent of my search and truth of my ancestry as well as I do."

When he reached her, he kept walking. As he hoped, she turned and began to walk with him.

"I want to know why you're here—the truth of why you're oceans away from the place you love and the people you love, trying to do something you obviously want, but makes no sense."

"I've told you. I'm here to marry and make a way for my sisters into society. It's no great mystery."

He clasped his hands behind his back and studied the grassy path beneath them. On the periphery of his vision, her shoes peeked out of her skirts with each step, then retreated like wary mice. She allowed him to see just so much of her. There was more—he was sure of it.

They came to an obstacle and she pointed left. "That way, I'm pretty sure."

He turned and continued strolling. She set a brisk pace.

"Why didn't your mother come—why didn't she bring you to England? Why are you here with your uncle and the countess?"

There was a hitch in her step, subtle but very much there.

"My mother is needed at home. It was my idea to come and I recruited Uncle Red and found the countess, who agreed to sponsor me."

"For a price," he said, wishing he could take it back the

instant it was out. She stopped and turned to face him, eyes flashing.

"Yes, for a price. There. Have you got what you came for? I have a companion who needed funds, but who has become a good and trusted friend. And who has advised me to have nothing to do with you."

"Smart woman," he muttered, just loud enough for her to hear.

She scowled and strode quickly for the next obstacle, disappearing around a turn before he got there. When he arrived, she was waiting for him halfway down the alley between the hedges.

"And just what are you doing here, Ashton Graham? Why are you dogging my steps? Is this part of your family's plan to find a way to disqualify me as a bride? Because despite what you and your family think of me, Arthur doesn't seem to think I'm unacceptable."

That was too close to the bone. He looked around the maze walls and then walked past her again, his hands clasped tightly behind his back. The only way he would get the truth from her was to be utterly frank. And that strategy was not without risk.

"Of course the family creaks and groans set me on you . . . with instructions to see that your lineage does not qualify you for life as a Meridian duchess. Is that such a surprise?"

She took a deep breath and caught up with him again.

"Not really. It's fairly obvious, in fact. The only confusing thing is that you have seemed to have helped more than hindered." She halted and looked sharply at him. "That's the puzzle. Why have you helped me?"

It took a moment for him to unpack a long-guarded truth.

"Perhaps because—in the course of my *ancillary* life— I have actually developed a few scruples. Perhaps because I despise what they've insisted I do. It goes against every scholarly principle I've ever known. And just perhaps, I'm sick and tired of being a family liability—a drain on the finances—a pawn to be moved and manipulated at will." His body tensed as old anger threatened to rise. He released his arms to his sides and rolled his shoulders. "They don't know me half as well as they think."

He walked a few more paces in silence, then turned to her.

"And perhaps because . . . I've come to like you more than I should."

Daisy watched him round the next corner and identified those words as the reason her heart began to flutter. He had said complimentary things to her before. . . . She was strong, sharp of wit, and passionate about life. But this was something new. He was admitting to having feelings for her, even if it was a lukewarm kind of confession.

Did it make things better or worse that he might return some of the feelings she had for him? Whatever it meant, the words were like rain on parched soil to her heart.

"Why are you telling me this? What do you want?"

"The truth about you. About why a young woman of twenty would take on the responsibility for her family's reputation."

"Twenty-two. Just. I passed my birthday a few weeks ago." She squared her shoulders. "So you know now: I'm mutton dressed as lamb. Overripe. Beyond the first bloom." The twinkle of disbelief in his eyes seemed more intimate than his hands on her skin. She suddenly wanted to let it all out, to have someone listen and truly understand.

"I came because I am the whole reason our reputation was tarnished."

"Ah." He nodded, turned, and began to walk again.

"*Ah?*" She stalked past him to plant herself in his path. "What does that mean?"

"It means there is probably more to it," he said with an earnestness that was infuriating.

"Aren't you clever." She crossed her arms and narrowed her eyes.

"What could you possibly have done that disgraced your family and imperiled your sisters so?" he asked, his gaze speculative as it sank over her.

How much had he already guessed?

"Good question," she said. "I bet you've even thought of an answer."

"Just possibilities." He studied her as openly as she had him.

"Such as?"

"You smiled too much. Probably at gentlemen."

"I am a friendly person."

"You laughed too freely," he charged.

"A body can't help laughing when the mood takes her."

"You rode too fast and too well."

"Where I come from, riding well is considered both necessary and admirable. Some of the finest ladies in England are devoted horsewomen."

"You danced with too much enthusiasm." He took one step closer, then another, his eyes glinting with mischief. "And you kissed too many fellows."

She took a step back, annoyed by his smug half smile.

"I'll have you know," she said with more heat than she wanted, "you are the only man I've kissed in five years. I did not bewitch, enthrall, or seduce the precious sons of the Four Hundred. I barely even spoke to one."

"Really?" He seemed genuinely surprised. "Zounds! Imagine how you'd kiss if you weren't out of practice." When her mouth dropped open, he added: "Not that there was anything wrong with your efforts. I'm just thinking you could probably start a fire with wet tinder when you're on your game."

"You—"

She whirled and stalked down the path, blinded to the twists and turns she negotiated from memory. How dare he? Her heart pounded. He was purposefully . . . teasing her. The warmth and hints of humor in his—She slowed her flight, feeling embarrassed by her touchy reaction.

After a few turns, she found herself at the heart of the maze, staring at a stone bench and the rose-draped arbor that shaded it. There was space for two on that seat . . . a place for lovers to meet and talk and kiss. She had planned to bring Arthur here to prove that her temptation-plagued nature could be made to focus on him and him alone.

Instead, she was here with the brother of the man she intended to marry. . . the one man she was coming to crave with every nerve and impulse in her being. She felt him enter the maze heart behind her and she headed for the bench, seating herself in the middle to leave no room for him.

Closing her eyes, she breathed in the light fragrance of the roses covering the bower. When she leaned to inhale more deeply, her hat brim banged the side of the arbor and she opened her eyes. He was standing in front of her, watching, and a second later he removed her hat and held it out to her. She snatched it from him to clutch against her.

"Scoot over," he said, lowering himself into the impossibly small area left unoccupied. "Make room, Daisy. Unless you'd prefer that I sit on your lap."

Chapter Nineteen

She moved. Glowering. Her heart began to make those little skips that created a disturbance in her pulse and sent a shiver through her. She was pretty sure he noticed.

For a time she sat in silence, awareness of his broad shoulders and strong legs slowly replacing her irritation.

"I behaved like a hussy," she finally said, watching for a reaction. He turned to look at her but said nothing. "I wore trousers beneath my skirts so I could ride astride and I rode with the men of the Bellington Hunt. Dancer and I took every fence in half a county—led the pack the whole way. And afterward, when a gentleman offered me a sip from his flask, I took it." She explained wistfully: "It was fine Kentucky bourbon. The best there is."

"Sounds like eminent good sense to me," he said with a wry twist that looked like it could turn into a grin at any moment.

"You don't understand," she said, thinking of the gulf between society's expectations for unmarried women and unattached men. He had probably never considered the constraints of a young girl's life—except perhaps to enjoy the reckless females who failed to abide by them.

"So, enlighten me."

"By all accounts you've spent your time outside the realms where pale young debs are led around ballrooms like prettied-up ponies out for bids. In such places, doubts about a girl's virtue are akin to eternal damnation."

"And your behavior"—he reached for her bare hand and traced it with his fingertips—"led to doubts about your virtue."

"That was the excuse. Mrs. Astor and her clutch of biddies are always looking for one." She met his gaze briefly. There was no cleverness or teasing in his expression; his earlier earnestness was back. "My stubborn, selfish behavior gave them the perfect excuse to exclude us. Brazen, they called me. I was too forward, they said, and I knew too much. As if 'knowing' somehow tainted my soul." She looked down, tears pricking the corners of her eyes. "My mother was devastated. She had worked so hard to polish our rough edges and get us into the right circles. I didn't see the reason for her endless rules and cautions until it was too late. I thought she was just being . . ."

She halted and it was a few moments before she swallowed the lump in her throat to continue.

"Passing judgment on others makes them feel important. We got to town after they did, so we had to be shown our place . . . *beneath them.*"

"What makes you think it is any different in England?" There was gentle chiding in his tone.

"Oh, I've learned it isn't, believe me. You Brits are just as stuck-up—'superior' you call it—and hide-bound as the old crows of the Four Hundred." She wanted to wipe her eyes, but refused to forfeit the comfort of his hand on hers. She took a ragged breath instead.

"But your society is old enough and worn down enough to have to face a few hard facts . . . like . . . when money is needed badly, exceptions must be made. American girls have married English noblemen before. We Americans might not be considered prime breeding stock, but when we have the money you need, you'll hold your nose and admit us to the family." Determination welled up in a bracing rush. "I'll do what I have to do. I intend to see that no one shames or belittles my family ever again."

"Daisy, Daisy . . ." He shook his head and ran his gaze over her heated face and liquid-rimmed eyes. "Only a stupid, ignorant, black-hearted jackass would judge you to be anything but remarkable." He leaned closer and she thought he was going to kiss her, but at the last moment, his hand came up to wipe away tears that had finally been dislodged and were drying on her cheeks. His touch was so gentle and the look on his face so tender that she sought his gaze with hers. His hand lingered to caress her cheek and at that moment, he smiled into her very soul. It was a rare moment of connection, of knowing and being known, that filled her with a kind of pleasure she had never experienced. He took her hand in his again, resting it on his thigh.

"So tell me about them," he said thickly, seeming as affected by that contact as she was. "Your mother, your sisters. What are they like?"

It seemed the most natural question in the world.

"There are three more Bumgarten girls," she said, smiling softly at the memories that tally summoned. "Frances, whom we call Frankie, is the next oldest. She's a pistol . . . never saw a puzzle she didn't try to solve. She's a wizard at mathematics and has a memory like a bear trap. Then there is Claire—we call her CeCe—who is a devil of a fiddle player and sings like an angel. Sarah is the youngest—cute as a bug and full of mischief. She's got a way with horses and most other animals that's downright spooky. They're all sharp as tacks and a little stubborn—though, I'm probably the worst in the family for that.

"Our mother is Elizabeth Strait Bumgarten." She gave a tuneless whistle. "Now there's a woman who demands respect and a wide berth. She's rail straight, tenacious, and tough as boot leather. Oh, and she reads the Bible. Got a verse for everything and an opinion on everybody."

"It would be interesting to see her take on Aunt Sylvia." He grinned.

"It would indeed." She met his expression with a smile of her own. "She talks tougher than she acts, though. As angry as she was with me, she never once mentioned sending me back to Nevada or disowning me. I know she cares about me, and she's only trying to do her best for us girls. I just wish I had seen that sooner."

"I believe that's what they call 'wisdom.'" He rubbed her hand with his thumb. "It comes with age. And sometimes experience."

At that moment a strange, calming warmth enveloped her. She looked to him and wondered what hard-won wisdom he had gained from experience.

"What about you? What was growing up like for you?"

He drew a deep breath and summarized.

"Lots of hungry nights in those early years. I was sent to bed without supper much of the time. Never knew my mother—she died soon after I was born. My father lasted a bit longer. At seven I was shipped off to school, where the gruel was as cold as the showers and the Latin masters had a perverse fondness for the rod. Small wonder we were little savages when they released us to the playing fields. I was pretty good at pitching and batting. Cricket," he explained. "I actually liked running—everything troublesome fell away when I ran." He rubbed a thigh with his free hand.

"And you stuck up for your brother," she said before she censored it.

"Where did you hear that?"

"From your old school friend, Reynard Boulton. We met at a dinner party in Oxford, and he told me that you defended Arthur when he was bullied at school. Surely that wasn't a secret."

"What else did he tell you?" His hand tightened around hers.

"Are you worried that he revealed your scandalous past?" It was her turn to tease.

"My flaws and mistakes are no secret. But the Fox is given to sensationalizing events. In fact, it's his stock and trade: making close-kept secrets into outright scandals."

"So I was warned. By him, no less," she said, surprised by his discomfort at the possibility that Reynard Boulton might have told her things about him. "He asked me about you . . . what I thought of you."

"What did you tell him?"

"Fishing for compliments?"

"Daisy"—he was instantly more serious—"he is not a nice man. He's trampled good names and ruined relationships and futures all over London."

She searched his face with surprise. "You're truly concerned."

"I said I have . . . I would hate for you to come to harm because of your association with me."

"You're more gallant than you admit," she said.

"I wouldn't use that term."

"And you've a broad streak of integrity running along your spine. Must be inconvenient at times."

"You're trying to turn my head," he said dryly.

"The mamas look at you and see the one they wished they'd hooked. And the papas look at you and wish they'd had half your charm and good looks. It's no wonder they can't bear to have you around their daughters."

It was his turn to stare in surprise.

"You and Boulton must have had quite a chat."

"He is a gossip, after all. It wasn't that hard to get him to talk." She raised her chin. "He gave a great deal more than he got, however. I'm an American, not an idiot. People here do seem to confuse the two. I knew better than to tell him I think you're smart and principled and considerate . . . and funny at times. And that I like you a great deal more than I should."

She felt his hand tighten on hers, but quickly looked out over the clearing to avoid his gaze. The last thing she needed right now was a bone-melting kiss. She'd find herself on her back with her knees in the air before you could say "whoa Nellie."

"Which brings me to something I've been wondering about." She cut a sidelong glance at him. "What are you still doing here?"

He frowned, turning toward her. "Clearly, the earl invited me."

"I don't mean here at Marlton, I mean here in England. You're unmarried, unattached, and probably have access to means. Why haven't you struck off in search of adventure or a fortune of your own?"

He was silent for a moment, then turned to face the clearing.

"I have thought about it," he said slowly, as if the confession were being dragged from him. "But the 'means' aren't exactly plentiful and there are the family obligations."

"Ah, yes. The duties of 'the Spare.'" She nodded gravely. "Remind me what they are again? Something about *waiting* . . ."

"You wicked girl." He turned to her with genuine surprise.

She laughed softly, enjoying this turnabout.

"Why don't you go to New York and find a rich wife and become a pillar of the community? *Ooooh*—or a professor. I imagine Harvard or one of those fancy colleges might find room for an Oxford man. Professor Huxley would write you a reference, I bet. Then you could find the rest of my ancestors . . . or maybe write the history of your *former* colonies."

Ashton bit his lip, staring at her as if she were morphing into something strange and terrifying. Like a praying mantis. The next second, that thought appalled him; it was something that would occur to insect-obsessed Artie, not him. And didn't female praying mantises devour their mates?

"Stop this, right now," he ordered.

"Or what?" Her chin tilted up, her eyes took on a provocative smoke.

"Or . . . I'll . . . have to leave."

"Go ahead," she said, her voice full of sensual challenge, "if you can."

He dragged his gaze from hers, dropped her hand, and would have stood if his body responded to halfhearted orders. Whatever happened, he wanted these few moments with her, wanted to tell her how she haunted his dreams and that he wanted her more every time he saw her. He wanted to tell her . . .

Then she nestled against his side and put her head on his shoulder. He closed his eyes and drank in that simple contact like a touch of the divine. In his mind he saw her again as she was that day in the cow shed—glowing with a uniquely feminine pleasure at bringing new life into the world. That was when it started . . . this breakdown in his commitment to his mission . . . this sense that he could not, would not ruin her without also destroying something good and vital in his own soul.

She was good-hearted and earnest and protective of those she loved—all things Artie needed but probably wouldn't recognize, even if they were offered to him on a silver platter. Marrying him, she would be throwing away the possibility of so much more in her life.

He disturbed her long enough to put the arm she leaned against around her and draw her tighter against his side. They sat for a few minutes in silence before he turned and pulled her full against his chest. *This*—he thought, staring into her eyes and feeling her warmth and sensuality flooding his senses—*is probably as close to Heaven as I'll ever get.*

And he kissed her.

"Daisy!"

"Daizeee girl, where the devil are you?" Red shouted as he trailed Lady Evelyn between the rows of maze hedges.

"Daisy Bumgarten, are you in here?" Lady Evelyn called, quickening her pace. Frantic with concern, she wrung her hands, halted, and turned to Red. "That's his horse out there. Daisy and I saw him ride out on it earlier. He has to be in here." She looked stricken. "If she's here, too . . ." She pressed a hand to her mouth, unable to speak of such horrors.

"She's got more sense than a house full o' congressmen," Red declared, scowling. "We'll find her." He struck off toward the next obstacle, bellowing: "Marguerite Bumgarten, where are you? You better speak up, girl, or you'll be in a world o' trouble!"

Ashton clamped a hand over her bee-stung lips and read the panic in her eyes as Red's voice wafted through the hedges and paths. She was astride his lap and wrapped around his body as tight as a birthday suit. Both of them were breathing hard and having difficulty reacting to the danger bearing down on them.

A blink later, she slid from his lap, stood, and straightened her skirts with trembling hands. One look at her rumpled skirts, flushed skin, and swollen lips would tell even the most sympathetic observer that she had been indulging in something forbidden. Instinct kicked in.

"We can't be found here together," she said.

"We have to go," he whispered feverishly, thrusting her hat into her hands as they both scanned the heart of the maze for an avenue of escape. She spotted the second opening and pointed. But as they neared the opening she glanced back and spotted her shawl on the bench, falling toward the rear.

"My shawl!" She groaned and he saw it in the same moment. He raced back for it and picked it up just as Red's voice broke into the heart of the maze. Wide-eyed, he waved her to go on without him and plopped down on the bench, tucking the shawl beneath him.

Daisy's heart was pounding as she slipped through the maze, trying to recall how the exit path was structured. She heard voices behind her, but they faded as she navigated the hedges' twists and turns. By the time she reached the maze's second opening, she was able to slow and walk at a sensible pace, despite her urge to run for the shelter of Marlton House.

This was the third time . . . or was it the fourth? . . . that Ashton Graham had saved her from ruinous discovery. She wasn't sure what would have happened if Red and the countess had caught them together, engaged in passionate embraces. But considering the countess's warnings about just such things and her exacting moral standards, Daisy couldn't imagine she would continue to support Daisy's marriage to Duke Arthur.

For the first time Daisy herself began to wonder if she was worthy of the eager, unworldly Duke of Meridian. Perhaps he deserved someone sweeter and less demanding, someone whose virtue was still hers to give. And perhaps she deserved to be known as the reckless, impulsive hussy she truly was.

"I was returning from a ride and realized I had never actually been in His Lordship's impressive maze," Ashton had said, calling on every skill of deception at his command. "That's my horse tied up outside." Outwardly he seemed cool and faintly disdainful as he was confronted by Daisy's uncle and sponsor.

"You're sure you haven't seen Miss Bumgarten?" the countess repeated, scrutinizing him through narrowed eyes. He prayed that the lumpy shawl he was sitting on was fully tucked and hidden.

"I have not," he lied smoothly, though at some cost to his self-esteem. He really was a wretch sometimes. A first class bounder.

"So, you're just sittin' here?" Red demanded, seeming bewildered by such a pointless pursuit.

"I've had a rather eventful week. I was seeking some solitude." He smiled at Red. "You should try it sometime. It's good for the soul."

The countess strode this way and that, pausing to peer down the path that Daisy had taken to escape. Her suspicious look said she wasn't convinced, but she gave a huff of resignation.

"Very well. We'll continue our search elsewhere." She turned back the way they had come. "Come, Mr. Strait, we need to find your niece."

Red lingered a moment, scanning Ashton's defiantly casual pose. Then his gaze dropped to a small piece of royal blue silk peeking out from under Ashton's rear, and he smiled with a sharpness that made Ashton reconsider his opinions of the old fellow.

"My Daize is a good girl." He paused a moment and

Ashton felt a heat creeping up out of his collar. The old boy noticed and his mouth twisted up on one side. "A bit wild betimes, and stubborn as all hell. But she's got a heart o' pure gold. If you're smart, you'll stay clean away from her. She's meant for better'n you."

Ashton sat for some time after Red left, hearing those words echoing around the hollow that developed inside him.

"She's meant for better'n you."

Yes, she was.

Chapter Twenty

Ashton Graham avoided dinner that night and left Marlton first thing the next morning, citing urgent family business. The countess was relieved, Red was gratified, and Daisy was privately disappointed. For a few hours.

She was dragged into Bristol the next morning by two determined countesses, who insisted she see the wonderful array of silks and unusual cotton weave fabrics that the shipping merchants of Bristol offered. They were fresh off the boat, Lady Regina said with some pride. Bristol ladies always got the finest first when it came to imported fabrics. Her boast proved true, and by tea time Daisy had selected a small haberdasher's worth of wonderful fabrics—most of which she declared she would send to her family in New York.

It was a most pleasant day, until the Lady Evelyn cornered her over tea and demanded to know what Ashton would report to the Meridian family council in a few days. Daisy had to admit that she wasn't sure of his intentions, but took hope in the fact that he had helped her uncover some of the material and knew it to be sound. The countess wasn't satisfied with that explanation, but she stiffened her spine and declared that they would deal with whatever happened. Meanwhile, she said as she leaned in to speak in confidence,

Daisy must work to see that the duke himself had a favorable opinion of the match.

The core of Betancourt was a Jacobean manor house that had been added to and renovated numerous times over the years. But the main impression presented to guests and visitors was of great long windows set in red brick with gray limestone quoins at the corners. It was only as the coach pulled into the entry court that the true age of the place became clear. The wooden window frames peeled and showed their age and the mortar of the brick of the main house needed repointing. The front doors were weathered, but had recently been subjected to a coat of oil that did little to hide their underlying parched and unattended state.

When the doors opened, a line of servants in black and white came trudging out, followed by a butler who had to have been around for the laying of the cornerstone of Betancourt. He walked bent and had jowls that quivered and made him look like a bloodhound on a scent.

Behind him came three faces Daisy recalled from that night at Mountjoy's ball: Aunt Sylvia, Uncle Bertram, and another old uncle whose name escaped her. At the very rear came the duke himself, striding quickly, looking astoundingly young and fit by comparison. He hurried past his elders to greet the countess and Red before turning to Daisy with a broad smile and hands eager for hers.

She gave him her hands and her best smile. He looked better than she had ever seen him—certainly better than a week before, when she'd had to help carry him back to the house and send for a doctor.

"Dearest Daisy," he said, sounding a bit out of breath. "Welcome to Betancourt. We're so pleased to have you here. Do come in and refresh yourself while my fellows see to your things." He gave a wave toward the coach that started several old servants shuffling forward to obey.

Inside, Betancourt seemed a place frozen in time. The furnishings and paintings hanging in the hall looked like they had been there forever. The wood of the great stairs had darkened, except for worn spots on the treads, and the carving and moldings overhead were half obscured by decades of candle soot. The floor of the entry was laid with marble that had cracked in places, some of which had been repaired noticeably. Still, there were abundant fresh flowers on the hall table and the place had a dignity about it that was undeniable.

Voices came from the grand parlor to the left and they entered a large receiving room filled almost entirely with septuagenarians. The gentlemen rose creakily as Daisy and her party entered and the ladies managed to turn and peer at them through smudged lorgnettes. One by one she was introduced to dowagers, aged "sirs," and the occasional baron or viscount. Each was pronounced a valued family friend, and several had an attendant standing by to help with a shawl, footstool, or ear trumpet.

Daisy looked to Arthur, who smiled indulgently when his guests called him "my boy," and saw no hint that he thought of this gathering as anything but expected. This was the old trots' idea of entertaining? These were the family friends who would try and test her under the guise of a social affair? She glanced at the countess, who merely raised an eloquent eyebrow and continued to make small talk in a rather loud voice.

A few additional visitors arrived over the afternoon and were introduced before dinner at a gathering in the grand parlor. These were mostly younger, some the offspring of the oldsters she had met earlier. But only one of them could rightly claim to be under forty: Reynard Boulton.

"Goodness, I didn't expect to see you here." Daisy extended her hand and he gave it a gracious nod before surrendering it back to her.

"I was surprised myself to receive an invitation. The

Meridians seldom entertain—I had to come and see what the fuss was about. And now I see. *You're* here."

"Me? I can't think they're celebrating my presence," she said, glancing up to find Uncle Bertram's gaze fixed on them. Boulton noticed and smiled.

"Perhaps 'celebrating' is waxing it a bit." He looked around at the abundance of white hair in the room. "They've assembled the troops. Whether for an honors brigade or a firing squad is yet to be determined."

She laughed in spite of herself and attracted curious glances. Within seconds she found the countess at her side to pry her away from London's premier gossip. Soon after, they were called in to dinner.

Daisy tried to steer the conversation away from the claims of gout, digestive problems, and dietary peculiarities that seemed to occupy the guests' thoughts. But none of her dinner companions, it seemed, had much interest in country pursuits like hunting anymore. A few of the men recalled the glory of past hunts and some argued over the lineage of long-dead horses, the skill of hound masters past, and the routs that followed the hunt's exertions. A few blue words escaped and no one batted an eye. She was regretting having brought up the subject when the duke himself stepped in to the conversation.

"Miss Bumgarten is something of a hunter herself," he said, loud enough for all of his guests to hear. "Brilliant rider, actually. And you should see her horse—black as night and seventeen hands at least."

The guests turned to look at her and to her credit she reddened under the attention—as a young unmarried girl should. When she looked down at her plate, she caught a glimpse of Boulton rolling his eyes for her benefit and smiled. It wasn't long before Red was called upon to repeat some of his best Nevada stories, and the rest of the meal was relatively genial. Red knew how to tailor his tales to an audience, and the older guests were enthralled by his larger than life depictions of the West and claims of derring-do.

There was no brandy-and-cigars part of the evening that required the ladies to retire to the drawing room. A number of the older gentlemen confessed to having strict orders from their physicians to avoid both, and some declined the coffee that was served on the same grounds. One by one they shuffled off to bed, leaving only the younger contingent of guests in the drawing room.

"Lovely dinner, Your Grace," Daisy said when Arthur finally managed to work his way through the remaining guests to reach her side.

"So it was. A bit dull for you, I expect. But, I say sincerely, your presence here made my night. You are so gracious and lovely."

"Why, thank you, Your Grace." She hoped her smile looked more genuine than it felt. "It is a pleasure to accept your hospitality. I confess surprise, however, at the number of older persons in your acquaintance."

"Oh, that." He chuckled and reddened a bit. "They're my aunts' and uncles' friends, actually. They planned the thing and since I have relatively few acquaintances near my own—"

"I say, Artie." Boulton sauntered up with a flask in one hand and a coffee cup in the other. "Thinking of opening up a boardinghouse for old-age pensioners?"

"Why? Do you need lodgings?" Arthur said with complete sincerity. "You're most welcome, Reynard. Stay as long as you like."

"Bloody hell, Artie," Reynard snapped. "That was a joke."

"Was it indeed? Didn't catch that at all." He looked to Daisy. "You have met Miss Bumgarten, haven't you? She's quite a horsewoman, you know. I intend to show her Betancourt on horseback first thing tomorrow morning. You're free to join us if you wish."

"It is my custom to sleep till noon," Reynard said archly. "And I'm no great lover of horses. No offense." He aimed that last at Daisy.

"None taken," she responded.

"I wasn't a devotee myself until Miss Bumgarten introduced me to the joys of riding," Arthur continued, looking to Daisy. "I've been practicing every day since. I think you'll find my seat much improved."

Daisy's eyes widened by the same amount that Reynard's narrowed. "I am glad to hear you're making progress, Your Grace."

"No doubt she could encourage your skill as well, Reynard. Do come with us tomorrow."

"I appreciate your largesse, Your Grace, but I'm a creature of habits."

"Bad habits," Arthur muttered as Boulton walked away, causing Daisy to look at him with surprise. "He can be a rotter, sometimes. But basically he's just lonely. When we were at school together, nobody liked him."

"That's rather sad," she said, considering Arthur's insight into Boulton's character. He noticed more than anyone gave him credit for.

"We were in the same boat. I didn't have many friends, either. Ash stuck up for us, though. And the other boys left us alone."

"Really?"

"Ash was like that. Always eager to fight and fierce to defend his family and friends. People think Ash is a bounder, I know, but he has a good heart. I'm glad he's coming home, even if it is just for a visit. I miss him."

Those were the words that echoed in Daisy's head as she prepared for bed that night in the once elegant, satin-lined bedchamber. *"I miss him."*

He wasn't the only one who missed Ashton Graham.

Sleep was a long time coming as she tossed and turned

and refused to think of any Graham but Arthur. He surprised her with his desire to ride and his efforts to follow through on his promise to gain skill in the saddle. And while he was still oblivious to the slights and subtleties of social interactions, she was beginning to think he wasn't as inexperienced as he seemed. She laughed softly, thinking of his exquisite rebuff of Boulton earlier. Yes, he showed promise, the Duke of Meridian. And she prayed that she could make him see the same in her.

The duke had indeed improved in the saddle, Daisy learned the next morning. She, the duke, Red, and a couple of the younger guests set off from the house when the sun was rising in the sky. Dew still drenched the grass, birds were chirping, and people in the clusters of cottages that dotted the estate were stirring. There were planted fields and woods and pastures ready for grazing, but there was little activity about them. Where were the cattle, sheep, pigs, and goats?

Interestingly, the people in those cottages ran into their yards to stare at the party riding by. The men doffed their caps and the women spread their aprons and dipped as they recognized their duke. There was a palpable excitement and no small bit of wonder in their expressions, as if seeing him were a rare treat. Arthur nodded graciously and squared himself in the saddle, as if their greeting reminded him of his role here.

By the time they returned to Betancourt proper, Daisy was pleased to be able to compliment Arthur on his horsemanship and his lovely home, the estate of Betancourt.

"The stable," Arthur said with chagrin as they handed off their mounts to a couple of aged grooms, "is not up to standards, I fear." He looked around the unpainted structure.

"As soon as I have means, I will be hiring a new stable man to take it in hand."

"Horses, horses," came a harsh voice some yards away and approaching. "They're all he's talked about since we returned from Marlton."

Uncle Bertram arrived with a taut look of displeasure for Daisy.

"Well, then, he's showin' good sense." Red stepped into Bertram's line of sight. "We always say in Nevada, 'you take care o' yer horses, an' they'll take care of you.'"

"A waste of oats, most of them," Bertram said with a sniff.

"Only because they haven't been attended properly," Daisy said, stepping out of her uncle's shadow and making straight for Arthur. "What say you, Your Grace? Shall we have a look at your carriage and riding stock?"

"Oh, I say, would you?" Arthur said with that innocent look she'd seen before. He looked to Red. "I would greatly value your opinions, Mr. Strait."

"Uncle Red, to you, boyo," Red said, grasping his own lapels proudly and waiting for the gasps that would follow. Daisy whapped her uncle on the sleeve and caused him to laugh wickedly.

The duke laughed, too, despite Bertram's wordless fury, and motioned them to follow along to the house.

A cold luncheon was served in the breakfast room amidst strong beams of light pouring through the great windows. They were joined by a number of the older contingent, who listened eagerly to news of the estate and spun a few stories of their youthful escapades in ponds, up trees, and pulling pranks in the great house. Daisy was surprised to hear that Betancourt's stables were once considered its prime feature.

Later, as they assessed the formation and movement of various horses from the stable, confusion erupted in the paddock at the far end. Knowing Dancer was stabled there,

Daisy jumped up onto one of the fence boards and stretched to see what was going on. A glistening black head was rearing and there was a lot of snorting and whinnying. The stable hands and grooms began to snicker. Red and Arthur pulled her back down and Arthur turned her by the shoulders and pulled her against him to shelter her from the sight.

"You mustn't look," Arthur said, horrified. "I fear your beloved mount has gone rogue and started to—"

"He's coverin' a mare, Daize," Red said loudly. "Must have found one in season."

"Oh." Daisy pushed back in Arthur's arms, looking a little abashed. "I'm afraid he's used to having his way with mares. I hope you don't mind."

Arthur was speechless for a moment, then quickly recovered. "I imagine your horse would be a splendid father."

Red burst out laughing and the stable hands scrambled to their duties while trying to hide their amusement.

"I mean"—Arthur reddened—"a foal from your stallion would be a wonderful addition to our stable."

"So it would," Daisy said, shooting a fierce look at Red. "He's a fine horse and a gentleman with mares. I had no idea he was put in with your horses."

The story reached the main house in record time, whispered and tittered about by the staff, who could scarcely recall the last time a foal was born on the estate. But by afternoon, when Daisy retreated to her room to rest and freshen up, the countess had a few choice words about the incident.

"Dearest Heaven—of all things! That beast of yours inflicting himself on the duke's riding stock! His family already thinks you're unbridled and uncouth, and unsuitable. And your presence is now marked with the taint of this reckless . . . 'mating.'"

"It wouldn't have happened if they hadn't put Dancer in with a bunch of Betancourt mares," Daisy declared defiantly. "It wasn't his fault or mine. And from what I've seen of the stock and stables here, Dancer's probably done them a big favor."

"Daisy!" The countess seemed truly appalled. "Watch your language."

"Well, the duke didn't mind—once he realized what was going on."

"He didn't realize . . . ?" The countess chewed on that for a minute. "He doesn't seem like the worldliest of gentlemen, but I would have expected him to at least know—well, no matter. We'll put it behind us and get on with the business at hand. Any word on when that rascal Ashton Graham will arrive?"

Chapter Twenty-One

The rascal arrived that very night, sometime after the duke and his guests had retired. The house staff were flustered and, lacking instructions, found him a room on the third floor, near the old schoolroom that had been converted into the duke's laboratory and display room. Once put to bed, Ashton was all but forgotten by a staff used to forgetting and overwhelmed by the number of mouths to feed and beds to make.

No one would have known he was there if the duke hadn't insisted on showing Daisy his workroom and collections. Accompanied by the countess and a pair of older gentlemen who professed to share the duke's love of nature, they climbed the wooden stairs to the long third-floor hallway.

"This used to be my schoolroom. Not much use for it since my tutoring days, so I converted it to my laboratory and display room. Wait until you see how I've arranged my collection."

Daisy looked up when he halted unexpectedly, and she froze. There in the hallway before them stood Ashton, bare-chested, shirt and stockings in his hands, his trousers and mouth both hanging open. He was just as shocked to see them as they were to see him.

"Great Galatians—what are you doing up here?" Arthur demanded.

"I—I—they put me up here last night." Ashton clutched his clothes a bit higher, flushing. "I arrived quite late and I'm not sure they knew who I was. Old Edgar seems to have completely lost his wits. . . . God knows he never had an abundant supply to begin with . . . but really . . . I am *family*."

Daisy made a faint strangling noise and the countess grabbed her and turned her away even as the duke stepped between her and Ashton.

"Ye gods, man, show some manners," one male guest declared.

"There are ladies present," another put in.

"So I see," Ashton said, and though Daisy couldn't see him she could tell he was smiling. She knew what he looked like when he got that low, teasing timbre in his voice. "Good morning, Miss Bumgarten. Fabulous to see you again." He paused for her response, but the countess's punishing grip on her forbade one. "Well, I was just on my way downstairs to find a bathing room. Got to freshen up after a long ride and a longer night." He leaned close to Arthur as he padded down the hall in bare feet. "You really must do something about putting a proper water closet up here, Artie. Especially if you're going to sentence children to this level someday."

It took a few moments for Arthur to collect himself and lead the group on to his laboratory. Daisy's shock at seeing Ashton's half-naked body was a perfect imitation of a young maiden's response at being exposed to such unsettling sights. But inside, she was grappling with an unholy urge to rush down the stairs, drag him into her room, and throw him on her feathered bed. Oh my darlin' Clementine— the man had a body just made for—A covert elbow from the countess brought her back to the duke's explanation.

". . . is where I do my preservations," the duke said,

gesturing to long tables set beneath the windows and the rows of brown bottles and tubes and peering glasses he called "scopes" arrayed on them. The gentlemen asked questions about the "micro-scopes" and he demonstrated by using one of his butterflies as a subject.

The countess shrank back with a look of horror when she saw what butterflies looked like up close. Daisy was surprised, then intrigued to learn the same thing. It occurred to her to ask if there were other things to view and before long, they were looking at flowers, leaves, onion skin, and twigs. There was a whole world, the duke declared, just out of sight.

When they moved on to his collections, Daisy found herself watching the duke with new eyes. With his microscope he had seen things few people had. It was little wonder that he had invested so much time and energy in such studies. With a home full of condescension, stinginess, and doddering elders, it was by far the best of the alternatives open to him.

"A marvelous collection, Your Grace," she said as he offered her an arm to descend the stairs. "I can see why you're so taken with them. The colors are so varied and so beautiful. I had no idea."

"Most people don't," he said a bit sadly. "It is actually of profound importance to understand and nourish the great variety of living things in our world. I have read widely about conservation that is what it's called, preserving nature and respecting natural processes—conservation. Only recently have I realized that it also involves tilled and planted lands and pastures. There are places on Betancourt that sorely need tending. And I've you to thank for giving me a nudge to get out and about the land to see what is happening."

"Oh, Your Grace, you credit me too much. You're an earnest and thoughtful lord with a deep sense of responsibility for your land and people. You just needed a spark to get you going. And I bet you'll have the place in top shape before long."

They trailed out to the butterfly garden, set a small way from the rear of the house. It was a pale cousin of the magnificent collection at Marlton, but she could see he was unhappy with the comparison and spent time going through the roster of flowers with him, trying to recall which ones Albemarle said were most hardy. In the less productive part of the garden, she stepped off a stone and felt the ground squish underfoot. It turned out, the area chosen for the plantings was poorly drained. The duke, not being a horticulturist himself, had trusted the selection of site and plantings to a fellow hired by his uncle Bertram.

Daisy saw the duke's irritation and took it on herself to tell him: "It's easily fixed, Your Grace. Most of the plants are sound enough for replanting. There must be a lot of places near the house that would be better for your butterfly garden. Shall we have a look and select a spot? Plenty of sun, good drainage—"

"Not just now," the duke said firmly, staring at his dampened shoes. A muscle twitched in his jaw, jolting Daisy with a memory of Ashton's doing the same when he was annoyed. "I need to have a bit of think, here. Be so good as to go on back to the house, dear Daisy." He gave her a pained smile. "I will join you later."

Daisy walked back to the house with the countess, who shook her head and gave Daisy a sympathetic look.

"He's upset about the garden," the countess said. "I've never seen him in a mood before."

"Nor have I," Daisy said, untying her hat as they reached the front portico. "But he has a great deal to contend with here, and I can't imagine he gets much help from family or the creaky old servants." She paused and glanced around the entry hall, lowering her voice. "The whole place feels like it needs a good scrub—"

"Miss Bumgarten," an aged but imperious voice interrupted.

"Yes?" She whirled about to find an old gent she recognized as the duke's uncle Seward standing a few steps away.

"Lady Sylvia and the rest of the family request your presence in the morning room," Seward intoned.

The time had come. She felt her heart begin to pound.

"Oh. I'll be there sh-shortly," Daisy said, stumbling over words. "I must fetch something from my room first." She lifted her skirts and headed for the stairs with the countess at her back.

When they were alone in the upper hall, she turned to the countess.

"Find Uncle Red. Tell him it's time and make sure he doesn't take a nip before he gets to the morning room."

The countess hurried down the west hallway to Red's room and Daisy turned toward her room to get the Temple Church document. She stood for a moment in the sun streaming through the windowpanes in her chamber, feeling light headed and a bit panicky. Her entire future, her sisters' futures, hinged on what occurred in the breakfast room a few minutes from now. And all she had to show them was one document proving one illegitimate baby's parentage. It wasn't much, but she prayed it would be enough.

She found Red and the countess waiting outside the morning room door, both gray faced and looking like they were facing a hanging judge. She squared her shoulders and produced a small, determined smile.

"Whatever the outcome," she said quietly, "everything will be fine. I know the duke thinks well of me—noble ancestry or not—and surely his opinion will count for something."

When the door opened and she glimpsed the six hoary

heads and hostile faces that would soon pass judgment on her heritage, her knees turned to rubber. It was all she could do to make it to the table and lay the ribbon-wrapped velum before them like a sacrifice before ancient gods.

"What is this?" Lady Sylvia demanded hoarsely, staring at the document as if it might grow legs and skitter across the table.

"This is the result of my search, at least what could be found on this side of the Atlantic. It is the birth record of Gemma Rose Howard, whom I believe to be my great-great-great-great-great-grandmother."

"On the Strait side," Uncle Red put in, crossing his arms.

"Very well." Lady Sylvia nodded to Uncle Bertram, who tugged the ribbon free and opened the document to read aloud.

"'Be it known that on this date, October third, in the year of our Lord 1747, Gemma Rose Howard, a female child, was baptized into the grace of God at Temple Church in the Redcliffe Fee of Bristol, England. Attending were her mother, Hannah Violet Howard, a member of this parish; her father, Commodore Fitzroy Henry Lee, Royal Navy; and two witnesses: Sadie Marie McLeod and Captain Eli Cornwallis, Royal Navy.'"

Uncle Bertram looked up with a vengeful squint. "The rest is the dean of Temple Church's signature and seal, which may or may not be—"

"Authentic?" came a deep voice from just inside the doors behind them. Daisy suddenly had gooseflesh and felt her stomach drop as she turned and glimpsed Ashton's flinty expression. He stood with his feet spread, one hand propped on his waist and the other wrapped around a thick book. "I can assure you, uncles, aunts, and all, that it is perfectly authentic."

"About damned time you got here," Bertram growled.

"Bertie, language!" Sylvia snapped. "You, Nephew, how do you know it is authentic?"

"I was there when it was discovered and when it was inscribed by the dean of the parish. I saw the citation in the parish book myself. There is no doubt it is authentic. But you would be sensible to ask next: Who are these people? And what claims do they have to nobility?"

There was a short silence before Lady Sylvia snorted and accepted the prompt. "Very well. Who are these people and what have they to do with English nobles"—she wagged a finger at Daisy—"or this *American* person?"

"The commodore listed as the father of the girl is none other than the seventh son of Charlotte Fitzroy Lee, Countess of Lichfield."

"Never heard of her," Bertram snapped.

"Fortunately *historians* have heard of her," Ashton said. "She was the daughter and favorite of King Charles the Second, our Restoration monarch."

That took a moment to sink in, and Daisy watched as the old gals' and gaffers' faces began to animate with interest. Only Bertram seemed unimpressed. He glowered, his eyes flitting back and forth as he made the connections.

"So this baby was the great-granddaughter of King Charles, and this girl claims to be related to her? How do we know this Charlotte even existed?"

"Because the king himself said so," Ashton said flatly, brushing past Bertram to drop the book on the table before Lady Sylvia and open it to a marked page. He tapped a section of print. "Right there."

"Read it aloud," Sylvia ordered, scowling. "So I can hear it."

Daisy stepped forward and picked up Huxley's book before Ashton could and began to read the now familiar passage.

"'Charlotte Fitzroy was born on September fifth, in the

year 1664, to Barbara Palmer, née Villiers, Countess of
Castlemaine, acknowledged mistress of His Royal Highness
King Charles the Second of England. The king acknowledged Charlotte from her birth and arranged a marriage for
her with a son of the wealthy Lee family, who held positions
of trust in his court. . . .'"

By the time she finished reading the entry, the oldsters
were wide eyed and murmuring among themselves about the
eighteen children and forty-two years of wedded life. Daisy
offered the book around and the old crones peeked, nodded
sagely, and waved her on. Only Bertram and Seward were
left unconvinced . . . and ready to play the ace up their sleeve.

"So, are you willing to certify that this female is indeed
the descendant of King Charles the Second of England?"
Seward demanded of Ashton.

Daisy held her breath, knowing his opinion on her marriage to Arthur and feeling strangely conflicted about his
testimony here. She wanted to marry Arthur; she wanted to
be a duchess—didn't she? She looked up at Ashton, whose
wicked, love-me-senseless eyes were clouded in a way she
had never seen before. She couldn't tell what was going on
inside him.

Seconds dragged by as he stared at her, deciding, weigh-
ing her fate in his capable hands.

"I am." He took a breath and turned to his family "creaks
and groans." "As a historian, I must say that there is documentation lacking from the other side of the ocean, but given
what Redmond Strait was required to learn and the lineage
of Charlotte Fitzroy . . . I would say it is more likely than not.
I would see no impediment to Miss Bumgarten wedding the
duke, should that be agreeable to them both. And should
the financial arrangements prove suitable." He swallowed
hard, meeting his uncles' gazes with a defiant spark. "I
believe my duty here has been discharged."

There were gasps and mutters as the full impact of Ashton's

report became clear. The uncles were appalled by the possibility of this courtship, despite the hint of a financial windfall, and Lady Sylvia was apoplectic.

Red, filled with indignation and stone-cold sober, pounded the table with a meaty fist and glared at the weaseling Meridian elders.

"Listen here, you sidewinders. My Daisy has passed yer damn-fool tests. She did it out o' respect for yer family and care for th' young duke's feelings. But this ends here. She's as noble as anybody in this room. So button yer lips and butt out. It's up to her and him now." He stuck his face in Bertram's, and the baron wilted around the edges. "If they decide to get hitched, then we'll talk *money*. Till then, there'll be none o' you lot standing in their way. Got it?"

Daisy was in shock as the countess took her arm and steered her out the door. It was over. Truly over. They had accepted her "proof"—with a push from Ashton and a threat from Red. She had a path to marrying Arthur. Daisy's relief was so great that it almost poured out through her eyes. Instead, she hugged the countess and Red, and in a burst of emotional excess, ran up to her rooms to write her mother a letter announcing that she intended to marry the Duke of Meridian and would soon be a duchess.

Chapter Twenty-Two

A shton watched Daisy leave with a warm kernel of satisfaction glowing in his chest. It was regrettably short lived.

"You black-hearted, double-dealing scoundrel! Damn your eyes!"

Bertram's curses ignited a storm of invective and vitriol. Ashton was momentarily stunned; he would never have guessed these desiccated gourds were capable of such violent emotion. Spittle and false teeth both flew.

"Out!" Aunt Sylvia snarled, rising halfway from her chair and flinging a bony finger toward the door before being overcome by her own fury, clutching her chest, and sinking back into her chair. "Get out, ungrateful cur. We'll see naught but the back of you, from this day forward!"

Ashton retrieved and tucked Huxley's book under his arm and strode out of the morning room, making sure the door slammed with a wall-trembling bang. He had done the right thing, skewered the old vultures who had held him and his brother hostage for most of their lives. It was probably a deathblow to his income and prospects, but just now it felt like a victory . . . no matter how Pyrrhic.

Reynard Boulton loomed up before him in the main hall.

One look at the fire in Ashton's eyes and the granite-hard set of his jaw told the Fox that something important was up.

"Ash, old chum—where are you off to in such a hurry?" He turned on his heel and kept pace as Ashton stormed out the doors.

"I'm going to get soused proper—probably drink twelve pints and start a fight." He glanced at the elegantly turned-out heir to the Tannehill title. "You interested?"

"Sikes, yes!" Reynard squared his shoulders with a sly look. "Always up for a good, old-fashioned tear."

They headed for the stable and the quickest transport available to the nearby Iron Penny Tavern.

Later that afternoon, Daisy freshened her hair and changed her dress into corded silk appropriate for a walk with a special gentleman, and hurried outside to find Arthur. He stood, a study in brown, scowling at a pond filled with water lilies and ducks. "Your Grace!" She approached with a beaming smile, but stopped dead the moment he looked up.

"Cursed ducks . . . I suppose they have to eat, but do they have to eat my water hyacinth?" He scowled and pointed. "Look at this—a ragged mess."

She was taken aback; she had never seen him so cross. It took a moment for her to regroup and understand both his pique and her disappointment. He had no idea what had just transpired in the morning room and no idea that they were free to court in earnest now. Her excitement drained, replaced by determination.

Now—she sensed with an insight that was uniquely feminine—was the time to be understanding and helpful.

"Good Heavens, Arthur." She swayed as she moved closer. "What has you in such a mood?"

He turned to her with an exasperated huff. "First it was

the stables, then the butterfly garden, and now the duck pond. I just noticed the roof is showing wear and the glazing on many of the windows is cracked or missing. I went around to the entry and, dang me if the front doors aren't in a sad state, too. What's happened to Betancourt? Everywhere I look something needs tending or mending or replacing."

"Well, houses do take upkeep," she said, inserting her arm through his and urging him forward, leading him away from the view that disturbed him so. "Weather and years take a toll. And Betancourt has stood for—what?—hundreds of years? It is probably time for another round of care."

"I thought Betancourt *was* being cared for. My uncles . . ." He halted and looked into her upturned face, conflict plain in his expression. "They have been my trustees since I was a boy. I expected that they were caring for the house and estate." His frown deepened. "And now I see so much has been neglected." He straightened and looked away. "I must bear the blame, for ignoring my duties. I'm not a boy anymore."

"You've been occupied with your studies," she said. "But now that you've taken notice, I'm sure you'll have things righted in no time." She turned to face him, alight with determination. "Tell you what—how about if I help you make a start. On the butterfly garden."

"You wouldn't think it too boring?" he asked, looking a bit less like a scarecrow that had the stuffing knocked out of him.

"I would love to help." She gave an impish grin. "Society—all that tea and talk—bores me. I'd love to have something to sink my teeth into. Who decided to put your butterfly garden in a bog in the first place?"

"I—I'm not sure."

After a fruitless search for the head gardener, who was reputed to be off fetching supplies of some kind, Daisy suggested looking for a plan or a map of the estate. That took them into the old duke's study, where they found Uncle Bertram and Uncle Seward involved in a letter that had just arrived. At the sight of his nephew, Bertram dropped it to the desk and covered it with his arm.

"What is that, Uncle?"

"Nothing!" and "A letter," Bertram and Seward answered together.

"From whom?" Arthur leaned across the desk and caught sight of the posting. "Addressed to me?"

"A note from the Countess of Dorchester," Bertram said, trying to sound offhand, while Seward nodded anxiously.

"What about?" Arthur pulled on the corner of the letter, and after a moment Bertram had to let it go. Arthur raised it into the window light and read it aloud.

"'. . . my heartfelt thanks for sending such a talented and remarkable soul as Dr. Edmonds to us. He has been a gift beyond price and has become almost a part of the family. Under his devoted care, the earl has rallied and is seen to improve daily. We believe he will soon be able to join us at table and to resume a healthy and fruitful life. Your Grace, we can never thank you enough for your kindness and generosity toward us. If we can ever be of service, you have only to ask. Your indebted servant, Rosalyn Lytton-Small, Countess of Dorchester.'"

He looked at his uncles in confusion.

"She thanks *me*? I've never heard of the woman, much less sent—"

"We—ahem—heard of the earl's grave illness and sent our personal physician to him," Bertram said, his manner so oily Daisy was surprised his hairpiece didn't slide from his head. "An act of charity that we knew you, with your generous nature, would approve."

"We made certain it was done in your name, Arthur." Tall, thin Seward attempted an ingratiating smile that came off like a bad case of dyspepsia instead. "Everything we do is done to your credit."

"Very well." With a troubled look, Arthur tossed the letter onto the desk and glanced about the overstuffed bins, shelves, and cabinets. "We've come for a map of the estate. I know I saw one in here somewhere."

"In my study? What were you doing in here?" Bertram stiffened slightly and glanced at Seward. Arthur was looking around and didn't notice, but Daisy caught it well enough.

"Not long ago. I saw—there!" Arthur headed for a wooden bin on the floor beside a stuffed leather chair. Seward reached him just as he began to look through the rolled up documents.

"Let me," Seward commanded, inserting himself between the bin and his nephew. "I believe I know just what you need."

"And plans for the garden," Arthur added, watching his uncle fumble with document after document.

"What garden?" Bertram came around the desk.

"The butterfly garden. The architect's plans. The fellow we hired to design and site the garden. *You* hired."

"Perhaps you have a plan of the garden itself?" Daisy suggested to Seward as he pawed through the maps.

"What business is this of yours?" Bertram snapped, drawing a dark look from Arthur.

"I just thought it might be good to consult the plan and learn why it was placed where it is," Daisy answered, checking her rising temper.

"I can't recall the fellow's name," Bertram said in clipped tones. "I shall have to consult the ledgers." He caught Arthur's displeasure. "We have a great deal to do, Arthur. We can't be chasing about after your whims day after day."

Arthur's mouth was a grim line as he took the maps from Seward's hands and escorted Daisy out.

They settled in the library, unrolling the maps on a table and looking them over to locate the various features of the grounds. After a while, Daisy paused and straightened.

"I don't mean to seem critical of your family, but did it seem to you that your uncles were anxious to have you leave?"

"It's always like that," Arthur said, frowning as he scanned a second diagram. "Uncle Bertram doesn't like his things disturbed."

"His things?" She had to bite her tongue to keep from using language that would have shocked Arthur. "Surely all the documents concerning the estate are yours."

Arthur sagged, and then braced himself on the table with his fists. "I suppose they are." He hesitated, frowning. "I should have been tending to Betancourt's affairs instead of . . ."

He didn't have to finish it; the look on his face said it all. He was suddenly feeling the weight of his title. Ashton's words in the Bodleian Library came back to her.

A duke's home wasn't his own. His time wasn't his own. And someday his children wouldn't be his own.

Such was the life she would choose by marrying Arthur.

It had to be worth it. Arthur had to be worth it.

Before she knew what she was doing, she stepped around the table and gave Arthur a kiss on the cheek.

He straightened with a look of surprise. And when she stayed close, he took the hint and lowered his lips to hers. It was soft and exploratory this time. More leisurely and vaguely pleasant. But in her mind and heart, there was an ocean of difference between her current response and the feelings she experienced when Ashton kissed her.

When the kiss ended, she lowered her eyes so he wouldn't see the disappointment in them, and forced a smile that she prayed would pass for the pleasure she hadn't felt.

Chapter Twenty-Three

Dinner that night was short and ill attended. A few of the oldest guests had elected to take a tray in their rooms instead of endure the formality of the dining room. A mere four courses were served, and plain fare it was: watery soup, overcooked turbot, bland beef with mushy vegetables, and a custard that had separated before it was served.

Ashton wasn't present, nor was Reynard Boulton or Arthur's aunt, Lady Sylvia Graham Upshaw. Uncle Bertram sat rigidly at the head of the table and didn't bother to try to foster good conversation or good appetite. Wine was poured short, and when Daisy asked for additional, the footman looked at her as if she'd asked for the head of John the Baptist. He only complied after he looked to Uncle Bertram, who was busy whispering to Seward, then realized the duke himself was tapping his goblet, demanding more.

Through it all, Arthur toyed with his food and turned his cutlery over and over, studying the tarnish that lay on the silver. But when he looked Daisy's way, his face brightened and he managed a bit of conversation with the guests seated nearest him.

The highlight of dinner came when a punctilious guest called into question Red's tales of cowboys' skills. Old

Baron Kettering declared that cattle roping from horseback was impossible and Red's claims about cowboy acumen had to be pure braggadocio.

Ever one for a challenge, Red declared he would demonstrate the truth of his claims after dinner. Daisy groaned softly as Red hauled out his flask and generously dosed his empty wineglass with whiskey. Arthur, seeming truly interested, sent for old Edgar and ordered torches be set around the perimeter of the main paddock to light the area for the demonstration.

"Uncle Red!" Daisy grabbed his sleeve as he headed outside ahead of the migration of guests buzzing about the challenge. "You haven't roped cattle in years."

"Like ridin' a horse, Daize." He grinned wickedly. "Once ye learn, ye never forget."

"But you need a real rope," she said, keeping up with him.

"I got rope." He leaned close. "I never go anywhere without a good cattle rope, girl. Thought you knew that."

He laughed roundly as he headed for the stable, peeling off his fancy tailcoat and tossing it to a stable hand. Sure enough, he exited the stable moments later with a suitable lariat that he had apparently brought across a continent and an ocean with Renegade's tack and western saddle.

"Can he really rope a running calf?" Arthur asked quietly as he settled by the paddock fence beside Daisy.

"I hope so," she said, shamed by her doubts about Red's skill. "He used to be a wonder at rope tricks, but it's been a while. . . ."

She watched with mounting tension as he produced his flask and took a couple of belts of whiskey before handing it off to another stable hand. He cut quite a figure in the torchlight, with his black trousers and tailored vest, and white shirt open at the collar. Every eye was on him as he unwound his rope, inspected its honda knot, and then addressed the odd mixture of blue bloods, stable hands, and house servants who ringed the paddock fence.

"A cowboy's workin' rope has to be stiff—made special for lassoin' cattle." Red played to his audience. "I never go anywhere without one!"

Daisy groaned. "He's three sheets to the wind."

"He does his best work when snozzeled," the countess responded.

Daisy gave her a surprised look and found her staring intently at Red, who was rolling his shoulders and limbering up.

"Might be a bit rusty." He made a puzzled face as if trying to remember. "Oh, yeah. This here's how it goes."

The rope *whoosh*ed up into the air and a second later it was spreading into a broad, swirling circle above him, sending a rustle of interest through the onlookers. There were some, however, who were less than impressed.

"Is that all you've got?" old Kettering called. "You said you could rope a calf."

"Get me a calf and I'll rope it!" Red called back, looking pleased. A second later he moved the spinning loop up and down like a piston, down around his shoulders, then his knees, then back up over his head again. There were *oooh*'s from the crowd. He spun the rope over his head for a moment, then dropped the loop in front of him and let it enlarge as he chuckled. "Gotta make this one big enough to dance in."

A second later he was jumping in and out of the loop while still spinning it, and applause broke out all around. Daisy applauded the loudest, though not by much; the countess was vehement in her appreciation. When Daisy looked up, the duke was grinning like a schoolboy.

"Oh, then there's this little bit." Red started vertical circles and bounced them back and forth to *oooh*'s and *ah*'s. He walked around the fence, giving the onlookers a close view of the process and teasing them with his western drawl and swagger.

When he came within a few yards of Daisy, he paused and issued a "Yip-yip-yippieo kyaaa!" and snapped the rope forward, sent it sailing past his niece to drop neatly around the countess. Lady Evelyn gasped as the lasso tightened around her and looked around as people laughed. She sputtered and blinked, uncertain what she should do as Red approached.

"That's no calf!" came a hostile male voice from across the paddock. "Ignorant American—can't tell a calf from a countess!"

A second later Red pulled the captive countess against the paddock fence and rushed over to give her a smooch on the cheek. Daisy was dumbstruck, but once the lasso was removed and Red moved on, the countess recovered with a flurry of "Oh, my's" and "Goodness sake's."

There was laughter at her reaction and she lifted her skirts and fled back to the house. Daisy would have gone with her, but the duke seized her hand and pulled her to his side, pointing to the paddock gate. Someone was pushing a calf into the arena, and as soon as it was released, it began to run.

Onlookers pointed and shouted at Red to lasso it. Daisy held her breath and watched while Red circled the rope over his head and took aim. He stalked the frantic calf for a few yards, then let the loop fly. Time seemed to slow as the lasso opened, sank through the air, and landed around the calf's neck. A second later the poor animal was yanked to a stop, struggling against the restraint. Red nodded to recognize the burst of applause. "Th' tricky part's gettin' the loop off," Red called as the noise subsided. A moment later he halted, let the rope slack, and as the stiff loop loosened, the calf slipped out of it and ran off.

It was a moment of triumph, well earned, but not without

its detractors. The old baron still insisted he rope a calf from a running horse.

"Nobody ropes from a horse in th' dark," Red declared, "unless they're lookin' to break a horse's legs. You need daylight an' a heck of a larger spread to work in."

"Thank you, Mr. Strait, for this marvelous demonstration." Arthur stepped in to declare amazement at Red's skill. "Your roping is unparalleled, exceeded only by your generosity in displaying it for us. I say—everyone back to the house for a bit of champagne to celebrate!"

They were halfway back to Betancourt before Uncle Bertram caught up with Arthur and pulled him aside to snarl into his ear, "What are you thinking—opening up the cellars after such an appalling display?"

Daisy heard enough to guess Arthur was being chastised, and stepped into Arthur's line of sight. Her smile was more defiance than pleasure.

Arthur straightened at the sight of her.

"Would you have me take back the invitation? Surely we can part with a few bottles of wine and some liquor, Uncle. We're not destitute." He paused and looked quizzically at Bertram. "Are we?"

Daisy walked the gravel path back to the main house with Arthur, missing the anger in Bertram's face as he stalked toward the servants' entrance to order the cellar opened. But Ashton saw it as he rode toward the stable, towing Reynard's horse—with Reynard sagging precariously in the saddle—behind him. He wasn't certain what had gone on in the paddock by the stable, but he suspected it had to do with *her*.

Despite his worst hell-raising intentions, he hadn't drunk nearly enough to purge the scene in the morning room from his thoughts and hadn't found a single opponent worth bloodying his knuckles.

He dismounted, helped Reynard sluice from the saddle, and handed off their mounts to an aged stable man. He called for a younger groom to help him get Reynard inside and to his room. They used the front hall and main stairs to avoid the people and noise from the grand parlor. In Reynard's room on the second floor, they let him fall with an "*uff*" on the bed and then loosened his tie and removed his shoes. Ashton looked around the mahogany and brocade-upholstered guest room and thought of his spartan lodgings near the nursery. He should have expected as much. He hadn't been welcome here in years, and after today, might never be again. His thoughts were confirmed when he found Uncle Bertram waiting at the bottom of the stairs.

"How dare you show your face in these walls?" his former guardian snapped. "You're banished from this house, this family. Set foot inside our doors again and I'll set the law on you, do you hear?"

"I have no doubt you would do just that. But I think Arthur may have something to say about it."

"Arthur is irrelevant."

"Are you sure about that?" Ashton shoved his face near Bertram's and let the words claw their way up out of the bottom of his soul. "You'd better pray he lives a long and fruitful life. Because if he should die without issue and I become duke, I'll see you begging in the streets before I'm done."

He strode to the tall front doors, threw them open with a bang, and exited, leaving them standing wide open.

Bertram narrowed his eyes as he watched Ashton stalk into the night and was soon dragging Seward out of the merriment in the parlor for an urgent conference. After a few words, they hurried upstairs to Lady Sylvia's chambers, knocked, and demanded the old girl's maid wake her up. It took a while for Sylvia's maid to make her presentable. When they were admitted to her elegant chambers—once the domain of the Duchess of Meridian—she was garbed in a nightgown dressing robe, a chin sling, and more than one nightcap. She waved them to the tea table by the window and demanded to know why they had disturbed her. Seward's explanation told her that serious discussion was required and she sent for her teeth.

"Mark my words, he'll cause trouble." Bertram mopped his forehead, then fanned himself with his handkerchief in Sylvia's overheated chambers. "He could go to Arthur, tell him what we paid him to do."

Seward shook his head. "Then he would betray his own selfish motives—agreeing to ruin the dollar princess for a few pieces of silver."

"How did this happen?" Sylvia swatted away her maid's attempt to wrap her in a shawl.

"We should have paid him more," Seward said resentfully to Sylvia. "I said we should pay him more."

"That's not it." Bertram's face twisted. "She got to him somehow—that Bamgarter chit. She got under his skin. He always was weak that way."

"Subject to the cravings of the flesh, that boy," Sylvia snapped. "Always has been ruled by his disgusting carnal . . ." Her glower took on a canny edge. "She got under his skin, did she?"

They looked at one another, each doing a variation of the same devious calculation.

"He's bedded her," Bertram said, smacking the table. "It can't be anything else, not with that brazen trollop." He smirked, impressed with his deduction. "She *seduced* him into abandoning the family's welfare."

"Dazzled him with her wicked charms," Seward declared, catching on.

"Diddled him to a stupor, you mean," Sylvia spat, quivering with fury. "Then cozened him into helping her."

"That's why he's suddenly developed a conscience—he's

passing his leavings off to his brother." Bertram oozed indignation. "He's mad if he thinks we'd allow—"

He stopped dead and stared into the distance for a moment, his eyes darting back and forth over a scene developing in his mind. Vicious delight spread over his face.

"That's it. That's what will end it forever."

"What?" Sylvia snapped. "What will end it?"

"Arthur could never think of marrying her if he were to find her in Ashton's bed—see it with his own two eyes. Sister, you were right about finding a use for Reynard Boulton this week. We can arrange for him to be in on the 'discovery' and in two days it will be all over London." His words came fast and hard. "That insolent chit will be finished in society. By the time we're done with her, she won't be able to get an invitation from a pox-riddled sailor!"

Red was in his element, telling stories and making terrible jokes while his audience drank liberally and collected around the piano to sing parlor songs that had traveled the Atlantic to become popular in England, too: "Beautiful Dreamer" and "Oh Promise Me." The duke had a rather nice baritone voice and blushed when complimented.

After a while, he sighed and turned to Daisy with a melancholy smile.

"I wish Ash were here. He has a brilliant voice. Used to sing me to sleep at school when I was—" He halted and forced a smile that ended the revelation. "A pity he had to return to London on urgent business."

Daisy's heart sank at the mention of Ashton. She wished he were here, too. She had no idea he sang, though now that she knew, she could almost hear it in the deep musical quality of his voice that made her want to listen endlessly.

At that moment she knew with heartbreaking certainty:

she was impossibly and irrevocably in love with Ashton Graham.

When the merriment ended and the guests drifted off to their rooms, Daisy walked through the darkening house with Arthur. In the entry hall, servants had doused lamps and trimmed wicks. Shadows settled in every corner and cast their faces in soft relief.

They walked side by side, the tension developing between them uncomfortable for Daisy. This was what it would be like, she thought, still reeling from her earlier discovery. For the rest of her life she would climb the darkened stairs at night with Arthur, dreading what would follow, thinking of Ashton and how different it would be with him.

She halted by the stairs and Arthur paused to see what had stopped her.

"I believe I'll go choose a book from the library," she said, spotting the candlesticks left on a side table for guests to use in making their way to their rooms. "After such excitement, I'm not certain I'll be able to sleep."

Arthur smiled his sweetest, most genuine smile and took her hands in his. "Shall I come and help you find one?"

"No, really." She squared her shoulders. "I'll only be a short time."

"Well, you might try *The Butterflies of Southern England*, by Stanford Jepson, PhD. It's put me to sleep a number of times."

She laughed softly, wondering if he'd meant it as a joke, and braced as he bent to kiss her. He managed to land one on her cheek, near her mouth, and seemed a bit flustered by his poor aim.

"Sweet dreams, Arthur," she said, retrieving her hands and taking up a candle to light.

He continued on up the stairs while she borrowed a flame from the candle burning on the sideboard and headed down the transverse hall, her mind and heart in turmoil. She entered the darkened library and stopped dead, staring at the shelves, stuffed chairs, and at the table where she and Arthur had gone over maps together. A presence loomed behind her, and she jumped, almost dropping her candlestick.

"Daisy." It was Ashton's deep, musical voice. He stepped into the light and steadied her hold on the candle by putting his hand around hers. His tie was missing, his hair looked windblown, and his eyes glowed like molten copper pools. She had never seen him looking more handsome. Or more serious. Her mouth went dry.

"I thought you were called to London," she said over the hammering of her heart.

"Is that what they've put about?" He seemed a bit strained. "In truth, I've been banished from the house and from the family."

"Banished? But why would you be—" She suddenly *knew,* and the guilt that knowledge brought weakened her knees. "Because of me. They're punishing you for helping me."

"Not such a huge loss." He affected a casualness that wasn't entirely convincing. "I've always felt more at home anywhere but here. I will miss Artie, however." He paused to gaze into her eyes. "And you."

She felt the weight of that settle like a boulder on her heart.

"If you're banished, what are you . . . ?"

"I came to collect my things. And to see you. I couldn't leave without letting you know. . ." He pulled her to a seat on the leather sofa near the windows and placed her candle on a nearby table. He settled beside her, took her hands in his, and took a deep breath.

"I want you to know that I want what is best for you . . . and for Arthur. He needs someone with courage and independence. Someone who can help him stand up to the family and become his own man. He has a good heart and a sound intellect. I'm sure he'll come to adore you, if he hasn't already."

"So, you're giving me your blessing?" she said, her throat tightening.

He rubbed her hands gently, tenderly.

"I am a second son." His voice was thick with unexpressed emotion. "That's all I have to give you."

"You cannot truly believe that," she said, searching the angles of his face and finding despair hiding in the shadows of each feature. "You believe your 'prospects' are all that matters to a woman? Has it never occurred to you that some women don't seek a title or fortune through marriage?"

"The only woman who matters to me . . . *does*."

She felt as if she'd been thrown from horseback—every part of her was jarred and shaken by those words. She had trouble getting her breath for a moment. He was right to think that about her; she had sworn it often enough in front of him. And she did care about it. She had to. Outside the soft candlelight and away from his resolve-melting presence, she had a goal to accomplish, a future to make for herself and her sisters. She had worked so hard and come so far, only to find that the price she would pay for success was higher than she could ever have imagined.

She looked into his eyes and reached up to cradle his cheek and then run her fingers over his lips. Her very skin ached for his touch.

He cared about her. He wanted her. And he refused to say so.

But if he said what she so desperately wanted to hear, what then? Would it change her determination? Even while making amends for her previous deeds, she remained stubborn and self-centered at heart. How selfish of her to want him to give his love, the best of his heart to her, when she was unwilling to do the same. Did she think she could wear it about her wrist like a bauble or set it on a shelf like a loving cup trophy? Would knowing he loved her satisfy some selfish, hedonistic urge within her?

Never in her life—not even on that awful day of the Bellington Hunt—had she been forced to face the flaws of her nature as she was forced to face them now. She was stripped bare under her own scrutiny and placed on the balance, weighed against the sacrifices of another's heart.

"You matter to me, too, Ashton." She picked her way through a storm of words so potent they had the power to change the course of her life. Forging on, she prayed that what she said would be the right thing. "I owe you a debt I will spend the rest of my life trying to repay. You are generous and kind and more gentlemanly than I deserved."

"I am no saint, Daisy." He glanced down at their joined hands. "I helped you only because . . . I couldn't seem not to. I couldn't betray the things I truly value, the foundations of my soul. At first all I could see was how different you and Arthur are, and I wanted to protect him." His tone changed, seeming richer, more nuanced. "Then after a while, after getting to know you, I found myself wanting to protect you, too."

She looked down, unable to bear the tenderness in his expression.

"You weren't wrong to try to protect him." She swallowed hard. "I'm not a simple little virgin. I'm stubborn and determined and independent as a hog on ice. I say what I want, I get what I need, and I ride astride . . . both horses and . . ."

She gathered courage for a moment and made herself say it.

"You see, I'm not exactly *pure*."

His hands on hers went perfectly still.

"Ah." His voice betrayed no judgment, no outrage, no emotion at all.

Chapter Twenty-Four

She looked up to find him watching her with a glint in his eyes.

"Ah?" She stiffened. "I just confessed to you the one thing that would disqualify me as the bride of a shop clerk, much less a duke—and all you can say is 'ah'?"

"It's not exactly news to me," he said, refusing to release her hands when she tried to jerk them away. "Daisy, you don't act like any tyro I've ever seen. You have to know that. You flirt with your eyes, and kiss like a goddess, and lick your lip when you're thinking pleasurable thoughts. A little hard to miss when you've been around experienced women."

"You knew that I'm not a virgin? And you let me go on and try to prove myself worthy of—why? Why didn't you say something?"

"I wasn't sure it mattered. You weren't exactly 'standard' in any other way, so why expect something as ordinary as sexual inexperience."

"It's not just inexperience; virginity means being pure and innocent."

"And terrified of a man's touch. Frantic to avoid 'the beast' in men. Told to stare at the ceiling and think of England. Sounds dreadful to me. Tedious and dull. Words, I might add, I would never associate with you."

She could scarcely believe what she was hearing.

"Then what words would you use for a girl of sixteen who thought she fell in love with a handsome wrangler and met him secretly . . . several times . . . until her mother found out, fired him, and sent him packing?"

"Headstrong," he said. "Curious. Adventuresome. Reckless."

"Not immoral? Not tainted and befouled and soiled?"

"Are we discussing women or bed linen?" He gave a short, ironic laugh, and she drew back. Seeing that he had offended her, he softened. "You're serious. You believe what you did was vile and unforgivable."

"Well, not exactly vile, but it was sinful and wrong."

"Because it turned you into a slattern who prowls the streets seeking to satisfy your base appetites in the gutters?"

"*No*," she said, emotion rising and pricking the corners of her eyes. "I'm not like that. I could never be."

"How many men have you slept with since that unforgivable episode?"

"None!" She was horrified that he might think she'd continued to pursue liaisons with men. "I've been with one man in my entire life."

"And he made you feel dirty and befouled and wicked," he pressed.

"*No.*" She scowled and made fists around handfuls of skirt. "He wasn't like that. He was sweet and gentle and did everything he could to make it good. But the aftermath —the fury, the humiliation—was so terrible, I've never been tempted to repeat it."

"Never?" He canted his head to look at her with that sultry, kiss-me-senseless stare, challenging that little white lie.

"I thought I had put away all of those longings and forgotten those feelings. Lots of people—doctors and preachers and even my own ma say women aren't supposed to have feelings like that. That women who do are wicked and immoral—sinners from the start." She couldn't meet his gaze anymore.

"And you believe them?" He sounded saddened by the possibility.

"I don't know what to believe. I mean the good Lord made us male and female, right? And we're supposed to marry and live together and have babies. Why make it plea-surable if we're not supposed to feel it? But then, I have those desires, those urges—maybe my thinking is muddled and sinful, too." She took a heavy breath and freed her hands from his.

"That is all history now, and it helped to make you the passionate and caring woman you are today." He turned her chin so she would look at him. "All that matters to me is that you are honorable and steadfast with Arthur. Promise me that . . ." He paused a moment, looking into her eyes, making that soul-penetrating connection that was coming to mean more to her than any physical pleasure. It was a knowing and being known, a belonging and acceptance, a commitment to caring.

Love; it was love.

She felt like she was crumbling inside—being demol-ished—then slowly, painfully reassembled into a different and not-yet-complete form. She was becoming something new, growing, changing . . . like one of Arthur's caterpillars transforming into a butterfly. She prayed she would be something better, finer than what she had been. And she understood now that her time with Ashton, their talks, their loving, their honesty with each other, was responsible for those changes. He was the one her heart had chosen. And she could feel in her depths that he felt the same about her.

"Promise me that you will be true to him," he said. "Promise me that when he seems tiresome and provincial and makes you want to pull your hair out with his rants about hugs and beasts—you'll remember he is more than that, and understand that he can be more still."

She rose and stood looking at him, barely able to get her breath. He rose, too, and stood before her, his heart in his eyes.

"Promise me, sweet Daisy, that when a handsome man pays you compliments and sweeps you across a dance floor, you will remember the earnestness of Arthur's heart and the steadfastness of yours. That you will not give in to the temptation coursing through your veins and burning in your loins. That you will not let your passions rule you and betray Arthur. I could not bear to think of either of you disgraced or in despair."

She stared at him, her love pouring through her eyes, speaking without words the truth she had just discovered.

"There is only one man who could ever tempt me away from Arthur."

She held her breath as tension charged the air between them.

Now. It was now or never. He had to confess his love—take her into his arms and heart. He had to ask her to be his instead, to marry him and cast her lot with his on the sea of Fate.

She saw the light dim in his eyes, but continued to hope. Please . . . please . . .

His shoulders sagged and he took a step back. Then another. Every inch he put between them tore a bit more of her heart.

He wouldn't say it.

He was ceding her to his titled brother. It was his duty.

He gave her a smile so filled with pain it was terrible to witness.

"I wish you the best, Daisy Bumgarten. I would be the first to say: Lady Marguerite, Your Grace."

Then he turned on his heel and left, taking the air in the room with him.

She gasped short breaths that didn't quite reach her lungs. It felt like she'd been dropped down a well and lay at the bottom, winded and broken. She took two steps to the sofa and collapsed, staring at the door in disbelief.

When the room became too blurry to see, she squeezed her eyes shut and forced her tears down her cheeks. Moments later, she doused the candle flame and sat in the cool gray moonlight from the window for a long time.

The countess was late rising the next morning and it was half past ten before Daisy decided to go down to breakfast alone. A number of the guests were still abed or taking trays in their chambers, and the two older gentlemen lingering over coffee and scones at a small table in the morning room were clearly dressed for walking. Their tweeds, field glasses, and notebooks marked them as birding enthusiasts. After she settled at the long table with a plate of eggs and sausage, Arthur entered dressed in similar tweeds with similar binoculars hanging around his neck.

"Daisy," he greeted her with a broad smile. "I was hoping to see you before I left." He blinked as if just struck by a thought. "I say, you wouldn't want to come with us, would you? I promised Cousin Ralph and Baron Kettering a bit of birding. I've seen some lovely songsters about the place."

"Oh. Thank you, but I think I would only slow your pace," she said, sensing the others' relief at her refusal.

"Very well. But I would love another riding lesson later."

"That would be wonderful," she said, sipping her coffee.

Moments later, the old gents trundled out the door behind Arthur and she found herself alone. It was a mercy, really. She hadn't slept well and feared the strain and puffiness around her eyes would tell on her. As she poured a second cup at the sideboard, Reynard Boulton lurched through the doorway, banging against the frame and planting himself just inside the room. He winced at the sunlight streaming in the long windows, rubbing his eyes with his knuckles. They were as red as sunset.

"Coffee," he rasped out, looking like a sheet just come out of the wringer. "If there's an ounce of mercy in you—"

She poured him the last in the silver pot and added milk and sugar as he staggered to the table holding his head. "Here. Sit."

He sank stiffly onto a chair. "You are a goddess, Miss Bumgarten."

"Not exactly, Mr. Boulton." She smiled as she carried her own cup back to the table and resumed her place, across from him. "But I do have sympathy for a drink-swollen head. I've dealt with Uncle Red's for years."

"You can tell a lot about a woman's character by how she treats a morning-after," he said, gulping the coffee with his eyes closed. "Jesus, I'm wrecked." He cracked his eyes open enough to glance around. "How did I get back here?" He wrapped both hands around the cup, greedily absorbing its warmth. "The last thing I knew, I was with Ash at the Iron Penny."

"The Iron Penny?" she asked, trying not to sound too interested.

"A local establishment," He buried his nose in the cup again. "Coaching inn at the edge of Betancourt. More tavern than way station these days. We went there to—" He halted and looked at her quizzically. "To have a few drinks. Ash seemed determined to drain a barrel or two and break any nose that got in his way. Mad as a wet cat over something."

"Did he say what?" Daisy asked, trying to sound casually interested.

"Not really. More of a sullen bastard when he's drinking."

He looked past her to the sideboard. "Could you be an angel and serve me up some eggs if they're still warm?"

She narrowed her eyes. He widened his, imploring.

With a growl, she rose and soon assembled a plate of eggs and cold ham. She rang for another pot of coffee and some hot scones, then came back to set the plate in front of him.

"My undying gratitude," he said with a sigh, and tucked into the food like a starving man. "I got the impression he was angry at the family for some reason or other."

"Not surprising," she said, wishing she could say how she truly felt. "They're not the nicest people. Except Arthur. He's dear and a little too accommodating to the old—his relatives."

Reynard looked like his head was banging like an anvil, and from the way he gripped his stomach he was in misery there as well. But his nose for gossip was working famously. He studied Daisy as he chewed and slowly came more alert.

"Not a great admirer of the Meridian clan, eh?"

"Not particularly." She sat back in her chair, cradling her cup. "And I am certain they would pour water on me if I was drowning."

He laughed, then grabbed his head with a wince. "Don't make me laugh, Miss B. In my grievous state it feels like a hot poker in my head." He took two more bites of eggs and brightened as a servant entered with fresh coffee, waving the fellow over emphatically. She could have sworn tears welled in his eyes at the sight of the scones and strawberry preserves.

A scone and several gulps of coffee later, he managed to focus on her again. "Don't take it hard that the Meridian elders aren't your greatest admirers. They don't like anybody. Not even themselves. God knows, most of the county hates their guts."

"They do? Why?"

"They've sold off every marketable commodity—sucked the wealth out of the farms, and when the tenants can't pay their rent they evict them. They quit buying from the local free-holders, and when the farmers became destitute they snatched up land that's been in families for generations."

"They're frantic to keep the place running," she said with a quick glance around the room, noting the fading drapes and yellowed paint.

"That"—he chewed thoughtfully—"or they're tucking away the money elsewhere." He traced the path of her gaze around the room with his own. "Doesn't look like they spent it here. God knows they've had Ashton on low rations for years. He's perpetually skinned."

"He doesn't have funds of his own?"

"Just what he wins at the tables. And the occasional boon from a friend. He lives in a house in Mayfair with a few other scapegraces at the largesse of the Marquis of Kirkland . . . who now resides with his wealthy wife in France."

"How do you know all of this?"

"I make it my business to know things."

"So I've heard." She finished her coffee. "And the duke knows nothing of this?"

"Artie? I doubt it. He's been otherwise occupied for years. They've seen to that."

"They've . . ." She halted, recalling the uncles' behavior in the study. It was worse than she thought. Heaven help him, Arthur was slowly waking up to the way things were being manipulated around him. But did he have the steel to set things right and take charge of Betancourt?

"I'm sure His Grace will find a way to sort it out," she said, dodging the Fox's all-seeing gaze.

"He might," Reynard said, returning to his food. The man did love to eat. "If he finds the right wife."

She glanced up to find him watching her with one eyebrow up. She was not about to respond to that.

"If you'll excuse me, I must check on the countess. She's late coming down this morning."

The Fox watched her go and smiled, despite the discomfort it caused. Miss Bumgarten was quite a package—bright, unconventional, levelheaded, and utterly bed worthy. He might consider making a run at her himself if he wasn't so sure she had already set her cap for the duke. Hard to compete with a duke in the marriage market.

Minutes later Daisy paced the countess's bedchamber, waiting for her to emerge from behind the screen where she soaked in a tub of rose-scented water. Elaborate bathing marked a major change in the countess's ordinarily utilitarian routine and Daisy might have been concerned if she wasn't already occupied with worries on three major fronts: Ashton, Arthur, and the double-dealing Meridians.

"Well, that explains the rumors of the duke's failing finances," the countess called from behind the screen. "Reynard Boulton probably started them himself."

"Perhaps. But they seem to be true. I mean, the house needs a lot of care and the whole estate seems oddly empty. The people who came out to see us on that first day seemed surprised to find there was still a duke."

"Hmmm." The countess sounded distracted. "Well, you still have a few days. Perhaps now you can get on with nudging His Grace to the altar."

Chapter Twenty-Five

"Nudging" was hardly the term for what she needed to do, Daisy realized as she watched Arthur arguing bird identification with Cousin Ralph and Baron Kettering. She needed to lasso him and tie him to a danged post to get him to pay attention to her.

Determination being her long suit, she succeeded in capturing his notice by the end of the day. They had ridden out on the estate and she asked innocent questions about the empty cottages they encountered and the families that had been forced to abandon them. The fields that were planted, on closer inspection, were ill-tended and full of weeds. He grew increasingly somber as the true state of Betancourt's lands became clear, and what was meant to be a pleasant outing became yet another reason for guilt over his inattention to his duties.

She hauled him to a stop by the stream that ran through Betancourt and insisted he dismount with her. There she faced him and told him about the rumors regarding Betancourt and his family.

"I don't know how much of it is true, but from what we've seen today, at least part of it is based in fact. Your uncles have kept things from you and I don't think it was because they have your best interest at heart. But that is something you'll have to decide. And when you do, I'll be there to help."

She reached for his hands and held them, feeling a surge of protectiveness toward him. She understood now how Ashton felt toward him and added that to the pile of reasons he had decided to bow out and wish her well as his brother's bride. When Arthur bent to give her a brief kiss on the lips, she tried hard to enjoy it.

Dinner was late and not especially memorable, except for Arthur's insistence that Daisy be seated beside him and that they both have seats at the head of the table beside Bertram. The old man seemed distressed to have his nephew so close at hand and outraged to have to suffer Daisy's presence and conversation throughout the meal. She caught the dark looks he shared with Seward and the disgust in Lady Sylvia's prune face.

There were readings in the grand parlor that night, mostly philosophers and political broadsides full of grand condemnations, meaningless claims, and proposals to cure all of Britain's ills with a return to "the old ways." Daisy groaned silently and could have sworn the countess rolled her eyes, but Arthur seemed to listen attentively to every word. Eventually they got around to some poetry from the library shelves and a couple of the verses brought forth chuckles from the aged guests. Reynard Boulton had the bad manners to snore through most of it, and when the lamps dimmed and guests retired, they left him there, sound asleep, propped on the wing of his chair.

Arthur escorted Daisy up the steps and paused at the top to smile at her and clasp her hands warmly.

"You made this evening bearable, Daisy. I would have you know, I am grateful for your presence and your caring nature." He bent to kiss her and she offered her mouth for a chaste meeting. She did not expect him to put his arms around her in an awkward embrace, but both it and the kiss were soon over. She smiled as he turned and strode down the hall to his room with an extra bounce in his step.

She was making progress.

When she opened the door to her room Collette was sitting in the stuffed wing chair by the cold hearth, head drooping. Daisy cleared her throat and the maid started awake and looked around.

"Oh, miss." She jumped up and swiped at her heavy eyes. "I'm sorry. I was waiting up to help ye, and give ye this." She brought a note to Daisy and then hurried to pour water into the basin for her mistress's toilette.

"Where did this come from?" Daisy asked as she opened the note and turned up the table lamp to read by.

"It was slipped under the door when I come up from dinner. I didn't dare open it."

The writing was not especially familiar, but her heart skipped beats when she saw it was signed "Ashton."

Daisy, I must see you, it read. *Come to the Iron Penny tonight at midnight. Yours forever, in all things, Ashton.*

She was stunned. He was staying at that inn at the edge of the estate, and the summons sounded urgent. Her breath came fast and her heart began to pound. Hers forever. In all things. He'd changed his mind!

It was all she could do to go through the motions of preparing for bed while planning how she might slip out of the house and make it to the Iron Penny undetected. There was such excitement thrumming in her blood, such anticipation in her skin, that she was unable to think of anything but him.

In her darkened room, listening for the hall clock's half-hour chime, she imagined his beautifully carved face, his strong shoulders and wicked grin. That was what she wanted. She wanted to wake up every morning next to that angelically handsome face and to go to bed every night with those devilish, strip-me-naked eyes. She wanted to go back to Nevada and make a home and a family with him . . . make a life for them both in a place where opportunity knew no bounds. For the moment, all thoughts of duty and sacrifice had fled in the face of the possibility of loving and having Ashton as her partner in life.

The clock struck half past eleven at last, and she threw the covers back.

She never really wanted to be a duchess, anyway.

Hair down, dressed in her split riding skirt, dark jacket, and riding boots, Daisy slipped from the house to the stable and found Dancer awake and more than ready for action. In ten minutes she had him saddled and was walking him out to the drive where she would mount. "Out along the road," Boulton had said, "at the edge of Betancourt." It couldn't be hard to find.

Seward sat in his darkened window facing the front of the house, watching her mount and give her horse a heel. With a smile he turned away and collected his hat and gloves. Moments later he was knocking quietly on his brother Bertram's door. Bertram answered blinking sleep from his eyes.

"She took the bait," Seward said, slapping his thigh with his leather gloves. "She left on her horse minutes ago."

"Excellent," Bertram said, rubbing his face with his hands. "We'll give them a few minutes to . . . get into it. Then we'll take off like the avengers of righteousness we are." He smirked. "Oh, and go find Boulton. He was last seen in the drawing room, snoring like a bloated hog. He may need time to collect himself, and we want him in top form to witness this outrage."

Seward nodded and struck off to find the Fox.

* * *

There was a half-moon to light the road and Dancer was eager to stretch his legs. In less than a quarter hour they approached a collection of modest stone and brick buildings that she knew from asking the servants was the village of Betany. Prominent by the road was a two-story building with windows glowing dimly on the bottom front. There were no people abroad in the village, and only the sound of Dancer's hooves on the ground and an occasional cricket or barking dog broke the deep silence. As she dismounted and tied Dancer to the post ring, she saw one of the windows go dark and rushed to the door.

A tug on the handle and then pounding with the side of her fist yielded a hoarse male voice from inside saying they were closed. She leaned to the gap in the frame.

"Please open up. It's important! I have to speak to one of your guests."

It took another minute before the man replied, "Hold yer britches."

The door swung open partway and the balding, grizzled fellow behind it scowled at her and looked around to see if she was accompanied.

"I've come to see Ashton Graham. I believe he is staying here."

"Nobody here by that name," the innkeeper said gruffly. "I run a respectable place, young woman. Now be gone." He started to close the door but she set her weight against it and kept it open.

"But, I need to see him. It's urgent. He sent me a note asking me to meet him here." She fished in her skirt pocket for the note and held it up.

"Sorry. Come back tomorrow!" he said aloud, then under his breath, whispered: "The back entrance. Bring yer horse around there."

She did as she was told, untied Dancer and led him around the rear of the inn, where the innkeeper quickly directed her to tie her horse in a shed beside the building. She hurried behind him into the back door and through a darkened kitchen, and into a tavern with a large fireplace and several tables holding the remains of the evening's consumption. He pointed to the stairs and said it would be the second room on the right.

She mounted the steps, heart pounding, feeling like she had climbed mountains to make it this far. She paused outside the door, bracing, running a hand through her wind-tousled hair. She was trembling at the prospect of seeing him.

She knocked softly, then again, and was soon rewarded by light coming from underneath the door. She could hear him moving about, possibly dressing. She smiled, thinking she should tell him not to bother.

Then the key turned in the latch and the door swung open.

Her heart stopped at the sight of him standing here with his shirt unbuttoned, his trousers half open, and his hair mussed from sleep. There was a faint odor of whiskey about him, but his eyes were clear and focused the instant his gaze struck her.

"What are you—" Ashton pulled her into his room and, after looking around the hall to be sure no one had seen her, closed the door and latched it.

When he turned, his knees weakened. Her hair was loose and tousled and inviting, and she was chewing her bottom lip the very way he wanted to. Her eyes glowed like a clear summer sky. Her jacket and blouse were unbuttoned at the neck—riding clothes, cut close to her curvy frame and carrying the stirring scents of horse and leather. He wasn't entirely sure she hadn't just stepped out of the erotic dream he'd just begun to enjoy.

"I got your note," she said, tension in her lovely face. "Here I am."

"Oh, God, Daisy." He groaned, his resolve melting. "I've told you I'm no saint. Please don't make me prove it."

"I don't care about what you're not, I care about what you *are*. I'm here because I'm crazy about you. I can barely sleep at night, thinking about you, remembering your kisses and the feel of you against me. I want more, Ashton Graham. I want all of you. And I know you want me."

Two steps were all it took and he had her in his arms, molding against him, taking away his power of speech and leaving him raw with longing that was as much pain as pleasure. He raised her chin and kissed those lips that had tortured his sleep and haunted his waking moments. She responded as if she were a part of his own body, with perfect intuition for what would satisfy him. When he lifted his head and focused on her face, she was smiling and saying something that took a moment to register in his head.

"Forever, you said. I'm here to make you honor that promise."

"Forever?" He blinked and gave his wits a quick throttle. "When did I say that?"

She prompted his memory with a seductive squeeze. "In your note. When you asked me to come to you."

"Wait—" He loosened his hold on her. "I didn't send you a note."

"You did." She pulled back to delve into her pocket and produce it.

He released her and opened the note, reading it with mounting dismay. "I didn't write this. This isn't my hand. My writing is smaller—with large capitals." He faced her. "How did you get this?"

"Collette said it was slipped under my door during dinner."

Something was happening, something very wrong.

"I'm sorry, sweetheart," he said, his voice constricted. "It seems like someone else wanted you to come here . . . to see me." His eyes flew wide as the implications slammed through him. Someone else. Someone who wanted them to be found together in an inn in the middle of the night. Someone who wanted to be sure Daisy would be there with—

"Damn them!" He stalked away, shoulders bunched, anger racing through him like a brush fire. "Damn their vicious, conniving souls to Hell!"

Daisy paled, her blue eyes washing gray with disbelief.

"Damn their black hearts. To do this to me is one thing, but to do this to you—to Arthur—" He grabbed her by the arm and hauled her to the door. "Come with me."

"Where? What are you doing? What's happened?"

"They'll be here shortly."

"Who? What are you talking about?"

"You'll see."

He led her down the steps and to the tavern, where the innkeeper and his boy were just clearing away the last evidence of the night's trade.

"We're about to have company, Bascom," Ashton told the innkeeper, while directing her to a table near the cold hearth.

"But we're closed," the fellow said, wiping his hands on his apron.

"Just unlock the door and stand by to witness. It will be over soon enough. Oh, and would your wife have any pins for the lady's hair?"

Daisy protested, but Ashton insisted she put up her hair, at least in a simple way. While she worked at that, he disappeared to his room for a few moments, donned a tie and jacket, and returned looking presentable.

She had managed to put her hair up and tuck it properly. He paused to look at her anxious face and felt a pull of pure longing that gave him second thoughts about the course he had chosen. She had spent years doing penance for her youthful passions and deserved so much more than the bargain she would enter into by marrying his brother. But, she had crossed an ocean and spent a small fortune to remake herself into someone acceptable in society. No matter what she might profess in the heat of a moment, she would never be truly happy or at peace if she abandoned her quest now.

The least he could do was protect her against their foul manipulations and allow her to make the marriage she wanted.

"You look quite ladylike," he said, approaching her, "except for this." He fastened the single undone button at her throat and then her jacket over it. The action felt intimate and bittersweet. "Now there can be no question."

"What now?" she asked in a small voice that didn't seem to fit her.

He squeezed her hand for reassurance before settling into a chair.

"Now we wait."

Chapter Twenty-Six

They heard the horses coming and soon a mix of voices in front of the inn. Daisy's heart fluttered like a caged bird in her chest. Someone intended to catch her here with Ashton, someone who knew he had defended her to the family elders and who was determined to disgrace them both.

Innkeeper Bascom hauled out his long gun and laid it on top of the bar, just in case, and Ashton nodded to him and pulled back his coat on one side to reveal a revolver tucked in a holster at his waist.

"Ashton," she gasped, "you can't—they're your family!"

They pounded on the door, demanding admittance, until someone tried the door and, finding it unlocked, thrust it open. It swung freely and banged back against a boot boy's stool by the wall.

In surged Bertram and Seward at the head of a pack that included a uniformed constable, who stepped inside and moved away from the group, his hand on his truncheon. Behind the old uncles came Arthur, Reynard Boulton, and the Baron Kettering, who had a hold on Arthur's arm. For a second, the intruders stared, confused, clearly not expecting to find their victims sitting respectably in the keeping room of the inn.

"There they are—just as reported." Bertram forged ahead, pointing at her and then Ashton. "She's come here for an assignation—foul harlot that she is—with His Grace's own brother!"

"You see, Arthur?" Seward stepped behind Bertram's shoulder, as always, needing his bluster for support. "Just as we said. She's faithless and immoral—a slattern who would deceive you with your own despicable kin."

"Good evening, Uncles, Arthur," Ashton said with defiant calm. "Oh, and you've brought the Fox with you, I see. Good evening, Reynard. And the good Baron Kettering, always a family accomplice. But I am puzzled by the constable. Did you think there would be some reason to—"

"He's here to close down this vile establishment where adulterers and fornicators are permitted to meet—making it a house of ill-repute." Bertram looked to the constable, who suddenly seemed less certain of his role here.

"How many times have you met him here?" Seward aimed at Daisy.

"There is no adultery going on here, nor has there ever been," Ashton said, waving to the innkeeper behind the bar. "As Mr. Bascom will attest, Miss Bumgarten arrived minutes ago, answering a summons from me."

"You see, he admits he invited her!"

"*Ostensibly* from me." Ashton rose, fists clenched. "I sent no such note."

Daisy watched in horror as history repeated itself . . . on a more devastating scale. She was caught again, accused again, shamed to the bottom of her soul. Her face flamed and she shrank within herself. What had she done to deserve such humiliation? Was she so wicked that her affections and longings now counted as sin?

"A likely story . . . You would have one concocted to

cover your misdeeds," Kettering put in, looking to Bertram, who seemed desperate to get on with it.

"Do your duty, Constable," he snapped. "Arrest them both!"

"Don't move," Ashton countered, slipping back his coat to reveal his gun. "Not until you've heard the whole story. The note that was sent was not my handwriting. See for yourself." He thrust the note toward the constable, who opened it, looked, and shook his head helplessly. Arthur wrenched free of Kettering's grip and shoved past his uncles to grab the note before Seward could.

He read it and looked up at Daisy and Ashton. Mercifully, there was no accusation in his face. Daisy's heart stopped for a moment.

"This is not Ash's hand." He sought out confirmation. "Look for yourself, Reynard. You were at school together, you would know."

The Fox pushed forward to take the note from Arthur and developed a wry half smile. Daisy thought she would expire before he announced slyly: "Definitely not Ash's writing. His has never been this legible."

Arthur snatched it back and glared at the script. "With an alteration or two, it could be Aunt Sylvia's." He looked up at Bertram with recognition dawning. "It is hers, isn't it? She sent this to Daisy."

"You're not sensible, Arthur." Bertram bulled his way over to his nephew, only to have Ashton meet him there with a look daring him to use the fists that were now clenched at his sides. "You've never had the judgment God gave an onion," Bertram snarled at Arthur, "and you're clearly over-wrought. She's worked her wicked charms on you and you're not rational. Look at her." He pointed at Daisy. "That harlot has lain with your brother and you still listen to her lies!"

"No!" Ashton thundered. "She has never dishonored

herself in such a way—nor dishonored Arthur." He turned to his brother. "She has nothing but the highest regard and concern for you."

"She's a whore!" Seward shouted, trembling. "How can you think of letting a whore into the bed where your mother gave birth to you?"

"There is already a whore in it," Ashton roared. "Sylvia could barely wait for our mother to die to claim her place at Betancourt. She moved into her chambers the very next day! Ask Edgar if you don't believe me. She and our uncles have schemed and lied and stolen from us our entire lives. Now that they see that their treachery is about to be uncovered, they set up this trap to disgrace Daisy and keep you under their control."

"Lies!" Bertram growled. "Foul lies from a proven adulterer who betrayed his own brother!"

"No!" Daisy found her voice, and stepped around the table to defend herself. "I am not an adulterer and neither is Ashton." She looked to Arthur, wounded by the pain in his face. "I am so sorry, Arthur. I knew they hated me, but I never imagined they would go to such lengths and drag you into such a foul scene." She swallowed hard and lifted her head. "I may not be what they wanted for your wife, but I met the test they set before me honorably. And I hoped that someday—"

"What test?" Arthur asked, glancing at Seward and Bertram.

"She lies! Don't listen, boy." Bertram seized Arthur by the arm.

Ashton moved to defend his brother, but Arthur stuck out an arm to hold him back. "No!" It was meant for both Ashton and his uncles, his voice deep and resonant with emotions he had never before expressed. When his uncle tried to pull him away, Arthur yanked his arm free and glared at him with outright fury.

"You think I can't see what is going on?" His chest heaved and his hands clenched. "You think I am so ignorant and isolated I know nothing of the world?" He looked to Daisy. "You might have been right before *she* came into my life. But my eyes have been opened, and I've seen for myself the scheming and malfeasance that have surrounded me for years. I might have forgiven your negligence . . . but now I see just how wicked and manipulative you are—to accuse and berate a young woman whose only crime is to desire a marriage with me."

Daisy gasped.

"Well, here is my answer to your treachery. I intend to marry Daisy Bumgarten and there is nothing you can do to stop me. Far from being the vile things you have called her, she is a woman of worth and decency." He looked to Daisy, who swayed and grappled for balance like her world was turning upside down. When he turned back, he was cooler, but no less angry. Determination had taken hold. For the first time in his life, Arthur felt the power he'd been born to wield.

"The lot of you will be out of Betancourt, by this time tomorrow. Do you hear?" He stalked forward making Bertram retreat with each step he took. "You're banished from Betancourt and will take nothing with you but the clothes on your backs. Every document, every sale or purchase of land, every foreclosure that turned tenants out will be examined by me and held in evidence against any claim you make of entitlement to compensation."

"You can't do this!" Seward declared, then grabbed Bertram by the arm. "He can't do this, can he?"

"Oh, I can. And I will. Betancourt is mine. The title and all of its holdings are *mine*," Arthur said, clipping each word. "I will no longer suffer your slights, dismissals, and insults. You and Seward are banished. Aunt Sylvia will be allowed to live out her days in one of the many empty cottages on the estate—cottages that you emptied of tenants and workers."

"You sniveling ingrate!" Bertram snarled. "You're nothing without us. We took care of you when you were a boy—we *raised* you—"

"I believe you have already taken your reward for that, in the form of a living that has beggared Betancourt." Arthur turned to the constable. "Please see them to the nearest station, Constable, and put them on a train bound for London. I'm sure they have forged connections there who will take them in."

Daisy's knees gave way and she sank into her chair with a plop.

"You forget—Boulton is here," Bertram said as the constable began to push him and Seward to the door. "He will let everyone know how infamously you've mistreated us. We'll see you pilloried in the London press for your crimes against us!"

"Who, me?" Reynard said as Bertram was shoved past him. He folded his arms and leaned against the door frame. "I haven't seen a thing. Just out for an evening stroll and maybe a drink at the local watering hole."

"Evil, backstabbing bastard—you're in it together, the lot of you—"

The constable had his truncheon out and seemed keen to use it to force the arrogant masters of Betancourt down the road on foot. Their curses faded into sputters and moans as the full horror of their banishment took hold.

"This is outrageous!" Baron Kettering declared, shaking a fist. "I won't stand by and see my oldest, dearest friends treated with such cruelty."

With an icy smile Ashton stepped between the baron and Arthur.

"If you feel that strongly, you're welcome to go after them, Baron, and offer them a place in your household," he said, challenging the baron to pay for his outrage with charity.

Kettering huffed and stammered, then pivoted on his heel and barged past Reynard and out the door. In short order he was mounted and giving his horse the spur—away from Bertram and Seward.

Reynard's laugh broke the silence as he clamped an arm on Ashton's shoulder. "Well done, old boy. Thought you were done for, at first." He turned to Arthur, but the duke was already moving toward Daisy.

Daisy watched in disbelief as Arthur knelt before her on one knee and took her icy hands in his.

"Daisy, my dear Daisy. I know I'm not the most aware of fellows or I'd have seen it earlier. It took something as dire and terrible as this to make me see what was before my face all along. I respect you and like you very much. I could not ask for a better or more capable wife and partner. I know this is hardly the time and you're probably in no state to answer—but, I have a feeling you are probably better prepared for this than I have been. You always seem to know more about what is happening than I do." He shifted on his knee, gripped her hand tighter, and swallowed hard.

"Daisy, say you will marry me and be my duchess—be my confidante and sounding board—my smarter, wiser half. Marry me and help me be a proper and worthy duke." He suddenly remembered: "And a husband."

It was not exactly the proposal girls dreamed of; no declarations of undying love, no promises of joy and bliss, not even a mention of making a family or growing old together. It was purely and truly Arthur.

His earnestness tugged at her heart and pricked her eyes.

This was what she had wanted and worked for two long years to achieve. It was a victory over huge odds, a restoration of her self-respect . . . the start of her family's redemption. Why did she feel so damned miserable?

She only had to look up to see the reason.

Over Arthur's shoulder she saw Ashton watching with his heart in his eyes. Their gazes met. She felt the pull of longing, of need, of a connection she had never felt with anyone else.

Then he turned his back, leaned heavily on the bar, and demanded that Bascom pour him some Irish.

She blinked to release tears down her cheeks and clear her vision.

With her heart breaking, she managed a smile.

"Yes, Arthur. I'll be happy to marry you."

She and Arthur rose together and he embraced her and held her for a moment. It was almost more than she could bear. She grabbed his coat, overcome, tears flowing. After a time, he turned her toward the door and led her out into the warm night.

Bascom watched Reynard stroll to the bar beside Ashton and scowled.

"I guess you'll be wantin' a gob full, too."

"What a perceptive fellow you are," Reynard said with a sardonic smile. He clapped Ashton on the back and tossed back the draught of whiskey as soon as it landed before him. Wincing as the liquor burned its way down his throat, he dragged a breath to cool if off and then fixed a look on Ashton.

"He's a twit, you know. Your brother. Any fool could see you and the Silver Girl are madly in love with each other."

"Reynard!" Ashton snarled, grabbing the Fox by the shirt.

Reynard just smiled. "Save your threats, old boy. I'm not cruel enough or stupid enough to try to ruin the lady's future. I just thought you should know that not everyone is as blind as good old Arthur."

Ashton had the grace to release him and smooth the front of his shirt before turning back to his drink. Three morose draughts of Irish later, Ashton turned and stumbled up the stairs to his room, leaving Reynard in the sole company of poor, sleep-deprived Bascom.

"I am usually a right bastard about these things. Don't know what the hell's got into me lately." Reynard lifted his glass, holding it to the light, considering his odd behavior. "Think I might be in love with her, too?"

Bascom's snort was reply enough.

"Yeah, I didn't think so, either."

Chapter Twenty-Seven

Daisy drank the sleeping powders the countess produced for her as she was tucked into bed, and she prayed it would work. Heaven was apparently closed for the night; it didn't. She had to pretend to fall asleep so the countess—who was roused in the dead of night to tend her traumatized protégée—would leave her.

She was going to marry a duke. Arthur chose the middle of the greatest disgrace of her life to assert himself as a man and propose to her on bended knee. Out of shock, despair, and utter gratitude, she had accepted.

Dear God, what had she done?

The desolate look Ashton gave her as he watched Arthur kneel and ask her to marry him was now all she could see. It cut her afresh, each time she closed her eyes and saw him withdraw and cede his love for her to his titled brother and her wretched ambition. She stumbled from her bed to pace her darkened chamber. Maybe the countess's medicine was having an effect after all . . . because her wits were running in a circle . . . scolding over and over that she was marrying the wrong danged man.

* * *

The next morning chaos reigned at Betancourt. The young duke had gone off the rails, the servants whispered. He used to be quiet and turned inward; now he invaded Lady Sylvia's and his two uncles' chambers with servants to pull things out of drawers and empty wardrobes! Heedless of the shock rippling through the household, Arthur ordered Sylvia's maid to pack her things and went toe to toe with the old girl herself, announcing her change of lodgings and assigning servants to carry her things—including the furnishings she claimed were hers by right—down to the hay wagons drawn up to the front doors. None of the staff were grieved to see the old girl go, though some were eager enough to see her depart with their own eyes.

Lady Evelyn and Daisy watched from Daisy's bedchamber window as the second wagon bearing Sylvia's things trundled off toward her new home. The countess allowed Daisy to move from bed to chaise, but refused to leave her side, insisting she rest, stay tucked in suffocating blankets, and drink smelly teas she emptied into an unused chamber pot the minute Lady Evelyn's back was turned.

Over the course of the morning Daisy gave her an account of the happenings at the inn. The countess was horrified by the treachery of the Meridian elders and genuinely surprised by the duke's valiant defense of her.

When she revealed the duke's proposal, Lady Evelyn almost fainted.

"Truly? Sweet Heaven." She blinked and fanned herself with her hands. "Tell me again—every blessed word!"

When Daisy recounted the duke's proposal a second time the countess sank, stunned, onto the chaise beside Daisy.

"You've done it, Daisy. You're to be the Duchess of Meridian. I had doubts at times, I confess." Her smile grew warm and her eyes grew wet. "But you persevered and you won the day." She seized Daisy's hands. "I am so proud of you."

Red was a bit more conditional in his acceptance of the news. He rose late, having slept through the night's dramatic events, and when he heard from Collette of Daisy's distress, he rushed to her room, threw open the door, and hugged her within an inch of her life.

"Good God, Daize—you about gave me a heart attack!" He released her long enough for her to take a breath. "What got into you—goin' to some damned tavern in th' dead of night? And what's this about th' old bastards findin' you there and the duke—hell, I don't care what his high-and-mighty-ness did, so long as it kept you from gettin' hurt." He pulled her against him and stroked her hair as he had when she was a little girl.

"What he did, Uncle Red, was propose," Daisy said, her throat tight.

"He did?" He set her back to search her face. "Well, I'll be jiggered. Th' boy's got more onions than I give 'im credit for." He thought for a minute. "That's what ye came for, a duke." He scowled. "You sure this is what you want, Daize? Bug-crazy Arthur for a husband?"

"Sure, Uncle Red." Her smile was as weak as her will to resist fate. "I'm happy as a pig in a summer wallow."

Red cocked his head, studying her, and his frown gradually transformed to a wry expression. "Always was a stubborn little thing." He straightened as if he'd decided and patted her blanket-smothered knee. "Hurry up and get better, girl—we got us some celebratin' to do!"

He rose and grabbed Lady Evelyn, dancing her around the room over her protests. "You did it, Evie girl. You got her a duke, after all!"

"Oh, out with you . . . you crusty old geezer," the countess said, dragging him to a halt and giving his shoulder a shove that could only be called playful.

Daisy watched with surprise as Red winked at the paragon of rectitude who had disdained his every word and action for nearly two years. "Evie girl" blushed. Was it possible Lady Evelyn—

"Now you," the countess said, tucking the blankets securely around her, "rest and regain your strength. We have so much to discuss—so many delightful things to consider." She paused at the door with an oddly wistful expression. "Planning a wedding for a duke. I never thought I'd have such a privilege."

As the door closed, Daisy groaned and dropped her head back on the pillows . . . relieved that she was finally alone and dreading the fact that her life was about to become a lot more complicated.

How complicated, she was to learn later that evening when she rose and insisted on dressing and going out to the garden for some air. She wore a simple cotton day dress and wrapped up in a thick crocheted shawl. Her hair was down and the rising breeze teased wisps around her face. Betancourt's garden was less than memorable, but just being out of doors lifted her spirits.

As she walked, she made herself remember the pain of watching Ashton turn his back on her after she had practically thrown herself at his feet earlier. Turning pain to anger and anger to determination, she forced her thoughts to settle on what would be, not what might have been. Her future husband was noble and gentle and, occasionally, even courageous. Sooner or later she would be able to take him to New York and fulfill both his dream of travel and her own of gaining entrance to New York society.

But first she had to find a way to move her stubborn passions from . . . *where they currently lay* . . . to her future husband. And there was no better time to begin than now. She marched back into the house to find Arthur.

Servants had been hauling faded rugs, curtains, and bed drapes down the stairs all afternoon, coughing and sneezing at the dust being stirred. Unused to such vigorous work, they were now exhausted and hungry, and they grumbled that the duke didn't have to clean the house all at once. When Daisy appeared, they nodded to her and quickly went back to work. It hadn't taken long for word to spread that she would soon be their new duchess.

She paused to ask where she could find the duke, and they pointed toward the rear hall.

The sound of his voice drew her toward the study that had once been Arthur's father's. He was probably busy, but—she squared her shoulders and adopted a determined perkiness—she intended to pry Arthur away from whatever occupied him and see they had some time together.

She strode into the study, still wearing her shawl, and stopped dead at the sight of them with their heads together, studying documents spread over the great desk. Ashton looked up and straightened. Arthur noticed Ashton's distraction, looked up, and smiled.

Damn his handsome eyes.

"Daisy!" Arthur hurried around the desk, hands out to take hers. "Are you well enough to be up and about?" He pulled her to a chair, but she remained standing.

"I'm of hardy stock, Your Grace. I recover quickly."

"What time is it?" Arthur looked around for a clock, finding none. "We haven't missed dinner, have we?"

"No. We have missed tea, however," she said, acutely aware of Ashton's gaze on her. "I think everyone forgot about it—even the cook." She pulled her shawl tighter. "I just wanted to see what you're up to."

"Ash and I are going blind from searching through this legal claptrap." He gestured to the stacks of papers, maps, and folios that covered every horizontal surface in the room. "There're piles and piles of it."

Just then Mrs. Ketchum, the housekeeper, came rushing in with her face ashen. "Your Grace—it's Edgar. He's sat down and can't get up."

"I'll come with you, Your Grace," Daisy said, moving toward the door. He stepped in front of her and took her by the shoulders. She looked up, surprised. "I may be able to help."

"You're barely out of sickbed, yourself," Arthur said in paternal tones. "No, no—I'll go. Promise you'll sit and rest until I return."

He didn't seem in a mood to take no for an answer. With genuine reluctance, she sighed and sat. Once she was settled, he hurried off with Mrs. Ketchum, leaving Daisy alone with Ashton . . . the one man in the world she couldn't bear to be alone with. The man she owed undying gratitude for saving her more times than she cared to count. The silence grew prickly.

"I suppose I should thank you for what you did last night." She couldn't bring herself to meet his gaze. "I never imagined it could be a trap."

"You came," he said quietly. Her fingertips started to tingle and she squeezed them into fists. Her response betrayed both her hurt and remorse.

"I did."

There were volumes to be read between his two words and hers, but neither was willing to open that painful book again. The desperate passion that sent her rushing to a country inn in the dead of night now seemed to belong to another lifetime. The decision was made. That moment was past. She had to find a way to get along without "love." She'd done it before—survived having her heart broken. She could damned well do it again.

"What are you doing at Betancourt?" She tried to sound casual as she eyed the door.

"Artie asked me to stay a while to help sort out the mess the grisards left behind. Who knew he had it in him to give that lot the boot? God knows he put up with plenty over the years." He looked around the study, seeming ill at ease.

"It took them threatening you to make him come out of his shell."

"I hope to be useful in other ways, in days to come," she said, feeling that traitorous tingle moving to her lips.

"I'm sure you will be." He strolled farther away, stopping near the window seat that for now was filled with ledgers and documents. "There are probably thirty years' worth of records in this room alone."

"When the sorting is done and the house is back to rights, what will you do then?" Imagine the torment of having him under the same roof while she tried to fulfill her duty to give the duke an heir! She groaned silently, convicted by her thoughts. Fortunately, he wasn't looking at her.

"I'll probably go to America." He had picked up a ledger and leafed through it. "I understand the people there are quite impressed by titles."

She could feel her face flushing. "You don't have a title."

"However, I *am* entitled to be called Lord Ashton Graham. That should be enough to get me an invitation or two. After that, I'll make a way on my own. Who knows, maybe I'll find a—" He paused to clear his throat. "But there's a lot to do before that. We're not even sure the death tax from my father's passing was fully paid."

She was stuck on the thought of him wooing, wedding, and bedding some bloodless New York deb. When she looked up, he was silhouetted against the golden glow of the late day sun coming through the tall window. His dark hair was flame-kissed, his skin seemed burnished, and his eyes shimmered with heat. Her breath caught.

She stared. Suddenly hungry.

He stared. Hungrier.

Chapter Twenty-Eight

"He'll be fine." Arthur's voice jarred their gazes apart as he burst into the room. "He's just ancient and gets winded easily." He paused beside Daisy and looked from her to Ashton in dismay. "I think we're going to need a new butler."

Relieved, Daisy slipped a hand through Arthur's arm and discreetly turned him toward the door. "Actually, Your Grace, we have a butler at our London house. Quite an efficient fellow. Keeps the staff on their toes—"

"You're feeling quite well?" Arthur asked as they reached the garden and he steered her to a bench overlooking the recently ravaged duck pond.

"I am." As she was seated, she looked up with a smile that was so sweet he postponed the questions on the tip of his tongue to enjoy it for a moment. "I want to tell you, Arthur, I will be forever grateful to you for what you said and did that night. You defended me against your uncles— you were courageous—heroic."

"What I was . . . was angry," he said, looking down at his clasped hands. "The last three weeks, I've learned a lot about my life and my family. I've learned who genuinely cares for me and who has used me for their own purposes." He leaned forward and propped his elbows on his knees. "And I realize now, there were things going on that I had no idea of." He glanced at her. "Daisy . . . why did you go to meet Ashton at the inn?"

"The note said—"

"I know what it said. 'Yours forever. In all things.'" He straightened and turned to her. "What did he mean? Why would he ask you to meet him in the dead of night?"

"As it turns out, he didn't," she said, looking down.

He swallowed hard. "Why would you go?"

He watched her shoulders sag and a guilty blush creep into her features, and he braced. His stomach seemed to slide lower in his middle.

"I will tell you, and I pray it won't make you think less of me—or decide I am unworthy of your trust and affection." She tugged her shawl tighter around her. "But if it does, then I will understand when you withdraw your offer of marriage to me. You see, I came to England seeking a husband. A noble husband with a title.

"My family's money is considered too new and our behavior too brash for us to be accepted socially in New York. I came to Paris to get some polish and to England to find a titled husband to help my family. I have three younger sisters whose futures depend on it."

"And you chose me?" He began to see things in a broader scope.

"There were rumors in London that you—your family—were deeply in debt and needed money. It seemed that you might be perfect for me, since I had lots of money and little else. The countess arranged an introduction."

"I had no idea," he said, thinking back to his London trip and the odd way his uncles steered him through it, insisting he attend events and meet people, most of whom seemed to be connected to some bank or brokerage and were keen to take his uncles aside for intense discussions.

"But your family got wind of my interest in you and wanted to prevent a courtship. They insisted I provide proof that I had noble blood myself, before they would consider letting us see each other. I had a short while to find proof, and they sent Ashton, as a historian, to certify that my 'proof' was genuine. That was how I came to know him.

"Truth be told, he wasn't very nice at first and made it clear he thought we would be a disastrous match. But as I searched for proof of my lineage, he came to know me and slowly changed his mind. When your uncles and aunts called me before the family council, after I arrived here, he confirmed what I had found and said there was no impediment to our courtship. Your uncles were furious—they banished him from Betancourt—which is why he moved to the inn. And when I got the note, I was sure something horrible had happened. Either that, or it was a warning of some kind."

She was silent for a moment, then looked up at him with eyes so blue and so deep that he caught his breath. She was telling the truth.

"Why didn't you tell me any of this?" he said, taking her hand and feeling the faint tremble in it.

"And admit to you that I was husband hunting?" She looked down. "That I had set my cap for you?"

"Everyone else seemed to know. Why not me?" He didn't mean it as a joke, but it did pull a small smile from her. Why was he always the last to be told things? His face heated. Because he was so blinkered and self-absorbed that he likely wouldn't have understood what it all meant, anyway.

"I wanted to know that if you married me, it was because you wanted me and not just my money. Just as you would want to know that I want you and not just your title."

"And do you?" he asked, searching her face as it came up. "Want me and not just my title?"

She straightened, looking distressed.

"You are the sweetest, kindest, most considerate man I know. You've shown courage and strength—how could I not want you?"

That was all he needed to hear. He put his arms around her and pulled her against him, holding her, feeling an odd warm spot in his chest.

"Thank you, my Daisy. For telling me. For liking me. For marrying me."

She looked up. "You mean, you still want to marry me?"

"Of course I do. You've opened the world to me . . . made me realize who I am . . . given me that courage to stand up for you and for myself." He lifted her chin to give her a sweet kiss. "You know, until I met you, I never even imagined kissing someone. I hope you'll let me know if I'm not doing it right." He watched her reaction, wondering if he'd been too frank.

"You're doing fine, Arthur." She laughed and put a hand to his cheek. "You're doing just fine."

That afternoon, Arthur penned an announcement for the *Times*, then rode into the village to meet with the vicar and arrange to publish the banns for the next three weeks. After that, they would be wed in the little church that had seen the vows of five previous dukes and numerous other Meridians.

Dinner was late that evening, accompanied by numerous apologies. The food was simple and needed more seasoning, and the head footman—Young Norton, a fellow approaching fifty—directed table service for the first time, generating more occasions for apology.

During dinner the countess and Red sparred amicably, Daisy and Arthur chatted quietly, and Ashton—annoyed by Reynard's presence and double-edged wit—drank most of his dinner. He excused himself as soon as possible and headed for the stable and a ride to the Iron Penny. Reynard chuckled at Ashton's display of temper and insisted on giving Red a trouncing over billiards after dinner.

It was a pattern that was to be repeated over the next week. During the days, Daisy and the countess hired some younger servants, visited the church where Daisy and Arthur would be married, and took stock of the house.

In the old duchess's quarters, they confronted the damage done by Sylvia's furious departure. They stared in dismay at the faded wallpaper, discolored floors where rugs had been removed, and missing furnishings and window drapes. The bones of a great tester bed remained, but had been stripped of hangings.

Something had to be done.

The countess sent for her lap desk to begin a shopping list for things the new duchess must have when she returned to Betancourt: a proper vanity, decent mirrors, a pair of matching wardrobes, a substantial mattress, a stylish and comfortable chaise, a writing table and another cedar-lined chest or two for storage in the massive closet.

Daisy didn't know whether to feel excited at the prospect of remaking quarters to suit her or to be overwhelmed at the work that lay ahead. That was before they entered the old duke's quarters—until recently the habitat of Uncle Bertram—and found it reeked of cigar smoke and a musty "old-man" smell that fouled every fabric and bit of stuffing. Furnishings were missing there, too, evidenced by pale outlines on the wooden floors.

An architect was needed, the countess declared, throwing up her hands. The whole place needed a fierce cleaning, fresh paint, and proper textiles and bathing rooms, not to mention a dozen more water closets.

Red rode out with Banks each day, inspecting the livestock—what there was of it. At dinner each night, he reported on his findings and quizzed Arthur about the history of the tenants and the estate's production.

Red disappeared for the better part of a day and night and came riding back onto Betancourt with Banks, a couple of hired hands, and a hundred head of cattle—some beef stock and some milk cows. Tenants came running from their home gardens, orchards, and empty barns to watch the return of hoof stock to the estate. At each farm they passed, Red and his men cut out a few cows and delivered them to the shocked tenants. Daisy heard what was happening and rode out with Arthur to see it for herself.

"Got to have some livestock," Red declared. "Seein' all those empty pens and pastures gave me the willies. Hey, watch this!" He produced his rope and before long had a calf in his loop. He released the animal and grinned. "Haven't lost my touch!"

In the tradition of such estates, the people bowed and curtsied to their duke to give thanks for restoring their livestock. Arthur was quick to introduce Daisy and give her and her uncle credit for such largesse. Red spoke up, terming it an early wedding gift from the future duchess's family.

Fortunately for Daisy, Ashton closeted himself in the study with Arthur during the day and made himself scarce at night. It was a relief in one way, a nagging void in another. Even as she chatted with Arthur and listened to Reynard's shocking gossip from every corner of England, she thought of Ashton and wondered what he was doing. She wished with all her heart they could draw him back into his family, give him an anchor in their caring and support. She hated the image of him walking out alone into the night, knowing it was her presence that drove him from his home.

After nearly a week of tiptoeing around Ashton, Daisy decided to take the countess's advice and travel to London to make preparations for the wedding and her reception into society as the Duchess of Meridian. There would be shopping, dressmaker appointments, more shopping, and answering the many invitations that would flood in upon news of Meridian's betrothal.

"The first thing you must do is pay a call on Lady Prudence Granville. She is an old acquaintance of mine and will arrange a tea or two to introduce you to some of the local nobs." The countess blanched in horror. "N-Nobles—I—I mean the nobility."

It was the first time Daisy had heard her use a common bit of slang. She chuckled. Uncle Red was rubbing off on her mentor.

The countess declared it must be a white wedding, after the manner of the queen's nuptials. It had become de rigueur among the moneyed and fashionable. Besides, Daisy would be stunning in pure white, the countess insisted. All eyes would be on her, as the new duchess, and she needed to make the proper impression, to demonstrate to all her virtue and sense of style. Daisy felt a little sick at that last part. Virtue? She groaned quietly and headed for the stable and a good, hard ride on Dancer to recover her priorities.

They were almost packed for London; valises, trunks, and hatboxes lined her bedchamber and the countess and Collette were taking inventory like a couple of store clerks.

"Miss Bumgarten?" Collette stood in the open window, staring at the long drive leading to Betancourt's front entry. "There's a coach coming. Fast."

A distant rumble and Collette's pointing pulled Daisy to the window to stare at the vehicle bearing down on Betancourt. As the countess came to look, Daisy saw her concern and realized they shared the same fear.

The old uncles were back!

Chapter Twenty-Nine

Daisy rushed downstairs to the library, where Arthur and Ashton were working with the family lawyer to understand the morass of family finances.

"There's a coach coming—I think it may be your uncles," she said, setting off an explosion of reaction. Together they rushed through the entry hall and ordered the front doors shut behind them.

As the coach neared they could see it was well sprung and glossy black with immaculate yellow wheels, clearly hired by someone of means. The minute it stopped, the windows were lowered and bonneted heads poked out. Daisy stopped dead on the small portico as the coach door swung open and a footman bolted forward to help a well-dressed lady descend.

"Mama?" Daisy choked on the word.

The tall, handsome, older woman shook out her skirts, smoothed her corded silk traveling ensemble, and straightened her hat before looking up. Three more familiar figures poured from the coach and stood gaping at the great house and the men who had come rushing out to meet them.

"Frankie? Claire? Sarah?" Daisy's heart thumped hard,

then lurched and pounded in her chest. "It's really you? You're really here?"

Her mother's rigid bearing melted as she hurried to Daisy with open arms. "My Marguerite—my sweet Daisy!"

Daisy stood frozen with shock until the warmth of her mother's arms melted her disbelief. She threw her arms about Elizabeth, incapable of saying more than "Mama." A moment later, they were inundated by young females, being hugged and jiggled and deafened by squeals of joy.

It took a few minutes for Daisy to extricate herself from their greedy embraces and onslaught of questions. Red came rushing out of the house, halted, and then howled with delight. He lifted and whirled his nieces about until they squealed and laughed. They had missed him as much as Daisy.

"Just look at you!" Daisy clapped her hands to her cheeks. "How you've grown, Sarah. And you, CeCe, you've blossomed—and howdy! Still playing, I hope." The auburn-haired beauty lifted the violin case in her hand. "And, Frankie—how I've missed you. I want to hear everything about everyone." She motioned the others to join their embrace and stood with her eyes closed, exulting in the rush of love and belonging between them.

When her mother joined them there was a moment of perfect silence. A discreet throat clearing caused her to come back to her senses and Daisy stepped back to look them over with pride. Three young women, dressed in dark-hued traveling silks and simple bonnets that framed their fresh faces to perfection. They were jewels, precious and beyond price.

"You look wonderful, too, Daisy," her mother declared, dabbing at her own wet eyes. "So very *ladylike*."

"And you, Mama—" She looked ten years younger than when Daisy had last seen her. "I can hardly believe you're here. How did you find us?"

"We docked at Portsmouth, took the train up to London,

and went to your house first. They told us you were in some place called Oxford, but opened rooms for us to stay. We asked after the duke and found that his name was well known. The staff had no idea when you would return, and we couldn't wait, so we decided to come and find you." She wrapped an arm around Daisy's shoulders and lowered her mouth to Daisy's ear. "Now which of these handsome gentlemen is to be my son-in-law?"

"Your Grace." Daisy held out an arm to Arthur. "I want you to meet my mother, Elizabeth Bumgarten. She's come from New York to see us."

"Arthur, Duke of Meridian. At your service." Arthur took her proffered hand and kissed it lightly while she made a stilted curtsy.

"Your Grace," Elizabeth said, her voice oddly small.

Daisy had never seen her mother at such a loss for words. Elizabeth couldn't meet his gaze, overwhelmed to find herself in the presence of true nobility. Her daughters, however, were eager to meet "Daisy's fellow" and crowded around to be introduced one by one.

Arthur reddened and was rendered speechless by their sweet curtsies and open adoration.

"And this?" Elizabeth had spotted Ashton leaning against a portico pillar with his arms crossed. The family resemblance was unmistakable.

"His Grace's brother, Lord Ashton," Daisy said, wincing at the way her sisters stared with interest at the handsomest rake in England. She was only mildly reassured when he gave them a smile of polite disinterest.

"Oh, and the countess, Lady Evelyn Hargrave, Countess of Kew . . . who has been my guide and companion through my travels and adventures."

"I owe you a great debt, Lady Evelyn," Elizabeth said. "You have been a blessing to my daughter, and through her, to our whole family."

The countess smiled and introduced Elizabeth to the continental greeting of kisses on each cheek. The younger Bumgartens were treated to the same dignified greeting and barely contained their embarrassment at not knowing how to respond.

"You must be exhausted," the countess said, then looked to Arthur. "Surely, Your Grace, there are a few guest rooms that have been freshened?"

"Bless me—of course. Daisy, you can put them in rooms near yours, so you can have time together." He looked around over their heads to locate the old butler in the doorway. "See to their baggage, please, Edgar." Opening his arms, Arthur shooed them through the doors and into Betancourt.

The Bumgarten girls gaped in amazement at the entry hall, staring at the paintings, gilt-work, and dignified old furnishings. Daisy felt an odd sense of pride in the old house. It was, after all, home to seven generations of Meridians. She led them up the stairs past portraits of long-dead dukes and duchesses, and down the hall toward her room.

The chambers closest to hers had been cleaned after their aged guests departed. She saw each of her sisters settled in and put her mother in the room next to hers. Soon they all were collected in Daisy's chamber, testing the bed and chaise, peering out the window at the view, and investigating her wardrobe and trunks and the bottles and brushes on her makeshift vanity.

"Girls, girls!" Elizabeth called them sharply from their nosiness. "Manners, please." She pulled Daisy to a seat on the chaise and ordered her sisters onto the bed and foot bench. "Now tell us—everything. How on earth did you meet the duke and manage"—she looked around and waved a hand—"all of this?"

"Duke Arthur and I were properly introduced by an acquaintance of the countess's. He was in London with his uncles. He's a naturalist and was not very sociable at first. In fact, I thought he was deadly dull when we first met. But the countess helped me set a course to get to know him better.

"We met again at the Earl of Albemarle's estate." Her sisters *ooh*-ed at the mention of another nobleman, an *earl*. "We got on wonderfully and he invited us here for a visit. His aunt and uncles weren't especially nice, and while we were here Arthur discovered they had been mismanaging his estate and drained Betancourt's accounts. There was quite a stir, during which he proposed to me, sent his vile relatives packing, and asked his brother to remain and help him set things right."

Elizabeth studied her daughter, sensing with a mother's intuition that there was more to the story. But she held her tongue and let the girls ask questions that betrayed their girlish sense of romance.

"Did he kneel when he proposed?"

"Did he give you a jewel? I thought dukes were supposed to give you a fabulous jewel when you married them."

"Did he kiss you?" Sarah giggled. "Is he a good kisser?"

"Yes—tell us about the kissing!" Frankie crowed, delighted by her mother's shock.

"And the music you hear," CeCe said with exaggerated dreaminess, "when he embraces you ever so tenderly."

Daisy grinned as she turned to her red-faced mother.

"They've been sneaking novels again, haven't they?"

The Bumgarten girls went down to dinner that night dressed in fetching dinner gowns. The colors they wore—sky blue, teal green, autumn gold—were chosen to complement hair and complexion and betrayed their mother's artistic eye. They pinned their hair up with simple elegance, all but Sarah. At fifteen she was still required to wear it down with ribbons.

Arthur, Ashton, Red, and Reynard Boulton were waiting in the grand parlor, along with the family lawyer, William Drexel, a dignified fellow with a shock of white hair and a ruddy complexion that betrayed a love of the outdoors. When the ladies entered, there was an audible intake of breath, followed by a stunned silence that was finally broken by Red.

"Damn, if you girls aren't a sight for sore eyes!" He bussed each one on the cheek with taunting pleasure. "Look at 'em. Pretty as pictures."

They were indeed. Fresh, lovely, ladylike, and filled with emerging sensuality, they were as potent a threat to bachelorhood as any man present had encountered. Only Arthur seemed to retain use of his faculties, greeting Daisy warmly and taking each offered hand with undisguised admiration. There, however, his social acumen was exhausted. Elizabeth quickly began to make rounds in the parlor, speaking to each gentleman in pleasant, gracious tones and making small talk as if she'd been born to the task of melting social ice. The countess and Red soon joined her.

By the time they went in to dinner, conversation had revived enough to permit the traditional seating of alternating lady and gentleman. To Daisy's surprise, Ashton managed to recall and insert into conversation that one of her sisters was a wonderful musician and another was something of a wizard with animals—horses especially. That left only the one who had a terrific memory and recalled absolutely everything and everyone. When he looked Daisy's way, their gazes met and she smiled at him with a softness that conveyed more than simple gratitude to any watching.

Arthur, seated at the head of the table, *was* watching. Ashton's identification of Daisy's sisters by characteristics only she would know, surprised him. It recalled to mind other looks that had passed between them.

By the time they quit the table for the parlor, the wine and laughter had warmed the company. When Daisy begged CeCe to get her violin and play for them, the others joined in requesting a performance. She went to collect her instrument while they served coffee and found seats.

Whatever they expected of a lovely young American girl, it wasn't the full, vibrant tones of a virtuoso violinist. From the moment she first dragged her bow across the strings, they were captivated. She played a piece that expressed her joy at being reunited with her older sister, then one that spoke of the beauty and desolation of her beloved home in the West. Not a muscle twitched as they absorbed the purity of the sound and the intense emotion of her playing. As they roused from the spell she had woven around them, she struck up a spritely dance that soon set their feet tapping and their hands clapping. Her music somehow compelled movement and joy.

Red jumped up and pulled the countess to her feet, leading her in a spirited country dance that delighted Daisy, Elizabeth, and the girls.

CeCe ended her performance on a more evocative note . . . playing a song of her own that was by turns simple and soulful and then wild and impassioned. It ended in a richly melodic movement that brought Daisy to the edge of her seat. She looked to Arthur, who smiled at her with delight and then looked back at CeCe. She glanced at Ashton and their eyes met. For a second time that night, feeling flowed between them. She looked away quickly, unsettled by the power of that brief exchange.

There was applause, of course, for Claire's performance. Arthur took her hand and kissed it with what could only be called reverence. But when the ladies retired for the night, the men groaned with relief and stared at each other, visibly shaken.

"God Knees, I need a drink." Reynard staggered to his feet. "Or ten."

"I know just the place," Ashton said, looking a bit unsteady himself. He turned to Arthur. "You coming?"

"Really? You want me to come?" Arthur brightened.

"Hell, yeah, son." Red clapped him on the shoulder. "After an evenin' with all my girls, a feller *needs* to get his beak wet. Why ya think I took up drinkin'?"

Chapter Thirty

The next day was filled with exploration of the estate with the Bumgarten girls, a horseback ride, and a better dinner than usual. Elizabeth took it upon herself to investigate the kitchen and made suggestions that Arthur asked Daisy to implement. The cook was relieved to find someone who understood the necessity of fresher food and a full complement of spices, and produced some surprisingly fine fare.

Lady Evelyn took it upon herself to coach the girls in the manners and customs of English society, and they practiced during tea. Arthur enjoyed giving them a "practice hand" when a gentleman was needed, but Reynard scrambled out of the way. No one was especially surprised when he announced at breakfast the second day that he had overstayed and had to leave for London immediately.

Daisy's sisters appeared at the front doors to see him off; one with a packed lunch, another with a book of poetry, and a third with a note containing several puzzles and riddles to occupy him on the journey. He acknowledged their generosity with a stiff nod, then bolted into the carriage as if the hounds of Hell were after him.

Ashton chuckled as he watched Reynard escape the threat

of respectable femininity. No one deserved the special Hell of Impenetrable Virtue more than the Fox.

That afternoon, a copy of the *Times* arrived, bearing the engagement notice of the Duke of Meridian to Miss Marguerite Bumgarten. Arthur sat in the study staring at it for a time before asking Ashton a question.

"Do you think women know if you haven't . . . um . . . you know . . . been to bed with a woman before?"

Ashton sat beside him on the window seat, considering the question.

"Some women might. If you're referring to a certain woman, I suspect it won't matter. You know, in the old days, twelve- and fourteen-year-olds were married and shoved into bed together. They managed."

"Twelve and fourteen? Really?" Arthur grimaced. "That's barbaric."

"So you would think. But some of those marriages lasted and were quite productive. Daisy's ancestress, for example. Twelve when wedded, thirteen at first childbed, and she had seventeen more children by the same fellow."

"Her ancestress? How do you know about that?"

"The old trots made her show proof of nobility in her lineage before they would let you two court. They paid me to guarantee it was genuine. I saw what she discovered, and it was real enough. She's a several-greats granddaughter of Charles the Second. On the wrong side of the blanket, of course. He didn't have children by his queen."

"So it's true, then. They really did demand she prove noble heritage."

"Oh, it's true. They were furious when I confirmed her findings. I guess she told you about it. That's why they sent the note and tried to trap us together—kill two birds with one stone." Ashton sighed. "I'm not proud of helping them. But at first I thought you and she weren't suited at all."

"You were trying to protect me. Again."

"Afraid so."

"And now? What do you think of me marrying her now?"

There wasn't the slightest hesitation in Ashton's response. "I think you'll do well together. She'll be a good wife."

Ashton patted his arm and walked out, leaving Arthur to ruminate. He had seen feeling-laden looks pass between Daisy and Ashton several times in recent days. He couldn't recall her ever looking at *him* like that. Even as a romantic novice, he knew it meant something important.

"A good wife, indeed," Arthur muttered. "But will she be mine?"

That afternoon, Elizabeth came across some papers in the bottom of her traveling case and carried them to Daisy.

"I almost forgot, I got your letter asking about our connection to the Howards and had a friend in Boston look up some records. This came the day before we left. It appears that a young woman came from England with a young daughter. It's on the ship's manifest." She pointed out the names. "Hannah Howard was the mother and Gemma Rose was the child. The girl grew up to have a child of her own, though I believe it must have been out of wedlock, because she gave the child her surname: Henry Fitzroy Howard." She sat back and handed Daisy the paper. "It turns out he was my great-great-grandfather, on the Strait side."

"She really was our ancestor? Gemma Rose?" Daisy looked stunned, then shot to her feet and headed for the door, where she paused. "You just confirmed . . . we are not only of noble lineage . . . we have *royal* blood!"

She rushed downstairs to the study where Ashton sat pouring over ledgers and waved the papers as she stopped before the desk.

"It's true! My mother had a friend in Boston go through shipping records, and they found Hannah and Gemma Rose.

Gemma grew up and had a son—out of wedlock—and gave him her last name. He was Henry Fitzroy Howard, my mother's great-great-grandfather!" She smacked the papers down on the ledger in front of him. "We were right! I am— *we are* descended from royal blood."

He shoved to his feet, gripping the letter and documents, and lurched around the desk. They bore the seals and insignia of the North Atlantic Shipping Company and the Massachusetts State Bureau of Records. The connection had been made; her ancestral trail *had* crossed the Atlantic. He grabbed Daisy's hands and began whirling her around and around.

"This is wonderful!" he declared, his face hot with excitement. "To have our suspicions confirmed, to solve a historical mystery that Broadman Huxley missed . . ."

He staggered to a stop, but didn't let her go. She knew she should break that contact, but the heat and raw pleasure of his touch was too compelling. Through recent restless nights, she had almost convinced herself that her responses to him had been embroidered by the lure of the forbidden. But now, as she stared up into his face, feeling his presence stirring her whole being to life, she knew it had been all too real. All too rare.

Then he lowered his head and—

A faint sound, a gasp or a hoarse word from the hall, made her turn her head sharply and his lips grazed her cheek.

Standing in the hall, Arthur stared at them in confusion at first, as if he didn't understand why they would be on the verge of . . . His eyes widened with hurt and disbelief mingled in them. He turned on his heel and strode down the hall, his footsteps echoing back to them.

She backed a step, then another, and then rushed into the hall.

"Arthur?" She hurried down the hall until she stood in the

entry and looked up the stairs. He was nowhere to be seen. Frantically, she raced up the stairs and summoned the courage to invade the west wing and knock on his bedroom door. With her heart pounding, she opened the door . . . to an empty room.

She stood for a moment looking at the displays of butter-flies under glass on the walls, the poster bed, and the order and simplicity of his private space. Feeling like the intruder she was, she backed out and closed the door.

She rushed down the hall, to her room, where a basin and pitcher of cold water allowed her to splash her face and try to regain her self-possession. She looked at herself in the washstand mirror and heard again her mother's harsh words—"selfish, thoughtless"—blended with the old uncles' vicious condemnations—"harlot, hussy, whore."

This couldn't happen again. She would not let this happen again. She had to find Arthur and make this right, no matter what it cost.

Arthur had done an about-face and run back down the hall. He paused by the library, but Red was there puffing a cigar while Lady Evelyn read the newspaper aloud from the window seat and waved his smoke out the open window. He tried the grand parlor, but her sisters were there, practicing dance steps and laughing while CeCe played for them.

Frustrated beyond bearing, he stormed out the main doors and stalked to the garden, where he kicked the dribbling fountain, ripped up dry stalks of flowers beyond their season, and let out a few curses he had never said aloud in his entire life. Chest heaving, he turned to the house and glimpsed the gusseted downspout he had used to climb to the roof when life inside Betancourt became unbearable.

Heedless of his suit and polished shoes, he climbed it and was soon creeping across roof peaks and valleys, avoiding places where the slate was loose or missing. The sight of so much roof needing repair was depressing, but by the time he reached the parapet overlooking the entry, the exertion had burned away much of his anger. He sat and dangled his feet over the edge of the wall, comforted by the breeze he usually encountered here and by the panorama of Betancourt laid out beneath him.

He hadn't been there long when he spotted Ashton exiting the house and heading for the stable, carrying a valise. Minutes after that, his brother reappeared on horseback and took off down the drive to the main road. He was leaving? He ought to leave, the bounder—trying to kiss Daisy—although, it hadn't looked like she was objecting, and, truthfully, that was the most hurtful part.

There was something between them . . . the way their eyes sometimes met and lingered. He had sensed it, but just hadn't wanted to face it. Now he couldn't scrub from his memory the sight of them embracing. He should be outraged, feel betrayed, furious. But mostly, he just felt empty.

It seemed like an hour later, it might have been longer, before he heard footsteps on the roof nearby and looked up to find her standing there, seeming a bit unsettled by their precarious location.

"I thought maybe I would find you here," Daisy said, taking in his dejected look and feeling utterly responsible.

"How did you get up here?"

"I remembered you said you walked the walls when you were upset. We couldn't find you anywhere else, and Edgar recalled you used to climb up the ladder from the attic onto the roof." She still had a cobweb in her hair and dust on her dress from the climb she'd made to find him. She sank onto the parapet beside him and looked around, pushing her hair back as the breeze teased it around her face. "This is quite a view. No one had used the ladder in a while." She brushed at her dusty skirt. "How did you get up here?"

"The drainpipe." He gestured over his shoulder to the rear of the house.

They sat for a few minutes in looming silence.

"He was kissing you," he finally said, frowning.

"He was. Sort of."

"No 'sort of' about it. He landed one." He pulled his legs up and rested an arm on an upraised knee. There was hurt in his eyes.

"I didn't mean for it to happen, Arthur. I thought you would both be there, as you often are. I was just sharing the documents my mother brought from New York—they show that the girl child born in Bristol was my many-greats-ago grandmother. It was the proof your family demanded and an answer to a mystery we had uncovered. I was thrilled to have it solved and he was, too. He whirled me around and we laughed and . . . he . . ."

It sounded worse the more she went on, so she stopped and bit her lip, waiting for his response. It wasn't what she expected.

"He knew all about your sisters."

"I told you I saw him several times as I was searching for proof of my lineage. I told him the truth about why I wanted a husband . . . that I needed a marriage that would help my sisters . . . that I was headstrong and selfish and felt responsible for the snubs and sneers aimed our way."

"You shared a lot with him, then," he said, looking pained by that.

"I suppose I did," she admitted, her mouth going dry. She had an awful feeling where this was heading. She said to herself as much as to him: "It seems I haven't gotten over being headstrong and selfish."

The difficult silence was ended by an even more difficult question.

"Did you and he . . . did you . . . are you lovers?"

"*No.*" She looked up in distress, unsure how or even if she could convince him of that. "I would never have done that. I didn't know you well, but I respected you enough to refuse anything that would disgrace you or myself. And Ashton is your brother. He would never do that to you."

He turned away for a moment, clearly deciding if he believed her.

"It's just . . . I've seen the way you look at each other when you think no one notices." He turned back, his gaze harder than she had ever seen it. "He wants you."

"I'm sure he's wanted a lot of women." She wasn't proud of using that to justify what happened between them.

"And you want him."

There it was. Tears welled in her eyes. It was no use pretending; he already knew the truth. What good would denying it do?

"Do you truly care for him?" he said, studying her as if she were under his microscope. "Or was he just a stepping stone for your ambition?"

The words cut her. If he saw her as ambitious and conniving, there was nothing she could do. But by damn, he would at least have the truth.

"I didn't want to like him. He was smug and clever and far too sure of himself. And he assumed way too much about me. But I began to see there was more to him than the disreputable rake everyone made him out to be. We worked together over library documents and church registers and I came to respect his mind and to understand why he wanted to keep us apart. He was honest with me about it. Just as I was honest with him about why I wanted a titled husband. I never meant to care for him."

"But you do," he said, frowning, studying her.

"I do." Tears burned down her cheeks. "I am so sorry. I never meant to hurt or disappoint you. I wanted to marry you and be a good and faithful wife to you. I hope you can find it in your heart to forgive—"

He pushed to his feet, his face set, his mind and heart now closed. He did, however, extend a hand to help her up.

"Please, Arthur, let's talk this through—"

"I think I've heard all I need to hear."

Everything felt so unreal as they negotiated the ladder and attic steps and made their way down to the upstairs hallway. He spoke not a word as he left her there, descended the main staircase, and strode out the front doors.

She made it down the east wing to her room without her family hearing or seeing her return. She sat down on the chaise, feeling drained and boneless. Her hands in her lap were white from clasping them so hard.

It was over. Now, how did she tell her mother and sisters that her fabulous marriage and their best chance at social acceptance were gone?

Chapter Thirty-One

Over dinner, which Daisy reluctantly had served despite Arthur's absence, she announced that they would all be traveling to London to shop and make preparations for the wedding. Lady Evelyn and Elizabeth both glanced at the empty chair at the head of the table, but her sisters were thrilled by the prospect. To them London was a trove of mysterious allure, riches, and adventure. Red, however, looked pained.

"Mind if I stay here with Arthur?" he asked. "A man can only take so much fittin' and sittin'. I've had enough to last three lifetimes."

Daisy smiled in spite of the twinge of panic his plea caused her. What if Arthur never came back? What if he came back with a constable to bounce them all out on their ears?

"We'll need you in London, Uncle Red. Besides"—she gave the countess a teasing grin—"who would keep Lady Evelyn in check. You know how carried away she gets in a haberdashery."

The countess seemed a bit miffed, but the girls' giggles undermined her indignation. She sighed and nodded, and it was settled. Coffee and evening music were cut short so they could retire early and begin to pack.

Dread settled over Daisy at the glint in her mother's eye as they mounted the stairs. When she gave Daisy's back a nudge and deftly stepped into her room behind her, Daisy knew she was in for it. Her mother had a nose for trouble unequaled in England's former colonies.

As soon as the door closed, Elizabeth turned on her.

"What's happened with Arthur?" she demanded.

"He had business in the—"

"I'm no fool, Daisy Bumgarten." Her voice was softer than Daisy expected. "Dukes do not conduct business in one-horse villages in the dead of night."

"First off, it's not the dead of night, and second, I don't oversee his whereabouts. He didn't say more than he was going out."

"On business," her mother prompted.

"So I assumed." She crossed her arms, feeling an anxiety that was familiar from her younger days creeping up her spine.

Her mother read her tension. "Did you quarrel?"

"What makes you think that?"

"What else could it be? Earlier today he was practically your shadow and now he is absent and doesn't bother to send word for dinner. That doesn't seem like him. Something's happened." Her mother pressed a handkerchief to her moist temples and lips and Daisy wondered fleetingly if it had smelling salts in it. "You may as well tell me. Sooner or later it will come out."

She felt herself shrinking inside, becoming sixteen again, disappointing her mother again. The same pursed mouth and "martyred" stance she saw before her had haunted her conscience for years.

"What happens between me and the duke is none of your—"

"You're my daughter, Daisy, and I've trekked halfway around the world to be with you when you marry. I have a right to know if something"—she halted, eyes widening—"or *someone* has caused . . ." She stumbled to a nearby chair and dropped into it like a wet hide. "That's it, isn't it? It's *him*."

Daisy took a step back, knowing too well what her mother meant; if she had trouble, her mother believed, there had to be a man involved. For a moment, she almost buckled, almost allowed that sixteen-year-old girl inside her to collapse under the combined weight of resurrected guilt and her mother's disapproval. But only for a moment, because in the next, her twenty-two-year-old self recalled how far she had traveled and how much she had overcome, including her own reckless and headstrong behavior.

More still, she recalled Ashton's reaction to her remorse over having given in to temptation and enjoyed it. Ashton had opened her thinking with his rational acceptance and caring response to the pain she'd carried for too long in her heart. He made her feel whole and worthwhile, and he refused to take advantage of her even when he knew her weakness for him.

Yes, someone had come between her and Arthur.

The man she loved.

"Yes, it's him," Daisy said, surprising herself, buoyed by a fresh conviction that being confused and trying to do the right thing in difficult situations shouldn't be grounds for eternal damnation. She had a problem, and she was going to handle it. Somehow.

"I care for Arthur very much. He's dear and good-hearted and upstanding. But I love Ashton. He's clever and mischievous and funny and gentlemanly. He stirs me—body, mind, and soul—and there isn't a single part of him I would change." Emotion welled up in her, filling her eyes.

"Oh, Daisy, don't you see—"

"I see a great deal. I'm a woman, not a child. And before you lay into me about how wicked and venal men are . . . about how they all want just one thing from a woman"—she stalked closer, eyes taut with challenge—"let me tell you: he could have had me six ways from Sunday if he'd only asked. But he didn't ask. And that, Mama dear, is all you need to know about him."

It was a hard, hard night.

Arthur, a pure novice at the sport of drinking, was mother-henned by an anxious Bascom at the Iron Penny, until he gave up the effort entirely and climbed back on his mount to mosey home. He didn't want to think anymore about her or his brother or the damned title that he wore around his neck like a noose. He hated being a duke. Despised it. He'd like nothing better than to sell up and take off and never come back to this miserable . . . Just let Ashton have the girl—the only girl he'd ever kissed, he groaned—just leave and let them forget he was ever born.

Halfway to Betancourt, he got a fierce urge and dismounted to pee in the brush at the side of the road. His horse took exception to the delay and took off—"Hey!"—leaving Arthur to walk the rest of the way home.

"Damned animal. Who needs you?" He shook a fist at his disappearing mount. "Horses only make me think of her. I learned to ride for her. I'm gettin' damned good at it." He straightened. "I was her hero. Stood up to Bertram and his cronies, I did. I'm stronger than they think I am."

He staggered on, not half as drunk as he wished.

"I was gonna marry her. But she's in loooove." He halted in the middle of the road and felt his chest and belly, wondering if he was in love. He had no idea what *looove* felt like, so how would he know if he was in it or not? He decided somewhere in his ramblings that he must not love her, that he would probably *feel* something in his chest if he did. Something like . . . dyspepsia . . . only nicer. The lack of such a guidepost meant it was probably wounded pride making him feel this banging in his head and lead in his feet.

"She loooves him. I never stood a chance. Well, he can have 'er. Serves him right—a vixen for a wife. *They deserve each other.*"

He shambled on down the road repeating that last phrase until it began to truly mean something to him. They deserved each other. By the time he reached Betancourt's kitchen and threw open the door, he was ready for some coffee and something to douse the fire that good Irish whiskey had started in his stomach.

He had some thinking to do.

Chapter Thirty-Two

Daisy put off going downstairs the next morning, enlisting Collette's help to cure her swollen eyes and prepare for the most difficult day of her life. A poultice of black tea, it seemed, was the remedy for such swelling. Collette fussed about, anxious because she had never seen her mistress so tense and dispirited, or with eyes puffy from crying.

When Daisy descended with flagging steps to the morning room, she was shocked to find Arthur sitting among her family, chatting amicably and looking only slightly more fatigued than she was.

"Daisy, my dear." He rose and poured her a cup of coffee, then ushered her to a seat. "I have decided to go to London with you," he said. "I know you will be busy shopping and visiting"—he covered her hand on the table with his   "but surely you can find some time for your future husband." His smile and his hand on hers were oddly determined.

"Of course, Your Grace," she said. "We have plenty of room."

"I have to meet with Mr. Drexel on marriage matters—contracts and such. But I'll have time of an evening for some socializing. Besides, your Uncle Red could use some male companionship. Yesterday the girls were using him as a yarn rack"—he held up his hands, a foot apart, in demonstration—"for their needlework."

And there it was—no scene, no hysterics, not even any discussion. Her future and the betrothal that yesterday had been in shambles would go on as planned. Harmony had been restored, though she had no idea how or why.

As they climbed aboard carriages later and headed for the train station, trailing a mountain of baggage and two horses, Daisy felt her mother's eyes watching her, even as she watched Arthur. But he showed no signs of his previous temper and rejection. He was in all things the doting groom-to-be.

It almost made her feel worse than if he'd railed, denounced her to her family, and tossed them all out on their arses. Almost.

By that night, as they settled into their London house, some of her angst and suspicion had subsided. She waited until dinner and some music from Claire's violin had mellowed her mood to invite him out onto the terrace with her. He took her hand, smiled, and accompanied her.

"You're wondering," he said, leveling a thoughtful gaze on her.

"I am. A day ago, you were ready to denounce me to the world."

"I never would have, Daisy. I was sore and my pride was singed. Fortunately I came to my senses in time to prevent real damage."

"You truly want the wedding to go on?" She searched his face in the light from the French doors. "Knowing"—she couldn't bring herself to say those hurtful words to him again—"what you know?"

"I am convinced that you and I can be amicable partners. And that love will grow between us as it should. Besides, we won't have Ashton around Betancourt forever. I'm making it part of the wedding settlement that he receive

funds to go to America to start a new life." He studied her
reaction without giving her any insight into his own. "Does
that comfort you?"

"Yes." She drew a deep breath and her tension drained as
she saw the sincerity in his face. Nobility seemed etched into
his every feature and texture. "Very much so."

He saw her to the bottom of the stairs in the entry hall,
and this time his good-night kiss fell exactly where he intended: square in the middle of her forehead.

Monsieur Pirouette, dressmaker to the wealthiest and
most elegant ladies of London society, dropped everything
to attend Miss Daisy Bumgarten's request for a wedding
gown and trousseau. Anything for the future duchess and her
lovely young sisters, he crooned, ushering them into his lair
a day later. The place was a warren of fabric stacks, cutting
tables, newfangled sewing machines, dressmaker forms, and
mirrors that created an illusion that there was no end to the
monsieur's domain. His assistants whisked the girls into
dressing rooms where they were measured, fitted, and dazzled
by a rich array of fabrics and the latest styles from Paris.

It turned out to be a small matter to get M. Pirouette to
dig deep into his contacts among London's elite for the
whereabouts of one Reynard Boulton, otherwise known as
the Fox. By midafternoon, a message Pirouette had sent was
answered in person by none other than the Fox himself.

No stranger to backdoor dealings, he appeared at the
alley entrance to Pirouette's and was quickly shown to a fit-
ting room where Daisy was dressing behind a screen.

"Ah," the Fox said as she peeked over the top of the
screen and broke into a beaming smile. "You. I would leave
this instant, but I am apparently a glutton for punishment."

"Good to see you, too, Reynard," she said, sliding gingerly
out of a skeleton of a dress that was full of chalk marks and

silk pins. "You probably know more about who goes where than anyone in London."

"Silver-tongued temptress," he said dryly. "You're trying to turn my head."

"Just to persuade you to help me find . . . someone." She stepped into another bit of the seductive armor fashionable females wore in the battle of the sexes and dragged it up onto her shoulders.

"Dare I guess who?" he said, picking up a pair of silky knickers with one finger and tilting his head, imagining.

"I suspect you know. I need to see him and I have no idea where to start. He's not at the place he usually stays—that Sever It House."

He smirked at her mispronunciation. "*Severin*. And that's because he's skinned, again, and spending his nights trying to enlarge what little coin he has left at the tables. Could be at any one of a dozen places."

"Is he . . . all right?" She gripped the top of the screen, standing on tiptoes, not caring that her anxiety for Ashton showed.

"He's Ash. He'll survive."

"Can you find out where he'll be tomorrow night and send me word?"

"I suppose I could. If I were sufficiently motivated," he said, rocking back, clearly considering how he might make use of such information.

"How about . . . I promise never to lock you in a room with my three sisters," she said, with wicked intent.

His jaunty mood dampened. "You don't have to be so vicious. A simple 'please, milord' would have sufficed."

An hour later, Reynard entered the bar of the Savoy and spotted Redmond Strait propped at the mahogany railing with a glass of fine Irish in his hand. The roguish old prospector had sent him an urgent message asking to meet at the elegant hotel's bar . . . about the same time Daisy's message arrived asking for a meeting. Red waved him over and offered him a drink.

"Scotch," he told the bartender, and they adjourned to a nearby table.

"What is this about?" Reynard asked, propping the head of his walking stick against the table and removing his hat and gloves, setting them aside.

"You know a whole lot o' folks, right?"

"I think that could be fairly said of me." Reynard had never considered modesty a virtue.

"Well, I need to find somebody." Red threw back the rest of his Irish and motioned to the bartender for another.

"And who might that be?" Reynard studied the westerner, dead certain now that the two favors he was undertaking would align, saving time.

"Ashton Graham. He's gone missin'."

"Ummm. And what do you want with him?"

"I wanna wrap my fingers 'round his throat and throttle him within an inch o' his miser'ble life." Red scratched his grizzled chin and narrowed one eye, taking on a piratical air.

"Oh, well, you may have to get in the queue, old boy." Reynard nodded to the bartender, who set his drink before him and sipped. "The way he's blowing through gaming establishments in the unsavory precincts of town, he's making a fair number of enemies. As clever at cards and dice as he is, he has only one neck, and far too many people want to wring it."

"Damn." Red turned that over in his mind, not liking the sound of it. "Looks like I'll just have to get to 'im first." He leaned over the table toward Reynard, who flinched in spite of himself. "Where do I find 'im?"

The Chancery was a gambling den where wealthy patrons from Mayfair dared to rub elbows with a dangerous, sometimes criminal crowd. It was quite the thing in certain well-heeled circles for men to dip their toes in an exciting bit of iniquity. Situated near the river, west and south of St. James, the gaming house occupied what was once a wealthy trader's town house, and was run by a woman whose beam and tonnage rivaled the White Star Line's best steamer.

Beulah MacNeal sat on a substantial settee on a mezzanine overlooking the bustling floor of the Chancery, and she spotted them the minute they came in, dressed in rumpled suits, with hair sparse and eyes shifty. . . . They were out of place and seemed to know it. The shorter, skinnier one jumped at every burst of laughter or crack of a dealer's shoe. The taller, heavier one was clearly looking for someone and maneuvered them to a clear space near the bar, where they could see the trade arrive. As they waited they filched food from the trays coming out of the nearby kitchen, filling their mouths and then pockets with stolen morsels.

They didn't have to wait long; in lumbered two robust specimens she knew to be knucklers—men who did messy jobs for people who didn't want to get their hands dirty. She watched as the pairs met, talked, and struck some kind of bargain.

"He'll be here any time," Bertram, Baron Beesock, told the hired bruisers. "I'll signal like this when he enters." He pulled on his ear.

"Remember," Seward put in, from behind Bertram's shoulder, "he's no novice to fisticuffs, so don't let him get in the first swing."

"Forget niceties. A knock on the head from behind is as good as a punch in the face to drop him," Bertram said, narrowing his eyes. "Once he's down, you can take your time breaking ribs and gouging eyes. Make him pay. But before he passes out, be sure to tell him his uncles say "Go to Hell.""

"What about th' money?" one of the punishers demanded.

Bertram handed over a small, worn bit of leather that jingled.

"Feels light." The fellow peeked inside and scowled. "The guv said we wus to collect first."

"We'll be watching from the roof," Bertram said. "When it's done, you'll get the rest." As the brutes backed off to watch the door, he smirked. "Ashton does well at the tables, he'll have money on him. There's a certain bit of justice, don't you think, in him paying his own punishers."

"We better hope he has enough on him to do so"— Seward watched the way one of their hirelings popped his big boney knuckles, and swallowed hard—"because we're flat broke."

Far above, Beulah beckoned over one of her muscular peacekeepers, handed him a scribbled note, and sent him with that message to the fellow who had been asking after this pair . . . the Fox.

Ashton paused a moment outside the door of the Chancery, feeling a bit too sober for the kind of action he would see inside London's most infamous gambling hell. Just setting foot in the place was asking for trouble and he'd already had more than enough trouble to last a while. He explored his tender jaw, moving it from side to side. Sore losers were becoming an epidemic in London's underbelly. But just a few more nights and he'd have enough to make his way to New York and a new life.

Grimly he set his face and shoulders and entered the place. Gambling was the one activity that seemed to stave off thoughts of all he was leaving behind. Of *whom* he was leaving behind. He strolled the perimeter of the playing floor, sizing up the competition and choosing a table of likely players. He had just snagged a brandy from the bar and was headed to a seat when a small mountain stepped into his path. Before he knew it, the bruiser was pushing him back behind a nearby column, where another big bloke waited to yank his arms behind him, and wrestle him to the back door.

He resisted, but calling for help never crossed his mind. This was a known hazard of his recent occupation—hard persuasions from unhappy tablemates and henchmen with more beef than brains. He'd dealt with such before and wasn't overly concerned when they shoved him out into the damp, ill-lit alley. He stumbled and righted himself, turning to spread his arms and flash a disarming smile.

"Gents, this is some sort of mistake." He watched one approach from the front with an ugly smile. He turned slowly, trying to keep both knucklers in view, but lost track of the second one. "I don't know who sent you, but I'm quite sure I'm not the object of your strenuous intentions."

"Yeah, you are, milord," the closer one said, showing yellowed and decaying teeth that made Ashton pray there would be no biting involved. The next instant he was reeling from a powerful blow to the back of the head—crumpling slowly, seeing stars—and struggling to remain upright.

He got both feet under him, just in time to look up at the ham-sized fist headed straight for his nose. Instinct kicked in and he dodged, sending that blow raking the side of his head. With his skull pounding and ears ringing, he staggered and scrambled to focus the pain into a some kind of response.

A heartbeat later, he dove at the big man, knocking him back against a wall and delivering a series of furious punches. Beneath his obvious fat the bruiser bore layers of protective muscle, but that was not enough to keep him from feeling Ashton's blows. Guttural curses and grunts of pain were all the bully-boy could manage. And then came another attack from the rear—something hard and heavy that landed across his ribs and knocked the breath from him.

Ash fell, rolled, and tried to fend off well-placed kicks and more blows with what looked to be a weighted truncheon. They'd come prepared to do real damage. In that split second, Ashton realized he was in a fight for his life.

Arthur arrived at the Chancery in a cab that refused to wait. As it drove away, he stood on the cracked pavement, eyeing the light and noise coming from the shaded windows, and the heavy door that opened only from the inside. If only he'd been able to convince the Fox to accompany him. The bounder said he had a previous commitment and flippantly wished the duke "good hunting."

The door was opened by a large fellow with a pox-ravaged face and a piercing glare. Arthur provided Boulton's name and that he was under instructions to consult Mrs. MacNeal, the proprietress. Whispers were passed to smaller men dressed as waiters, who led him to the rear of the establishment and up a set of substantial stairs. He had noticed the mezzanine overlooking the playing floor as he followed them, but had failed to see the very large woman sitting above it all, watching the trade below with a keen interest.

"The Fox sent you?" she asked, looking him over.

He nodded, momentarily dumbstruck.

She waved a hand at a nearby chair and he perched on the edge of it, trying not to stare at her greatly exaggerated curves and overly abundant bosoms. The candlelight surrounding her was kind, but couldn't soften the calculating glint in her eyes. Her melodious voice was as compelling as a stage magician's.

"You are looking for someone," she crooned. "Who?"

"Ashton Graham," Arthur said, feeling very much out of place. "My brother. I was told he would be here tonight."

She looked to the runner standing nearby, dressed in black. He bent to her ear and after a moment she nodded. "He was here. I believe he met with some gents who escorted him outside . . . into the alley. Not really my business, what happens outside my walls. Perhaps you'd like to go and see if he's still there." She nodded to her assistant, who led Arthur down the steps and around tables of well-lubricated gamblers and revelers to a rear door.

The heavy door slammed behind him the minute he stepped into the dim alley, and it took a moment for him to realize that the thrashing bundle on the ground was Ashton and that the hulking fellow nearby was kicking the living daylights out of him. Shocked, Arthur looked around and saw a second bruiser rising from a pile of refuse with a vicious smirk. His brother—they were beating Ash!

Before he realized what he was doing, he seized the first thing at hand—an oak stave from a broken barrel. Raising it with both hands, he came up behind the bastard who had just gained his feet, and with a fury he'd never experienced before, swung that wood for all he was worth.

The force of the blow exploded up his arms and jarred his very teeth, but he lunged forward and swung back the other way in a blind fury. The thug bent with the first blow, gasping for air, but the second blow connected hard with the back of his head and he dropped like a plank.

Arthur's presence registered with the second man, who turned from Ash to brandish his truncheon at Arthur with a sneer. "You wanna taste o' this, pretty boy?" The second bruiser's foot caught as he lunged, and he stumbled straight into Arthur's swinging club.

Arthur called to Ash and headed for him, but his opponent shook off the blow and came upright. Ash whipped around on the ground to grab his ankles and send him sprawling. Seconds later, Ash was on him, landing blows of pain and fury, snarling, incoherent with rage.

Arthur came to his senses first, and grabbed Ashton—
"Enough! He's done!"—pulling him back, then off the
inert thug.

Everything was still except their pounding hearts and
heaving chests. As the roar of blood receded in his head,
Arthur helped Ashton to his feet and led him over to a pile
of discarded pallets and broken barrels. He pushed Ash to a
seat on an overturned half barrel and inspected his face.

"You look awful," he said, wincing and producing a
handkerchief.

"Then not half as bad as I feel," Ashton said, gripping his
ribs beneath his battered coat and then dabbing at his bleed
ing mouth and forehead with Arthur's accessory. "God. That
was damn near the end of me." He looked at the motionless
forms splayed nearby. "Those bastards are pros."

"Pros?" Arthur felt his chest with a hand and took a deep
breath.

"Professional muscle, bully-boys, thugs. They had
weighted truncheons and brass knuckles. Somebody paid to
set them on me."

"Who hates you that much?" Arthur scowled. "Besides
family."

"Don't make me laugh," Ashton said with a chuckle that
sent pain spearing through his midsection.

"Who's laughing?" Arthur said, remembering his irritation. "You're a real bounder, you know that. The old trots
weren't half wrong about you."

"Wh-a-at?" Ashton stared at his elder brother in disbelief.
"You just rescued my arse and now you're calling me every
name in the book. What's gotten into you?" He was struck
by another thought. "What the hell are you doing here in the
first place?"

"I came here to have it out with you."

"Over what?" Ashton turned to him in dismay. "What
have I ever done to you?"

Arthur shoved to his feet and a second later Ashton followed. He was none too steady, but he was not about to take his brother's ire sitting down.

"You know damned well!" Arthur snarled, and a moment later his fist landed in the middle of Ashton's face with a *crunch*.

"Aghhhh!" Ashton staggered back, stunned by the fact of the blow as much as the force behind it. "Shit, shit, *shit!*" He held his nose and felt blood run. His milquetoast, bug-obsessed brother had just broken his nose! He straightened— holding his damaged nose—into Arthur's righteous glare. "What the hell was *that* for, you little shit?"

"For taking my bride away from me before I ever had a chance with her," Arthur bellowed, and swung hard at Ash again. This time, Ashton was better prepared and blocked the blow, though at some cost. His entire body was aching, throbbing, and in some places on fire. Instinct honed by years of down-and-dirty fighting made him retaliate with a counterpunch.

"Owwwwww!" Arthur grabbed his jaw, staggered, and then wiped blood from his mouth. Looking at it, his eyes flew wide. "You *hit* me!"

"You deserved it, you horse's arse."

"After I just saved your bloody life? You hit me after I saved you?"

"I've saved yours a hundred times, you numskull. You only survived Eton because I fought for you every damned day! I had more nosebleeds—" It registered that Arthur's anger had to do with Daisy. He thought Ashton had—"I never did anything to Daisy or with Daisy. She was yours from the first day we met and that never changed. She was determined to marry you and she deserves to." For a moment his physical misery gave place to the ache in his heart and a growing sense of dread.

"Something happened." Ashton glared back at his elder brother. "What happened? What did you do?"

"What did *I* do?" Arthur stuck out his chin. "I asked her to marry me, honorably and decently. She said yes. Then I found out she's in love with you, my own brother. You went and stole her heart before I had a chance to win it."

"What makes you think she's in love with me?" Ashton felt his heart pounding harder than when he was fighting.

"She told me so. I asked her flat out and she said she did."

"You asked her? What kind of damn fool move was that?"

"I saw the way you looked at each other, the way she glowed when she talked to you, the way you softened around her. I may not be the sharpest tool in the shed, but even I could see the truth when I caught you kissing her!" And he threw another punch.

"Goddamn it, Artie, don't make me—"

But he did. Again and again. They traded blows that rocked their senses and sanity and finally brought them, bruised and bloodied, to their knees.

On the nearby roof, Seward pulled on Bertram's arm, trying to get him to abandon the spectacle unfolding in the alley below.

"Come on, Bertram." His voice was constricted. "We've got to get out of here."

"And miss this? It's even better than what we planned—the bastards are bashing each other senseless." He almost giggled with pleasure.

"But when those bruisers wake up, they'll be mad as hell." Seward inched back to the parapet of the Chancery's roof for another peek.

"We'll be long gone and they'll have no clue who we are or where to find us," Bertram scoffed, then brightened.

"Wish we could hear what they're saying. Whoa, did you see that one?"

"This is one bad idea, Daize," Red said as they exited the cab onto the pavement before the Chancery. "If he's here, what'll you say to 'im?"

"It's no good talking to her." Reynard Boulton turned from paying the cabbie, then ushered them toward the forbidding front door. "She's in love."

"I never said that," she said, frowning at Reynard.

"You didn't have to," he said dismissively, then pounded the knocker on the door. It swung open and the beefy doorman with the scarred face broke into an odd smile at the sight of him.

"Your Lordship." He nodded and opened wide to admit them.

"Is she here?" he asked.

"She's always here," the fellow said, snapping his fingers for a servant to take the men's hats and walking sticks. Daisy surrendered her shawl. The doorman led them across the bustling gaming floor to the stairs at the rear.

Daisy had never seen such a place—music fast and loud, men in evening clothes and women in scandalous gowns, crystal chandeliers glowing, champagne flowing. Gaiety was everywhere, but with an edge that took her to her limit of comfort. As they climbed the stairs she asked Reynard who "she" was and he just smiled.

Moments later she was stunned to be introduced to a woman of middle years and prodigious bulk, with the fashion sense of a Parisian madam. Mrs. MacNeal was in the unique position of owning this establishment because of either remarkable talents or a remarkable life. Daisy had no right to judge either, so when she offered her hand and smiled, the woman seemed surprised and produced a lovely smile.

"You've had business tonight," Reynard said as they stood before the lady.

"Two brothers," she said, sipping from her champagne glass. "Two rough boys. And two old fellows who ate like they were starving." She threaded her fingers together with a sly expression. "They fit into one story. And now you, Reynard, and this lady and this gentleman, who is no gentleman." She gestured to Red, who flushed and grinned.

"The old men," Reynard said. "What did they look like?"

"One with a bull neck and a belly and temper to match. The other a weasel, quick and easily frightened. I believe they're on my roof at the moment."

"Could you see they come down?"

She smiled and nodded. "For you, I can."

"Where are the others, Mrs. MacNeal?" Daisy ventured. "It is important we speak to them."

The proprietress turned to her majordomo. "Show them the rear door."

"As ever," Reynard said, kissing her hand without a trace of mockery, "I am in your debt."

Moments later, they stood just inside the rear door, gaping at the sight of Ashton and Arthur in the alley beyond, battered and bloodied, propping each other up in order to take swings at each other.

"Say you're going to marry her," Ashton snarled, giving him a shake. "She's got her heart set on being a duchess—she's worked for years to come this far. You're not goin' to let her down, you hear?"

"You're so keen to see her wed—marry her yourself!" Arthur snapped, locking his knees and leaning against Ashton's shoulders.

"You're the one with the damned title. You're the one who *can* make her a duchess, so you're the one who's *going to do so*."

"S-says who?" Arthur was beginning to slur his words through bruised and swollen lips.

"Says *me,*" Ashton panted, scarcely able to see for the sweat and blood running in his eyes.

"Yeah, well, I decided I don't *want* to get married." Arthur was struggling to stay upright. "Did you know there are women everywhere? I did not know that. All kinds of women. Like those sisters of hers. Have you *seen* them?" He tried to whistle, but it came out as mostly air. "Pretty as pictures—no, as butterflies. There's women all over th' place, and I never even had *one*! It's not fair that the one I get stuck with wants *you.*"

"You're not stuck with her, you jackass. You're lucky to have 'er. She's an angel, a marvel among women. She knows stuff you can't imagine. I saw her pull a calf out of a cow, single-handed. She can make a horse dance in time to music, and she's not afraid of coyotes or sidewinders or polecats— just ask Red." He shook Arthur by the coat. "She spent two damned years tryin' to catch a duke and you're gonna marry her or else."

Daisy stood, dumbfounded, watching her betrothed husband and the man she loved threaten and beat each other, each trying to convince the other to marry her. It was shocking and absurd and utterly humiliating.

She reached for Red's hand as he stood beside her, and when he would have charged out into the alley, she held him back, pleading for restraint with hurt-filled eyes. He put an arm around her as she listened and her heart seemed to slide to somewhere in the vicinity of her knees.

Then it came, the final blow.

"So, she loves you, but you don't want to marry 'er." Arthur seemed to be running out of steam for this head-to-head collision. He pulled out his most devastating charge:

"Either you don't love her, or you don't want to get married. Which is it?"

She froze, listening, blinking away the tears collecting in her eyes.

The pause seemed to go on forever.

Ashton dropped his arms and disengaged from Arthur.

He stood looking down, and his shoulders rounded slightly.

"I love her. Curse your eyes, I love her with everything in me." He looked up with anger so old it had grown cold and grim. "Don't you see? I have nothing to give her. *Nothing*. No home, no position, no income, no title. No future. And she deserves all of that and more."

Watching him recount his lack of worldly goods, rank and position, her heart protested that none of that mattered to her any more. A moment later, she finally understood; it still mattered a great deal to him. More, in fact, than she did. It was pride, his precious male pride, that kept him from seeing that he could have all of that and so much more . . . if he would only open his heart and let go of the past to embrace the future.

Frustration boiled up in her, hot and potent.

How dare they toss her back and forth like some damned *cricket ball*?

She pushed away from Red and dashed through the door before Reynard could stop her. She halted a few feet from them, spread her feet, and propped her fists on her hips. If their ears hadn't been ringing from the blows they'd taken, they probably could have heard the lightning flashing in her eyes.

"You miserable, low-down, yellow-bellied—" She halted and turned to Arthur. "I thought we had settled the matter of our marriage. You told me it would go forward, and in good faith, I believed you. Now I hear you whining about how you'd rather enjoy the entire field before settling on just one flower. You regret not having sampled the charms of many women? What a heart-warming complaint from a man who two months ago hardly knew how to ask a lady for a dance. You say you don't want to marry me because I love someone else? Well, I'm not sure that will be a problem for long."

She turned on Ashton, who stared at her as if her hair were on fire.

"And you. You love me so dearly, you would give me everything *you* desire. How gallant. Did it never occur to you to give me what *I* want? I as much as told you that I love you, and you stood as dumb as a doorstop, refusing to say what was as plain as the nose on your face."

"I didn't want to burden you. I thought it would be easier if—"

"If you didn't say it out loud, it would be easier on your conscience when you handed me over to somebody else?"

"You were determined to marry a duke, to make a future for your sisters." He looked into her eyes. "I was trying to give you what you want."

She narrowed her eyes and stepped closer, landing equidistant between them. "Well, how lovely. Here is what I want: a husband, a week from Saturday at the church in the village of Betany. I'll be there in my white wedding gown with flowers and organ music and the vicar all ready to go. One of you idiots had better show up with a ring and a damn big apology."

She advanced on Ashton, considered his injuries up close, and grabbed his shirtfront, pulling him down so they were nose to nose.

"Just to help you make up your mind . . ." She pulled him down further and planted a bone-melting kiss on his damaged mouth that more than made up for the pain it caused.

She turned to Arthur, said, "I don't believe I ever got to demonstrate the real possibilities in a wife's affections," and kissed him with enough heat to cauterize the splits in his swollen lip. He staggered, dazed, when she released him.

As she headed for Red and Reynard Boulton, who stood gaping at her from the gaming house's rear entrance, down the alley came the Chancery's doorman and another burly employee. Before them, being shoved roughly along by grips on their collars, came Bertram and Seward, looking considerably worse than at their last encounter. "You." She approached near enough to see their unshaved faces, rumpled clothes, and the resentment burning in their eyes.

"You'll never be a duchess," Bertram snapped. "Even Arthur—that worthless, ungrateful dolt—knows better than to mingle his noble blood with the likes of yours."

Ashton moved like quicksilver and landed a fist hard on the wretch's jaw, sending him reeling. If it hadn't been for the doorman's grip on his collar and coat, he'd have sprawled in the filthy alley. He turned to Seward, who put up his hands, pleading to be spared.

"We didn't mean to. We thought . . . you needed . . . a-a—"

"A few broken ribs?" Ashton gave him a tap on the jaw, after all.

Daisy, head held high, blew through the knot of people in the doorway, and Uncle Red and Reynard Boulton—both torn between watching what would happen next and following her—exchanged looks and then headed after her. As one of the Chancery servants hailed them a cab, she recovered enough to spear Reynard with a dangerous look.

"I'd better not hear a word about this—now or ever. Because if I do, and I'm not married nine days from now, I just might decide to marry *you*."

Reynard blinked, looking truly unsettled by that threat.

"My lips are sealed."

* * *

In the alley, Bertram and Seward were dropped between their hirelings and sat mutely trying to recover. The doorman looked around and gave Ashton an approving nod. "Anything else you need, milord?"

"A constable or two," Ashton said, trying not to grin and make his lip bleed further. "Or four."

"Yes, indeed." Minutes after he ducked inside, they heard constables' whistles in the nearby street.

The hired thugs were roused and taken into custody along with Bertram and Seward. "They're good friends," Ashton put in. "If I were you, I'd be sure to put them in a cell together."

Wicked delight bloomed in the head constable's face.

"A fine idea, guv."

"What?" Bertram froze as he was being hauled to the Black Maria. "You can't do this. I demand a separate cell. I am the Baron Beesock—"

"Never heard of ye."

"I'll have your job for—"

Ashton threw an arm around Arthur's shoulders and turned him toward the still open door of the Chancery.

"If she ever kisses you like that again," he said a bit too calmly, "you're a dead man."

Arthur laughed, despite how much it hurt.

They were met by the doorman with a tray containing two substantial glasses of liquor. "Mrs. MacNeal thought you might need this. But she asks that you take it where you are." His grin was wry and a bit chilling. "Wouldn't want to scare the customers."

Chapter Thirty-Three

"It's a good day to marry a duke," the countess said as she threw back the drapes in Daisy's room and let in the newly risen sun. Fresh, cool air wafted in, and she breathed deeply. "It's finally here—the day you've been hoping for, planning for, and waiting for."

Daisy groaned silently. The desire to curl up and pull the covers over her head was overwhelming, but not to be. Her mother sailed in without knocking, carrying a tray of coffee, scones, and fruit.

"Morning, Your Grace-to-be," she declared cheerily, placing the tray on the table. "What a good day to marry a duke!" With that, she ripped the covers back and rocked Daisy with insistent prodding. "Up, daughter-of-mine. You've a lot to do and we have to be at the church at half past ten."

Daisy closed her eyes and groaned aloud.

"No, no." The countess saw her retreating into a stubborn mood and joined Elizabeth by the bed, where they exchanged worried glances. "We can't have His Grace waiting at the altar, now can we?"

The door that her mother had left open was seen as an invitation to one and all. Daisy's sisters came barreling in, talking excitedly, squealing with awe and delight at the white satin gown hanging from the wardrobe, and climbing onto the bed with her. Her mother's prodding was gentle by comparison to their shaking and pulling and teasing.

She finally sat up and glared at them all.

"Coffee. I need some coffee."

"What you need is a husband," Elizabeth declared, pouring her a cup and carrying it to the bed, where Daisy was now upright against the pillows. "And in a few hours, you'll have one. You'll be a wife and a duchess."

Daisy forced a smile while groaning again inside. She hadn't seen Ashton or Arthur since that night at the Chancery. She'd had a couple of ambiguous notes from Arthur regarding times and places. And a bouquet of stunning white roses that she'd carried on her lap all the way from London . . . making her sisters swoon at the romance of it. And that was all. Her ultimatum hadn't been addressed and, despite her belief that the two men would take her seriously, she had a niggling fear that it still might all go arse over teakettles.

God, she was starting to *think* like a Brit.

They primped and powdered and curled and buttoned her—the countess teary eyed, her mother alternating between sniffling and issuing hushed advice as to how she should behave in the marital bed, and her sisters laughing and teasing her about her husband-to-be's manly qualities. Collette soldiered on through it all, styling Daisy's hair elegantly and buffing her nails. By the time she was fully buttoned into her wedding gown, she was half frozen with dread.

Surely Ashton would make the right choice. Surely he would step up and marry her. He did love her. She knew he did. Down deep. Surely he wouldn't be so selfless and boneheaded a second time.

She found it hard to enjoy the fervent admiration of her family and the Betancourt staff as they gathered to watch her descend the main stairs in her trained gown and silk illusion veil. A cold hand gripped her insides as she waved and climbed into the newly acquired Betancourt coach. It was large enough for Daisy, Red, her mother, and the countess, but the girls rode behind in an open carriage rented for the occasion. At that moment, she would have gladly traded places with any one of them.

The vicar stood just outside the church doors, wearing his vestments and a nervous smile. A few latecomers stretched their necks to catch a glimpse of the bride, then scurried into the church for a seat. There weren't many nobles present; the duke hadn't yet made connections among the younger generation of titled folk and gentry in the neighborhood. So, there was plenty of space for tenants and ordinary folk from the village. A peek through the main doors showed the pews to be packed.

"Is he here?" she paused to quietly ask the vicar, while her mother and the countess arranged her train and fussed over her veil and bouquet.

"Oh, yes." He seemed a bit unsettled to add: "Both of them are."

Both? What the devil did that mean?

The countess and her sisters entered and were seated at the front. Her mother kissed both her cheeks, smiled tearfully, and entered on the arm of none other than Reynard Boulton. Daisy didn't know whether to be pleased or alarmed that he had come from London to observe the nuptials.

As she and Red moved forward, into the small narthex, Red pulled a small flask from his breast pocket and held it out to her. Much as she wanted a pull of whiskey, she shook her head and let him finish his "snort" before moving forward to stand at the rear of the sanctuary.

Her knees went weak. At the front of the church, at the vicar's left, stood Ashton and Arthur, both dressed to the nines, but with faces lightly swollen, cuts healing but still visible, and black eyes only now turning that sickly greenish yellow. A glance around the congregation showed that most attendees were surprised by their appearance. Over the wheezing music from the pump organ, the whispering was audible. Even the countess and her mother and sisters were confused. She could feel Red vibrating against her arm and realized he was chuckling. He found it funny! She so wanted to kick him.

The Graham men were standing equally close to the empty space before the vicar, space she would soon occupy. So which was her groom?

At a change in the music, she and Red started down the aisle, which made the congregation turn and stare. She heard the comments: "lovely," "a stunning gown," and "pretty as a picture," but her gaze was fixed on Ashton's battered face. He broke into a smile as warm as summer.

Unfortunately, Arthur smiled, too.

When she paused before the vicar and he said a few words that sounded like "*gurgle, toggle, waggle, waddle*" to her, Red abandoned her to take a seat at the front, by the countess. Daisy panicked, standing there, facing the two of them. Arthur stepped forward to take her hand and she swayed, halfway to a full-blown swoon.

Then he turned to Ashton with a broad smile and placed her hand in his brother's.

Ashton's warm hand closed over her icy one and he stepped up to steady her. Reeling, all she could think was, *You're going to pay for this*.

"Daisy Bumgarten, I'm here to declare my enduring love and devotion to you. You're my heart of hearts, the light of my soul, the foundation of my hope, my dreams, and my future." He sank onto one knee and reached into his pocket for a gold ring set with a sizeable cut diamond. He held it up to her and asked, "Will you be my wife?"

There was not a breath taken in the silence that followed. Every eye was focused on her response. She swallowed hard, searching for the love-me-forever in his battered eyes, and melted inside.

"Took you long enough. Of course I'll marry you," she said, tears running down her face as she opened her arms and he shot to his feet to fill them. She held on to him, breathing in the reality of him, absorbing the fact of his strong arms around her, dimly aware of the confusion that broke out and of the frantic fanning and smelling-salts-sharing in her family pew.

Arthur addressed the congregation, arms raised to signal for quiet.

"For years, my beloved brother, Ashton, has been my rock and my anchor. It may seem strange, the way this wedding has changed, but it is with the deepest love and the highest pleasure that I acknowledge his choice of the smartest, sweetest, strongest woman I know to be his wife." He turned to Daisy and Ashton with a broad smile that probably cost him a little pain, then looked to the stunned vicar. "Let's get on with it, shall we?"

"B-but the banns—"

"A special license," Arthur said, producing a document from his pocket and handing it over, "courtesy of my new friend the bishop. I think you'll find it all in order."

A bit of stammering and some raised eyebrows later, the vicar did indeed get on with it. There were a few very fervent prayers, some vows, some music from the lovely Claire Bumgarten's marvelous violin, and then Ashton was placing the ring on Daisy's finger.

There was hardly a dry eye in the church. Even sentiment-shunning Reynard Boulton was effected. Then he looked over to find one of the Bumgarten girls staring fixedly at him and jerked his gaze away in horror.

Oh, no. Not him. No one would catch him voluntarily putting a ring through his nose.

Music from the wheezing organ escorted the newlyweds

down the aisle and out into the sunshine. They kissed lovingly and were congratulated by everyone, including Arthur and the Baron Kettering. After signing the church register, they were showered with rose petals as they ran to their carriage.

On the way back to Betancourt and the wedding breakfast, Daisy looked down at the sparkling ring on her finger and then up at her husband.

"Are you sure this is what you want?" she asked.

"Are you kidding?" he answered, pulling her into his arms and tenderly stroking her cheek. "It's what I've wanted since . . . I'm fairly sure it was the calf pulling that sank me. From that moment on, I kept trying to talk you out of marrying Arthur, but what I really should have been doing was talking you into marrying me."

"Yes, you should have. Selflessness and sacrifice are noble and have their place . . . but their place is not in bed beside me at night."

"I'll remember that." He chuckled and kissed her with purely scandalous intent . . . a promise of the joys of the nights to come.

Betancourt hadn't seen such a celebration in generations. The front doors were thrown open to welcome invited guests, tenants, and villagers, but the meal was served at long tables in the side yard overlooking the garden. Music was provided by a trio of local musicians, and into the afternoon, Claire joined them to strike up a vigorous country dance. Barrels of ale and casks of wine had been hauled out of the cellars, and before long spirit-and-ale warmed camaraderie spread through the guests, both great and small.

Elizabeth helped her daughter remove her veil and pin up her train, then hugged her again and searched her face. "You're really happy with him?"

"I am," Daisy said, sensing a sadness in her mother. "I know he's not a duke, but he is entitled to be called Lord Ashton."

"Oh, Daisy, I'm not disappointed. I won't say I wasn't surprised, even shocked—but not disappointed. I was afraid I had pushed you to marry someone you didn't care for just to make amends." Elizabeth stroked her hair and let her hand settle on her daughter's shoulder. "I've had a lot of time to think, and I am so sorry for the misery I put you through in Nevada. I was trying to do what was right and I ended up hurting everyone involved. If only your father had been there to help me see the right, I probably would have made different choices. He was always so deep-seeing and sensible."

"It's all right, Mama." Daisy put her hand over her mother's. "It worked out fine in the end. I'm married to a wonderful man and I'm going to have a good life. Please don't be sad."

Elizabeth sighed. "If I'm sad, Daize, it's because your father isn't here to see the woman you've become. He always had great faith in you. I should have remembered that." Tears collected in her eyes. "He would be very proud of you, but no prouder than I am."

She hugged Daisy, and for the first time in years Daisy felt her mother's love, freely given, warming her heart.

As the day wore on, she showed her sisters the "jewel" Ashton had given her. "It was a ring given to his mother at her wedding. He said he and Arthur retrieved it from a bank vault in London last week."

"Oooh, and he's not even a duke!" Sarah said with an acquisitive gleam in her eye. Daisy laughed; they were going to have to watch that one.

Later she watched Ashton with her uncle and Reynard and a couple of the local squires, tilting cups and laughing. Even beaten, bruised, and still recovering, her husband was the most handsome man present. Handsome beyond bearing.

She felt a delicious stirring in her body as she watched, and realized that for the first time in her life she was free to have sensual pleasure with no holds barred, nothing held back. She swayed on her seat and took another big swallow of champagne.

Eyes sparkling, she joined her sisters and a group of young people dancing in the grass near the duck pond. They joined hands and stepped to a pattern easy to follow. She was soon flushed and breathing hard.

The minute the music stopped, the dancers fell out of their circle in exhaustion. A hand grabbed hers and she found Ashton leading her toward the house. Even inside, people were strolling, staring at paintings, portraits, and the worn but still impressive entry hall.

He pulled her down the rear hallway to a niche, clamped arms around her, and kissed her like he was a starving man and she was manna. She responded with everything in her and was soon pressed hard against him, undulating, inviting greater response. They were both panting when he broke the kiss.

"I saw you dancing," he murmured thickly, kissing her temple, then sliding down to nibble the side of her neck.

"I saw you watching me," she answered. "I was dancing for you."

"Sweet Jesus." He drew a ragged breath, then he straightened and pulled her out into the hall. She barely kept up as she tried to smooth her hair and gown. He surprised her by leading her up a narrow, little used set of stairs to the next floor.

"I didn't know these were here," she said, looking around.

"Servant stairs," he whispered with a wink. "Very useful."

She had an idea where they were headed and licked her well-primed lips in anticipation. He waved to the doors they passed and said, "Which is yours?" She darted ahead and led him to her room. Once inside, he turned the key to lock out the rest of the world and pulled her between him and the door.

She opened to his kiss, eager and buoyant—all out of patience, circumspection, and self control. She wanted to feel his body, to see him, taste him, hear him hum with pleasure as she nibbled her way up and down his—

"I love you, Ashton Graham," she said between deep, ravishing kisses that went on and on. Her body was so hot that her bones seemed to be melting.

"And I love you, Daisy Bumgarten. Lady Daisy. My luscious, maddening, inventive temptress of a wife. And if I don't get this coat off, I'm going to burn to a cinder."

He straightened enough to wrestle his coat from his shoulders and started on his vest . . . while she stepped away and twisted frantically back and forth, trying to reach the long row of silk-covered buttons that fastened her wedding gown. It was impossible—there were a million buttons and she couldn't reach more than a handful. With a growl, she tugged at the lace-covered satin and found it the equal of her strength and impatience. She bent and twisted and tried to make at least part of the gown slide around to the front so she could reach the cursed fastenings.

Her dance of frustration brought a husky laugh from him. He stood clad in his shirt and trousers with his legs spread, arms crossed, and a heart stopping I-want-you-naked look on his handsome face. She stilled and stared back, with a make-me tilt to her chin.

"You need help, I see." He approached, running a hot, appreciative gaze over her every curve and feature, then doing it again with his hands, covering her body in naked adoration. He turned her and began to undo the small, silk-covered buttons that streamed down her back. For every one he dispatched, he laid a kiss on her bared flesh. Goose bumps rose all over her and she shivered and pulled what she could of her gown off her shoulders. More, she wanted more.

"This, I believe, is how it all began," he said, running into undergarments and having to tug them up and aside to reach bare skin.

"What is how it began?" She could barely stand, much less think.

"Buttons," he said. "In Mountjoy's library. Who would have guessed it would come to this?"

She managed to slip her corset cover up and off as her gown loosened, then her front-fastening corselet. Moments later she raised her skirts and dropped her petticoats and knickers. By the time her gown was fully undone, she was naked underneath. The heavy satin and lace creation drooped delectably over her breasts, bringing to mind another early encounter.

His hands trembled as he pulled the gown from her grasp bit by bit. She made no move to stop it and soon stood naked in a pile of satin and frothy lace. He ran his hands over her bare shoulders, down her tingling breasts, and over her waist. His voice was soft with feeling.

"You are so beautiful, Daisy. I can't believe that you're mine."

For a moment she felt her eyes pricking, then she shook it off and grinned at him. "Off with them, husband!" She attacked his clothes and in a much shorter time, he stood naked as his birthing day, seeming a little embarrassed. Fading yellowed bruises on his ribs and a massive one that was still blue-green on his left hip made her gasp.

"Oh, Ash, I had no idea they hurt you so badly." She stepped over their clothes and went to him, brushing his injuries and wrapping him gently in her arms.

"Nothing critical to a wedding night was damaged, I promise." He pulled her hard against him in demonstration and tilted her chin.

"Thank Heaven. I've been waiting for this night for . . . forever."

Their lips glided and tongues danced, enjoying, exploring as they moved with a single mind toward the bed. Soon they were throwing back covers and falling together into the welcoming softness.

He lay beside her, kissing, nibbling his way down her bare body, finding the places that made her gasp, sigh, or squirm. He licked and suckled her nipples, spread searing kisses over her belly, and nuzzled the curls that covered her woman's flesh. By the time he was through, she was hot-eyed and determined to have her fill of his body, too.

She rolled him onto his back and, careful to avoid his bruises, kissed her way across his chest and up his throat, to nibble his ears. He moaned as she started down again, pausing at the base of his throat, then licking his nipples in slow, hypnotizing circles.

"Oh, God, Daisy . . . you're . . . where did you ever learn to . . ."

Her leg slid over his and she pressed her body against him, rotating her hips to let him feel her wet heat. "See what you do to me?" she whispered.

In a heartbeat she was on her back with him above her, kissing her, and settling between her thighs. She rocked against him, wanting, inviting, even as her fingers dug into his shoulders and she tasted his salty skin.

When they began to join, she stilled and looked up into his hot bronzed eyes, wanting to see his passion there, wanting him to see the rich response it produced in her. But moments later his eyes closed, as did hers. Their bodies pressed and strained and thrust until they reached the limits of sensation. She gave a soft, throaty cry and tensed around him, locking her legs, riding a wave of pleasure as she pulled him deeper into her.

He buried his face in her neck and soon went rigid and quaking with a climax. It seemed to go on and on . . . thinning the boundaries between them until she couldn't tell where her responses ended and his began. They were one in this pleasure, in this life, in this future.

When he slid to the bed beside her she curled against him with a dreamy smile that made him grin.

"You look like a kitten with a belly full of cream," he said, stoking her face with his fingertips.

"I've never felt so happy, so complete in my life." She ran her palm over the plane of his stomach and up the mounds of his chest. "I wish everyone could feel this way." She looked up at him. "I wish Arthur could."

"He may. Someday." He turned and propped up on his arm to face her. He stroked her arm and the curve of her waist. "I have to tell you something."

"That sounds serious."

"We won't be going to New York right away."

"Oh?"

"I know you have your heart set on showing me off to the 'hundred' or whatever, but we'll have to postpone that for a while."

"Why? What's happened?" She thrust up onto one arm, facing him.

"Arthur . . . won't be here . . . and I've agreed to stay on at Betancourt and take care of the place."

"You and me, you mean. Why won't Arthur be here?"

"He's going to travel. He told me he needs to see the world before he settles down . . . if he settles down. He signed documents when we were in London making me his heir and abdicating the title to me if something should happen"—he watched her taking it in—"or if he doesn't return in five years, I become duke in his stead.

"Are you all right? I know it's a bit to take in."

"So you two just cooked this up between you? Without a word to me?"

"You had already talked with Arthur. He said you encouraged him to travel and see something of the world." He stroked her cheek. "I didn't think you'd mind. You'll be the duchess here in all but name."

"And you'll be the duke." She saw the irony in it. "Are you sure this is what you want? I don't think you owe Arthur anything more. Don't you want to travel yourself? Go to Nevada. See New York?"

"I've already traveled and seen the continent." He looked thoughtful for a minute. "Somehow . . . I feel that things aren't quite finished for me here. Would you mind staying and helping me put Betancourt to rights?"

The hope in his eyes, the love in her heart—how could she say no?

"With one condition." She lay down and snuggled against him. "The minute I'm pregnant, we make plans to sail for New York. I want my children born in the U.S. of A."

He laughed and pulled her close, breathing in the scent of her hair.

"I think that can be arranged."

Chapter Thirty-Four

The celebration lasted until sunset, during which time people occasionally asked after the newlyweds, but were not concerned enough to search for them. Later, Collette's discreet and unanswered knocks on Daisy's locked door confirmed for the immediate family that the honeymoon had begun in earnest and there was no cause for worry.

Oddly, no one thought to look for Arthur until dinner, when Daisy and Ashton appeared with an answer to his whereabouts that no one expected.

"He's gone." Ashton pulled a letter from his breast pocket and read it to the family at the dinner table. In it, Arthur handed control of Betancourt to Ashton for the period of his absence and claimed a small traveling stipend for himself from the wedding settlement. Red was downright delighted for him, the countess and Elizabeth were aghast, and Daisy's sisters were glum at the thought of missing Arthur's *eligible* company.

It indeed had been a great day to marry . . . a duke's brother. That marriage and that wedding night were the start of a new era at Betancourt. There were guests at the grand old house frequently in the months to come. Former tenants returned from the city to take up their old occupations, and herds of sheep, passels of pigs, and flocks of ducks and geese grew increasingly common on the estate. The roofs were fixed, plumbing was installed, and new furnishings were ordered for many of Betancourt's rooms, including the old duke's and duchess's chambers. By the year's end, they were making plans to install wires for electrical lighting and there was even talk of a newfangled telephone someday.

Elizabeth and her girls moved into the London house, found new servants, and were introduced by the countess into society as the young duke's relations and Lord Ashton's sisters-in-law. They were a success and had their choice of invitations to parties, soirees, and balls.

It all came to a head eighteen months later, when Daisy walked into Ashton's study, holding both her stomach and head. "Ashton, dear"—she looked deathly pale—"it's time to make plans for New York."

"Really?" He rounded the desk in a heartbeat, picked her up and whirled her in his arms. When he set her on her feet, his eyes twinkled. "About time. I was beginning to wonder if I'd ever get the chance to charm that old gorgon, Mrs. Vanderbilt."

Afterword

I hope you enjoyed Daisy and Ashton's story. I have so enjoyed crafting the Bumgarten family and charting their challenges and triumphs. Stay tuned: there is more adventure and discovery and romance to come!

And just a historical note: the Meridians bemoaned the tidal wave of "dollar princesses" who descended on England in the late Victorian era and inveigled their way into noble marriages, but not everyone was quite so judgmental. One count puts the number of wealthy American brides who married English lords and gentry at over two hundred— which means that a good bit of American blood was injected into the family trees of the British aristocracy. These marriages were sometimes resisted by English families, but money and influence were persuasive and time eventually put to rest most tensions.

The marriages, however, were not necessarily happy. Ashton's observations on the restrictions and demands of an English lord's birthright and the problems that faced their American brides are based on known accounts. One of the most prominent examples was Jennie Jerome Churchill, Winston Churchill's mother. She and her family were indeed shunned by "the Knickerbockers" of New York high society because their money was too new. Jennie's mother whisked her off to London, dressed her in 450,000 dollars' worth of Charles Worth gowns, and quickly saw results. Jennie soon married the dashing Lord Randolph Churchill. Not long into the marriage, the affairs began, and though Jennie continued to love Randolph, and even cared for him as he died of syphilis, they seldom shared more than a name and a large, lonely house.

Another American bride was Consuelo Yznaga, later the Duchess of Manchester. She met the Viscount Mandeville when he went to the U.S. on a "hunting" expedition— though, in fact, what he was hunting for was a rich bride to cover his gambling debts. He was a womanizer, a gambler, and a notorious patron of prostitutes. Needless to say, Consuelo did not find happiness in her marriage, but she did seem to enjoy her title . . . and the additional noble husbands who added to her status over time.

No accounting of the influence of America's dollar princesses would be complete without the mention of Frances Ellen Work, an American heiress who married the scandalous James Roche, Third Baron Fermoy. Roche was also a gambler and very fond of debauchery—so fond, in fact, that Frances's father reached across the Atlantic to recover his poor daughter and her children—stripping his grandsons of the name "Roche" and renaming them "Work," like himself. The sons eventually returned to England to assume their father's much diminished title and lands, and their sister's great-granddaughter became Diana Spencer, Princess of Wales. Through Diana, the unhappy Frances's descendants—princes William and George—have become future kings of England. Not too shabby for a "dollar princess."

So . . . Daisy Bumgarten's brash determination to marry "up" had many real world counterparts. And Ashton's battle to become his own man or stay a loyal "second son" was regrettably similar to the struggle of many younger sons in England's hierarchical society. Sibling rivalry being what it is, it is hard to say how many of the nobility's younger sons were as loving and devoted to their elder brothers as Ashton.

* * *

Coming next in the SIN AND SENSIBILITY trilogy: Daisy's younger sister, Frances "Frankie" Bumgarten, takes London society and a certain nobleman by storm, and finds that love is one secret that is *very* hard to keep.

Connect with U s

Visit us online at
KensingtonBooks.com
to read more from your favorite authors, see books
by series, view reading group guides, and more.

Join us on social media

for sneak peeks, chances to win books and prize packs,
and to share your thoughts with other readers.

facebook.com/kensingtonpublishing
twitter.com/kensingtonbooks

Tell us what you think!

To share your thoughts, submit a review,
or sign up for our eNewsletters, please visit:
KensingtonBooks.com/TellUs.